THE GANNET HAS LANDED

Peter Kerr

Published by Accent Press Ltd – 2008
ISBN 9781906373290

Printed and bound in the UK

Cover Design by Glen Kerr

Illustrations by Peter Kerr
(Reproduced by arrangement with Summersdale
Publishers Ltd.)

Peter Kerr's website: *www.peter-kerr.co.uk*

About The Author

Peter Kerr is Scotland's best-selling travel writer. *Snowball Oranges, Manana Manana, Viva Mallorca!* and *A Basketful of Snowflakes*, his critically acclaimed Mallorcan-based books, have sold in large numbers worldwide and have been translated into ten languages.

The inspiration for Peter's Spanish books comes from his own experience. When the recession of the 1980s hit he threw in the towel as a farmer of barley and beef cattle in Scotland and moved his family out to Mallorca to take on a run-down orange farm – something that he knew absolutely nothing about!

Peter is also an accomplished writer of fiction: his books include three adventures of humorous Scottish sleuth, Bob Burns – *Bob Burns Investigates: the Mallorca Connection, Bob Burns Investigates: The Sporran Connection* and *Bob Burns Investigates: The Cruise Connection*, as well as the adventures of Jack-the-lad Scottish farmer Jigger McCloud in *Fiddler On The Make*.

For more information please visit
www.peter-kerr.co.uk

CHAPTER ONE

'VIVA MALLORCA!'

BACK HOME IN SCOTLAND, young Doogie O'Mara had wakened up to a few hangovers just like this one, with all sorts of crazy thoughts having three-legged races round his mind against a motley selection of guilty doubts and twinges of downright panic. But this was different. For one thing, he hadn't been sleeping, and for another, he hadn't been drinking either!

Yet here he was, fresh out of second year at vet college, sitting on a Merryweather Holidays' charter jet, surrounded by a couple of hundred *Viva España*-singing, half-cut holidaymakers, seven miles above the Pyrenees and irrevocably en route to Palma, Mallorca.

God, how he hated that place, or what little he had seen of it. It had been a long time ago, when he was about nine or ten: just him and his mother and father and his kid sister, stuck for a whole week of monsoonal storms in some crummy dump of a one-star hotel up a dingy back street in Ca'n Pastilla. But he could remember just about every miserable detail of that holiday as though he had endured it only yesterday… The wall above his bed spattered with squashed mozzies; the shower over the bath that peed cold water on you while you stood gagging at the stench wafting up from the plughole; the flamenco-wailing of the labourers building an apartment block that he could almost touch from his bedroom window; the endless nights of playing Scrabble in his parents' room, until he thought he would truly die of boredom; that tiny, gypsy-type girl with the rotten teeth and skinny, bow legs, who used to come in to make the bed and do the room, grinning '*Hola, guapo!*' at him and leering in a way that he didn't understand then and could scarcely bear to contemplate even now; and worst of all, perhaps, that sadistic bastard of a cockerel that was hell bent on waking him up before five o'clock every morning, crowing his broken-voiced yodel from the midst of a ramshackle little vegetable patch that was still being gamely cultivated down there among the cement bags and heaps of breeze blocks littering the building site across the street. God, how he hated bloody Mallorca!

'Y'all right, mate? Ya look a bit peaky-like.' It was the first that the shell-suited Mancunian slob now sitting next to him on the plane had said, apart from ordering half the contents of the drinks trolley for himself and his shell-suit-co-ordinated wife. ''Ere, 'ave a slugga this voddy and Coke, pal. It'll settle yer stomach.'

'No, thanks all the same, I –'

'Ya should've ate the nosh, that's your trouble. Get plenty in yer guts, that's the secret. Yeah, never spewed in a kite in me puff, I 'aven't.'

As much as it had turned his stomach at the time, Doogie – for one of those inexplicable, masochistic reasons that tend to creep up on us all on such occasions – had been unable to keep the corner of his eye off this guy scoffing the most nauseating trayful of in-flight food that he had ever turned a nostril from. And the appearance of the food had been debatably even less appetising than the smell, the indeterminate green splodge clinging to the outer curve of a sausage suggesting that the cook had either had a major mushy-pea disaster or had inadvertently rediscovered penicillin.

'Yeah, great nosh on them 'ere Merryweather kites,' the male shell suit enthused. 'Ya should've got yours down ya, mate – that's your trouble!'

So great, in fact, had his chance flying companion considered the Merryweather nosh that, having consumed everything laid before him except the scented contents of a freshen-up sachet, he had enthusiastically gobbled up his wife's left-overs, and then, with a permission-seeking grunt, had relieved Doogie of his untouched tray and had dispatched its entire contents down his cakehole as well.

'Yer first time to Mallorca, is it?' he asked Doogie, the announcement that they were commencing their descent to Palma having put the mockers on any further booze-ordering, and freeing his mouth for uninterrupted conversational purposes.

'No, I –'

'Still, ne'er mind, eh? When ya've been to Mallorca as often as me and 'er 'ere 'as, ya know every bugger and every bugger knows us. In't that right, chuck?' He half turned towards his wife, who was already too busy sucking a freebie mint, poking her ears and puffing down her finger-clamped nose to even hear. 'Yeah, mate, there ain't an English pub in Magaluf don't know ol' Jack Dean – or Torvill to me mates, like. Er-uhm, where ya headed yerself – Hotel Barracuda, Trinidad, Maggie Park? I know 'em all. Yeah, there ain't a hotel in Magaluf don't know ol'…'

Doogie decided to do his popping ears a double favour by following Mrs Shell Suit's example, while asking himself just what the hell he had let himself in for on this trip.

''Ow long ya stoppin'?' Torvill asked, once he had expertly led a relief-charged 'round o' applause for the driver' following the plane's safe touch-down. 'Two weeks? Me and 'er 'ere never come for less than a fortnight ourselfs, like. Nah, not worth the bleedin' bother. Mind you, we never stop longer than a month. Creates too much hassle wi' t' invalidity benefit payments. Bad back, see – council dustman – early retirement.' He gave Doogie a wink that wouldn't have been out of place following the donation of a hot tip at the races. 'Say no more, mate! Yeah, anyway, so ye're 'ere for a fortnight, are ya?'

'No, worse luck, I'm here for –'

'Only a week, eh? Very wise. Gorra watch the pennies at your age. Oh aye, it's true, is that. Yeah, look after the pennies and the pounds'll look after –'

'A year, actually,' Doogie interrupted. 'I was about to say I'm here for a year … at least.' He then had to pull himself into the back of his seat as the two shell suits elbowed past at the start of their well-practised lunge up the aisle to claim pole position at the as-yet-unopened exit.

'Oh yeah?' Torvill called back, patently miffed. 'Won the bleedin' lottery, 'ave ya?'

Wet cement! That was the smell Doogie had been trying to remember. Wet cement – everything in Spain seemed to have smelled of it on that holiday, and it hit him again now. It permeated the whole airport terminal, sweating out of every precast concrete pore in the stifling midnight humidity. The smell of wet cement mixed with the scent of Ambre-Solaired bodies and the faint but unmistakable pong of distant sewage.

Doogie took a quick glance around the vast arrivals hall. It was even bigger than he had remembered. Bigger, busier, noisier, worse! Anyway, no turning back now. Look for the Merryweather Holidays rep, that's what the man had said. Just make yourself known to the nearest sky-blue blazer. It didn't take long.

'Hi!' he said, homing in on a plumpish, exhausted-looking girl with 'Angie' emblazoned beneath the Merryweather logo on her lapel badge. 'I'm Doogie.'

'Hi, Doogie,' Angie replied with an air of forced cheeriness. 'Which resort are you booked for, love?' She lowered her red-rimmed eyes to the clipboard she carried like a permanent extension to her left arm. 'Surname?'

'O'Mara.'

'O'Mara,' she repeated, then ran her forefinger down the list of names. 'Resort?'

'Search me. I'm not here on holiday. I'm here to work … for Merryweather!'

Angie clapped a hand to her forehead. 'Shit! I'm sorry, love. Ingrid told me to look out for you coming off this gannet, but I completely forgot. Just been one of those nights, you know. Pandemonium.'

'No problem,' Doogie breezed, while doing his best to disguise his growing feeling of misgiving by shaking her hand warmly. 'Just point me in the right direction, and I'll be on my way.'

Angie was staring glassy-eyed at the wall of trolley-pushing humanity, led by a familiar shell-suited duo, now bearing down on her from the direction of the Baggage Reclaim area. 'Where's your luggage, Doogie love?' she asked distractedly.

He pointed to the solitary canvas grip at his feet. 'This is it. Got it over as hand luggage. That's how I'm first through.'

'Smart thinking, kid.' Angie was bracing herself for the onslaught. 'OK, just dive outside smartly and look for bus number seven. It's got the Merryweather sign on the side. Grab the front seat and keep the one next to you for me. Hey, and don't let *any*body nick it, even if they've got a wooden leg. I'm gonna get the weight off my feet, even if it means one of these holidaymaking sods standing all the way to bloody Santa Ponça!'

Doogie's confused senses didn't take in much of the coach trip – only the robotic drone of Angie's voice telling the punters over the mike about the charms of Mallorca and which hotel they had arrived at now and who should get off where. In the dark, everywhere looked much the same to Doogie: the predictable procession of one gaudy *Bert's London Bar* after another, punctuated by the occasional *Dortmunder Pils* sign

5

and a plethora of pizza joints and Chinese restaurants. A twenty-minute dash along an *autopista* that could have been any motorway in the world only led to more of the same. Welcome to Spain!

Eventually, Angie had to dig a soundly-sleeping Doogie in the ribs. 'You're here, kid. End of the line for you, this is.'

Doogie blinked at his watch. Nearly two o'clock in the morning. He peered out of the window onto the pavement terrace of a bar teeming with a fifty-fifty blend of suntanned and milky-white bodies, all kitted out in holiday clobber and looking as though they were just getting warmed up for a night on the bash.

'Where are we?' he yawned.

'Palma Nova – outside Papi's Bar,' Angie said. 'Where all the reps hang out – on the odd occasions when we're not working or trying to snatch a couple of hours' kip, that is. Oh, and if Ingrid isn't back yet, just hang about until I've dumped the last of this lot. Shan't be long.' Then, noticing the forlorn expression on Doogie's face, she tweaked his cheek and chirped, 'Cheer up, kid. It'll be all downhill from now on, I promise.'

'Just what I was bloody well afraid of,' Doogie muttered to himself, forcing a grin as he jumped down from the bus. 'Thanks for the lift, Ange,' he shouted. 'Catch you later!'

After the relative coolness of the air-conditioned bus, the midsummer Mallorcan heat, even at this wee-small hour, enveloped Doogie like an invisible electric blanket. For all that, the briny smack of the sea mingling with a breath of unseen pine woods reminded him suddenly of home. Yet the air here was suffused with a heady scent of exotic flowers and herbs that was uniquely Mediterranean. Doogie liked it.

He also liked the look of Papi's Bar. It was a brightly-lit, spacious place that exuded bonhomie. Two entire walls of adjoining French doors were thrown open to the night, which fairly rang with the high-spirited sounds of Papi's youthful patrons. Everything was sparkling and vibrant. People were having fun, intoxicated as much by the atmosphere, perhaps, as by alcoholic intake. It was holiday time and the night, like the clientele, was young.

This was a face of Mallorca that Doogie had been unable to appreciate as a storm-imprisoned ten-year-old in Ca'n Pastilla. He felt the clouds of depression magically dispersing with his travel weariness. Maybe coming on this trip hadn't been such a bad idea after all.

'Yes please?' a barman yelled at him through the clamour of guffaws, squeals and pop music.

'Ehm, I'm looking for Ingrid...'

The barman shrugged impatiently as half a dozen raised voices competed for his attention. 'You wan' drink, o' no?'

Before Doogie could answer, the overwrought barman had succumbed to the inevitable and was already repeating the order of the loudest voice: 'Two beer, two Bacardi Coke. You wan' ice, leemon?'

Lesson number one – you had to be quick off your mark to survive around here.

Doogie was bundled out of his contemplation, and his place at the bar, by a seven-foot giant with enough rings in his ears to curtain a bay window. He reeked of beer, fish-and-chips and vinegar, and was wearing a sleeveless T-shirt sporting the tell-tale legend:

What Drink Problem? I Drink, I Fall Down,
I Get Up, I Drink Some More ... No Problem!

'One side, skin!' the giant piped in an incongruously high-pitched Liverpool accent. 'Let the fookin' dog see the fookin' rabbit, a'right!'

Lesson number two – the age of chivalry, if it had ever existed, was well and truly gone from this scene. Toughen up, O'Mara.

'Did I hear you mention Ingrid, squire?'

Doogie looked down at the seated owner of the head his elbow had just collided with. The guy had a face that was fairly good-looking in a shifty, Jack-the-lad sort of way, and his expression suggested he'd asked the question more through nosiness than genuine interest. He appeared to be in his late

7

twenties or early thirties and spoke with a slightly nasal south-east England accent.

'Yes, I – I'm sorry I knocked into you there,' Doogie flustered. 'It was the, uhm –'

'Ingrid, you said?'

'Ingrid – that's right. Do you know if she's about? I'm supposed to –'

Deadpan, Jack-the-lad motioned him to sit down at the low table opposite the couch he was lounging on. He was flanked by two gum-chewing girls, both identically dressed in skin-tight jeans and floppy cotton tops, crudely cut off just below the bust line to reveal painfully-pink midriffs that looked hot enough to fry eggs on.

'You're a Merryweather man yourself, I see,' Doogie smiled, his eyes drawn to the guy's sky-blue blazer. He offered his right hand across the table. 'I'm Doogie O'Mara.'

'Nick Martin,' said the poker-faced Merryweather man, not bothering to remove his own hands from the shoulders of his two groupies. 'Friend of Ingrid's, are we, squire?'

There was something slightly condescending about the way he had posed that question, Doogie thought. And there was something a bit disparaging in the permanently drowsy look of his eyes, which were now wandering over Doogie as if weighing up some tatty merchandise at a car boot sale. The two groupies followed suit, each pinging a length of bubblegum from between her lips with one hand, while fondling a Nick Martin thigh with the other.

Doogie tried not to look too self-conscious. 'No, I don't know her at all,' he said. 'I've come to work for Merryweather Holidays myself actually, and Angie sort of mentioned that … well, is Ingrid here?'

Nick Martin shook his head, the makings of a smirk playing at one corner of his mouth. 'Up at Son Amar with a coachload of gannet crap.'

'Son Amar?'

'Big, flash nightclub place up the island. An absolute *must* for the punters.' The sarcasm in Nick Martin's voice matched the expression on his face. He leered into the bubble-blowing faces of his two companions in turn. 'Except them with better things to do, huh, girls?'

The girls giggled and swapped suggestive remarks in what Doogie took to be Cockney accents.

Those nagging, fish-out-of-water feelings were beginning to swim back into his mind. 'So, when's Ingrid likely to be back, then?' he asked.

'Buggered if I know, squire. Not in a hurry, are you?' Nick spoke the words as if Doogie wasn't even there, his eyes focused now on the better-endowed of the two bubble-blowers. ''Ere, give's a feel of yer dumplin's, darlin',' he growled, then shoved his hand down the top of his feebly objecting victim.

'Hmm, Dougal,' her chum muttered as she eyed Doogie up and down again. She blew a meditative bubble. 'That's that 'airy mutt in the Magic Roundabout, innit?'

If Doogie had heard this clichéd crack once, he'd heard it a thousand times. 'The name's Doogie, not Dougal,' he stressed. 'That's Doog-*ee* – i-e, right?'

'Whatever, mate,' she replied disinterestedly. 'I'm off for a bleedin' leak.' She hauled herself to her feet. 'That's leak, i.e. slash, right?'

''Ere, 'ang abaht, Samamfa,' her chum piped up, while wriggling reluctantly away from Nick's groping fingers. 'I'll come wiv yer. I'm burstin' for an 'ose an' all!'

'Fuckin' slags,' Nick grunted. He grimaced as he watched the two young 'ladies' pause to pluck the clinging denim from the clefts of their backsides before wobbling off loo-wards on stilt-like stilettos. 'Still, any port in a storm, eh?' He glanced sceptically at Doogie. 'Then again, maybe not.'

'Meaning?' Doogie scowled. His patience with this bloke's offensive manner was rapidly running out.

Nick Martin dismissed Doogie's query with a sweep of his hand. 'What'll you have? Beer, is it? Hey, Pablo!' he shouted over his shoulder, not even bothering to turn round. 'One *San Mig* for the squire here.'

If the barman heard him, he gave no such indication. He got on with what he was already doing and ignored Nick's offhand order completely.

Nick's eyes were everywhere, except on Doogie, as he asked him, 'And what world-shattering tale of woe drives you into Merryweather's merry band, squire? Failed romance, failed career, or just failed to get yourself a proper job, was it?'

'Nothing like that at all, as it happens,' Doogie began, his hackles rising. 'In fact –'

'Yeah, yeah, yeah, tell me the old, old story.' Nick Martin was already standing up and gazing over Doogie's head, his randiness radar fixed on a reject from a Victoria Beckham lookalike contest who had just shimmied into the bar. 'Yeah, tell us all about it sometime, Magic Roundabout. But do me a favour,' he added dryly, 'wait 'til I'm not around, huh. I've heard it *all* before.'

He ran a hand through his hair, pulled down the cuffs of his blazer and was off on a Posh Spice conquest.

Doogie was still muttering anti-Nick Martin curses when Angie collapsed into a chair beside him.

She kicked off her shoes. 'Why *do* we do it?' she puffed. 'Of all the crazy ways to make a living...'

Doogie looked at her blankly.

'Sorry, love,' she said, realising that a word of encouragement probably wouldn't go amiss. 'Pay no attention to my moans and groans. It's not always as bad as this.'

Doogie thought for a few moments about something appropriate to say, then came out with the blatantly obvious, 'Rough night, was it?'

'Tell me about it! You do a double shift to cover for one of the girls who's down with the flu, your first batch of punters arrives from Gatwick at eight in the morning and, just to get things off to a good start, a toddler throws his breakfast up over the head of the woman sitting in front of him on the coach. Then you've got a pensioner deciding to have a heart attack in the check-in queue for the Luton flight, a kid with a

10

dose of the Eartha Kitts fills his pants as he comes off the Bristol gannet – which just happened to be on a two-hour delay that brought it in only minutes before your Manchester lot, by the way – and now they tell me I'm on the early shift again tomorrow, because one of the other girls has had a nervous breakdown. Yes, love, a rough night … and day!'

'All downhill from now on, eh?' Doogie said with a wry smile.

'God, I'd commit murder for a coffee!' Angie gasped, then dabbed a refreshing touch of perfume behind each ear. She glanced at Doogie's empty hands. 'Aren't you drinking, love? Cor, don't tell me they're sending us teetotallers now!'

'No – I mean, yes please. But that Nick Martin bloke already ordered me a beer … I think.'

'Ah, so, you've met Tricky Nicky.' There was a note of foreboding in Angie's voice. 'Did he pay for your drink, by any chance?'

Doogie hunched his shoulders. 'Not that I saw.'

'You've got a fat chance of getting it, then. The barmen have got Nick Martin's number. No kidding, love, he's got a slate in here that's longer than one of old Sam Merryweather's cigars.' She nodded at Pablo behind the bar, held up an imaginary cup and saucer, then mimed a pint being pulled. 'If you take my advice,' she continued, looking Doogie squarely in the eye, 'you'll give our Mr Martin a wide berth. He's bad news.'

'Thanks, I'll remember that. But why does the company employ a creep like that anyway? Not very good for the image, from what I've seen.'

'Because he's bloody good at his job. Simple as that. And don't be fooled by the way he's carrying on in here – sniffing after all the silly little tarts just arrived from Leeds-Bradford or wherever. He can be as smooth and sophisticated as it takes, when it suits.'

'That takes a bit of imagining,' Doogie frowned, rummaging in his pockets for money to pay for the drinks Pablo had just brought to the table.

Angie slapped him lightly on the wrist. 'This one's on me, kid. There's no sex discrimination when it comes to buying rounds in this firm.'

'Cheers, Ange,' Doogie grinned. 'Here's to a smooth trip downhill – for both of us.' He followed Angie's gaze round to the doorway, where Nick Martin was already touching up the mini-skirted bum of the Posh Spice clone. 'How the hell does such a bloody sleazebag manage it?'

'Over here, all a bloke needs to pull a bird like that is a Merryweather blazer and a pulse. Yeah, when they come on holiday, most of these bimbos leave what little brains they've got at their home airport – along with their knickers, if you ask me.' Angie whistled a cooling blast over her coffee, then took a tentative, luxuriant sip of the steaming, black liquid. 'Ah-h-h, that's better. Every nerve end in my system's been screaming out for that since God knows when.'

Doogie watched her closely as she slumped back in her chair – head back, eyes closed, her comfortably-upholstered body relaxing into a careless heap like a punctured Lilo. She had a pretty enough face, he reckoned, but with a decidedly well-lived-in look about it. About thirty, she'd be – give or take a year or two – with that resigned, almost defeated air of someone who'd already taken a bit more than her fair share of life's kicks in the teeth and had finally decided just to bend with the wind and make the best of things.

'So, what's your story, young Doogie?' she murmured without opening her eyes, just as he was turning over in his own mind the same question about her. 'You've got a Scottish first name, an Irish surname, and you flew in from Manchester. There's got to be a story there somewhere.'

'Well, to answer the last bit of your question first, I had to report to Merryweather's Manchester office for my interview today – or yesterday now – and they stuck me on the first plane to Palma Mallorca here.'

'Good old Merryweather Holidays, always thinking of staff welfare first.'

'How do you mean?'

'Well, they could have sent you to Benidorm!'

'But I'd asked to be sent to Kenya.'

Angie opened one eye and blinked incredulously. 'Kenya?'

'Well, Kenya, The Gambia, anywhere in Africa, really. I thought it would give me the chance to study the wildlife at first hand *and* get paid into the bargain.'

Angie closed her eye again. 'You've come to the best place if you want to study wildlife, love,' she chuckled softly. 'Just wait 'til the Glasgow Fair holiday starts. You'll see more wild animals in a fortnight round the corner here in Magaluf than you'd come across on the entire continent of Africa in a whole bloody lifetime.'

Doogie peered lugubriously into his beer. 'Christ!' he muttered, 'I can hardly wait.'

'Anyway,' Angie suddenly chirped, 'you were about to tell me the Doogie O'Mara story.' She sat up in her seat and put on a commendable show of interest. 'Come on, tell me all about this exotic name of yours.'

'Nothing much to tell, really,' Doogie shrugged. 'It was my Dad's name before me, that's all.' There was an awkward pause before he continued. 'We're from Arran, you see.'

'That's Ireland somewhere, isn't it?'

'No, you're thinking about the islands with the one *r*, where the pullovers come from. I'm from the one with the two *r*'s – off the west coast of Scotland, way out in the Firth of Clyde. It's sort of on the way to Ireland, so…'

'So, we have Scottish Doogie, Irish O'Mara, coming all the way to Mallorca from the island of Arran via Manchester Ringway, is that it?'

'Yeah, I suppose that's about it.'

Angie couldn't help but notice that a wistful look had come into Doogie's eyes. She left him with his thoughts for a moment, then said, 'One good thing, being from an island, you should soon feel well at home here.' Then, seeing his sceptical frown, she added, 'Give it a chance, kid. It's not *all* Palma Airport and Coca Cola signs, you know. And anyhow, you still haven't told me how you come to be working for

13

Merryweather.'

'Saw their ad in a students' mag and, hey presto, here I am!'

'Didn't fancy being a student, then?'

'Yeah, I loved it. It was just that…' Doogie fingered his beer glass nervously. 'It was just that…'

Angie laid a hand on his arm. 'Listen, you don't have to explain *anything* to me, love. It's none of my business. I was only trying to make conversation, that's all.'

'No, it's all right, really it is. I mean, it'll maybe do me some good to talk about it … if you can bear to listen, that is.'

Angie settled back into her seat again and raised her coffee cup in a theatrical flourish. 'Fire away, kid. You have my undivided attention.'

'I've always wanted to be a vet, you see. For as long as I can remember. Ever since the first time I saw my dad delivering a calf, when I was, I dunno, four or five maybe.' A reflective smile lit up Doogie's face. 'I've lost count of the number of animals I've seen being born since then, but I still get a lump in my throat every time I see it. Magic – that's the only word I can ever think of to describe it. Pure magic. Especially a calf. Up on its wobbly legs in no time, the mother sniffing it, then speaking to it in gentle little moans, reassuring it as she licks it dry. She's proud as well. As doting as any human mother. I tell you, Angie, it's the bonniest sight you could ever set eyes on.' He shook his head and gave a contented little chortle. 'Aye, pure magic.'

'Your father,' Angie said, 'he's a vet as well, then, is he?'

The bluntness of her question jolted Doogie out of his reverie. 'No, no,' he replied, leaning forward and lowering his eyes as he pensively traced invisible patterns on the table top with his fingertips, 'not even a real farmer, in the full-time sense of the word, at any rate. Just a handful of acres outside the village, that's all. A croft, they call it in our part of the world. Not enough to make a living off nowadays, you know. Just a way of life that's handed down from father to son … or used to be.'

It was Angie's turn to watch Doogie closely now, quietly sipping her coffee while he sifted through his thoughts.

'He drove a truck, and a bus as well – in the summer mainly – just to help make ends meet. Even worked behind the bar in the local hotel during the busy season.' A little chuckle escaped his lips. 'The busy season. The same Glasgow Fair holiday that you were talking about. At one time, it seemed as if the entire population of Glasgow came pouring off that Ardrossan ferry at the start of the second fortnight in July. Now they all come to Mallorca, I suppose.'

'They used to, love, but a lot plump for Bulgaria or Croatia these days. A bit cheaper, like.'

Doogie was still smiling to himself, not really seeming to hear what Angie was saying. 'Every summer, my mum would rent out the house – two months, even three, if she could get the bookings – and we'd all move into what we called the holiday villa, which was actually nothing more than a big sort of wooden shed in the back garden. A lot of the families in the Arran villages used to do that.'

'Sounds a bit, well, desperate, if you don't mind me saying so. A bit rough on your poor old mum especially.'

'Nah, she never thought anything of it,' Doogie laughed. Then, as if considering it for the first time, he said quietly, 'She never complained anyway. But maybe you're right. Maybe I just took it all too much for granted, the way kids do…'

Angie patted the back of his hand and gave him a reassuring smile. 'I shouldn't let it worry you, love. We all do that at times – take our mums and dads for granted, I mean. I've got to own up that I still do, and God knows I'm old enough to know better.'

'They live over here too, do they?'

'No, back home in Nottingham. Hardly ever get time to visit them in this job, mind you. Yeah, but they usually try to get over here for a week or two every year, though – if Dad's feeling up to it, that is. Anyway, I know they're always there if I need them. Which is exactly what I said,' Angie grinned, '–

taking them for granted, right?'

Doogie nodded and took a gulp of his beer.

The earlier crush of people in the bar was beginning to thin down now. The barmen were clearing tables as they became vacated by groups of customers who were leaving, perhaps to go to bed, or, in some as-yet unattached cases, for an optimistic trawl round a couple of all-night clubs.

'So, you're a vet, young O'Mara?' Angie prompted, picking up the threads of the flagging conversation. 'I didn't think you looked old enough to –'

'I've only done two years at vet college,' Doogie butted in, unable to disguise a look of guilt, which, to Angie, made him appear like a schoolboy who'd just been caught stealing apples.

'Whatever happened?' she said. 'I can't believe you blew your exams, a smart-looking kid like you!'

Doogie shook his head. 'No, no, I passed the lot with flying colours actually.' He spoke without a hint of bragging, yet almost as if the passing of exams with ease had been a foregone conclusion.

Angie could hardly believe her ears. 'And you've jacked it in to work as a bloody *Merryweather* rep? You must be off your tiny chump! Whatever did your folks say, for heaven's sake?'

'Well, ehm … nothing,' Doogie mumbled, the colour rising in his cheeks. 'That's the whole point, sort of – or part of it, anyway.'

'Sorry, love, but you've lost me completely!' Angie was beginning to bristle. 'Quite obviously, your folks have had to work damned hard to send you to university, and now you've thrown it all up and you're trying to tell me they're not even fussed? Come on, pull the other one!'

Doogie stroked his bottom lip, hoping that Angie wouldn't notice his chin quivering. 'No, it's not like that,' he murmured. 'Not as simple as that…'

Angie could see that she'd touched on a sore point, and she felt bad about it. 'Look, I didn't mean to upset you, kid. I'm sorry, really I am. It's, well, it's none of my business, and I shouldn't have jumped to conclusions.'

Doogie managed a smile. 'No, it's OK, honest. I've been needing to talk to someone about it, and it's just…' His voice broke and he faked a little laugh. 'And it's just your bad luck to be in the wrong place at the wrong time, that's all.'

She squeezed his hand and gave him a sympathetic wink. 'Right, get it off your chest, Doogie boy. If nothing else, your old Auntie Angie's a good listener.'

Of course, she had been absolutely right in what she'd said, Doogie admitted. His parents *had* worked damned hard to give him and his sister Mo a good start in life. Qualifications, that's what you needed to get on, his father had always said. A few letters after your name, that was the secret, if you didn't want to end up like him, slaving away for all God's given hours with precious little to show for it at the end of every month except an aching back and always that one bill more than you could afford to pay.

Doogie had taken his father's words to heart, sticking in at school, working for the local vet at weekends and school holidays, always striving for that one goal. And when the news finally came that he had won his place at the vet college in Edinburgh, his parents couldn't have been more delighted. He could see them yet, standing proud as Punch at the end of Brodick Pier on the day he left, waving 'til the steamer was almost out of sight.

Doogie never saw his father again. He died just two months later, an old man before his time – struck down at the age of only fifty-one.

'He'd done it all for me,' Doogie told Angie, 'and I hadn't even noticed it happening. All the time I spent helping the vet, I should have spent helping him. Now I just feel that if I hadn't been so damned self-centred, maybe he'd…' His voice trailed away and he sat looking disconsolately down at his hands.

Angie sighed deeply. 'Look, I know I wasn't blessed with too many smarts, but I do know this – you're blaming yourself

17

unfairly. Your dad worked as hard as he did because he wanted the best for his kids. And if that's the kind of man he was, nothing, and I mean *nothing*, would have changed things.' She thought for a moment before saying, quietly but firmly, 'Listen, I don't want to seem cruel, love, but instead of thinking about yourself like this, you should be thinking about your mum. You've still got to repay her for everything she's given you as well, you know, and you can best do that by making sure you achieve the things your dad worked for … if you can understand what I'm trying to say.'

Doogie didn't answer. He didn't need to. The confused, lost look in his eyes said enough. Angie fumbled with her fingers – embarrassed, regretful and not knowing what to say next.

'Sorry. Dammit, sorry's no use,' she finally blurted out. 'God, I should keep a sign hanging permanently in front of my eyes – *Engage brain before opening bloody mouth*!'

'Six months after Dad,' Doogie said, staring straight ahead. 'She was all alone – Mo at college in Glasgow, me in Edinburgh. Nothing he could do for her, the doctor said.' Doogie fell silent for a few seconds, then murmured, as much to himself as to Angie, 'They still haven't found a cure for a broken heart…'

A seemingly endless quiet followed, Angie more unsure than ever of what to say, Doogie gazing into his beer, lost in a maze of private thoughts.

'I was just sitting there in my bedsit a few weeks after Mum's funeral,' he said after a while. 'On my tod in a dingy Edinburgh basement on a rainy Sunday afternoon. I was skint, fed up, with a mountain of notes to revise, and dreading to think of how many dozens of miserable Sundays just like that I'd have to suffer before I finally qualified.' He gave a sad little laugh. 'Funny, the rain took me back to the one and only family holiday we ever had. Here in Mallorca, it was. In Ca'n Pastilla, I think. I was too young to appreciate it then, of course, but my folks must have skimped and saved for years to pay for that holiday. And it rained all bloody week!' He shook his head remorsefully. 'Yeah, and to top it all, all *I* could do was moan about it. Jeez, what a pain in the neck I must have been!' Pensively, he swilled the beer about in his glass. 'Too bad you only realise these things after it's too late to apologise.'

As delicately as she could, Angie offered the suggestion that it would be pretty insensitive parents who'd expect a kid to say sorry for every childish thing he did. All part of the joys of having sprogs, she reckoned it was.

With a wistful smile, Doogie said that he supposed she was right enough.

Angie sensed that he was far from convinced, however.

In any case, he continued, recalling that holiday had got him thinking about his own life and what might lie ahead for him. Admittedly, his parents' sacrifices had given him a better start than they had ever had. But for all that, he had come to suspect that he might be heading into a similar quagmire – a more lucrative quagmire, perhaps, but one from which there might be no escape either. All of a sudden, everything had seemed too pre-ordained, too cut and dried, right down to having been promised a partnership by old Hyslop, the vet at home, on the assumption that he would eventually take over the practice.

That, Angie suggested bluntly, sounded more like the stairway to heaven than a path into a quagmire. 'My God, most aspiring young vets would give their eye teeth for a chance like that, surely!'

'Oh, absolutely,' Doogie readily agreed, 'and none more so than me, believe me.' He shifted uneasily in his chair. 'But there's something else. Well, some*one* else. A complication that I hadn't properly weighed up before.'

Angie nodded her head knowingly. 'A girl. The inevitable *femme fatale*, right?'

'Well, no, not *exactly* that. Just Margaret Hyslop, in fact.'

'And don't tell me – she just happens to be the old vet's only daughter, correct?'

'That's right. And, I mean, Margaret and I have known

each other all our lives. Even sat at the same desk on the first day at primary school. Then, later on, with me always being around helping her old man and everything … well, I suppose we became good chums.'

'Aha, but you were more than just chums, right? In *her* eyes, at any rate.'

Doogie's brows gathered into a perplexed little frown. 'To tell the truth, I can't remember ever giving her any encouragement, but she just seemed to drift into this crazy idea that one day we'd be… I mean, it just sort of became the accepted thing, even with her parents.'

Angie couldn't resist a mischievous dig. 'OK, young O'Mara, *now* we're getting down to the nitty-gritty. You've joined Merryweather because you're on the run – from a *woman*! Oo-oo-oo, naughty, naughty!'

But Doogie's frown only deepened. He ran a finger absent-mindedly round the rim of his tumbler, making the glass whine a note that was as melancholy as his expression. 'Yeah, but you don't know Margaret,' he mumbled, slouching forward and resting his chin on his fist.

Angie summoned up a playful giggle. 'Hey, come on, she can't be *that* awful! *And* she comes with a nice little dowry of a veterinary practice on the picturesque island of Arran. Take my word for it, love, you'll meet a few people in this firm who've tied the knot for far less attractive reasons than that. Yours truly for starters!'

'But it's not just the marriage thing, you see. If only it was.' Doogie's face had now taken on a look of approaching doom. 'I mean to say, nest-building is one thing, but Margaret's empire-building tendencies… Hell's bells, they're something else again!'

'Empire-building on *Arran*? What, got ambitions to be boss of the sheep-shaggers' union or something, has she?'

'Her sights will be set a bit higher than that,' Doogie lamented. 'She's studying medicine, you know.'

'And what's wrong with *that*, may I ask? Think about it, kid – if things work out, she'll be the local doctor some day and you'll be the local vet. You'll have the whole scene stitched right up. Sounds like a nice one to me, I must say!'

'Hmm, could be, if it stopped at that. But I know Margaret. Honest, before long, she'd be pushing me to stand for the local council, then she'd want me to be the leader of the council, then the local MP, then the Secretary of State for Scotland. I'm telling you, Angie, she wouldn't be satisfied until she was ringing up Pickfords to move our stuff into Number 10!'

'The solution to that little problem is simple,' Angie shrugged. '*You* tell *her* what the score is. Put the old foot down. Assert yourself. Show her who wears the pants. Women love to be dominated, and you can take my word for that, kiddo.'

'Aye, but you don't know Margaret,' Doogie dolefully repeated.

Angie stifled a yawn. 'Christ, look at the time! Nearly three o'clock in the bloody morning again.' She looked first over one shoulder then the other. 'What the hell's happened to Ingrid? I've got a kid to say hello to before I leave for work again in four hours. Poor little sod must be beginning to wonder who the strange woman is who pops into his bedroom for a couple of seconds now and again.'

Doogie was mortified, and he was quick to apologise. He had been a right selfish pillock, he told Angie, to have kept her there listening to his hang-ups, when all the time she should have been at home with her own family. 'Doesn't your husband worry when you're out this late?' he asked.

Angie merely raised a shoulder and said that he might have at one time, but as he had done the permanent off the day he found out she was pregnant (and that had been nearly five years ago), she had long since been obliged to concede that it looked as if the bastard didn't give a monkey's any more. It had been the typical holiday rep's romance, she volunteered, while Doogie took his turn at suffering the remorse of spontaneous tactlessness. She'd been a wet-behind-the-ears English rose, she admitted, arriving starry-eyed in Spain with her dyed blonde hair and doing a Mills & Boon for the first

21

dago waiter who told her that he couldn't resist a woman of such classic Nordic beauty. What the Latin louse had conveniently failed to mention, however, was that he couldn't resist *any* woman, and the alleged qualifications of classic, Nordic and beauty didn't even come into it. As long as she was breathing and preferably a gullible, foreign empty-head, she would do nicely.

If it hadn't been for her neighbour, old María, acting as a surrogate granny, Angie concluded with a rueful dip of the head, she and young Pedrito would have been submerged in the deep stuff long ago. Oh, and as much as she loved him, she said as an afterthought, if ever Pedrito showed signs of inheriting his father's wayward ways, she reckoned she'd snip the *cojones* off the little bugger without giving the matter a second thought. Bloody men!

'Ehm, I hope you don't mind me asking, but who exactly is this Ingrid we're waiting for?' Doogie enquired by way of steering the conversation towards a less ticklish topic.

'Talk of the devil!' Angie proclaimed, gesturing with her coffee cup towards the door. 'Doogie O'Mara, meet our head rep in Mallorca!'

Doogie turned his head to see a tall, graceful figure, ebony skin aglow with good health, athletic frame immaculate in Merryweather Holidays uniform, ambling rhythmically towards them through the now almost empty bar.

'Hi there, Doogie O'Mara!' the graceful figure boomed in a rich bass that would have done justice to the lead in *Othello*, half an acre of gleaming white enamel exposed in what might have been euphemistically described as a saucy grin. 'I'm Björn Bergman – or Ingrid to me friends. You'll be rooming with me until you've found a pad of your own, sunshine, so once you've popped your eyes back into their sockets, let's hit the road for Ca'n Pastilla!'

CHAPTER TWO

'IN AT THE DEEP END'

'*DÉJÀ VU.*'

'De what, sunshine?'

'This street, that hotel. I've seen it all before. It's where we came on holiday about ten years ago!'

A chortle rumbled in the depths of Ingrid's chest. 'That's Ca'n Pastilla for you. Once seen, never forgotten.' He pulled the car up at the kerb. 'Grab your bag, Doog. We're in this apartment block here.'

Ingrid led the way into a bleak lobby, in which the only sign of life was a half-dead rubber plant in a stone planter.

'No news is good news,' he grinned, fleetingly opening and

closing the flap of one of a rash of rusting mailboxes on the wall. 'The only things I ever finds in there are lizards and bills. Oh yeah, and the annual Christmas card from me granny in Jamaica.' With another chortle, he shepherded Doogie into the lift.

'Yes, I actually saw this apartment block being built,' Doogie said as he emerged in Ingrid's wake onto the fourth floor landing.

'Spare me the details, man. I like to sleep *ee-ee-z-ee* in me bed, you know.'

But Doogie was still in reflective mood. 'There used to be a cockerel, in a little sort of vegetable patch at the side of the building down there.'

'Used to be is right,' Ingrid droned. He rolled his eyes at Doogie and licked his lips while unlocking the door. 'But I ate 'im! Chopped off his head with me machete and drank the warm blood in a voodoo session with me mates right here in me kitchen!' His laughter echoed along the empty, terrazzo-floored hallway like a roll of jovial thunder. 'Step inside, sunshine. Welcome to me hut.'

Doogie didn't quite know what to make of this character – Ingrid or Björn or whatever he chose to call himself – other than that he seemed to be a living conundrum, and bordering on a permanent one-man fiesta to boot. Even the half-hour drive from Palma Nova in his ancient little SEAT 600 car had proved to be something of an event, choosing, as he did, to forego the speedy convenience of the city's *Via de Cintura* by-pass in favour of a laid-back, open-windowed cruise along the palm-fringed, neon-bathed razzle-dazzle of Palma's bay-hugging Paseo Marítimo boulevard. Every stop at traffic lights had been an excuse to holler, '*Bienvenido a Mallorca, amigos!*' and release a flood of cheery banter at bemused groups of nocturnal ravers. You had to keep 'em happy, brighten up their dismal little lives, he had beamed at Doogie. That was what it was all about, man. And it appeared to Doogie that he genuinely meant what he said.

But the most noticeable thing about Ingrid was that his

tongue never lay still. A quip about the dodgy seafood in this restaurant, an anecdote about the sailors who frequent that bar, a dirty joke about the night porter in one particular hotel, and a stern warning about those gippo greasers hanging about across the street from a certain night club.

Then there was his name, Björn Bergman.

'Not your typical West Indian, Rastafarian handle that, man,' he had laughed as he dug Doogie in the ribs. 'But I'm gonna let you into a secret – I grabbed it by deed poll as soon as I was eighteen. Well, you know, how would you like to live for thirteen years in Brixton with a label like Winston Satchmo Fats Montgomery Waller?'

'Hmm, when you put it like that,' Doogie had said, opting for a reasonably non-committal reply, 'I can see what must have attracted you to a more clean-cut, Scandinavian name, right enough.'

Ingrid had laughed like a drain at that, his guffaws booming over Palma harbour like a recording of a foghorn that had got stuck in the groove. 'You said it, man! The Scando with the best suntan in Mallorca, that's me!'

The first thing to strike Doogie when he entered the flat was the overwhelming smell of spices: exotic odours of colourful Caribbean dishes that he could instantly imagine Ingrid cooking up in the tiny shambles of a kitchen, which was separated from the spartanly-furnished lounge area by a breakfast bar littered with an assortment of tins, bottles, coffee mugs and an untidy pile of magazines and newspapers.

'It may not be Buckingham Palace, sunshine, but it's me home.'

'Yes, very comfy,' Doogie lied, then ambled over to the balcony window. As he instinctively knew it would, it looked onto not only the hotel, but the very room in which he had been incarcerated those ten years ago. For a moment he wondered if the little gypsy girl still turned up in the mornings to make the beds. Yeah, probably would, with her unfortunate dearth of career-advancing attributes. Still, comforting to know that there was always somebody worse off than yourself.

Or was there?

Doogie was startled by the sound of a whimpering yawn behind him. He spun round just as a petite figure with shapely, olive-brown legs protruding from the shortest of red silk dressing gowns slunk sleepily into the room and nuzzled up to Ingrid, murmuring some suggestive-sounding Spanish words into his ear, long black eyelashes fluttering seductively.

Ingrid coughed and gestured towards Doogie. '*Aquí Doogie O'Mara – representativo nuevo de* Merryweather.' He then turned to Doogie. 'Sunshine, meet me live-in lover, Fidel. I won't bore you with his other names. Spanish, like West Indian – they go on too long, man.'

Doogie was patently gobsmacked.

Fidel was patently unimpressed. He surveyed Ingrid's newly-arrived house guest with all the welcoming warmth of someone who had just clapped eyes on a large turd lying in the deep end of his swimming pool. Without another word, he pouted sulkily then minced, head lowered, back from whence he had appeared.

Ingrid cast Doogie a searching glance, an impish twinkle glinting in his eye.

Doogie just stood there, fiddling with the straps of his Adidas holdall. He could see it all so clearly now – Nick Martin's snide comments about him being a friend of Ingrid's and so on. And Angie's cutting little remark about him being on the run ... from a *woman*. Hell's bells, they thought he was one of those!

His mouth started to speak of its own volition: 'Please excuse me if I looked a bit surprised there, Ingrid – ehm, Björn, but it's just that, well, you seemed too sort of... That is, when I say *sort* of, I don't actually mean...'

Ingrid treated himself to a few more mischievous seconds of relishing Doogie's fit of verbal floundering before throwing the lifeline: 'What you're trying to say is that I seemed too butch to be a horse's, right?'

'A horse's?'

'Rhyming slang, man. Horse's hoof, you know. Poof!'

Ingrid was enjoying this.

'No, no! Oh, absolutely *not*!' Doogie flapped. 'I mean, it never even crossed my mind that you might be a – that you were a...' Cornered by his own embarrassment, he lowered his voice with his eyes. 'A horse's.'

Ingrid's bass bellow of laughter rose with disquieting ease to a soprano giggle. 'Don't get your pibroch in a twist over the butch stuff, sunshine,' he sibilated, planting one hand on his hip, the other raised and hanging limp-wristed by his ear. 'I can be as camp as a reservation full of wigwams when I want to be!'

Doogie didn't know whether to laugh, cry or make a dash for the door. But before he could even start the mental process of making such a vital decision, Ingrid announced that it was way past his bedtime.

'So, what do you say, honky-tonk?' he grinned. 'Fancy sleeping in the middle for the first night, do you?'

Ingrid's ensuing laughed confession that he had only been winding him up about the *cosy* sleeping arrangements didn't help Doogie get much shut-eye during the few hours that remained of the night. His tiny room's only window was a modest rectangle of louvred glass high on one wall, which suggested to Doogie that his designated dormitory had originally appeared on the building's plans (if, indeed, there had ever been any) as some kind of pantry-cum-broom cupboard. In any event, it now presented him with the choice of either slowly suffocating in a stifling, claustrophobic fug or leaving the door sufficiently ajar to allow a life-sustaining through-draught from the narrow corridor that separated his cell from the flat's only bedroom.

Having come out in favour of the life-support option, he was then obliged to endure a barrage of grunts, giggles, creaks and, eventually, snores reverberating across the hallway. But even then, every time he felt himself drifting off, he would jump up with a start, convinced (despite Ingrid's earlier wind-up assurances) that one or both of his hosts was en route to pay him a surprise visit.

To crown it all, his sleep-craving senses were finally introduced to their first Mallorcan dawn in a decade by the neighbourhood crowing of not just one cockerel, but a whole choir of the infernal creatures. Their reveille was quickly augmented by the manic barking of a widely-dispersed chorus of keen but confused guard dogs, which in turn was complimented by the definitive Spanish din of two-stroke motorbikes rasping off in all directions. Finally, the whole caboodle was drowned out by the deafening scream of an endless procession of jets skimming the roof of the apartment block as they descended towards the nearby runway at Palma Airport. Good God Almighty, his dreary basement pad in sleepy old Edinburgh had been like the presidential suite in the bloody Hilton compared to this!

'The jets?' Ingrid pooh-poohed over a seven o'clock breakfast of burnt toast and treacly black coffee, which had been prepared by a pointedly silent Fidel, now standing on the balcony in his dressing gown, staring huffily out at nothing in particular. 'Nah, you never notice them after a while, sunshine. Anyhow, the jets is why I live in this place. Nice and near the airport, see. I gets a phone call from one of me mates on the Merryweather desk to say the gannet has landed, and abracadabra! I'm there in five minutes. Gives me more time for me sunbathing, man,' he chuckled.

Doogie gave a nervous laugh. 'Yes, with a name like Ingrid Bergman, I suppose you've really got to work hard at maintaining the bronzed Swedish look,' he replied in an attempt at levity, then immediately wished he'd kept his mouth shut. Ingrid making wisecracks at his own expense was one thing, but... 'Uhm, I notice you all call the planes gannets,' he said, quickly changing the subject.

'Yeah, only the Merryweather ones, though.'

'Really? Why's that?'

'Well, you know what the old sailors used to say – open up a gannet and you'll find all the rubbish on earth stuffed inside there.'

28

The phone rang and Ingrid got up to answer it...

'Hello ... Yep ... Shit! ... OK, doll face, I'm outta here!'

He grabbed his blazer and made for the door. 'Sorry about this, sunshine,' he called back to Doogie. 'Gotta rush. Two more reps down with the flu this morning. Anyway, you've gotta get yourself into the Merryweather office in Palma pronto. It's in the Plaza España, opposite the railway station. You'll get a bus just round the corner here.' He opened the door and paused halfway through. 'Oh, and when you get there, ask for the boss, Manolo. He'll tell you what's happening. *Adiós*!'

Manolo was the archetypically-dapper, middle-aged mainland Spaniard. He was of medium height, with fine-boned features reflecting his Moorish extraction, his upper lip concealed under a heavy black moustache, his harassed brown eyes ever alert but seldom smiling. He was on the phone, speaking animatedly in Spanish while drawing flamboyant doodles on a large notepad placed exactly in the centre of his neatly cluttered desk.

The attractive Mallorcan girl, who had shown Doogie in, wrote what he took to be his name on the pad, smiled shyly and returned to the outer office.

Manolo took a deep, exasperated breath, placed his hand over the telephone mouthpiece and told Doogie bluntly: 'You will have to go immediately to Magaluf. To the Hotel Magaluf Park. A coach full of clients is waiting to go on a guided tour of La Granja. You are the guide.'

He resumed his phone conversation before Doogie had time to stop his jaw from dropping.

'But I haven't a clue what to do,' he objected at the first break in Manolo's telephone outpourings. 'What's La Granja? I mean, when I applied they said I'd be given full training for the job.'

'Also, when you applied you said you wanted to go to Kenya,' Manolo countered in English that was as precise as his haircut. 'You are working for Merryweather Holidays now,

29

Mr O'Mara, and you had better get used to it.' He pressed a button on his desk. 'Catalina here will show you where to find a uniform,' he continued as the Mallorcan girl came back into the room, 'and Angie will be at the Hotel Magaluf Park to give you instructions.' He returned to his telephone conversation without as much as giving Doogie a shrug of apology.

The row of sky-blue blazers and beige trousers hung in a walk-in cupboard opposite an identical row of ladies' jackets and skirts, looking for all the world to Doogie like inanimate versions of the gender-segregated ranks who, at one time, would line up on either side of the village hall at the start of the Saturday night dances back home on Arran. A dark thought occurred to him that the previous occupants of these garments had probably either committed suicide or had simply gone AWOL for ever, the latter of which he was seriously tempted to do himself.

The girl handed him a jacket and slacks from the rack. 'I think for you these are OK,' she said. 'You will encounter white shirts and the ties of Merryweather in the drawer there. Please to approve the clothes for size, but make quick. Manolo he does not smile today, for we have absent four reps too few with the sicknesses.'

They had four reps too bloody *many* absent with the sicknesses, and number five getting sicker by the second, Doogie thought to himself. He knew what she meant, though, so he said nothing.

A couple of minutes later, he reappeared in the main office to the concerted wolf-whistles and catcalls of the dozen or so Brit girls, who had previously seemed too engrossed in their PC screens and telephones to even notice he existed.

'Wow! Who's the new hunk in the company kit?' one yelled. 'Hubba, hubba! What's *your* brochure price for bed-and-breakfast, big boy?' another shouted amid a chorus of cackles.

Catalina mercifully came some way to easing Doogie's embarrassment by walking up and pinning to his lapel a Merryweather ID badge, complete with a hand-printed inscription of his name, which, to his way of thinking, she had charmingly misspelt as 'Dugi'.

Spanish-style, she kissed him lightly on both cheeks. 'Now everyone is knowing that you are legitimate,' she said softly, then retreated blushing to her desk amid a hail of jibes about love at first sight and some indelicate words of advice on the subject of what surprises a nice Mallorcan country girl like her could expect to find under a big, hairy Scotsman's kilt.

One of the less vociferous of the Merryweather admin team beckoned Doogie urgently towards the door. Handing him an envelope and a slim paperback book, she said, 'That's the euro equivalent of a fifty quid sub on your first wages – I presume you're skint? – and a Mallorcan guidebook. You'll find a paragraph on La Granja in there somewhere, and I suggest you mug up on it smartly between here and Magaluf.' Before Doogie could even utter the first word of the string of questions piling up in his head, she went on, 'Now, there's a taxi waiting outside for you, so get your little Highland bum into gear before Manolo comes out and inserts a well-polished winkle-picker up it!'

'There you are, love,' Angie said as she shooed Doogie from the taxi towards the waiting coach, 'your university background's gonna come in nice and handy on your very first shot at being a tour guide.'

'Oh yeah?' Doogie's heart was already skipping beats. 'How d'you figure that out?'

'Well, you must've learnt *something* about bullshit in two years at vet college.'

'You mean –?'

'I mean there's gonna be fifty punters on that bus who'll be looking to you and your detailed knowledge of Mallorca to make this a trip to remember long after their holidays on the island are over.'

'Fantastic! And I know as much about Mallorca as I do about the dark side of the bloody moon!' Doogie's feet were now relaying top-priority leg-it messages to his brain. 'Play

31

the game, Angie. You can't just stick me in there with that lot and expect me to –'

Angie was already harassed to breaking point and in no mood for any of this. 'I thought Julie at the office was supposed to give you a guidebook, for Christ's sake!'

'She did.'

'Well?'

'And all it says about La Granja is that it's an old sort of manor house and farm place up in the mountains, and there's a bit about it dating back to Roman times or something.'

'OK, so it's a farm, with animals and everything. You'll be in your element, so go for it!'

She grabbed Doogie by the scruff of the neck and bundled him into the coach, where they were greeted with a semi-good-natured chorus of *Oh, Why Are We Waiting?* from the twenty or so day-trippers already on board.

'Right,' Angie shouted in Doogie's ear, 'this is the punter manifest and a note of the hotels where you've to pick up the rest.' She handed him a clipboard, then nodded towards the driver, a surly-looking blob of a fellow with oily, thinning hair and a fat cigar stub wedged between his lips. 'Carlos here knows where to go, but other than that you're on your Jack Jones. He's only interested in helping Merryweather reps if they've got short skirts and big tits.'

Picking up the mike, she clapped her hands to bring the rowdy singing to an end. 'Good morning once again, ladies and gentlemen, and please accept our apologies for the short delay in setting off. I'm sure it won't spoil your enjoyment of the trip to La Granja – one of my own favourite spots on the whole of Mallorca, as a matter of fact. Unfortunately, though, I won't be coming with you today. They need my happy, smiling face at the airport, worse luck. But my loss is your gain. For, due to a last-minute change in staff schedules, you're privileged to have as your guide today Merryweather Holidays' leading expert on Mallorca, its history, geography, and in particular its flora, fauna and wonderful rural customs and traditions. Ladies and gentlemen, it is my great pleasure to introduce you to … Mister DOOGIE O'MARA!'

'Thanks a million, Ange,' Doogie grumped out of the corner of his mouth during the explosion of cheering that followed. 'A real pal you turned out to be!'

'You better believe it, kiddo,' Angie muttered ventriloquist-fashion through a cheesy grin, while joining in the applause. 'Bluff your way through this trip without getting thrown off the bus and you can count yourself one of the team!' With that, she was out of the coach and off at the trot towards the waiting taxi.

To his great relief and even greater surprise, Doogie's initial state of almost incontinent panic had subsided considerably by the time the coach was drawing up outside the fourth and final hotel on the list. Until then, it had merely been a matter of allowing Carlos to weave the lengthy bulk of the coach through the warren of bar- and shop-crammed streets that constitutes the hub of the twin resorts of Magaluf and Palma Nova. All Doogie had to do was step down from the coach at each hotel-stop, smile and say good morning to the patiently waiting huddles of customers, check their names against the manifest as they boarded, then wave goodbye to each hotel's head porter, who was invariably to be seen peering out with a discreetly expectant expression from the foyer as the coach drove off. This was a piece of cake!

But his bubble of elation was about to be burst, for there, slumped uncomfortably on the forecourt wall of the Hotel Barracuda, were two familiar shell suits…

'What the bloody 'ell kep' ya?' Torvill Dean puffed, while hauling his perspiring blubber up the coach steps a chivalrous pace ahead of his holdall-lugging missus. 'Half an hour me an' 'er 'ere 'ave been stranded out in that white man's hell. I'm piggin' knackered and I'll be claimin' a full refund from your employers, young man!' Frowning, he scrutinised Doogie's face. ''Ere, I know you, mate! Where 'ave I clocked your coupon before?'

Doogie's heart skipped another beat. His oh-so-short honeymoon with tour-guiding was about to come to a humiliating end. Suddenly, it was bullshit or bust.

'Ca'n Pastilla?' he chanced, stumbling back as Mrs Shell Suit lurched past and surrendered her amplitude to the seat immediately behind Carlos the driver. 'Ever spent a Merryweather holiday in Ca'n Pastilla, sir?'

Torvill's face lit up. 'Spot on!' he declared. 'Hotel Casa Blanca, Ca'n Pastilla, two summers ago, it was. Never forget a face, I don't.' He dumped himself into the seat beside his wife and stabbed a podgy finger at her holdall. 'Ee, chuck, give's one o' them sugary crow-songs ya whipped offa the breakfast buffit. All that 'angin' about in the heat's got me fair peckish. Er, yeah, and ya might as well fish me out a tin o' lager when ye're at it. The chill should be nicely off it by now, like.'

Carlos uttered a Spanish oath and set course for the open road, the diesel engine at the rear of the coach growling obediently in response to his every jab on the accelerator pedal, his cigar stub rolling magically from one side of his mouth to the other in concert with his corresponding rotations of the steering wheel. True to type, he blared the coach's twin horns menacingly at every vehicle or pedestrian that even threatened to hinder his progress. And there appeared little doubt that, the smaller the vehicle and the more aged and infirm the pedestrian, the more satisfied was the leer on Carlos's face.

With Mr and Mrs Shell Suit well to the fore, a spontaneous outburst of *Here We Go, Here We Go, Here We Go*! issued from the more extrovert element among the passengers when the coach left the outskirts of Palma Nova and roared towards the highway and the untold pleasures of rural Mallorca that awaited.

Doogie, learning fast, didn't hesitate to grab this opportunity to duck down low into his seat opposite the driver and get stuck into the contents of the guide book with a vengeance. But, as he feared, that solitary sentence he had read in the taxi was all there was on La Granja. He was already beginning to formulate a desperate plan to collapse and fake a full foaming-at-the-mouth wobbly on arrival at the dreaded destination, when he felt a gentle tap on his shoulder.

He looked up into the face of an elderly woman he remembered coming aboard with a companion of similar cut at the hotel before last. Although suitably dressed for the midsummer Mediterranean heat, they both still retained a certain tweedy appearance that set them apart from their predominantly tee-shirts-and-shorts travelling companions. This prompted Doogie to toy with the speculation, however unlikely, that they were a pair of retired schoolmarms over for a genteel rave-up in the fleshpots of Magaluf.

'I'm so sorry to disturb you,' the woman said with a prim smile. 'My name is Wood – Miss Wood – and I am here with my sister Amanda – *Miss* Amanda – on a short painting and nature-study holiday.'

Doogie felt like asking her if she couldn't see that he was trying to work himself into a bloody epileptic fit here, but, remembering his manners, he stood up and offered her his seat instead.

Miss Wood came straight to the point. While she did not wish to appear in any way forward, she felt obliged to mention to him that some of the more academic passengers, like herself and Miss Amanda, (they were retired schoolteachers, he would perhaps be interested to know), considered that the journey to La Granja presented an ideal opportunity for them to learn a little about the passing countryside from someone as well-versed in the subject as he. Although she and her sister had been regular visitors to Mallorca for more than thirty years, and had made (in their own amateurish way) a fairly comprehensive study of the island's indigenous plants and wildlife, a chance such as this to learn from a professional seemed just too good to miss. Would he consider it too much of an imposition if she were to ask him to broadcast brief details of any items of particular interest over the coach's public address system? For instance, in the space of only the past five minutes she herself had already seen a golden oriole in flight through a grove of holm oaks *and* a hoopoe perching on the upper branches of a jacaranda tree. Why, she believed that even the more – how could she put it? – *frivolous* of the passengers would be absolutely thrilled to have such delights pointed out to them.

Doogie cast a fevered glance at the speedo on the dashboard in front of Carlos and tried to calculate what the odds would be in favour of his surviving a leap from the bus at over 100kph. No chance, no escape and no hiding place! He would have to stand his ground and bullshit like a man.

'How interesting that you should make that suggestion, Miss Wood,' he gushed, 'because I do normally like to make just such an informal in-transit talk a feature of this particular journey.'

Miss Wood nodded sagaciously.

'However,' Doogie continued, his brain groping madly for a straw to clutch, 'I have, ehm, rather foolishly left my specs in the office, and without them I can't see a thing beyond the end of my arm. Myopia, you know. Runs in the family.'

Miss Wood's hitherto benevolent demeanour changed instantly to one of acute irritation. Although she had hesitated to mention it until now, she felt compelled to remind Doogie that she, like the others, had come on what had been advertised as a *guided* tour and, having paid for such, they expected to be provided with such, and the fact that the guide was short-sighted and had misplaced his spectacles was really no concern of theirs. She would see to it when she returned to London that a formal complaint would be made to Mr Merryweather himself, a gentleman of proven solicitude, who had always attended personally to any other small gripe that she had felt obliged to register over the years. She knew from experience that Mr Merryweather took a very dim view indeed of any slackness, no matter how slight, in his staff's treatment of clients.

Indeed Mr Merryweather did, Doogie agreed. There was no greater stickler for staff excellence in all departments than Mr Merryweather, and he endorsed his employer's attitude one hundred percent. How fortuitous then, Doogie continued, that two such keen aficionados of the Mallorcan countryside as the

Misses Wood just happened to be on the coach on the very day he needed an extra pair (or two) of eyes, so to speak.

Miss Wood cocked an ear.

'What I'm suggesting, Miss Wood, is that you and your sister might consider doing me the great honour of acting as Merryweather Holidays' guest guides for the remainder of today's trip.'

Miss Wood half closed a sceptical eye, while Doogie prayed silently that the air conditioning would prove sufficiently powerful to disperse the aroma of bullshit that he feared must now be permeating the entire interior of the coach.

'Naturally, you and your sister would have the price of today's excursion reimbursed in full,' he went on. While trying gamely to ignore the mental shin-kicking that his innate sense of Scottish canniness was giving him, he produced the envelope which Julie had given him earlier and thumbed through the contents a few inches in front of Miss Wood's face. 'And it goes without saying that there would be a little something extra for you both, as a small token of Merryweather Holidays' appreciation of your stepping into the breach.'

Miss Wood's eyes moved from the money to the microphone. 'So, Miss Amanda and I would be broadcasting to the class – er, to the other passengers – via the public address system?'

'After a suitable introduction, of course,' Doogie truckled.

'AMANDA!' she shrieked in headmistressly treble towards the rear of the coach. 'COME HERE *IMMEDIATELY*!'

CHAPTER THREE

'CHRISTMAS COMES EARLY'

'Oh, I've just come down from the isle of Arran –
I'm no very bright 'cause I've fleeced ma sporran.
Dougal, where's yer troosers?'

NICK MARTIN'S JEERING PARODY of the old Andy Stewart song was clearly intended to impress the girls in the office and to embarrass Doogie. It failed on both counts.

'Nice one, Magic Roundabout,' Nick continued, undeterred by the knock-back. 'All the other guys I've known in this job have had to fight off women offering *them* loot. Now you turn up, and on your first day you've only given two old bints a free trip to La Granja *and* you've lobbed them even more dosh for doing *your* job for you! Get real, squire – you're not in the Outer bleedin' Hee-brides now!'

'Shove a sock in it, Nick,' one of the girls piped up. 'The kid was only doing his best.'

'Oh yeah, all rushing to protect poor Dougal now, are we, girls? Just as well, 'cause he's gonna need all the protection he can muster when Manolo gets his hands on him for throwing away the company's money.' Swaggering away from Doogie, he barked, 'If it was down to me, I'd dock it off your bleedin' wages, squire.'

Though his powers of restraint were being tested to the limit, Doogie didn't rise to the bait. He noticed Catalina, the young Mallorcan girl, working at a photocopier at the far side of the office. She looked up and exchanged glances with him, smiling coyly and lifting her shoulders into an apologetic little shrug – a revealing piece of body language that didn't go unnoticed by Nick Martin.

He ambled over to the copier, checked to see if Doogie was looking, then wrapped his arms round Catalina's waist from behind and whispered something into her ear. Catalina blushed violently and squirmed away.

Doogie realised that this familiarity act of Nick's had been performed for the sole purpose of riling him, and, much as it surprised Doogie himself, it had worked. He wanted to shout at him to keep his pawing hands off, but he checked himself, knowing that this was precisely the reaction that Nick Martin was trying to provoke.

Satisfied, nonetheless, that his little ploy had had the makings of the desired effect, Nick swaggered back into the middle of the office and announced, 'Would you believe, ladies, that young Magic Roundabout here was actually waving bye-bye from the coach to the head porters yesterday, when the poor geezers were standing there wondering why the hell he hadn't slipped them their backhanders for flogging the punters tickets for the trip?' He forced out a mocking laugh. 'Yeah, Carlos the coach driver told me all about it when he came back last night. *And* Carlos had to organise his own whip-round on the way home from La Granja and all! I ask you, has this tartan twonk got a natural gift for being a tour guide, or what?'

Doogie was beginning to see red, and Nick was well aware of it.

'Still, I guess the coach drivers all get paid in haggis where you come from, squire. Or don't they have coaches on Arran yet? Still getting about on bullock carts, are they?'

Nick's self-satisfied guffaws were met by an uncomfortable silence from everyone.

Doogie counted to ten, then said coolly, 'I'll tell you something, *squire* – after studying a fair bit of veterinary science, I thought I'd seen every aspect of the commoner forms of animal anatomy. But how wrong I was.' He walked up to Nick and clapped him lightly on the cheek with the flat of his hand. 'Now I've seen the impossible. A horse's arse with teeth!'

At a stroke, the palpable tension that had been building up in the office was relieved, and a wave of tittering into computer keyboards spread across the room. Nick Martin picked up his clipboard from the duty controller's desk and sauntered towards the door with as much nonchalance as he could fake. He paused before he left to throw Doogie a look that left him in no doubt that he'd eventually be made to pay for that put-down.

'*Olé*! *Viva* Doogie O'Mara!' Julie the cashier whooped the moment the door closed. 'That bastard's had that coming for years!'

There was an eruption of giggles as the 'horse's arse with teeth' crack was repeated back and forth. But this outbreak of hilarity was abruptly halted when a distinctly down-in-the-dumps Angie emerged from Manolo's office.

'In you go, love,' she mumbled at Doogie with a backwards jerk of her head. 'It's your turn in the lion's den now.'

If Manolo's smile still didn't quite reach his eyes, Doogie reckoned that his general disposition appeared to be significantly more agreeable than it had been the day before.

'I hope you will accept my apologies for yesterday,' Manolo said, shaking Doogie's hand and motioning him to be seated, 'but, in addition to the unforeseen staff shortages of which you are aware, I also had to cope with several cases of hotel over-booking which, unless resolved immediately, would have meant over one hundred of our clients arriving on the island last night with no accommodation available for them.' He strode round behind his desk and sat down. 'But that is the package holiday business, Mr O'Mara, and it's our job to ensure that our paying customers don't suffer because of our little difficulties. *Your Happiness Is Our Reward* is the Merryweather motto, after all.'

Doogie was already suspecting that Manolo's initial show of affability had only been a well-mannered way of softening him up for a verbal going-over – a suspicion reinforced by the ominous pout that appeared beneath Manolo's moustache as he reached for a small piece of paper on his desk. He leaned back in his chair and silently read the hand-written message, his face expressionless now, except for a nervous twitch that pulled occasionally at his left eyebrow. Doogie was about to suggest that he might as well save the company time and trouble by asking for his jotters right there and then, when Manolo looked up and tapped the piece of paper with the back of his fingers.

'Angie was given this by a guest at the Hotel Antillas first thing this morning. Apparently a copy has already been sent to Mr Merryweather in London. It's a memo from one of our clients – one of our most *valued* clients – who was on the guided tour to La Granja with you yesterday.' He tapped the paper again. 'Can you guess what it might be about, Mr O'Mara?'

Doogie fumbled nervously with the Merryweather ID tag on his lapel. 'Well, I've a pretty shrewd idea, and before you go any further, I'd just like to say that –'

'Come, come!' Manolo interrupted, a tetchy tone to his voice. 'I'm not about to ask you to hand in your badge just yet.

41

Believe me, I'm not the ruthless villain you may have been told I am.'

'You aren't? I mean, of course not.' Doogie was becoming confused. Maybe he should save his resignation speech for a moment or two yet, though. 'So, ehm, that letter's not what I *think* it is?'

A fleeting smile travelled from one side of Manolo's moustache to the other. 'I have no idea what you *think* it is, but I *know* what it is. It's one of the most glowing testimonials we have ever received from any of our clients in relation to that or any other guided tour. And all thanks to you, it would appear.'

'Ah, but I don't think you understand,' Doogie began. 'You see, it's actually a Miss Wood – well, a Miss Wood and her sister Amanda – who are to thank for –'

'But this *is* from Miss Wood.' Manolo handed Doogie the letter. 'Go on, read it for yourself.'

Doogie was flabbergasted. Miss Wood's comments read like the school report that every kid dreams of, but few ever get...

'*Mr O'Mara was the epitome of courtesy and consideration, did not insult his listeners with a parroted diatribe of mindless pap as most tour guides do, but instead skilfully involved the more enlightened travellers present in sharing their own particular knowledge with those less well-informed than they. Sterling effort. Excellent!*'

Signed, Maude Wood (Miss) BA.'

'There is a postscript on the reverse, which you should also read,' Manolo remarked blandly.

Doogie turned the page and scanned Miss Wood's immaculate handwriting in a state of increasing amazement:

'*Enclosed herewith is the sum of seventy-five euros in cash, and I would appreciate your being so good as to pass this on to Mr O'Mara as a donation towards a spare pair of spectacles. My sister Amanda and I sincerely hope that he will accept this in the spirit in which offered.*'

Doogie was unable to stop himself uttering a silly little laugh. 'I – I don't know what to say...'

'No need for you to say anything. I've already conveyed the company's thanks to Miss Wood, so we can now regard that short chapter as ended.' Manolo glanced at his watch, and his manner instantly became more abrupt. 'You have the 10am flight from Birmingham to meet with Angie. You'll spend the next two weeks working with her and learning from her, after which you'll take over her duties entirely. She will explain. Now, Mr O'Mara – Doogie – since you are now a member of the team, you must excuse me.' He lifted the phone. 'I have many other urgent matters to attend to.'

Unable to respond with anything more articulate than a stunned 'Wow!' and a stammered 'Thank you', Doogie had almost reached the door when Manolo called after him:

'*Oiga*! Don't forget this – the money from Miss Wood.' He held up the banknotes. 'Interesting, don't you think, that this is exactly the same amount that I instructed Julie to give you as an advance against your first salary yesterday morning?'

Doogie gulped and felt his cheeks flush.

Manolo handed over the money, that curious little smile traversing the shadow of his moustache once again. 'If I were you, Doogie, I would regard seventy-five as my lucky number from now on.'

Doogie piled into the passenger's seat of Angie's aged Renault 5. 'But why so glum?' he asked her. 'Let's face it, promotion's got to mean good news in anybody's language.'

Angie hurled the little car headlong into the inside lane of crowded traffic dashing down the wide Avenue Alexandre Roselló, acknowledging the ensuing fanfare of blaring motor horns with a flamboyant V-sign in her rear-view mirror and a mouthful of shouted curses in Spanish.

'Oh, don't get me wrong, love,' she eventually replied. 'I'm dead chuffed about the promotion. The extra money'll come in handy as well. Yeah, and don't you go thinking I'm miffed that you're gonna be stepping into my shoes after only a fortnight in the job. No, no, I'm delirious for you, really I am.'

'So,' Doogie shrugged, 'what's the problem?'

'The problem, kiddo, is that the promotion means a move off the island. I've been appointed head Merryweather rep in Ibiza, that's what.'

Doogie closed his eyes and grimaced as Angie jumped a red light and finally slipped the gear lever into third at a rattling forty miles per hour. 'Excuse me changing the subject for a moment, Ange, but is this a diesel?'

'Not as far as I know. Why?'

'It sounds a bit like one.' He looked back at the puff of blue smoke still hovering above the scene of the last gear change. 'And it farts like one too.'

'Nah, petrol, definitely.'

'When did you last have it serviced, for God's sake?'

'When I bought it, five years ago. Well, the guy said he'd serviced it, anyway … I think.'

'Angie, I don't want to put the wind up you –'

'That's considerate of you, love.'

'– but you're gonna have to get that engine overhauled, and smartly.'

'Listen, kid, it'll get a long enough rest once I bugger off to Ibiza.'

'Oh right, Ibiza,' Doogie said, realising that Angie had her own priorities. 'Head rep and everything. Congratulations, Ange. Magic!'

'Hmm, maybe.' Angie shook her head and sighed, not seeming in the least concerned that they'd come within a hair's breadth of being bulldozed into kingdom come by a thundering great juggernaut as she swept onto the airport-bound *autopista*.

'You're not having second thoughts, are you?' Doogie asked. 'I mean, a chance like that mightn't happen again for a long time.'

'It won't happen again for me *ever*, and that's why I've got to grab this chance now.' She brushed a tear from the corner of her eye, simultaneously exchanging abusive gestures with the overtaking juggernaut driver. 'It's little Pedrito, you see. I'll have to leave him here with old María until I get a suitable pad fixed up for us over there – and that'll be the end of the season, at least. Four whole months! Jesus, I'm missing the little bugger already.'

The remainder of the short journey to the airport was spent in relative silence, with Doogie reflecting on how paltry and selfish his problems now seemed in comparison with Angie's, while she sniffled and muttered incomprehensively to herself.

'Of course, I'll have to rent out my flat here if I'm ever gonna be able to afford to pay the rent for a place that'll do us in Ibiza,' she ultimately said out loud, as much to herself as to Doogie. Then, suddenly inspired, she added brightly, 'Hey, love, I don't suppose you could bear to wrench yourself away from the luxury of Ingrid's dosshouse to take my place on, could you?'

Doogie felt as if Christmas had come early to Mallorca. 'You're pulling my leg!'

'I'm bloody not, kid. *And* I'll keep the rent as low as possible. But you only get the place on the understanding that you look after it like a baby. No sub-lets to other reps – I know that game. No wild parties – old María's just next door. And no bonking in my bed. Agreed?'

'You've got yourself a deal!'

Angie thought for a moment while she took a ticket from the machine at the entrance to the airport car park. 'Do you know much about petrol engines, by any chance?'

'You don't grow up on a croft without learning plenty about *any* machine that helps with the work.'

Angie braked the little Renault to a spluttering stop in the nearest parking space. 'OK,' she said, 'put Humpty Dumpty here together again and you can have the use of him while I'm away – provided you promise to keep him in tip-top nick and pay all the necessaries, and that includes parking fines. Oh, and no bonking on my back seat, either. This is *not* a shaggin' wagon! Agreed?'

Doogie's look of absolute delight was the only answer needed. So what if the temperature was climbing to ninety in the shade? For him, Christmas really had come early.

Angie hustled him towards the terminal building. 'Right, young O'Mara,' she breezed, 'I think you owe me a coffee!'

CHAPTER FOUR

'A BOOGIE FOR DOOGIE'

EVEN WITH A FULL compliment of reps on duty, Doogie found that the schedule which had to be completed each day took some getting used to. Not that he wasn't accustomed to hard work, for he had known nothing else, but this job was in a league of its own.

For a start, there was the heat: incessant, humid, burning heat that sapped the energy, drained the patience, shortened the temper and stung the eyes with sweat. It was a heat that made him yearn at times for a nice, dull summer's day on Arran, with a fresh westerly wafting drizzle in from the Atlantic, and the Summit of Goat Fell floating above the mist like an island in the clouds.

Then there were the hours. Work was neatly chopped up into eight-hour shifts in theory, but extended in practice into endless days and sleepless nights of trying to be in several parts of the island at once as flight delay built upon flight delay. Life became a procession of shuttling successive herds of high-spirited or bellyaching passengers between airport and hotels; of cheerily declining (at the risk of losing a few teeth) cans of beer being thrust at you by bunches of 'the lads' on the coach; of sensitively redirecting old Mr and Mrs Smith to the back of the Edinburgh check-in queue after they'd stood for almost an hour waiting to reach the front of the East Midlands line; of politely telling young Mr and Mrs Smith where to put their reeking bundle of used nappies and what to do with their folding baby buggy; of helping newly-arrived and near-hysterical Widow Smith to ascertain which of a possible two dozen other airports across Europe her luggage had been flown to; and, last but not least, of parrying the advances of the ubiquitous Ms Smith by making it apparent (without hurting her feelings) that you weren't really turned on by having your bum repeatedly groped by a gin-reeking old dragon with hair that resembled a wig made of bleached Brillo pads.

But that, as Manolo had said, is the package holiday business, and under Angie's tutelage Doogie was quickly learning the ropes and slowly coming to terms with living in a near-permanent state of physical and mental exhaustion. One consolation, however, was that the long working hours left little time for sleep, which meant being obliged to spend less time in the stifling cupboard room at Ingrid's runway-end apartment. This, in turn, diminished any obligation he might have felt to break the ice with the patently unsociable and possibly (though Doogie dreaded to think it) *jealous* Fidel. Ingrid, for the most part, was akin to a ship that passed in the night, never failing, for all that, to buoy Doogie up with a few good-humoured words of advice and encouragement whenever their courses happened to cross. He was an enigmatic mixture of avuncular dependability and almost exotic mystery: a puzzling personality, of whom Doogie couldn't help but feel slightly in awe. But he liked him. Ingrid, he felt sure, was OK.

As for Nick Martin, on the couple of occasions he'd chanced to come within nodding distance of Doogie at the airport, there had been a distinctly cold and uncommunicative reaction, and that suited Doogie fine. He had resolved to take Angie's advice by giving the guy a wide berth anyway. As far as he was concerned, Nick Martin was nothing more than a ten-a-penny dickhead and didn't merit wasting time even thinking about. Yet he instinctively knew that he hadn't heard the last of Mr Martin's malicious mouth. The dent to his vanity caused by Doogie's put-down in front of the girls in the Merryweather office would not be readily forgotten.

The eve of Angie's departure for Ibiza was a Sunday, only a few days before the onset of the July invasion of the massed holidaymaking hordes from the north, and the end of what some of the more seasoned Merryweather reps considered to be the lull before the storm.

In what Angie regarded as an uncharacteristic lapse into compassion, Manolo had actually arranged for both her *and* Doogie to have the day off – Doogie's first since arriving on the island, and Angie's first, she claimed, in God knows how long. In any case, it presented the first and last chance for her to show Doogie her flat, and to explain how everything worked, where and when to pay the municipal taxes, the phone and electricity bills and the contributions towards the communal upkeep of the building.

The Calle Rosas Bermeso is situated at the residential end of Palma Nova. It's a relatively tranquil little avenue of mature villas and apartments set within a shady pine grove, only a couple of streets back from the shore and the resort's little yacht marina. Doogie was immediately impressed. Perhaps predictably, Angie's apartment block, though small and unpretentious, had a homely, lived-in look. It sat in well-tended gardens boasting a handsome palm tree by the entrance, and there was a profusion of geraniums cascading over several of the building's small balconies. There was no

49

lift, so Doogie shouldered his grip and climbed the outside stairs that led to Angie's third-floor flat.

'What do you reckon, kid? Is this worth a feature in *Hello!* Magazine, or is this worth a feature in *Hello!* magazine?'

'Centrefold, at least,' Doogie enthused, thinking that wonders would never cease. He had expected something all chintzy and twee and wall-to-wall Laura Ashley. Something all, well, something all … Angie.

'Not my taste, love,' she said, as if reading his thoughts. 'The place used to belong to a retired lawyer or something from Barcelona. Holiday flat. I bought it fully furnished when he kicked the bucket. All this stuff's far too olde-worlde and macho for me. Once I can afford it, I'm gonna have it redone all modern – all, you know, chic, sophisticated and slinky like.' She patted a well-padded hip and winked. 'A bit like myself, right?'

Wide-eyed and rubber-necked, Doogie merely nodded and secretly hoped that Angie would remain financially strapped for a long time yet. Not that he wished her anything less than the best of personal fortune, of course. No, it was just that he couldn't have imagined a more perfectly decked-out bachelor pad in his wildest dreams. In every detail, it was the archetypal Spanish stately home in miniature – tiled floors of mellowed terracotta, dark wooden furniture with those pernickety little raised square panels and forged metal appendages, overstuffed chairs squatting solidly on carved wooden feet with complementary inlays on the arms, and cool, white walls adorned with gilt-framed copies of antique maps and prints of mediaeval hunting scenes.

'I've tried to jazz it up a bit with a few Mexican-style rugs and all these bright flowers and stuff,' Angie said, almost apologetically, 'but I know it won't be right 'til I can turf out all that doomy old Spanish gear. Gives me the bloody heebie-jeebies, that does.'

'Turf it in my direction when the time comes, then. I reckon it's magic.'

'Yeah, you would, wouldn't you? All them pictures of dead

animals and everything.'

Doogie was feeling right at home already. 'How often do I water the plants, Ange?'

'Don't you dare! They're all fake – but good quality fake, mind. I got them for nix in a five-star hotel here when they closed it down a few years back. Yeah, the only real ones are them geraniums or whatever in the boxes out on the balcony here.' She led Doogie out through the French doors. 'But old María sees to all their needs, so you may as well forget any agricultural tendencies you're still harbouring.'

Doogie was becoming more impressed by the moment. The balcony, like the apartment, was small. It was just big enough to accommodate one sun-lounger and a round metal table with four chairs, but it faced due south, with a view over the treetops to the little yacht marina. From there, the crescent of Palma Nova bay swept away to the right, its sprawl of hotels and villas looking, from this distance, like a toy town backed by a ridge of pine-clad mountains.

'It must be a heartbreak to leave this, Ange,' Doogie said. 'I mean, you've got your own little bit of paradise right here.'

Angie's expression became pensive. 'Oh, I'll miss it all right, but it's leaving Pedrito behind that's really gonna slay me. The flat – well, at the end of the day it's only bricks and mortar and a view, and there's plenty more of that about. But Pedrito…'

'So, where is he?' Doogie asked, trying to keep the mood as bright as possible. 'I've been dying to meet the wee fella.'

'He's next door with old María … as usual,' Angie sighed, then added, 'Poor little sod obviously couldn't believe I was actually going to be at home *all* day today. Just took his cornflakes this morning and buzzed off to María's. Yeah,' she sighed again, 'just force of habit, like.'

Doogie could see that attempting to maintain a cheery atmosphere was likely to prove fairly futile. 'He's bound to be feeling pretty cut up about you going away tomorrow, though,' he said, opting for the realistic approach as he followed Angie into the kitchen.

'But that's the real kick in the guts,' she muttered dolefully, 'because I honestly don't think the little bugger could care less. And if that's what it's like when he sees me every day – even if it is only for a few minutes sometimes – what the hell's it gonna be like when he only sees me once every two or three weeks?'

'Can't you get back any more often than that? I mean, Ibiza's only a twenty-minute hop by plane, isn't it?'

'Yeah, but they're all scheduled flights. There's no Merryweather gannets between the islands, so I'd have to pay full whack. Coming back once or twice a month will be stretching the finances to the limit, believe me. Put it this way, there's no point in taking the promotion if I'm just gonna spend the extra dough on air fares, is there?'

Doogie stood listening quietly while Angie gave him an increasingly down-in-the-mouth rundown on the working of the various kitchen appliances.

'And don't forget,' she concluded glumly, 'you have *got* to take your rubbish out and bung it in the communal wheelie bin along the street *every* day, otherwise the kitchen will be crawling with *cucarachas* in no time.'

Doogie scratched his head and made an exaggeratedly gawky face. '*Cucarachas*? They're Latin-American formation dancers, aren't they?'

Angie turned on him, ready to snap his nose off for being so bloody dense. But then, noticing the twinkle in his eye, she burst into a kind of weepy laugh and punched him on the shoulder. 'They're fucking cockroaches, you daft Scotch lummox!' she warbled, then grabbed a piece of paper towel from a roll on the wall and gave her nose a big, noisy blow. 'And that's the first and last tears you'll see from me.' She took Doogie's arm and bundled him towards the door. 'Come on, kid, let's round up María and Pedrito. Yeah, bugger sitting about here sniffling. We're all going out for Sunday lunch. And sod the expense. I'm paying. But you, young Doogie O'Mara, will be driving Humpty Dumpty, because I, your old Auntie Angie, am gonna get nicely pissed!'

But for the very real possibility of Angie's little Renault 5 giving up the ghost at any moment, the half-hour drive to Sant Elm was an experience that Doogie thoroughly enjoyed. Apart from the traumatic trip to La Granja, during which he had been too uptight to appreciate much of what he saw in any case, this was his first opportunity to get out of his workplace, the ever-expanding spread of tourist developments that crowd the vast shoreline on either side of Palma city. He was relishing this escape into a relatively unspoiled corner of the *real* Mallorca. And he was soon to discover that, no matter how flattering their words, none of the guidebooks on which he had been boning up since coming to the island had adequately described the stunning beauty of the place.

Doogie was totally bowled over by the rugged grandeur of the mountains, with forests of pine and holm oak carpeting their rolling foothills and reaching their green fingers to the highest ridges. He was enthralled by the sight of trees miraculously clinging to great, riven outcrops of rock as if rooted to the very stone itself. The hint of myrtle and thyme and a thousand other bewitching perfumes drifted on the limpid air, while birdsong trilled over the chirrup of crickets basking in the clumps of withered grass bordering the winding country lanes. Over roadside walls, dwarf palms, ageless carobs and scarlet-flowering pomegranate trees could be seen growing wild. And everywhere, the glorious Mallorcan sunshine painted the landscape in sharp contrasts of light and shade.

Old María, whose range of English vocabulary appeared limited to 'OK?' and 'Is nice, no?', had opted to sit in the front beside Doogie. There were two likely reasons for this. Firstly, because she recognised that Angie would want to have as much of Pedrito's company to herself as possible. And secondly, because she probably also recognised, even more astutely, that to attempt to manoeuvre her short but perfectly globular frame through one of the little car's two doors and into the back seat would have been to court the likelihood of a

Palma Fire Department call-out, oxyacetylene cutting gear at the ready. Regular exclamations of '*Hombre*!' and '*Madre mía*!' peppered her cheerful running commentary on choice details of the passing scene. This enthusiastic narration, uttered in a childlike treble typical of many Mallorcan matrons, helped keep Doogie's mind off the distressed grunts and coughs emanating from Humpty's engine as he coaxed the toiling little vehicle up one seemingly endless succession of hairpin bends after another.

'*Mira*!' María would squeak. 'Look! See that farmhouse – the one with the yellow shutters? Well, it was in there that old Grimalt did for his wife on the night of the Fiesta of Sant Pere in 1964!' And María knew every detail of the scandal, for was it not she and her late husband Bartolomé who sold the evil old goat the rat poison from their hardware store back along the road there in Andratx? And there – that water *cisterna* by the torrent – that had been where the youngest daughter of Serra the blacksmith had drowned her newborn babe the very night before she departed for Palma to be a nun. And her own father the father of the babe at that! '*Madre mía*!' María made the sign of the cross. 'Pray that the Mother of God restored the gift of virginity to the wretched girl!' And now, the village of S'Arraco. This, she continued, had been where some German hippies had established a witches' coven in 1975 and had cast a spell that resulted in all the potatoes in the valley dying of blight that year. Tomatoes too! And all because the village storekeeper had refused to stock bratwurst and sauerkraut. '*Hombre*!'

A brief flurry of crucifix-fingering and muttered invocations would follow before María drew breath and launched herself, smiling broadly, into yet another series of ghastly tales of tragedy, pestilence and woe.

While all this was going on, Angie was chattering away nineteen to the dozen to Pedrito in the back, ostensibly oblivious to María's jabbering and intent only on trying desperately to make up for a little of the precious time which was about to be lost. Doogie glanced at them in the mirror from time to time: at Angie's laughing face and sad eyes, at her hands holding Pedrito's, stroking the shock of black hair from his forehead, brushing off non-existent smudges from his T-shirt. Then, her eyes downcast, she returned her hands to her lap, where she wrung them nervously as Pedrito innocently asked some little question or other about things he saw outside. His questions were in Spanish, though, and always spoken to María.

The last mile or so into Sant Elm was all downhill, the road snaking through a gully shaded by overhanging pine trees. On one side, the ground fell away into a glen that followed the course of a dry stream. Doogie noticed, however, that sufficient winter moisture had been retained in the slivers of fertile land on its banks to support lush colonies of bamboo and even a tiny field or two of vegetables. Though a world apart in certain ways, this idyllic scene reminded him of the humble croft which had once been his family home.

'Drive straight on up the main street,' Angie instructed as they rounded the last bend. 'The place we want is at the far end.'

Doogie closed his ears to old María's gleeful discharge of vitriol about the scandalous second wife of the cousin of the husband of the woman – the drunken bitch – who used to own that bar on the right there. Instead, he concentrated on enjoying the latest feast Mallorca had laid before his eyes. For, while Sant Elm hasn't been left totally unsullied by the advance of tourism, it is, nevertheless, a haven of relative restraint. Most of the village skirts one shore of a breathtakingly beautiful bay, its far side shielded by a mountain ridge that ends abruptly in headlands plunging vertically into the sea.

Following Angie's instructions, Doogie drove the length of the narrow main street and parked the car in a sleepy little lane, where the only signs of life were two mean-looking cats hissing and growling over the spilled contents of a plastic garbage bag. The air was rich with the Sunday smell of roasting chicken.

'It's early yet,' Angie said to Doogie. 'Only one o'clock. Another hour and this place will make Notting Hill at carnival time seem like a church fête on Arran. Let's nip round the corner and grab a decent table while the going's good.'

Donning a straw hat with its brim turned up at the front, which made her resemble an outsize incarnation of Paddington Bear in drag, old María led the way. Her verbal outpourings were now focused on detailed historical notes (accurate or otherwise) on the island of Dragonera, a sprawling, scrub-dappled bulk of beige rock dominating the skyline beyond Sant Elm bay.

Since Doogie no longer had to keep his mind on the rigours of driving, he decided that this would be an ideal opportunity to get in some much-needed practice in spoken Spanish. 'There's an island very similar to that in Arran's Lamlash Bay, where I come from,' he haltingly told María, hoping to stimulate a conversation on a mutually-interesting subject. 'The Holy Island, they call it back in Britain – *La Isla Santa.*'

Aha, but Dragonera was holy also, María pointed out, drawing Doogie's attention to a tiny building perched on the island's summit. That was the famous hermitage of Dragonera, and it had been occupied by holy men long before *Las Islas Británicas* were even discovered by those Roman sailors who just happened to drop off there for a *pipí* on their way past.

'*Pipí*,' Angie explained to Doogie, 'is the Spanish for piss!' End of conversation.

The *Restaurante El Pescador* could hardly have been more aptly named, since it is genuinely the lower half of an old fisherman's cottage, sitting snugly beside the similarly converted *Restaurante Vistamar*. These two unassuming little eateries enjoy one of the most privileged views of the dramatic south-western tip of Mallorca. All that stands between the two stone cabins and the sea is a canopied terrace, which both establishments use as an alfresco extension to their limited indoor dining areas.

Doogie wandered across and looked over the wall to a small jetty and a few wooden, ladder-like slipways that connect little boathouses to the rocky shore. Across the bay, a scattering of tall-masted yachts swayed lazily at their moorings alongside little local fishing *llauds*, their hulls gleaming white in the sunshine, their red-and-gold stern flags hanging limp in the still, hot air.

'We're gonna sit inside,' Angie called over to Doogie. 'You don't want to be out there, love, believe me.'

'Why not? It isn't too hot under the awning here, and the view's amazing.'

'It's not the bloody heat I'm bothered about, and you can see the same view through the window, so just get yourself inside here, and don't argue!'

María sagely nodded her agreement. 'Is OK, Boogie. Is nice.'

Doogie didn't bother to correct her about his name. At least Boogie was nearer the mark than Magic Roundabout!

'Boogie – that's a funny name,' Pedrito commented in perfect English, while sitting himself down beside Doogie at the table and staring at him with a forefinger rammed to the second knuckle up his nose.

'Yeah, well, it's Scottish,' Doogie replied offhandedly, not wanting to complicate matters. 'We've all got funny names up there.'

'It's *Doogie*, Pedrito, not Boogie,' Angie chipped in. 'That's D-oogie, with a D not a B, all right?'

Pedrito mulled that over for a couple of moments, then said, 'Are you going to be my new daddy, Boogie?'

'No! Certainly not!' Doogie blurted out, totally taken aback. Then, not wishing to offend Angie, who was now trying to hide a smirk behind her hand, he swiftly added, 'I mean, it would be very nice and all that, Pedrito, but … but, ehm, no.'

'Well, why did my Mummy tell me that you're going to come and live in my house?'

Doogie let out a little laugh and was about to explain, when Angie, clearly ill at ease, cut in:

'Oh, look, Pedrito! Here's the waitress with some bread

57

and olives and wine and water. *Fabuloso*! I take it you do like olives, Doogie, do you?' Without waiting for a reply, Angie hurled herself into a spirited conversation in Spanish with the waitress, then said to Doogie, 'In case you didn't get all of that, the sardines come highly recommended today.' She made an oblique gesture towards the waitress. 'Fresh as a virgin's kiss, according to her husband. He must have a bloody good memory, eh!' She forced a nervous giggle. 'Anyway, she says he only caught them this morning, so...'

Doogie shrugged. 'OK, sounds fine to me. Sardines it is.'

Pedrito, despite old María's fluttering and scolding, was now too busy cramming as much crusty bread as possible into his mouth to be bothered about an answer to the question he'd asked Doogie. For his part, Doogie suspected that he knew the reason for Angie having made sure he didn't answer it anyway.

With a chastening look, he stage-whispered over the table to her, 'You haven't even told the wee guy yet, have you?'

Frowning, Angie held a finger to her lips.

Doogie frowned back. What the blazes, he wondered, was Angie playing at? Surely it would have been better to give the kid as much time as possible to get used to the idea that his mother was going away. She'd had two weeks to break the news to him after all. But now... Well, he told himself, far be it from him to interfere. He poured himself a tumbler of water, then raised it to Angie's glass, which she had already charged with red wine.

'Cheers, Ange. Here's to you-know-who in you-know-where!'

'*Salud*, kid.' Angie gulped back a tear with her wine. 'And if you say another bloody word about you-know-where today, I'll personally –'

Her impending threat was cut off by an excited squeal from Pedrito. He pointed a bread-filled fist seaward, to where a large pleasure boat, loaded to the gunnels with upwards of a hundred singing and dancing holidaymakers, had rounded the headland and was making all haste towards them across the bay.

'*Jumbo One!*' Pedrito yelled.

'And that, young Doogie O'Mara,' Angie declared, patently grateful for this fortuitous opportunity to change the subject, 'is only one half of why we're lunching indoors!'

'One half?' Doogie queried.

Angie motioned towards the approaching pleasure cruiser. 'Before you can recite "it's a braw, bricht whatsitsname", there'll be another floating gannet stuffed with raving, sangría-soaked punters following in that one's wake.' She nodded her head knowingly. 'Yeah, and whatever did a nice little place like Sant Elm do to deserve this? I hear you ask. Well, that, as our great benefactor Sam Merryweather would say, is the package holiday business, my son.' Angie poured herself another wine. 'Say no more … already!'

Angie's grasp of the situation turned out to be spot-on. By the time the waitress had delivered them a large platter heaped with grilled sardines, day-trip vessels *Jumbos One* and *Two* had indeed tied up at the jetty. Their human cargoes clambered up the sea-wall steps like hordes of plundering pirates and seized every available table outside the two little restaurants. Then, as if by magic, the lone waitress was joined by several others, each running a non-stop shuttle service of food and drink between restaurant and terrace.

'God almighty!' Doogie groaned. 'And I thought Brodick Pier on Arran at the start of the Glasgow Fair fortnight was frightening!'

'I told you you'd feel at home here,' Angie shrugged.

Somewhere, a guitar strummed stridently, and a rich, baritone voice boomed out a reprise of the *Viva España* chorus the passengers of both boats had been bellowing as they approached Sant Elm jetty. A sombrero-shaded black face appeared over the sea wall, and a wild cheer rose from the wine-scoffing, food-gobbling multitudes.

'*OLÉ, BJÖRNO-O-O!*' they yelled.

Doogie almost choked on a sardine bone. 'Christ!' he coughed. 'It's Ingrid!'

'What the hell's he doing here?' Angie gasped. 'He's supposed to be covering for me at the airport!'

Ingrid, resplendent in Hawaiian shirt and Bermuda shorts, and thrashing a guitar flamenco-style, strolled round the tables, grinning and singing and inciting his audience to join in, mouths full or not. The pink-kaftan-draped figure of Fidel minced rhythmically behind, tapping a tambourine and sporting a *Kiss Me Quick* sailor's hat tilted jauntily on the side of his head.

Angie did a double take. 'Blimey! I've heard of all hands to the pumps, but this is ridiculous! Bloody hell, Manolo would throw a right wobbly if he knew Ingrid had deputised that bleedin' fairy cake into the Merryweather posse!'

'More flu victims, honey,' Ingrid explained, popping his head round the door on catching a glimpse of Angie's stunned features through the window. 'The musical matelots who usually do this gig are down with it, so…'

Angie gawped at him. 'But the airport! I mean, the Newcastle and Luton gannets and everything. I thought you were supposed to be –'

'Hey, don' you go gettin' yo' liddle-ol' lily-white butt all jambalaya'd, Miss Angie,' Ingrid crooned in mock plantation-speak. 'Massa Manolo is a-doin' it fo' us his-self, sho' nuff.'

'Man*olo*? Yeah, yeah, pull the other one,' Angie retorted, '– it plays *Somewhere Over The Rainbow*!' But all she got back from Ingrid was a wide-eyed shrug. 'Come on,' she objected, 'Manolo hasn't been reduced to doing the airport slog for about twenty years! I mean, he's a *manager*. He doesn't *work*!'

'I hasn't been reduced to doin' this Captain Singalong caper for years either, pumpkin,' Ingrid countered dryly, all traces of frivolity dispensed with. 'But needs must, and you and young Doogie here best count your blessings that your day off wasn't given the chop, that's all.' Then, sensing that Doogie was about to express his gratitude, he promptly added, 'And don't kid yourself, sunshine – you'd've been back on duty pronto if we could've got a hold of you in time.' He gave

Doogie a conspiratorial wink. 'So make the most of it, huh?'

Young Pedrito, meantime, had clambered onto Doogie's knee, the better to reach the communal dish of sardines, which he was getting stuck into, Doogie noted, with the de-boning dexterity of an Aberdeen fishwife.

Ingrid gave Doogie's back a playful punch. 'Hey, man, you really got a nat'ral way with kids, don't you!'

Doogie returned Ingrid's leg-pull with a bashful smile.

Delighted, Ingrid bellowed with laughter. 'And that, sunshine, gives me a great idea. Wow, and you better believe it, boy!'

'Uh-huh?' Doogie charily replied, reluctant to even begin considering the possibilities.

Pedrito pointed a whole sardine at Fidel, who was loitering by the doorway, moodily fingering the bells and ribbons of his tambourine. 'Why is that man wearing a lady's dress?' he asked. 'Only *maricas* wear frocks,' he reasoned, his fledgling bilingualism innocently replacing the word 'pansies' with its Spanish counterpart.

He was too young to have that one explained, Ingrid told him through a booming guffaw. The swiftness of Ingrid's response took the heat out of a potentially awkward situation, though it failed to forestall a fit of sniggers from old María, who, thanks perhaps to that one Spanish word, had clearly understood the gist of Pedrito's observation. It also failed to prevent Fidel from chasséing off in a fit of pique.

Ingrid glanced out towards the terrace, where his boisterous charges were wolfing down all the solid and liquid sustenance that came their way. 'Well then,' he sighed, 'I'd best be off and delight the Merryweather music lovers with another of me old Spanish folk songs.' Prudently not mentioning Angie's imminent departure for Ibiza, he bade them a flamboyant farewell and hit the terrace singing the chorus of *We're Having a Gang Bang Against The Wall*.

'What's a gang bang, Boogie?' Pedrito enquired.

'I think your mum could be better qualified than me to answer that,' he replied, while giving Angie an impish wink in an attempt to brighten up her increasingly morose mood.

'I should be so lucky,' she mumbled in return, before gloomily pouring herself another measure from the rapidly diminishing contents of her wine jug. 'The nearest I get to a sexual experience these days comes out of a Tampax packet.'

Doogie's explosion of laughter startled Pedrito at first, but he then started to giggle as well, irresistibly infected by this outbreak of adult jollity. Neither was old María immune to the tickle of this welcome merriment bug, albeit that she didn't understand what she was laughing at any more than young Pedrito did.

'Stuff it,' Angie finally sniffed, then stood up and hauled a bewildered Doogie to his feet. 'Come on, kiddo,' she blubbed, smiling through wine-fuelled tears as the beat of Ingrid's guitar pulsated through the open door, 'let's me and you show them gannet droppings out there what boogie *really* means!'

CHAPTER FIVE

'MISTER SUNSHINE'

DOOGIE NEVER DID FIND out whether Angie had finally plucked up enough courage to tell Pedrito the truth about her move to Ibiza. The little chap certainly never mentioned it during his regular breakfast-time visits next door to Doogie. He seemed content to talk to his mother on the phone every day and to carry on his life in old María's company in the way he had long become accustomed to. Doogie was glad for him, though child welfare was a subject he was loath to concern himself with when he finally crept exhausted into the sanctuary of his adopted new home every night ... or, more usually, every morning.

'*The Mister Sunshine Club* is what Sam Merryweather decided to call it,' Ingrid had said to Doogie, while shepherding him through the revolving doors of the Hotel Tiempo Alegre in Magaluf on the morning after Angie's impromptu farewell shindig at Sant Elm. 'This place is the flagship of the Merryweather chain on the island, so it's here Boss Sam wants to launch his bright new idea, *comprende*?'

Doogie had been gripped by a terrible sense of foreboding as he followed the striding Ingrid over the marble floor of the foyer. 'But how do I figure in this?' he'd asked gingerly.

'Because, matey, you are about to be *Mister Sunshine*

himself!'

And that, due to the unfortunate fact that the children's entertainer recruited for the job had lost his bottle (or, perhaps, had consumed too much of its contents) before he was due to leave the UK the previous morning, is how Doogie O'Mara, veterinary student turned rookie holiday rep, suddenly found himself dressed up as a clown. Before he fully realised what was happening, he was doing his inadequate best to provide poolside fun – combined with all-too-frequent life-saving activities – for a couple of dozen bedlam-raising brats. These founder-members of the *Mister Sunshine Club* were dumped in his charge every day during the bleak, sweltering, post-lunch hours when sensible natives were in bed having a siesta, and when the kids' parents, if they weren't playing bingo in the bar, were probably also in bed, either sleeping it off or having it off.

'Could be worse, though,' Doogie had philosophically told himself on that first embarrassing stint in the Coco-the-Clown kit. 'I could be on the dawn shift at the airport, or even the suicide-zone slot at three in the morning.'

Despite such stoical reasoning, however, he found himself on *both* dreaded duties the very next day, and that was in addition to his poolside duties as a mass childminder. In the view of the Merryweather Holidays management, his afternoon *Mister Sunshine* stint was, after all, only a recreational interlude in his normal work schedule.

'Look on the bright side, sunshine,' Ingrid grinned at him at the end of the first week. 'Just think, man – all them young mums in the hotel here a-letchin' after you when they brings their sprogs along of an afternoon. Yeah, this gig's a passport to nookie paradise for a good-lookin' young dude like you!'

Doogie looked forlornly at the two-foot expanse of clown's boots protruding from beneath his calf-length tartan flares. 'Hmm, I've had a fair demand for my stud services, right enough,' he grumped. 'You've seen the spotty bird with the six kids and the white stick, have you?'

Ingrid bellowed out his usual drain-like laugh. 'Never

mind, sunshine,' he beamed, 'I've fixed up an assistant for you. Startin' tomorrow. A nice one – trust me!'

Young Catalina from the Merryweather office was really on a rep-training course, or so she genuinely believed. It was part of the company's policy of providing employment opportunities for young local people, according to the Merryweather corporate propaganda, but in reality only an excuse for hiring gullible, out-of-work youngsters to do dogsbody tasks for a pittance of a wage. Sam Merryweather had learned the financial benefits of such dole-queue-reducing scams from successive British governments, and he hadn't been slow to adopt the system wherever possible throughout his overseas holiday empire.

Doogie was in the pool pumphouse that doubled as his changing room when Catalina arrived for her first day as *Mister Sunshine*'s sidekick.

'Already I learn to making tea the English way and working the *máquinas* of *fotocopia* and fax,' she keenly confided. She proudly fingered the lapel of her newly issued Merryweather blazer. 'Now I have the *oportunidad* to being a real rep, no? Also to improving of my English with speaking to the *clientes* here, yes?'

'Well, yes and no to both questions,' Doogie replied, trying to appear serious as he pulled a ginger, bald-pated wig over his unruly shock of hair, 'but not necessarily in that order.'

'*Qué*' Catalina queried with an expectant smile. 'I no understand.' She touched the mop-like fringe of his wig and giggled.

Doogie felt his cheeks flush under their coating of white greasepaint. What a complete fanny she must think him, he reckoned, then proceeded, however reluctantly, to stick on his red nose and test his revolving bow tie.

'It's just that, well, how can I put it?' he said at length. 'The actual rep side of this *Mister Sunshine Club* job is a bit, you know, unorthodox. *No ortodoxo, sí?*'

'*No ortodoxo?*'

Despite himself, Doogie was becoming captivated by the inquisitive look in Catalina's big, brown eyes as she probed for an answer she could understand. However, it was a dead cert that mixing pleasure with work would be a non-starter in the Merryweather rule book, so he smiled at her as platonically as he could. She giggled again. A glance at the upwards-sweeping makeup of his mouth in the mirror told him why.

'You'll find out as we go along,' he shrugged, unaware that raising the over-padded shoulders of his coat had only exacerbated his already-ridiculous appearance. 'And the language,' he gamely continued. 'Yes, well, the clients here do speak English ... of a kind. But whether it's the kind you'd really want to learn is a moot point, I'm afraid.'

'Moot? *Qué* is a ... moot?'

Doogie knew when he was beaten. He took her by the elbow with one hand, picked up a bashed-about ghetto-blaster with the other and led her towards the door. 'You'll get the hang of it as we go along,' he assured her, then ushered her into the blaring sunlight.

'Oy! 'Oo's the sexy bird?' a seven-year-old London lad called out from the far side of the pool. Doogie had already nicknamed him the Artful Dodger. He was squatting in front of the bouncy castle that had been dubbed the *Sunshine Clubhouse*, systematically relieving a group of less streetwise kids of their pocket money in a dodgy pitch-and-toss game. 'Been flashin' 'er a butcher's at yer 'aggis in yer shed there, 'ave yer?' At that, he let rip with a peal of cackling laughter that sounded unbelievably filthy for such a baby-faced tyke.

'See what I mean about the quality of the English language spoken hereabouts?' Doogie asked the suddenly apprehensive-looking Catalina. He gave her arm a reassuring squeeze. 'Don't worry, they're not all as horrible as that little – well, let's see – what can I call him?'

'Fucking arsehole?' Catalina enthusiastically suggested, borrowing freely from the Anglo-Saxon vernacular with a smile so chaste that she might equally well have been reciting a string of Ave Marias to the Pope.

Doogie fingered his red nose. 'Ehm, yeah, I suppose that'll do,' he said, trying to keep a straight face. Obviously, the girls in the office had been coaching her in the use of such English colloquialisms, so he decided it would be simpler just to leave it at that, for the present at least.

'YIPPY-HI-HO-O-OH!' he yelled to the motley gang of sprogs gathered by the bouncy castle.

'YIPPY-HI-HAY-Y-Y!' they hollered back, in accordance with the rallying cry that had been devised by Sam Merryweather himself.

'SHUT YOUR BLEEDIN' CAKEHOLES!' a voice thundered through the open patio door of a first-floor balcony directly above. 'WE'RE TRYIN' TO GET SOME BLEEDIN' KIP HERE, FOR CHRIST'S SAKE!'

'Kip?' Catalina hesitantly enquired of Doogie. 'Cakeholes?'

He flashed her a don't-worry-about-it smile and pressed the play button on the ghetto-blaster. The *Mister Sunshine Club* song honked out, the banal lyrics again penned by Sam Merryweather himself, and sung, apparently, by a tone-deaf hag (his wife, it was rumoured) trying to sound like a five-year-old girl.

Doogie launched his outsize boots into a soft-shoe shuffle for the final approach to Club HQ.

'YIPPY-HI-HO-O-OH, Sunbeams!' he called out. 'And what are we going to do for fun today?'

'HOW'S ABOUT A ONE-HOUR SUNBATHIN' SESSION IN THE BOTTOM OF THE PIGGIN' SWIMMIN' POOL?' the voice of the sleep-deprived gent bellowed from above.

'A chance would be a fine thing,' Doogie told himself while he surveyed the host of expectant faces gaping up at him. They were literally daring him *not* to entertain them. 'Hey, just look, Sunbeams,' he grinned, making a theatrical gesture towards Catalina. This is our brand new *Mister Sunshine Club* lady. So, come on, everybody, let's have a big, happy hello for … CATALINA-A-A!'

Doogie applauded optimistically as the group of children monotoned a dull, 'Hell-o-oh, Cat-a-lee-na-a-a,' in response.

''Ere, give's a look at yer knickers, Mrs Sunshine darlin'!' the London kid called out, then led the others in a chorus of giggling.

Clueless about the cause of the merriment, Catalina giggled naively along.

Doogie shuffled round to where the cocky little leader of the hilarity was slouched, pulled him aside and hissed in his ear, 'Any more of that, Dodger, and I blow the gaff on your pitch-and-toss caper, right?'

The kid eyeballed Doogie with a look of defiance that also belied his tender years. 'Dunno what the bleedin' 'ell ye're talkin' about, mister,' he smirked.

'The two coins – one with two heads, the other with two tails, right? I've seen it all before, sonny boy.'

The youngster chuckled to himself, his cocksure expression never wavering. 'Yeah, yeah, in yer dreams, mate.'

'Whatever you say, wise-guy, but if I see you ripping one penny off any of these kids again, I'll bring in the *Guardia Civil*, right!'

'The wot?'

'The local rozzers, the fuzz, the pigs, get me? I can call them now, if you want, and we'll watch you emptying your pockets right here in front of your new chums, OK?'

The smirk faded from the boy's face. 'Bleedin' charmless Scotch git!' he muttered, then slunk back into the refuge of the throng.

After such an unpromising start, the remainder of the afternoon somehow passed remarkably smoothly – relative, at any rate, to the mayhem prevailing when Doogie had been trying to cope on his own. The immediate benefit of Catalina being there was that all the little girls in the group (and several of the little boys too) were naturally drawn to her, huddling around to listen to island nursery rhymes and fairy tales. This allowed Doogie to concentrate on trying to control the club's more rumbustious element, who were patently not interested in such sissy stuff. Instead, they delighted in giving free vent to their nascent lager-lout tendencies by testing the impregnability of the bouncy castle walls with flying sun loungers or anything else that wasn't nailed down.

The other invaluable bonus Catalina's presence provided was that she could attend to the toilet needs of the younger female Sunbeams: a tricky chore that Doogie had previously felt prudent to delegate to one or two of the more senior girls – themselves only seven years old at most. Predictably, this had resulted all too often in some pathetic, little soul or other returning prematurely to her mother's care with tear-stained face and sodden pants... or worse. Conversely, Doogie had observed on his first day at the job that none of the boys ever even *asked* to go to the bathroom, leading him to the logical conclusion that they simply peed in the pool during supervised splash-abouts at the shallow end. *Viva* chlorine!

''Ere, ya won't really grass on me pitch-and-toss scam, will yer?' an unusually subdued Artful Dodger asked Doogie while the rest of the club members were being reunited with their parents at the end of the afternoon.

'Depends if you keep your nose clean,' Doogie shrugged. 'Entirely up to you, kid.'

The boy rolled his shoulders uneasily. 'It's only... well, I mean... it's only that me old man would kill me, see.'

Doogie pulled a wry smile when he saw the look of genuine angst contorting the young tearaway's face. 'You're lucky to have a dad with principles,' he said, ruffling the Dodger's hair. 'You'd do well to follow his example.'

Lowering his eyes, the little boy shook his head. 'Nah, ya don't understand, mate,' he groaned. 'See, it's me old man's dodgy coins what I been usin'. Yeah, and he'd do his bleedin' nut if he sussed it was me what nicked 'em.'

At that, he turned and wandered glumly off, leaving Doogie to contemplate reality after such a brief reunion with his faith in human nature.

'*Please, miss. Please, miss*. This is what the little children are saying to me always,' Catalina grinned at Doogie after she had seen the last of her charges safely off. '*Miss* – this is the name they are calling their teacher at school in England, no?'

'One of them,' Doogie grunted as he flopped exhausted into a chair under the shade of a Carling Beer parasol.

'And the other ones?' Catalina keenly questioned.

Doogie closed his eyes and let his head fall back, his hands dangling loosely by his sides. 'You don't want to know, believe me,' he mumbled through a yawn. 'Jeez, I'm knackered!'

'Knackered?'

Doogie opened one eye to see Catalina canting her head in that seductively inquisitive way of hers.

'Knackered?' she repeated, a worried frown wrinkling her brow. 'This is meaning you are *enfermo*, no?'

'*Enfermo*?'

'*Sí*, the, uhm…' Catalina paused to think of the word in English. '*Sí*,' she finally ventured, 'the infirmary-ness.'

Chuckling to himself, Doogie sat up. 'No, no, I'm not sick, just tired. *Cansado*, you know?'

Catalina's eyes lit up. 'Ah, so "knackered" is "tired", yes?'

Doogie couldn't help laughing. 'Yes, it is. But "knackered" – well, it isn't a word a nice young lady like you might want to use, if you see what I mean.'

Catalina caught her breath.

No time like the present, Doogie thought. He raised a gently admonishing eyebrow. 'And the same goes for words like "fucking" and "arsehole", I'm afraid.'

Catalina didn't know where to look. 'But the girls in the *oficina*,' she gasped, blushing violently, 'they are teaching me that "fu-"–' She clapped a hand to her mouth, the shocked look in her eyes gradually turning to one of amusement as the truth dawned on her. She let out an embarrassed little laugh, before muttering a string of quick-fire Spanish words that Doogie guessed didn't add up to much of a commendation of her mentors in the Merryweather office.

Time to drop the subject, he decided. He pulled off the clown's wig and ran a hand through his sweat-matted hair.

'I'm not supposed to remove my disguise in public,' he confided, 'but if I leave this thing on my head any longer, I'll go stark-raving doolally.'

A pensive smile came to Catalina's face. 'Doolally,' she murmured. 'I have so many beautiful words of the English still to learn.'

They sat quietly with their own thoughts for a while.

When Doogie eventually broke the silence, he was somehow only half surprised to find himself fumbling for words. 'It's, ehm ... well, it's been really good having you around today, you know. I mean, come to think of it, I don't know how I ... well, how I sort of managed to do this *Mister Sunshine* job without you – before today, if you know what I mean.'

Catalina dipped her head. 'I like very much this job,' she said, then added shyly, '*Sí*, and is really good to having you around today also.'

Doogie cleared his throat and took a diversionary look at his watch. 'Wow, ten past five, would you believe! Hey, I'm off-duty now until I go to the airport at midnight!' He hesitated briefly, then asked, 'How about you, Catalina? Working this evening, are you?'

Still looking down, Catalina shook her head. 'I work no more until *mañana*. Then I go again to the *oficina* at the nine of the morning.'

Doogie hesitated again, giving Merryweather's don't-mix-workmates-with-pleasure maxim due consideration. 'Look,' he said at length, having concluded that what he did in his own time was his own business, 'I don't suppose you'd like to ... I mean, how would you fancy –?'

'You like to coming with me?' Catalina cut in, looking up suddenly, her eyes wide with anticipation. 'You are *veterinario*, no?'

'Well, yes – no, not exactly a vet yet. But, yes, I –'

'*Bueno*,' she grinned, 'so you like to coming with me to my home, to the farm of my *padres*, my parents, *sí*?' She shook her head persuasively. 'No is far from here.'

Doogie was slightly taken aback by Catalina's swiftness in coming forward. 'Your – your parents have a *farm*?'

'*Sí*, a farm,' she enthused, her eyes sparkling. 'We have a farm with many *animales* and many almond trees. Is very beautiful. *Sí*, and for you my *madre* will making the food, no?'

Doogie was momentarily lost for words. 'Well, yes … thank you,' he finally replied, unable to disguise his pleasure at the thought of having someone cook him some *real* food, after existing for so long on polystyrene airport sandwiches and microwaved midnight pizzas. 'That would be absolutely, well … great!' Then he looked down at his outlandish *Mister Sunshine* garb, and his face fell. 'But this clown's stuff… I mean, I'll leave the clothes in the pump house here, but I'll have to go home then. You know, have a shower and everything.'

'*Muy bien*,' Catalina smiled with a casual shrug. 'This for me is *no problema*.'

The sound of a female conversing cheerily with Doogie on the landing as he fumbled with his keys had old María out of her door in the wink of a keyhole-peeping eye, her suspicion radar on full beam. But just as she was about to give him the third degree, a glimmer of recognition flickered in her eyes and her mouth opened wide.

'Cati!' she squealed, rushing forward and clasping the equally astonished Catalina to her ample bosom. '*Mi pequeña*!' she exclaimed, while planting kisses on Catalina's cheeks. 'My little Cati! What a *fantástica* surprise!' The old woman held Catalina at arms length, tears of joy glinting in her eyes as she gazed adoringly at her. '*Jesús, María y José*!' she gasped. She dabbed her eyes with her apron and clucked with all the delighted surprise of a fat old hen that had just laid a double-yolker.

She and Cati's family had been neighbours out in the country, María explained to Doogie. Of course, that had been before her husband died, after which she had moved into this *apartamento* here in town. It had been so long since they'd last met, Cati and her – ten years or more, she reckoned – when Cati was maybe eight or nine – all awkward and gangly and just sprouting new front teeth. And, *madre mía*, she went on, hardly pausing to draw breath, just see what a beautiful young *princesa* she had turned into now! '*Dios mío*, a prize catch for any young *caballero*!' she declared. She then flashed Doogie a puckish wink. *Sí*, she assured him, she would produce many strong sons, this one.

Catalina covered her embarrassment by returning old María's hug.

Doogie busied himself unlocking his front door.

Meanwhile, little Pedrito had appeared from old María's apartment and was staring up appraisingly at Catalina. 'Is she going to be Mrs Boogie, Boogie?'

'Ehm, no, Pedrito,' Doogie mumbled self-consciously, picking up an envelope from inside his door. 'We just sort of work together, you see.'

Catalina bent down to shake Pedrito's hand. 'My name is Cati,' she smiled. But, she continued confidentially in Spanish, even if she wasn't going to be Mrs Boogie, he could call her Mrs Sunshine, if he liked.

Doogie pretended not to understand what she had said to Pedrito, but allowed himself an inward smirk of approval nevertheless. A look of gloom spread over his face, however, as he opened the envelope and scanned the enclosed note. It was from Margaret Hyslop, the old Arran vet's daughter, who had designs on Doogie and ambitious plans for their mutual future. And now – *now* of all times – she was coming to Mallorca!

'Shit!' he grunted.

Old María tutted.

Young Pedrito sniggered.

'Is bad news?' Catalina enquired, a little knot of concern on her forehead.

'Yeah, bloody right it is!' Doogie spluttered, stuffing the letter back into the envelope, then quickly amending, 'I mean no, no, nothing really. Just something I wasn't expecting, that's all.' He feigned a placid smile and motioned them to come inside…

'Anyone care for a drink?'

CHAPTER SIX

'HOME FROM HOME'

HAVING LITTLE PEDRITO ACCOMPANY them wasn't exactly the image of a sojourn into the Mallorcan countryside that had been forming in Doogie's mind while taking a shower. But Pedrito, it transpired, had asked Catalina in his habitual, innocently-forthright way if he might join them, and she hadn't hesitated to give her consent. It would be a lovely treat for the *niño*, she suggested to Doogie when he emerged from the bathroom, *and* it would also give Señora María a welcome break from looking after the little fellow.

'Fine by me,' Doogie said, thinking to himself that it could have been worse. Old María might have been coming along as well!

'Is OK, Boogie,' María grinned as she saw them off on the landing. She was clearly revelling in the sight of this newly-formed trio of surrogate familial bliss. 'Is nice!' But the little one would have to be back by ten at the latest, she called after them down the stairwell. '*Hombre*! Late enough that for a four-year-old!'

Humpty Dumpty, Angie's faithful Renault 5, was running a treat now – for its age. Doogie's timely execution of an oil change and his fitting of new sets of points and spark plugs had worked wonders for the performance of its long-neglected engine. The little car fairly purred along the westbound *autopista* from Palma Nova, heading into the late afternoon glow with windows and sun roof opened wide to the balmy air. Humpty's radio was blaring out strange, Arab-rhythmed pop tunes from *The Voice of Algiers*, or whatever obscure North African radio station it was tuned into – or, rather, stuck on. Doogie reminded himself that this was another little job he would have to see to sometime. Then again, the more he heard it, the more he liked this hypnotically-monotonous music. Today's electric guitars notwithstanding, it evoked images of Spain's colonisation by the Moors many centuries earlier. To him, at this moment in time, the music seemed absolutely appropriate to the setting – exotic, vibrant, mysterious, Mediterranean.

And Catalina didn't seem to mind the sounds coming from the car radio either. She was sitting there beside Doogie, her fingers gently tapping out the beat on her knees, her dark hair billowing in the slipstream while she gazed over the expanse of sea away to their left.

Suddenly, Doogie's thoughts were drawn to Arran; to silver-gold sunsets on the Firth of Clyde; to summer glens, where dancing midges bobbed swarming and stinging in the limpid evening air; to cool, twilight shadows creeping down from the purple mountains. His thoughts were drawn to home.

Yes, to home … and to Margaret Hyslop.

Hell's bells, that letter from her was all he needed! Oh, not that he minded seeing Margaret again. But maybe not just yet. Maybe not until he had sorted out his future in his own mind. Maybe not *here* of all places. Maybe not *now*. And the *now* part was the worst of it, because she hadn't even said *when* she'd be turning up, only that she was on a back-packing holiday in mainland Spain and that she'd pop over to the island to meet up with him at the first opportunity. God, she could arrive on his doorstep at any moment! And what was he supposed to do to with her then? Typical Margaret, this – never giving a thought to the fact that he was working his nuts off for eighteen hours or more most days. And, horror of horrors, what if she just happened to turn up at the Hotel Tiempo Alegre one afternoon and caught him acting the kids' minder in that ludicrous clown clobber? A dainty dish that would be to set before her father. Dammit, if only he hadn't sent her that postcard with his new address on it. But on the other hand, even if he hadn't, she'd only have wheedled it out of his sister Mo and would have gone ballistic into the bargain.

Doogie exhaled a lungful of troubled air. 'Why, Margaret?' he moaned under his breath. 'Why bloody *now*, Margaret?'

He was eventually retrieved from his brooding by Catalina touching his arm and indicating that they should turn right up ahead.

'It is the road for Capdellá, my village,' she said, her look combining pride and apprehension. 'I hope you will like.'

'Oh, I kinda think I will,' Doogie replied with a reassuring nod of his head.

He surveyed the pretty countryside which surrounded them now that they had escaped the featureless tarmac ribbon of the *autopista*. It was a softly rolling landscape of small, stone-walled fields, of ochre hillocks flanked by almond and olive groves, where skinny, panting sheep hugged what little shade they could find beneath the trees' spindly branches. Here was a scene of timeless tranquillity, a world apart from the tower-block tourist traps where Doogie now spent much of his working life.

'In fact, I *know* I'll like your village,' he grinned. 'Once a bumpkin, always a bumpkin, if you know what I mean.'

Catalina knew what he meant, even if she didn't understand what he'd said.

Driving on, a quick glance in the rear-view mirror told

77

Doogie that little Pedrito, in contrast to his incessant outpouring of questions that had dominated the earlier part of their journey, had finally succumbed to the drone of the engine and the heat of the evening. He was slumped, sound asleep in the dubious security of his ill-fitting seat belt, a succulent thumb in his mouth, a comforting forefinger up his nose. Doogie motioned Catalina to take a peep over her shoulder, and they both chuckled quietly at the little chap's pose of careless relaxation. So careless, Doogie silently noted, that the slumbering Pedrito had involuntarily released the contents of his bladder into his jeans, and over a fair area of the rear seat too. Ah well, so much for thoughtfully offering him a drink back at the flat!

Approaching Capdellá, the road began to snake its way upwards, skirting a pine-wooded hillside and overlooking a little valley dotted with beige-coloured stone farmhouses. A few still showed the cluttered evidence of workaday life in the aged farm implements lying scattered around. But other houses, doubtless owned now by rich foreigners, sported grandiose, stone-arched extensions to their original simple form. Close to one, an elegant swimming pool occupied a tiny terraced field where an entire family's sustenance once grew. Outside another, a shiny BMW coupé was parked in a manicured courtyard that, not so very long ago, would have been the muddy province of rootling pigs. Progress.

The same warm-hued masonry was replicated in the houses of Capdellá, an unassuming little village nestling in the foothills of the Tramuntana Mountains. At first glance, there seemed to be no more than a couple of tiny shops, a post office and a bar to provide for the needs of the folk who lived in the sleepily-shuttered houses fronting its two intersecting streets. The place had a simple, laid-back charm, though, and Doogie smiled his approval to Catalina as she signalled him to turn left at the crossroads ahead.

'We take the mountain road for Andratx,' she informed him. Then, sensing his unease at the thought of coaxing the little Renault over the towering ridges that suddenly loomed before them, she quickly added, 'But *no problema*. The farm of my parents is not now far.'

The road began to twist upwards again once they cleared the village, the cultivated contours of the slopes stepping up in terraces all the way to where craggy cliffs glowed like amber in the evening sunlight. *Finca Sa Grua* was the name seared into the bleached wooden sign at the head of the track down which Catalina asked Doogie to turn. It meant The *Grua* Farm, she explained – its name taken from the mountain in whose lower folds the farm lay. Not insignificantly, the mountain of *Sa Grua* also protected her father's fields from the cold Tramuntana northerlies of winter.

From this vantage point, Doogie at last began to understand why Catalina had appeared so proud of her native village. While passing through, it had struck him as attractive enough in a plain sort of way. Viewed from here, though, it was a living picture postcard: a cluster of terracotta-roofed houses and small, ramshackle farmsteads, back-yard citrus groves and bougainvillea-draped pergolas cradled together at the centre of a valley of breathtaking beauty. And all this set against a backdrop of serene, majestic mountains.

Catalina noted Doogie's enthralled expression. 'Is like Arran, no?' she asked.

'Aye, I suppose it is,' he kidded, 'except we've maybe got a couple of better-looking palm trees up there!'

'Better than that one?' Catalina queried, a twinkle in her eye as she pointed to the magnificent fifty-foot specimen dominating the gateway to what she announced was the home of the family Ensenyat.

Doogie's jaw dropped. 'Yeah, well, maybe that one does kinda put the two wee Arran ones in the shade right enough.'

He pulled up in the farmyard, then got out to savour the ambience of what he could already see was a place rich in character and charm. The old farmhouse was in the traditional, unfussy Mallorcan style – a rectangular two-storeys of stone the colour of weathered straw, topped with a gently-pitched roof clad in mellow tiles. At the front, chunky wooden beams supported an open verandah, or *porche*, which, judging by the presence of two dilapidated easy chairs and a portable TV, provided an airy sitting-out sanctuary for Catalina's parents on hot summer evenings. A few hens and a strutting cockerel scratched and pecked around the yard, in which the resinous smell of pines drifting down from the mountains mingled with that warm, pungent odour of farm animals so familiar to Doogie. This was, he concluded, the Mallorcan equivalent of the small, no-frills, working farm on which he had been brought up.

If, on emerging from her kitchen to greet them, Catalina's mother felt perturbed at the sight of her daughter arriving home unannounced in the company of a fair-haired foreigner with a black-haired, wet-trousered infant in tow, she managed to disguise her feelings extremely well. Indeed, she welcomed both visitors so heartily that Doogie, at least, felt instantly at home. As might be expected, though, the newly-awakened Pedrito was more withdrawn than usual. Señora Ensenyat's diplomatic offer to swap his 'accident-damaged' jeans for an old pair of Catalina's childhood shorts did go some way, however, towards restoring the little fellow's customary self-confidence.

'These are boys' shorts anyway,' he privately assured Doogie at the first opportunity after changing. 'Girls' ones smell different.'

Doogie gave him a pat on the shoulder. 'No doubt about that, Pedrito,' he said with a suitable degree of solemnity. 'Yeah, definitely boys' ones, them.'

A grin and a satisfied sigh indicated that Pedrito's macho self-esteem had been duly restored.

Catalina had been chattering away to her mother in *mallorquín* all the while, and although Doogie could understand little of the local language, he had managed to grasp enough of what she said to gather that he, Pedrito, Angie, old María, Humpty Dumpty and their respective relationships had now been fully defined.

Señora Ensenyat's resultant smile showed just a hint of

relief, Doogie fancied. In any case, she then informed him in 'standard' Castilian Spanish that, while Cati showed Pedrito and him round the farm, she would prepare them a meal of good, old-fashioned Mallorcan country fare.

'After all,' she added with a wink, 'playing the clown must make a young man very hungry, *si*?'

The sun was already descending towards the summit of Sa Grua Mountain when Catalina led Doogie and Pedrito back towards the farmstead. They had wandered through field after little stone-walled field, in which oats had recently been harvested between regularly spaced lines of almond trees. As they passed by, lop-eared goats looked inquisitively up at them, their neck bells tinkling while they moved about grazing on any tufts of weeds they could find growing in the stubble.

Apart from answering Pedrito's occasional questions about what was what and why, little had been said during the stroll. Doogie and Catalina had seemed content to quietly enjoy the sense of well-being that this little farm engendered in them. It was a feeling made all the more precious since both knew that, by leaving home to seek 'better' ways of life, they had done their bit, no matter how reluctantly, to end for ever the age-old lifestyle of their respective families. Eventually, the fancy extensions and shiny BMWs would smother the Finca Sa Grua as well. Progress.

Catalina pointed out a neglected-looking farmhouse a couple of fields lower down the valley. 'It is the *finca* of Señora María, your neighbour in Palma Nova,' she informed Doogie, adding that the house had remained unoccupied since old María's husband passed away about ten years previously. Catalina's father now worked the land and tended the almond trees for the old woman. But, Catalina went on, as María had no family, the whole place would eventually fall into disrepair and become abandoned, like so many of these little farms.

'But why doesn't she sell it?' Doogie asked. 'I mean, I've no doubt your father could do with the extra land on a permanent basis.' He made a sweeping gesture with his hand. 'And with a view like that, she'd have no problem selling the

81

farmhouse to some money-bags foreigner.'

Catalina gave a resigned shrug. The answer to Doogie's question was two-fold, she explained. Firstly, her father couldn't afford to buy the land, and secondly, old María didn't need the money anyway. Selling her hardware store in Andratx, together with the savings she and her husband had salted away over the years, had provided her with more than enough to see out the rest of her days. Yes, Catalina confirmed, the fate of old María's farm was sealed. It would, in effect, die with her.

Doogie shook his head in despair, recalling that his family's croft on Arran, rented from the local laird, had been taken back into the estate after his parents died. It meant one less crofter, certainly, but at least the land was still being put to good use.

'Cati! Cati!' a voice called out from the Finca Sa Grua farmstead. A dark-haired fellow in his mid thirties, dressed in working clothes, had been rushing from one of the farm buildings towards the house when he noticed Catalina. He shouted some garbled instructions to her in *mallorquín*, then dashed back into the building.

Clearly concerned by what he had said, Catalina began to run towards the house herself. 'Please excuse,' she called back to Doogie. 'I must to telephone quickly.'

'*Qué pasa*?' Pedrito asked, wide-eyed. 'What's happening?'

'I haven't a clue, pal,' Doogie shrugged. 'But it's kinda urgent, whatever it is.'

He took Pedrito by the hand and they set off towards the barn that appeared to be the source of all the anxiety. As they approached, the sound of moaning drifted out through the open door. Animated words were being exchanged by male voices. With Pedrito clinging to his trouser legs, Doogie stepped hesitantly inside. He could just make out the shape of two men crouched over an animal lying on some straw bedding at the back of the shed. As his eyes became accustomed to the gloom, he saw that the men were tending a cow, a young heifer, and it was obvious the poor animal was in distress. She groaned as she lifted her head and looked round at her own heaving flanks.

'A bad first calving, I'll bet,' Doogie muttered to himself.

Just then, Catalina came rushing into the shed. Breathless, and looking even more concerned than before, she blurted out something to the men in Spanish. Doogie managed to grasp that the vet wouldn't be able to come for at least an hour, as he was doing some sort of emergency operation on a dog.

'*Mierda*!' the older of the two men cursed. '*Hijo de puta*!'

No point in standing on ceremony in an emergency, Doogie thought. 'Hi, I'm Doogie,' he announced, then stepped swiftly into the fray, his shirt already off. 'It's all right, I'm a vet,' he said to the patently mystified older man. '*Veterinario*, OK?' He then spoke to Catalina. 'Fetch a bucket of warm water and some soap, please. And be as fast as you can, right?'

Doogie lost no time in appraising the situation. He ran his hands over the heifer's body, whispering soothing words to her as she moaned pleadingly, her eyes staring in bewildered agony.

'It's all right, lass,' he murmured, 'we'll soon get the wee bugger out, never fear.' He turned to the older man. 'How long has she been like this?' Noting the puzzled look on the man's face, he repeated the question in faltering Spanish.

The man raised his shoulders, then said, almost apologetically, '*Dos horas.*'

'Two hours! That's two hours too many,' Doogie said under his breath. 'I just hope the poor little sod's still alive in there, that's all.'

Catalina came rushing back in with the soap and water, her mother following a few paces behind.

'OK,' Doogie said to the two men as he lathered his right arm, 'make sure she doesn't try to get up.'

Then, realising that neither probably understood a word of English, he pointed to his arm, made a crunching sound, and indicated that the heifer should be kept in her present position.

Nervous mumblings of '*Sí, sí*' and '*No problema*' indicated

83

that his two assistants had got the message. Not that it made much difference, Doogie reminded himself. If the beast decided to make the wrong move while he was up to his armpit in midwifery, there was precious little the two blokes could do about it. Anyway, in for a penny...

Lying down on the floor behind the heifer, he handed the younger chap the end of her tail and signalled him to keep a safe distance. As Doogie instinctively knew she would, the frightened creature then proceeded to empty the contents of her bowels over his bare chest – an understandable enough response to the crude intrusion of a human arm.

'Pooh!' he heard Pedrito exclaiming somewhere in the background. 'Dirty cow!'

Doogie's probing fingertips touched the calf's fore-hooves. 'Good,' he grunted. 'At least you're the right way round.' He thrust his hand even deeper, his eyes already stinging with sweat. 'Now then, calfie, where's your nose got to, eh? Dammit!' he gasped. 'That's all we need!'

Even if they didn't understand what he was saying, the look on Doogie's face told his anxious audience that there was a problem. A big one.

'The calf's head's turned back,' he said. 'No way can we get it out like that.'

The heifer let out a woeful moan, as if to say that she could have told him so without being subjected to all this indignity.

Doogie tensed as he felt the animal's hips move. 'Steady, lass. Just stay put,' he told her, trying to keep his voice as calm as possible. 'Bad enough with a calf stuck inside you without having a broken-armed vet student hanging out of your behind as well.'

An apprehensive hush had now descended on the scene.

Catalina knelt down beside Doogie and dabbed the sweat from his forehead. 'Is still alive, the baby cow?' she asked in a whisper.

'Could be. I don't know. Won't be much longer, though, even if it is.'

Carefully, Doogie then eased himself round on the hard

mud floor in a desperate effort to add another inch to his searching fingers. It worked. 'Gotcha!' he panted on taking hold of the calf's slippery muzzle. 'Now, come on, wee fella,' he urged, 'let's have that head of yours pointing towards the exit!'

At that, the heifer's abdomen started to heave as she tried to rid herself of the source of all her agony.

'Not yet, for Christ's sake, pet,' Doogie pleaded, feeling the pressure of the heifer's contractions crushing his arm and fearing that he would lose his tenuous grip on the calf's nose. 'Just hold on a wee minute more – there's a good lass.' Just then, the heifer's muscles relaxed momentarily and Doogie grabbed the chance to give the calf's head an almighty tug. 'There,' he puffed, 'that's got it round the right way!' He extracted his arm and gave the heifer a pat on the rump. 'OK, now for the hard bit, darlin'!'

He turned to Catalina again. 'She's going to need some help with this. The calf – it's a big one, you see. Huge shoulders. We'll need some rope. A clothes line would do.'

Catalina stared blankly at him. 'Sorry, *no comprendo.*'

'Ehm, rope … *cuerda,*' Doogie said, frantically searching for the Spanish words. 'Yeah, *cuerda* for the…' He pointed to his shirt lying on the floor. '*Cuerda* for the washing. And make it quick!'

As Catalina hurried out, Doogie, drenched in sweat, stood up and started to rub down his muck-covered chest with straw.

The older of the two men came forward and handed him a half-full bottle of water. 'I am the *padre* of Cati,' he smiled. 'Her father, *sí*?' He gestured towards his companion. 'And Rafael, he is my neighbour.'

'Doogie – Doogie O'Mara,' Doogie responded, eagerly accepting the water bottle, then taking a refreshing slug. 'Ah, that's magic … thanks!' He glanced down at the filthy state he was in and shrugged apologetically. 'Oh, and please excuse me if I don't shake hands.'

Catalina rushed back in with a coil of washing line, which Doogie grabbed and quickly tied in a noose at both ends.

Without wasting a second, he lathered his right arm again and readopted his prone position at the heifer's rear.

'Right,' he muttered, 'once more unto the breach, dear friends!'

The task of looping the nooses round the calf's front ankles was relatively easy, compared to righting the attitude of its head. For all that, it was still as awkward as trying to thread a greased needle in the dark, as old Hyslop had often grumped whilst struggling through this same procedure on wet byre floors back on Arran. What the mums in labour thought of it all wasn't hard to guess, and Doogie knew from her increasingly distressed breathing that this one couldn't take much more. They would have to get that calf out quickly, dead or alive, if the heifer was to be saved.

He scrambled back to his feet, then gave Catalina's father and Rafael one piece of the rope, holding onto the other himself and beckoning Catalina to lend a hand.

The heifer gave a low groan, her hind legs twitching involuntarily as she started to strain in what Doogie feared might be a last desperate attempt to give birth.

'Together!' he called to his helpers. 'Come on now! Pull as she pushes! PULL!'

As the heifer bellowed in pain, Catalina's mother knelt down and cradled the wretched animal's head in her lap.

'Don't give up now, lass,' Doogie implored. 'Come on – another big shove!'

Seemingly endless minutes of concerted heaving and pushing passed, but all to no avail. Then, just as Doogie was about to admit defeat, the tip of one of the calf's hooves appeared, then the other, and then its pink muzzle. A bubble of mucus appeared at a nostril, then popped.

'It's alive!' Doogie grinned. 'The wee bugger's alive after all!'

He pressed his team into yet another strength-sapping heave. The heifer responded, and out popped the calf's head. Doogie's growing feeling of euphoria ended abruptly, however, when he saw that the calf's tongue was blue and dangling ominously out of the side of its mouth.

'Quick!' he shouted, redoubling his efforts and urging the others to do likewise. 'We'll lose it if we don't get it out fast. Now PULL!'

As if sensing that her ordeal might almost be over, the exhausted heifer made one final, supreme effort that had her groaning in agony into Señora Ensenyat's apron. Then, as the calf's membrane-shrouded body finally slithered out onto the barn floor, a cheer went up from little Pedrito, who had been watching this crudely-assisted miracle of nature from a suitably safe distance.

'Yippee-ee-ee!' he yelled. 'The cow just pooped a little cow out of her bottom!'

But Doogie was only too aware that it was a tad early for celebrations. Crouching over the calf, he opened its mouth to clear it of mucus, then, with a piece of straw, did the same for each nostril. 'Come on, wee fella,' he pleaded. 'Breathe, dammit, breathe!'

Endless moments passed without any sign of life appearing in the prostrate little animal. Doogie vigorously rubbed its rib cage, trying to stimulate breathing. But nothing.

'Is it dead, the baby?' Catalina asked him, her eyes imploring him to do something, anything.

Doogie knew its chances of survival were growing slimmer by the second. A feeling of desperation was building inside him. He bent over and took the lifeless head in his hands. Prising the jaws open, he put his mouth to the calf's and exhaled a great lungful of air down its throat. Then another, and another. Still no sign of life.

He felt a hand on his shoulder, and looked round to see the forlorn face of Catalina's father. 'Come,' Señor Ensenyat said softly, a sad smile of resignation on his lips. 'You can do no more, *amigo*.'

By now, Pedrito had ventured forward and was standing by Catalina's side, looking down in awe at the newborn calf.

'Look, Boogie!' he whispered, as if in the presence of a sleeping child. 'The little cow ... he's waking up!'

Doogie quickly redirected his attention to the calf, hardly daring to hope that Pedrito hadn't been mistaken. But, sure enough, one big brown eye blinked open, then the other. The calf gave a little sneezing snort, a cough, and took its first glorious breath of life, startling itself with the loud 'Moo-oo-oo' that then escaped its mouth.

Instinctively, the heifer turned her head towards the sound and returned her calf's cry with a motherly murmur of reassurance.

Doogie made no attempt to hide his delight while bending down to lift the still sneezing and blinking calf into his arms. 'OK, wee one,' he grunted, 'better let your mum see what the cause of all the fuss looks like, eh?'

'*Gracias, amigo*! *Muchísimas gracias*!' Señor Ensenyat beamed, then threw a congratulatory arm round Doogie's shoulder, with no apparent regard for the unsavoury stuff smeared all over it. He pointed to the calf, standing on long, wobbly legs where Doogie had placed it by its mother's head. 'It is a baby girl cow, *sí*?'

'Aye, a wee heifer, sure enough – and a right braw one at that,' Doogie automatically replied, as if he was back home on Arran and sharing the delight that the birth of a female addition to his herd brings to the dairy farmer everywhere.

'Braw … wee … heifer?' Catalina enquired, puzzled by the strange-sounding words.

'That's right,' Doogie grinned back. 'And a right wee stotter, in anybody's language!'

The evening meal that Señora Ensenyat presented, despite the interruption to her preparations caused by the maternity crisis in the barn, turned out to be a simple but wholesome treat, the likes of which Doogie hadn't enjoyed since he lived at home with his own parents. Also, there was a definite air of celebration around the big wooden table which had been carried from the kitchen and set in the relative cool of the *porche*. Doogie felt quite flattered, though not a little embarrassed, by the near hero-worship that was being directed at him by everyone. By everyone, that is, except Rafael.

Although the Ensenyat's strapping neighbour had done at least his fair share of hard work in helping deliver the calf, he'd seemed in a singularly sombre mood since joining them for supper. More than once Doogie caught him staring darkly at him when he glanced up from his plate, only for Rafael to quickly look away, deliberately avoiding eye contact. Also, Doogie couldn't help but notice the little admiring glances that Rafael cast in Catalina's direction from time to time: glances, Doogie perceived, which Catalina did not return. Nor did these little flashes of body language go undetected by Catalina's parents, who would then discreetly exchange knowing looks across the table.

You didn't need to be an agony aunt to grasp what was going on here, Doogie thought. Anyway, on checking his watch, he realised that he had other more pressing things to worry about at the moment. It was already well past old María's curfew hour for Pedrito's return.

'And now you go home to sleep?' Catalina's mother smiled on noticing Doogie stifle a yawn after he had expressed his thanks for her hospitality.

'No,' Doogie replied with more than a trace of regret, 'now I go to the airport to start work!'

CHAPTER SEVEN

'PAINFUL RETRIBUTION'

FOR ALL HIS INITIAL aversion to being saddled with the role of Mister Sunshine, Doogie had to admit to feeling a slight pang of sadness at the eventual arrival from England of a man-and-wife duo of professional children's entertainers, hired on a permanent basis to take over what he had come to call his daily zoo-keeper's turn at the Hotel Tiempo Alegre. For one thing, the *Mister Sunshine Club* had provided him with a welcome, though gruelling, break from routine Merryweather Holidays duties every afternoon. For another, it had given him a chance to get to know Catalina a bit better, albeit that there was a strict limit to how well you could get to know anyone when in the company of up to thirty rumbustious little

'Sunbeams'.

On the plus side, though, Doogie was relieved that he would not now run the risk of Margaret Hyslop seeing him in what she would surely have regarded as a totally demeaning situation for a future pillar of the community on Arran. For, no matter how much he hated to admit it, Doogie still couldn't escape the weird feeling of subjugation that Margaret somehow managed to provoke in him, even in her absence. He remembered all too vividly how appalled she had been at his decision to take a year out from his studies to work as a holiday rep, so her likely reaction to his dressing up as a clown every day hardly bore thinking about.

As Doogie was the only Scotsman in the Merryweather Holidays' Mallorcan team, manager Manolo, in his wisdom, had singled him out for special duties at the start of the Glasgow Fair holidays in the middle of July – duties including, but not restricted to, meeting every one of the four Glasgow flights to arrive on the first Saturday. And it didn't take Doogie long to realise that what Angie had said about the 'wildlife' aspect of this particular fortnight was no exaggeration. OK, he had seen the phenomenon of the mass annual exodus from Scotland's largest city often enough on Arran in years past, but the excitement-charged and (in some cases) well-lubricated state of the hordes pouring from the steamer onto Brodick Pier had been like the arrival of a Sunday school outing compared to what he now encountered at Palma Airport.

Not that all the Glaswegian holidaymakers were particularly boisterous or had necessarily had even the merest whiff of a cork during their southward migration. Far from it. In fact, the first plane of the day had delivered three hundred or so passengers whom any self-respecting metropolis would have been proud to have as its citizens: a grand assortment of families, ranging from the obviously well-heeled to the not quite so affluent.

The only black mark had been awarded to a diminutive grandfather with a fear of flying, who had partaken of too much Dutch courage prior to departure. He had then proceeded to lose his false teeth in the plane loo, 'while shoutin' doon the big white telephone tae Ralf an' Hughie,' as his wee Hairy Mary wife had so eloquently put it to Doogie. She had then asked him (in vain!) if he could persuade 'wan o' the conductresses tae go back in therr and fish ma man's wallies oot the airyplane's cludgie'.

But each successive flight delivered increasingly large numbers of young 'singles', paradoxically in groups, and most of them noisily intent on having a bloody good time from minute one of their holiday. In the main, though, their high spirits hadn't been to the excessive discomfort of their more mature and, usually, less ebullient fellow travellers. Not until the last flight of the day, that is.

'Rather you than me, chum,' one of the stewardesses said to Doogie as she exited International Arrivals displaying the general demeanour of someone who had just scrambled out of a bear pit. 'We had a bunch of loonies on that gannet who had the captain within a whisker of turning back to Glasgow, and I kid you not!'

'Pissed, I take it?' Doogie asked, rhetorically.

'Or whatever. They're out of their tiny skulls anyway. And the language!'

'A pity you let them on the plane in the first place.'

'No, honestly, they weren't that bad when they came on board. Well, OK, you could see they'd had a few, but nothing out of the ordinary.'

Doogie hunched his shoulders. 'Why did you keep serving them bevvy during the flight, then?'

The stewardess shook her head. 'That's it, we didn't. Not more than a couple of beers apiece, at any rate.'

Doogie nodded. 'Dope,' he concluded. 'Yeah, they've probably been popping loco sweeties – just using the beer to wash them down.'

The stewardess squirmed as the sound of bagpipes wailed through from the Baggage Reclaim area. 'Anyway, they're all yours now, mate,' she said, 'and the best of British luck!' With that, she scampered off to catch up with her cabin-staff colleagues, who had already made themselves prudently scarce through the nearest way out of the terminal building.

Although Baggage Reclaim is essentially off-limits to anyone except bona fide passengers, Doogie felt that this was an eminently excusable occasion for breaking the rules. With an assenting nod from the official on duty, he slipped through the customs area. Then, following the skirl of the pipes, he made his way past bemused legions of newly-arrived Germans and Scandinavians, past clutches of tutting French matrons still waiting for their luggage to appear, and into a cat-calling squad of skinheads just off the Luton flight. Things looked – and sounded – ominous!

'Ship them bagpipe-stranglin' plonkers back to 'aggis land, why don'cha?' one beer-bellied skin with a Union Jack tattooed on his forehead bawled. 'Bleedin' animals!'

'Yeah!' one of his mates yelled as he ripped the ring pull off a can of Carlsberg Special. 'Get them Jock bastards to show some fuckin' decorum, right?'

'Oy! Shut yer peebrock, will ya!' another bellowed in the general direction of the bagpipes, while a sea of multi-national faces looked on in stunned silence. 'Some of us is bleedin' music lovers 'ere, for Gawd's sake!'

Raucous skinhead hilarity ensued.

'Trouble brewing,' Doogie said to himself, his stomach starting to churn. Yeah, and where the hell were the Guardia Civil when you needed them most? Not a single policeman in sight! 'Brace yourself, O'Mara,' he muttered as he tried to select the most human-looking of the Luton bunch to approach. 'Once more unto yet *another* breach, dear friends,' he further muttered, 'although I'd settle for stuffing an arm up a cow's backside any time, rather than stick my nose into this mess!'

'Where's the bleedin' coach, Little Boy Blue?' a bare-torsoed skinhead belched in Doogie's face. At the same time, he inadvertently, though totally without concern, battered a bottle-clinking holdall against Doogie's shin. 'Me an' me mates 'ere is bound for...' A baffled scowl on his face, he turned and shouted back into the pack, 'Oy! Where the fuckin' 'ell we goin' anyway, lads?'

'Spain somewhere, I fink,' a mate blandly ventured, casually goosing a passing and distinctly unamused frau from the Frankfurt flight as he spoke. 'Auf Wiener schnitzel, pet!' he guffawed after her. 'Yeah, 'owja fancy nine inches a' Cumberland sausage, Mahleen Deetrick?'

Doogie took a deep breath. Time to nip this potentially nasty situation in the bud. 'Everything's under control, gentlemen,' he loudly announced to the skinhead gang with as much confidence as he could fake. 'Your transport's waiting for you. Hurry on now, please!' He pointed to the nearest exit gate. 'All Luton passengers that way. As quickly as you can, please. Your coach is about to leave.'

'What's the bleedin 'urry, mate?' the Union Jack tattoo grunted. 'Ain'cha never 'eard a' yer *mañana* syndrome?'

'Yeah, bleedin' right!' one of his companions concurred, gripping his distended gut and looking frantically about. 'I gotta lay a cable 'fore I go anywhere, so where's the fuckin' gents' khazi, eh?'

Doogie could see that he wasn't going to get anywhere fast with this lot. Deciding to try the softly-softly approach, he laid his hand on the facially-tattooed one's elbow, then removed it rapidly as a get-yer-poofter-mitt-offa-me-or-I'll-remove-yer-liver look darkened those classic missing-link features. 'Entirely up to yourselves, of course,' Doogie then said, feigning indifference, 'but it *is* the Fiesta of San Miguel, you know.'

The Union Jack guy's black look graduated to one of suspicious optimism. 'Saint Meegwell? 'Ere, that's beer innit?'

Doogie forced an irony-loaded chuckle. 'Aha, but that's my point entirely, though.'

'Yer wha'?'

'The Fiesta of San Miguel, unlike the beer named after its hallowed patron, is the one dry day on the Spanish calendar,'

Doogie lied brave-faced.

The flag on the forehead furled into a frown. 'Meaning?'

Doogie pointed to a wall clock. 'Meaning, that one hour from now – that's at two am, the hour of the Saint's birth, by the way – all the bars put up the shutters.' With a gloomy look, he added, 'Yeah, illegal for anybody to be seen touching a drop for the next twelve hours. Same all over Spain.'

'Shit,' said Union Jack, dejection tugging at the rings on his lower lip, 'if we'd knew that, we'd 'ave wenta fuckin' Torremolinos!' He wheeled round to muster his troops. 'Right, lads,' he barked, 'let's get onto that bleedin' coach smuckin' fartish!'

'But what about sortin' them Jocks out?' a companion queried.

'Forget 'em! Plenty more where they came from!'

A look of panic contorted the loose-bowelled skin's face. 'But what about the kházi?' he pleaded.

'Stuff a cork up, my son! We got some serious drinkin' to do – and fast an' all!'

At that, the Luton Airport brigade joyfully followed their leader through the indicated exit, bellowing out xenophobic football chants as they went.

Doogie inhaled a great sigh of relief. 'Right, that's got rid of *them*. Now for the dangerous bit!'

'It's at times like this you feel proud to be British,' an elderly gent in a Panama hat commented cynically, gesturing towards the departing skinheads, then towards the Glasgow flight's luggage carousel. There, appearing through the plastic curtains amid a scattering of suitcases and golf bags, lay a comatose kilted figure, flat on his back, raised knees splayed, his wedding tackle exposed for all to marvel at, fresh vomit stains decorating his *Flower of Scotland* T-shirt.

A roar of ridicule exploded from his delighted mates, while protective mothers turned their young daughters' heads away. A clutch of teenage girls, meanwhile, swapped comments behind cupped hands and tittered as they took sidelong peeks at the evidence of what constitutes a true Scotsman.

Doogie edged his way through the melee of Glasgow passengers now jostling to collect their baggage. He had to dodge indiscriminately steered trolleys and feverishly back-passed suitcases until he reached the group of culprit kilties. A couple of them were making a token effort to spot their luggage as it trundled past on the conveyor belt. Others stood clapping their hands and shouting bawdy words of encouragement to the remainder of the clan, who were doing a wild improvisation of the Eightsome Reel to the accompaniment of their piper. Despite the fearsome amount of noise they were generating, there seemed to be only about ten of them, Doogie estimated. A dozen at the most.

'One versus twelve,' he mumbled under his breath, his heart pounding. 'Ah well, say goodbye to your teeth, O'Mara!' He braced himself, then tapped the nearest hand-clapper on the shoulder. 'I'm sorry, friend,' he shouted in his ear, 'but you're gonna have to get your pals to cool it. We've had complaints, see, and –'

The lad spun round, scrutinised Doogie's face, scowled incredulously, then exclaimed, 'Jesus Christ! What the hell are you doing here, O'Mara? I thought you were in Africa somewhere, studying the copulation technique of porcupines or something equally daft!'

'Jimmy Brown!' Doogie gasped, finally recognising the blue-and-white-painted face of one of his colleagues from vet college back in Edinburgh. 'What brings you to –'

'And what's with the poncey gear?' Jimmy cut in, a mocking smile on his lips as he fingered the lapel of Doogie's sky-blue blazer. He glanced at the ID badge. 'Merryweather Holidays? What the hell's all this shite about, eh?'

Doogie could have countered by asking Jimmy what the hell he was doing with his face painted the colours of the Scottish flag, but this was neither the time nor place for mickey-taking student banter. 'Never mind that right now,' he said dryly. 'It's a long story.' With a jerk of his head, he gestured towards Jimmy's Eightsome Reeling mates. 'But I'd advise you to get that bunch to belt up pronto, or the whole bloody lot of you are gonna spend the night in the local slammer!'

A silly grin creased Jimmy's face. 'Nah, they're just normal Edinburgh medical students. All stark, raving bonkers.' He nudged Doogie in the ribs and winked. 'Daft but harmless, eh!'

'Listen,' Doogie snapped, 'the Guardia Civil won't care whether they're studying to be doctors or dustmen. You'll all be out of the same football-hooligan bag to them, and...' He paused as something odd about Jimmy caught his attention. 'Your eyes,' he frowned, peering at the vacantly-smiling face. 'Your pupils. Look at them. My God, they're like piss-holes in the snow! What the blazes have you been on, man?'

Jimmy raised his shoulders. 'Ach, just a few wee eckies.'

'*Ecstasy*?'

'Aye, well, something like that anyway.' Jimmy nodded towards his medical student chums. 'These guys can get their hands on all sorts of stuff, you know. Saves on the booze money.'

Cringing, Doogie looked round to make sure no one had overheard this conversation. 'Well, I hope to hell none of you have brought any *stuff* in with you. I'm telling you, Jimmy, the Spanish police, they'll –'

Jimmy laid a placating hand on his shoulder. 'We might be daft, O'Mara, but we're not *that* fucking stupid!' He flashed Doogie a sly wink. 'Anyway, if you know your way about these parts, no doubt you'll be able to point us in the right direction for a wee fix, huh?'

A cheer went up from some of the more broad-minded passengers as Jimmy's two luggage-retrieving colleagues finally managed to haul the collapsed kiltie off the carousel, only to let him flop down on the marble floor, where he rolled back into his previous immodest pose. He was out of it, and contentedly so.

Doogie noticed two green-uniformed policemen standing at one of the exit gates. They were watching this pantomime through cold eyes, their hands resting menacingly on their gun holsters. Doogie was sorely tempted walk away and let the inevitable happen. Maybe a night in the cells was what this bunch of selfish nutcases needed. Then again, dammit, he was a student himself, after all.

He barged into the midst of the Eightsome Reelers. 'Right, you guys, that's enough!' he yelled, then strode over to the piper and snatched the blowpipe from his mouth.

'Hey!' the piper cried as his instrument collapsed yowling about him. 'You could've had ma fuckin' teeth out there!'

One of the disrupted dancers squared up to Doogie. 'Yeah, what's your game, arsehole?' he snarled while his mates closed ranks. 'Fancy yourself as a hard man, do you, eh?'

'No, but they do,' Doogie came back. He pointed out the two Guardia Civil officers, who were now ambling towards them, revolvers at the ready.

The piper blanched. 'Oh, shit!' he droned. 'The pigs!'

'Yeah,' said Doogie, 'and these guys aren't about to give you a nice, wee verbal slap on the wrist like the ones that catch you pissing up closes in Edinburgh on a Saturday night.'

Jimmy Brown, for one, was learning fast. 'Better listen to what he's saying, lads,' he urgently advised. 'He's one of us and he seems to know the score here!'

'Correct,' Doogie confirmed, his confidence rising. 'And the score is that you numpties are gonna go home with broken bones, lice, dysentery, scurvy, stretched arses and worse after a few months in the company of the human dross that's locked up in the local nick, *if* you don't get your act together right now!'

The Guardia Civil duo, meanwhile, had paused a few paces away. With typical poker faces, they were weighing up the ongoing situation, while pointedly ignoring the pleas of some aggrieved passengers from the same flight to 'chuck the ignorant yobs in jail', or, conversely, to 'run the foul-mouthed bastards off the fuckin' island!'.

'See yer Merryweather Holidays?' one irate Glaswegian woman squeaked at Doogie after being reunited with her luggage. 'Ye're crap! Imagine allowin' Edinburgh scum like that on a Glesca plane!'

A gravid silence had now fallen on the kilted student band.

'Hey, lads, I don't like the look of this,' Jimmy Brown quavered, his eyes darting from one exit to another – all of them now guarded by pairs of armed police.

'The pilot would've radio'd ahead, you know,' Doogie stated matter-of-factly. 'So any more silly-bugger stuff out of you guys and you're right in the deep stuff.'

Jimmy Brown's look was becoming more sheepish by the second. 'What do you suggest, Doogie mate?' he asked.

'I suggest you get your gear off the carousel, haul your stoned chum off the floor and onto a trolley, then quietly make your way to Exit-A along there. Yeah, and it won't do any harm to apologise to as many people as you can on the way.' He made to leave. 'I'll see you in the Arrivals Hall, and we'll take it from there.'

A chorus of throat-clearing stuttered through the gathered clan. Doogie felt a hand on his shoulder and turned to see the object of their sudden unease.

'*Lo siento, señor, pero estos chicos no pueden salir.*' Even for those who didn't understand Spanish, the tone and expression of the Guardia Civil officer made it obvious that he wasn't here to play games.

'He says you can't leave,' Doogie grimly translated. He cast his eyes round the dejected huddle of students. 'Any of you blokes speak Spanish?'

A concerted mumble indicated the negative.

Exasperated, Doogie looked at his watch. 'Just like the thing,' he grumped. 'Now I'm gonna have to nursemaid you bampots through a police grilling when I should be getting the rest of the passengers organised and onto the buses. What a pain in the arse!'

Ah, but there would be no need for him to wait, the Guardia Civil officer informed him in Spanish. He and his colleague knew enough English to give this bunch of young *lunáticos* a fright. All he needed from Doogie was confirmation of their holiday address on the island. In addition, however, he should note that the lads' passports – and their bagpipes! – would have to be surrendered to the Guardia Civil for the duration of their stay.

'I'm afraid you're on your own, boys,' Doogie announced to his glum-faced countrymen. 'My presence won't be required after all, it seems.'

'I suggest we demand to see the British consul,' one supercilious-looking youth ventured.

'If I were you,' Doogie retorted, 'I'd keep my trap shut until spoken to.' He surveyed the pathetic coterie with a wry smile, then added, 'The way things stand, you're not really in a position to demand anything, are you?' He looked at his watch again. 'Now, if you'll excuse me, I've got that planeload of your fellow passengers to face.'

'Thanks a million for standing by us, *mate*,' one trainee medic shouted after him. 'I hope I get the chance to return the compliment if I ever find *you* in a jam!'

Without breaking his stride, Doogie raised a hand and waved as he called back over his shoulder, 'The wound was self-inflicted, physician. So why not have a bash at healing thyself!'

Perhaps the teeming clamour that was Papi's Bar at 3am wasn't the most sensible port of call for someone who'd been on the go since first thing the previous morning. Bed was where Doogie's common sense told him to be, but after the hassles of first pacifying and then delivering to their various hotels the understandably irate passengers from that last Glasgow flight, common sense didn't enter the scheme of things. A long, cool beer was all that mattered to Doogie.

'Well, if it ain't Magic Roundabout himself! Still acting the clown, are we, squire?' Nick Martin was the last person Doogie needed to bump into right now.

'Only when I'm paid to,' he retorted, while simultaneously trying to catch the barman's eye. 'What's your excuse?'

Allowing that to pass as if he hadn't heard it, Nick snapped his fingers at the barman. 'Oy, Juan! A drink for the squire here. My shout.'

'*Una caña, por favor*, Juan,' Doogie said, ordering a draught beer and surprised to see Nick dip into his breast pocket and pull out a wad of euro notes that must have amounted to five hundred quid in old money.

'Oo-oo-oo, *una caña*!' Nick aped. 'Quite the Spanish linguist all of a sudden, aren't we? Yeah, course that's the benefit of going native with the Mallorcan totty, innit? A quick shag while you're copping for the lingo lessons under an orange tree, huh? Yeah, nice one!'

Doogie let that pass as if *he* hadn't heard it. He raised his glass. 'Cheers, Nick. Thanks for the beer.'

Nick didn't bother to respond, but instead began making a performance out of peeling two notes from his roll and slapping them down on the bar. 'Oy, Juan!' he shouted to the barman again. 'One for yourself and the rest of your muckers, OK? On me!'

'Feeling a bit flush tonight, are we, squire?' Doogie quipped, po-faced.

Nick pulled a facial shrug. 'Yeah, well, can't take it with you, Magic Roundabout.'

What the blazes was all this sudden generosity about? Doogie wondered, recalling what Angie had said, just a few weeks earlier, about the size of Nick Martin's slate in this same bar.

'Yeah, the lovely Catalina Ensenyat,' Nick muttered into his glass, his eyes fixed on nothing in particular behind the bar. 'Goes like a rabbit, no doubt. All them peasant bints are the same. Half rag-head, know what I mean?' He turned and leaned back against the counter, glass in hand, his eyes still avoiding Doogie's. 'Not that I speak from personal experience, of course.' He motioned towards the heaving selection of Brit holiday floozies gracing the room in all their come-and-get-me subtlety. 'What's the point in stooping to the local donkeys when there's all this thoroughbred nookie about?'

Doogie waited a moment, then said, 'Excuse me if I dip

101

into vet-speak, friend, but I think you're getting your equine and canine a bit mixed up, aren't you?'

'Oh, yeah, very droll,' Nick sneered. 'And we've certainly got *plenty* dogs on the island now, haven't we? What with your newly-arrived Glasgow gannet crap an' all!'

'Only the accents are different,' Doogie muttered, then downed the last of his beer. 'Anyway, what's your poison? My shout this time.'

Nick rebuffed that offer with a shake of his head. 'Save your bawbees for impressing your little *señorita*, Dougal. I'm buying. Hey, Juan – another beer for the squire here, right!'

'Thanks all the same, but I'll buy my own,' Doogie said bluntly. 'I think it'll taste better.'

But his words fell on apparently-deaf ears. Once more, Nick Martin was employing his habit of staring straight through Doogie while he spoke. 'Just take a butcher's at *that* piece a' crumpet!'

Doogie half turned to look at the cause of Nick Martin's excitement. Dressed in a pelmet-sized micro-mini and a see-through boob tube, she was standing in full I'm-available pose in the doorway.

Nick gave a self-satisfied snort. 'And has she got the hots for me, or what!'

Doogie shrugged. 'Yeah, well, she looks a right slapper, so that would explain it.'

'Don't push it, Magic Roundabout,' Nick muttered, while directing a cheesy grin at his latest female target. 'We've seen plenty of you so-called *educated* smart-arses come and go.' He shook his head. 'You never last the course.'

Doogie gave him a thin smile. 'Maybe, but if *you* ever get dumped by Sam Merryweather, you'll have no worries, I'm sure.'

'Oh yeah?'

'Yeah. You could start your own sperm bank. I mean, you've got all the basic qualifications, haven't you? All you'll need is a mirror ... and a thimble!'

That stung Nick Martin. He stabbed a finger into Doogie's

shoulder and snarled, 'You'll regret that, James bleedin' Herriot! And that is a fucking promise, all right!'

'Jeez, I haven't been so scared since I was threatened by a rogue frog in the biology lab.'

With a conceited smirk crawling over his face, Nick was staring past him again, so Doogie turned his head to double check this latest 'stunner' to catch Nick's fancy. He'd thought there was something vaguely familiar about her at first glance, but after taking a moment to look through the newly-applied war paint, it all came back to him. The peroxide-blonde thirty-something had arrived on one of that morning's Glasgow flights and had made her availability blatantly obvious to Doogie at every opportunity on the coach between the airport and her hotel.

'Right up your street, this one,' he said to Nick Martin. 'Hasn't even bothered to camouflage the white circle on her third finger, left hand!'

'Least of my worries,' Nick Martin came back. His grin grew cheesier as the blonde grooved towards him. He got off his bar stool and brushed Doogie aside. 'Look and learn, Florence,' he said out of the corner of his mouth. 'Look and learn.'

'Hi, handsome! Remember me?' the blonde drawled in a broad Glasgow accent, ignoring Nick Martin totally as she approached the bar. 'It's Doogie, intit?' She held out her hand. 'Senga – Senga McDuff.'

Doogie decided to play it businesslike. 'How do you do, Mrs McDuff. Hotel Tiempo Alegre, wasn't it?'

'Tut, tut!' she simpered, while maintaining a determined grip on Doogie's hand. 'Ah don't go for all that formal stuff, like.'

Doogie inclined his head towards the slack-jawed Nick Martin. 'You'd better meet my colleague, then. They don't come much less formal than him.'

But Senga McDuff continued to ignore Nick. 'Well, Doogie,' she purred, not taking her eyes of him for a second, 'are ye no gonny buy me a wee drink?'

'I'm outta here,' Nick Martin grunted. 'The pullability level in this joint just went through the bleedin' floor!' At that, he set off muttering through the crowd, in search, Doogie assumed, of another conquest.

Doogie shifted his thigh away from where Senga McDuff had strategically placed her knee. 'Look Mrs – ehm, Senga,' he began, 'I don't want to appear rude, but firstly, it's against company policy for staff to fraternise with clients of the opposite sex, and secondly –'

'Aw, come on now,' Senga interrupted with a suggestive wink, 'ye're no gonny tell me it's all Nancy boys and dykes that works for that firm o' yours, are ye?'

'And secondly,' Doogie resolutely continued, 'I don't think your husband would be too chuffed if he came in here and –'

'Och *him*?' Senga pouted. 'He's tucked up nice an' safe in his bed back in Glasgow, so he is.' She ran her fingers down the inside of Doogie's lapel. 'So, he's not gonny be a problem, is he, darlin'?'

This was getting a bit too up-close and personal for Doogie. 'Look, no offence, right, Mrs McDuff, but I've just finished an eighteen-hour shift, and as soon as I've downed this beer, I'll be heading for the same place as your husband.'

'*Glasgow*?'

'No, bed.'

'Hmm,' Senga hummed, 'sounds promising.'

'To bed, to *sleep*!' Doogie quickly qualified. 'Alone!'

'Yes please, *señora*,' a barman chipped in. 'You wan' order drink?'

Senga batted her eyelashes at the harassed and totally disinterested Spaniard. 'Well, at least there's *one* gentleman in Mallorca. Aye, Ah'll have a vodka and Coke, *amigo*. Oh, and don't you go holdin' back on the Coke, eh. Ah like it *all* in.'

'Subtle as an earthquake,' Doogie silently mused. 'You can't hide class!' He necked the last of his beer and was just about to make his exit when a voice rasped in his ear:

'Well, well, well, we meet again, Little Boy Blue!'

Doogie turned round to look straight into the bloodshot

eyes of the leader of the skinheads he'd had the run-in with at the airport. 'Shit!' he gulped. 'I mean, well – fancy seeing you here.'

'Yeah, just fancy!' the skin croaked. His nose was almost touching Doogie's, his breath an explosive mixture of booze and curry. 'Oy!' he called to three of his mates, who were elbowing their way towards the bar. 'Look what I've found!'

Doogie wished the floor would open at his feet. 'So, then, I take it you boys got settled into your hotel or apartment or whatever,' he blustered.

'The fuckin' Fiesta of Saint fuckin' Meegwell, is it?' the skin snarled, saliva splattering Doogie's face. 'All the boozers in Spain close at two am, is it?' He shoved Doogie in the chest, forcing his back against the bar. 'Take us for bleedin' reetards, do ya, Boy Blue?'

'Look, I was only trying to keep you away from those Scottish guys, that's all. Didn't want any trouble flaring up. Only doing my job, you know.'

The other three skinheads were now crowding round. No escape.

The Union Jack on the forehead of the lead skin wrinkled into a knot. 'That accent a' yours,' he growled. 'Scotch, innit?'

Before Doogie could answer, the skin grabbed the ID badge on his blazer.

'Mmm, O'Mara … Irish, eh! Same fing as Scotch, only bleedin' worse!' He took Doogie's lapels in both hands. 'Well, *that*'s for bein' Scotch!' he barked, head-butting Doogie on the bridge of his nose. 'And *this* is for bein' Irish!' he added, kneeing him viciously in the groin. ''Ave an 'appy Fiesta of Saint fuckin' Meegwell, my son,' he grunted as Doogie sank unconscious to the floor, blood gushing from his face. 'Yeah, an' fink yerself bleedin' lucky we didn't give ya a good bleedin' kickin' an' all!'

When Doogie came to, the pain pounding in his head was only marginally less ferocious than the throbbing in his private parts, to where his hand was instinctively and instantly drawn.

'Don't rub them,' Senga McDuff scolded, while she

gingerly dabbed the gash on his nose.

Doogie was trying to focus. 'I'm not,' he groaned. 'I'm counting them.'

'Couldn't have happened to a nicer guy,' he heard the voice of Nick Martin comment from somewhere beyond the crush of people surrounding the scene of the drama.

'Ye'll need a doctor, Doogie,' Senga McDuff said. 'That gash where the guy nutted ye is gonny need stitches.'

Doogie looked about him as the haze began to clear from his eyes. He was still on the floor where he'd dropped, but sitting up now, his back propped against the bar. 'H-how long w-was I out?' he stammered.

'Only a wee minute or two,' Senga McDuff said. 'Aye, but ye'll still have tae see a doctor, though. Ye never know – concussion an' that.'

Doogie grimaced and blinked his eyes.

'Heh, come on, everybody,' Senga called out to the gathered sightseers. 'Stand back an' give the guy some air, for Christ's sake, eh!'

'Well, at least I'm not talking like a boy soprano,' Doogie panted, gently caressing his vitals while struggling to get up off the floor.

'Aye, sep' ye'll maybe be about as much use as wan for a while, but,' Senga McDuff quipped. 'Thank God Ah didnae manage tae pull *you* for later!'

One of the onlookers helped Doogie to his feet as another fetched a chair.

Flopping onto it, Doogie looked down at his bloodstained clothes and shook his head dolefully. 'Blessed are the peace-makers, right enough. Next time there's gonna be a brawl at the airport, I'll let the daft idiots get on with it.'

In spite of her brassy façade, Senga McDuff turned out to be an angel in disguise as far as Doogie was concerned. Unlike Nick Martin, who disappeared into the night once the disappointment of seeing Doogie regaining consciousness had worn off, she organised a taxi to take him to the all-night clinic in Palma Nova, hung about in the waiting room while he had his injuries attended to, then accompanied him in another taxi to his flat. She even took the trouble to climb the stairs with him to make sure he got through the door safely in his distinctly wobbly state. In response to Doogie's outpourings of thanks, all she had said on leaving was that he owed her one.

But one what? That was the question that bothered Doogie.

'Which lamppost did you walk into, sunshine?' Ingrid said on seeing Doogie hobble stiffly into the Merryweather office the next morning. Then, as Doogie raised his sunglasses to reveal the full extent of the bruising round his eyes, he added, 'Or should I say express train? Man, are you a *mess*!'

Doogie sighed. 'And all sustained in the execution of my duties, more or less. Maybe I should sue Sam Merryweather,' he suggested, half-heartedly.

'Yeah, that'll be the day,' Ingrid laughed. 'Listen, I gotta rush. But I'll get the highlights from you later, right? And, hey – better see Manolo about some special duties, kid. He won't be wantin' you hangin' about the airport lookin' like that.' Ingrid gave one of his rumbling chuckles. 'No shit, man, you'd go frightenin' the goddam customers' kids!'

He certainly frightened Catalina, who had now returned to her old job as office junior, following her brief interlude as Doogie's assistant at the *Mister Sunshine Club*.

'*Madre mía*!' she gasped from her post at the photocopier. 'What is happen to your face, Doogie?'

'If you think the face is bad, you should see the bits that are covered up,' Doogie said in a somewhat forlorn attempt to make light of things.

'*Perdón*?' Catalina queried, clearly confused.

'It's, well, it's a kinda complicated story, but don't worry – I'm OK, honest.'

'But, Doogie, your nice nose!' she replied, her face a picture of concern. 'He is *roto* – broken, *sí*?' She stroked his face lightly with the back of her fingers, a gesture that elicited an outburst of catcalls from the other girls in the office.

'No, no, it's not broken,' Doogie insisted, trying to smile

107

reassuringly, but finding it too painful. 'Just a couple of stitches under the plaster, that's all.'

'Stitches? Plaster?'

'Yeah, you know…' Doogie mimed a sewing motion.

Catalina shuddered and clasped a hand to her mouth. '*Dios mío*! The stitches, the plasterings! *Qué terrible*!'

Doogie was beginning to feel a tad embarrassed by Catalina's public display of anxiety. 'Look,' he whispered,' I think I'd better have a word with Manolo, don't you? Is he free right now?'

Manolo's reaction to Doogie's appearance was exactly as Ingrid had anticipated, although his attitude towards his account of how he had received his injuries seemed surprisingly unsympathetic. Or so Doogie felt – initially, at least.

'You should *not* have gone into Baggage Reclaim,' Manolo stated flatly. 'If you were concerned with what the air stewardess said about the behaviour of some of the Glasgow passengers, you should have alerted the police. They are experts in dealing with such situations. You are not!'

'Maybe so, but my fib about the Fiesta of San Miguel did avert a battle taking place *and* it cancelled out the possibility of a lot of innocent people being hurt. I mean, if the pilot had warned Palma Airport in advance about the out-of-order students on board, as I presume he must have done, why the blazes weren't the police in Baggage Reclaim waiting for them?'

'Not my concern.' Manolo was adamant. 'And it shouldn't have been yours, either.'

Doogie couldn't hide his resentment. 'Well, thanks a million,' he muttered, pointing to his nose. 'I'll know better next time, won't I!'

But Manolo was having none of it. 'Count yourself fortunate that there may even *be* a next time!' he snapped. 'We do not approve of in-uniform Merryweather employees being involved in bar-room punch-ups, no matter what the circumstances!'

Doogie was feeling really hard-done-by now. 'It was a bit too one-sided to be called a punch-up,' he objected. 'I mean, like I explained, this crazy caveman just stepped up, stuck the head on me and kneed me in the balls.' He snapped his fingers. 'All over, quick as that!'

'Yes, and as the caveman told you, you were lucky they didn't give you a good kicking too.' Manolo wagged an admonishing finger. 'When you've been in this business as long as I have, you've seen it all before – too many times. Young men left bleeding to death in the gutter, a knife in their guts, or their heads kicked in. Believe me, my friend, you were *very* lucky to come out with only a cut nose and swollen *cojones*!'

Doogie found himself stuck for words. Much as he disliked admitting it, Manolo was absolutely correct in what he said. Now that he thought about it clearly, what would have happened if the skinheads had bumped into him out in the empty street at that hour of the morning, instead of inside a bar full of potential witnesses? A shiver ran up his spine.

He hung his head. 'Yeah, you're absolutely right,' he conceded. 'I was bloody stupid.' He raised his eyes, looked at Manolo and shrugged. 'What can I say? The ruined uniform and everything. All I can do is pay for it out of my –'

'The uniform will clean,' Manolo cut in, a twinkle in his eye, a little twitch of a smile tugging at his moustache. 'And your nose will heal.' He leaned over his desk and gave Doogie a manly slap on the shoulder. 'And I will light a candle for your *cojones*, eh!' Chuckling, he settled back into his chair and folded his arms. 'Now, what are we going to do with you until you are fit to be seen in public again?'

CHAPTER EIGHT

'FEMININE INTUITION'

SWIMMING POOL MAINTENANCE HADN'T been one of the strings Doogie ever thought he'd need to collect for his bow, but the old man who was contracted by Merryweather Holidays to do the job at their various hotels, apartment complexes and holiday villas on the island had fallen ill. So, after a half-hour crash course on how to operate the underwater 'vacuum cleaner', back-wash the filters and adjust chemical levels, Doogie was let loose in a little blue van. He was clad, appropriately, in shorts and Merryweather tee-shirt, with baseball cap to match, and equipped, even more appropriately, with an outsize pair of shades to cover as much of his bruised face as possible.

This was a bit of all right, he thought to himself when setting out on his rounds for the first time. To all intents and purposes, he was his own boss, with no coachloads of punters to pander to and ferry about. It would be just himself, the sun and swimming pools, and no hassles, as long as he got through the jobs on his daily list and didn't foul up. Yeah, he could get used to this!

It transpired that the clients he met were a friendly lot, by and large, and generous too – particularly those families renting some of the bigger villas in choice locations like the Costa d'en Blanes hillside on the chic western flank of Palma city. There would always be a cool drink for him, and sometimes even an invitation to join in an alfresco lunch by the pool, if he *happened* to time his visit right. If not, there were always the unassuming little bars and restaurants where other 'tradesmen' – builders, joiners, plumbers, delivery men and even swimming pool cleaners – congregated for a bargain-priced *menú del día*, the set menu of the day. You could always tell the best establishments, simply by the number of vans parked outside. Doogie soon drew up a short list of favourites on his beat: places where he could eat a hearty three-course lunch, complete with a jug of wine (if he was going to have time to snatch a quick siesta in his van!), and including an up-front *ración* of olives and crusty bread. And all this for less than the price of a pie and a pint back home. Boy, the 'workies' in Britain didn't know what they were missing. This was the life!

One particular day, when his schedule was to include the Palma Nova area, Catalina called him on his mobile phone to suggest they meet for just such a *menú* at one of a selection of eating places lining the sunny side of a back street in the Son Caliu outskirts of the resort. These were unpretentious but good-value eateries, once mainly frequented by in-the-know local taxi drivers, but nowadays also the favoured lunchtime haunts of many astute expat Brits. The aptly-named 'Churchill's' was Doogie and Catalina's chosen rendezvous on this occasion.

They sat down at a pavement table under an awning that provided essential shade from the fierce late-July sun. Catalina

111

looked worried as she scanned the bill of fare chalked on a blackboard by the door.

'Nothing tickling your fancy?' Doogie enquired.

That characteristic puzzled frown of Catalina's creased her brow. 'My *fancy*?' She canted her head inquisitively. 'What is this *fancy*, Doogie? *Sí*, and why should it be tickling me?'

Doogie couldn't help laughing. 'Sorry – it's just a daft expression. No, I only meant to ask if there's nothing on the menu you like, that's all.'

Catalina still looked ill at ease. 'Yes, I like. But also I worry about Señora María, your neighbour.'

'Old María?' Doogie shrugged his shoulders. 'She seemed fine when I saw her at seven this morning. What's up?'

'Well, my mother, she phone me at the *oficina* this morning, at the ten hours. She saying the Señora María been phone her, and no is sounding good.'

Doogie raised an eyebrow. 'How do you mean?'

Catalina shook her head. 'I don't know. My mother just ask me come to Palma Nova to seeing Señora María. To making sure she is OK.'

'And?'

'Well, I been seeing her before I coming here. But…'

Doogie was starting to worry now as well. 'So, how was she?'

'Oh, she telling me everything is OK. She smiling and saying "is OK, is nice" – *como siempre* – as usual, no?'

'Hmm, but you're not convinced, eh?'

Catalina frowned again, and there was no mistaking her anguish. 'She is very old lady, Doogie. *Sí*, and little Pedrito … he has got, how do you say, a big handful, no?'

Doogie laughed again. 'Well, something like that anyway.'

Catalina smiled an embarrassed little smile. 'I say something stupid, *sí*?'

'No, no,' Doogie assured her. 'I know what you mean. But, ehm…' He hesitated. 'But it's just that we say Pedrito *is* a big handful.' He coughed and tried to keep a straight face. 'You see, to say he *has got* a big handful could mean – well, it would mean something slightly different.'

Catalina blushed to the roots of her hair.

Prudently, Doogie decided to terminate this impromptu language lesson. 'Anyway,' he breezed, 'I wouldn't worry too much about old María, if I were you. She's a hardy old bird, and Angie will be back soon to give her a break from Pedrito for a day or two. And, hey, I'll tell you what – I'll try to knock off early tonight just to make sure she's all right.' He looked into Catalina's eyes. 'OK?'

'*Sí*, OK, Doogie,' she said quietly, but her smile didn't disguise her continuing concern for the old woman.

Doogie waited a moment, then whipped his sunglasses off in a flamboyant attempt to lighten things up a bit. 'Right!' he beamed. 'You didn't tell me what you think of my nose now the stitches are out!'

Catalina grimaced, pursing her lips as she reached out to gingerly touch the wound crossing the bridge of Doogie's nose. 'Oo-oo, is still very hurting you, yes?'

'Getting better every day,' Doogie grinned, then tried to catch a reflection of himself in the restaurant window. 'Yeah, and the swelling's gone down a lot, don't you think?'

Catalina nodded, but still looked anxious. 'But your leather, it is –'

'Skin, Catalina. I'm human and still alive, so it's my skin, OK?'

'*Sí*, the *skin* – the skin by your eyes, he is now very *amarillo*, I think.'

Doogie peered into the window. 'Aye, you're right,' he muttered. 'It *is* going yellow now, right enough. Dammit, at this rate, Manolo's gonna have me back on airport duty in a couple of days!' He nudged Catalina's arm and gave her a wink. 'Here, maybe I should slap on some black and blue makeup, eh?'

Catalina looked down at her hands. She paused, then coyly asked, 'And the bits that are covered up … they are already getting better also?'

Doogie cleared his throat, then said with eyebrows arched,

'Well, you might say they *were* a bit of a handful at first. But, yeah, everything's getting back to normal proportions now, thanks very much.'

The arrival of the waiter spared Catalina's further blushes.

Over post-lunch coffees, Doogie asked, 'Your father's new heifer calf – doing fine, is she?'

Sí, it was thriving, Catalina cheerfully assured him. It was growing well and none the worse for its adventurous arrival into the world. Indeed, the calf would become a valuable addition to her father's little herd of milkers one day ... thanks to Doogie.

Doogie liked the way Catalina slipped so effortlessly into such conversations about farming. It was in her blood, second nature. Without doubt, her current 'career' in tourism notwithstanding, she would make a fine wife for some fortunate young Mallorcan farmer one day.

His thoughts were drawn inescapably then to Margaret Hyslop, and what the future might or might not hold for them. *Them*! He repeated the word in his mind. Why was he still conditioned to think of Margaret and himself as an item? Hell, he had got away from Scotland to try and make some sense of all that foregone-conclusion stuff of hers. Get a grip, O'Mara! Get your head together.

'Did you like the neighbour of my parents – Rafael, who helping you with the birthing of the baby cow?' Catalina asked out of the blue.

Doogie was caught off guard. 'Well ... yeah,' he faltered. 'Yeah, seemed a fine bloke. And a good strong pull on the ropes as well. I mean, we couldn't have done the job without him, you know. Yeah, I liked him fine.'

Catalina shot him a knowing glance, then lowered her eyes. 'He ask me to being his wife.'

'Well, congratulations!' Doogie said, perhaps a little too quickly and certainly a lot too effusively. He attempted what he hoped would pass for a delighted smile. 'Yes. Yes, as I said – a fine bloke. And, ehm, your folks ... well, I mean, they're bound to be extremely –'

'I cannot do it,' Catalina blurted out. 'I cannot to marrying Rafael, and I am already saying this to him.' She looked Doogie briefly in the eye, then diverted her stare back to her lap and murmured, 'And I am already telling my parents also.'

Doogie didn't know what to say. Granted, he had suspected that this sort of scenario had been in the air when they'd all been having the evening meal at the Ensenyats' farm after that eventful calving. But he had also been doing his best since then to turn a deaf ear to what a still, small voice had been telling him about his own inevitable involvement in it all.

Jeez, first Margaret Hyslop, now this. And Margaret wasn't even *on* the island yet! Those familiar, mixed-up thoughts of Doogie's were having three-legged races round his head again. Dammit, maybe he should never have taken time out from vet college after all…

Catalina eventually rescued him from his agonising by divulging (for her own alleviation as much as anything, he guessed) that the 'understanding' with Rafael's family went back a long way. Oh, not that there was anything *binding*, she hoped Doogie would understand. Indeed, it was a long time, she was certain, since anything approaching an arranged marriage had taken place between Mallorcan farming families. But it was sometimes hoped, even *assumed*, that, if a farmer had an only son and a neighbour had an only daughter, and both families had only a small amount of land, a betrothal leading to an eventual amalgamation of the two farms would just, well, sort of happen. She looked at Doogie with big, baleful eyes. 'Business he is business, no?'

The tension broken, Doogie smiled and nodded his head. 'Tell me about it! Just about all the biggest farming dynasties in my own country have been built that way. And still are!' He laughed out loud. 'Yeah, and how about all the so-called *royal* families, eh?'

Catalina brushed a tear from her eye. 'But I cannot do it, Doogie,' she sniffed, gazing blankly ahead. 'I can never to marry Rafael.'

Doogie sat silently for a while, gathering his thoughts and allowing Catalina to nurse her own.

'You have to be true to yourself,' he eventually said, almost as if to himself. 'Let's face it, when all's said and done, the decisions we make when we're young shape the rest of our lives.'

Catalina turned her head to look at Doogie. 'Be true to yourself,' she quietly echoed, a look of admiration lighting her face. 'It is a very beautiful thought you are making.'

'Aye, a beautiful thought,' Doogie concurred with a rueful smile, 'but I think a guy called Shakespeare came up with it first.'

Another few moments of pensive hush.

It was Catalina who broke the silence. 'The, uhm, the letter you did find in your *apartamento* before we go to birthing the baby cow on that day,' she tentatively began, her expression suggesting that she already wished she hadn't broached the subject.

Doogie wondered what the hell was coming next. 'Uh-huh?' he prompted guardedly.

Catalina was struggling with herself. 'Please, it is not my business, I know…'

Doogie shifted awkwardly on his chair. 'Uh-huh?' he said again.

'The letter – it – the letter, it was from your *novia*, yes?'

'*Novia*?'

Catalina summoned up all her courage. 'Yes,' she said, her face flushed, 'from your young lady, your *señorita* in Scotland, no?' She immediately held up her hands in apology. 'Oh, please, please, you must not to answer. It is not my business.'

Doogie heaved a sigh heavy with resignation. 'No, no, it's all right. If I don't tell you, Angie will, I'm sure.' He paused. 'But, tell me, what made you suspect the letter was from a … girl?'

Catalina couldn't resist a smile. 'Two things only.'

'Yeah?'

'*Sí*. One, the look of your face when you did read the letter…'

'Uh-huh? And two?'

Catalina gave a demure little laugh. 'Oh, only something we are calling in Spanish the *intuición femenina*.'

CHAPTER NINE

'POOLING INFORMATION'

THE NEXT MORNING, DOOGIE made a point of knocking on old María's door before leaving at seven, even though she had said she was fine when he'd called in to see to her after work the previous evening.

She was just a little tired, she had assured him. The heat of the summer, the humidity. *Madre mía*, it seemed to exhaust her more with each passing year. Made her a little breathless at times. A sign of getting old, that was all. Ah, how lucky Doogie was to have the precious energy of youth, she had sighed, flopping into her easy chair and cooling her face with butterfly movements of an extravagantly-decorated fan. '*Hombre*! Do not preoccupy yourself with me,' she'd smiled on noticing the look of concern on Doogie's face. '*Va bien todo*, Boogie! Is OK!'

Doogie could only take her word for it. But still he worried. He wondered if the strain of looking after a boisterous four-year-old was beginning to take its toll. He didn't want to complicate matters for Angie, of course. Didn't want to add to her anxieties. But all the same, maybe he'd better have a quiet word with her about it ... when the time was right.

'Ah, *buenos días,* Boogie!' old María beamed, opening her door and reaching up to pinch his cheek. '*Buenos días*, Don Juan O'Mara, eh!'

Catalina had phoned her the previous night, she teased, and had said that Doogie had treated her to lunch. *Carám*! The *restaurante* of Sir Winston Churchill sounded very grand! Doogie was *un pícaro*, a rogue, she giggled – trying to sweep the girl off her feet with his big spending and everything.

'It was only a six-euro *menú del día*,' Doogie confessed with a limp smile. 'Not likely to raise any girl's feet far off the ground, I'm afraid.'

Aha, but Catalina was not just *any* girl, María pointed out, while wagging a censuring finger in front of Doogie's nose. No, no, her little Cati was not just a beautiful girl to look at, though that was *muy importante* too, of course, but she also had a beautiful heart, the heart of an angel, the soul of a saint. Plus, and this should not be overlooked, she had the strength, the loyalty, the *carácter* of the true Mallorcan country woman. '*Absolutamente incomparable*!'

Doogie had a chuckle to himself at María's blatant, and now frequent, attempts at match-making. God, if only she knew the complications involved! However, the old dear was in good spirits, and that was all that concerned him at the moment. The sounds of Pedrito cheerfully having breakfast inside the apartment confirmed that all was normal, and María's parting information that Catalina would be popping in to see her on her lunch break again today put Doogie's mind even more at ease.

*   *   *

Since becoming a 'tradesman', Doogie had latched on to his Spanish counterparts' custom of stopping off en route to work at one of the many small bars already open at that early hour: not for a *coñac-* or *anis*-laced *café carajillo*, as was the wont of the iron-livered natives, but just for an eye-opener of strong, black coffee and a quick flick through one of the morning newspapers lying on the counter. Today's front-page headline, and the talk of the all-male clients crowded into the bar, was the tragic news of a fourteen-year-old Danish girl, who had died the previous day in a Palma hospital after taking drugs – Ecstasy it was suspected – at an all-night dance club in Magaluf.

'*Las drogas*!' one cigar-chewing taxi driver loudly croaked. '*Un catástrofe* for the youth of today!' He threw the contents of his *coñac* glass down his throat. '*Sí,* and the filthy *bastardos* who push them should be garrotted. *Coño*!'

The barman, who was busy drying glasses, raised a shoulder in mute agreement.

By chance, Magaluf was the location of Doogie's first call this morning. He was still reflecting on the senseless loss of that young life as he connected up the hoses of his pool-cleaning gear at the Merryweather *Under-30 Club* apartments. Because of the noisy nocturnal habits of the young-singles clientele, these self-catering holiday flats were judiciously situated in one of the less 'sophisticated' backwaters of the resort. As might be expected at such an ungodly hour for youthful ravers, there was no sign of life anywhere about the complex, save for the sound of an occasional snore or fart drifting out from one of the windows of the grubby apartment block that towered above the pool.

'Christ!' he heard a voice declare, 'if it isn't bloody O'Mara again!'

Startled, Doogie spun round, and there was the dishevelled figure of his erstwhile college chum, Jimmy Brown. He was staggering over the forecourt towards him, the crotch of his Bermuda shorts drooping low as an elephant's scrotum, his bleary eyes now resembling, in Doogie's veterinary view, the arseholes of two seriously constipated cats.

Doogie waved his hand. Jimmy waved a beer bottle.

'Jesus sufferin', first a holiday rep, now a swimming pool skivvy!' Jimmy slurred. He grinned vacuously and offered Doogie a slug from his bottle. 'What the hell's the score, man?'

Politely declining the beer, Doogie told him that the reason for his latest apparent career change was another long story, the details of which he wouldn't bore him with right then.

'Aye, well, they say spice is the life of variety,' Jimmy laboriously articulated. 'Somethin' like that, anyway.' One of his eyes was closed against the offending daylight, his body swaying back and forth at the edge of the pool while his left leg tried to circumnavigate its doggedly stationary neighbour. 'Yes, and listen – nice work, if you can get it, pal.' He attempted to pat Doogie's shoulder, but succeeded only in fanning fresh air.

Doogie smiled as he watched his friend's unintentionally-daring balancing act. 'Had a long night, have you?'

'Belter's ... Downtown Magaluf ... Different class.'

Doogie frowned. 'Belter's. That'd be the club where the Danish lassie who just died came by the Ecstasy, right?'

Jimmy wobbled a couple of paces away from the pool as his right leg jolted momentarily back to life. 'Ecstasy? See Belter's? No problem. Piece o' cake.' After a brief struggle, his hand found the pocket of his Bermudas and he produced a fistful of small tablets, several of them escaping through his fingers and bouncing away over the tiled terrace. 'See what I mean, son?' he slavered. 'Eckies? Not a problem.'

'Hell's teeth!' Doogie gasped. 'That lot must have cost you a packet!'

'Nah,' Jimmy countered. He was looking hazily pleased with himself. 'Got them for nix, didn't I?'

'For *nix*?' Doogie shook his head. 'I don't get it.'

Jimmy proceeded to explain that the club had been mobbed last night, and, naturally enough, the talk among the punters had been about the girl who'd died. The place had been crawling with cops as well, some Spanish bird had told him. Plain-clothes guys doing their undercover bit. Then this bloke had come up to him, looking kinda furtive like and talking out of the corner of his mouth. He'd slipped Jimmy an envelope, saying the Ecstasy tabs in it were for free, if he'd agree to do him a favour before getting on the plane back to Glasgow tomorrow.

Doogie was fascinated. 'So this guy knew you were looking for dope before he even approached you? Is that what you're saying?'

Jimmy shrugged. 'Well, you know how it is. Me and the boys, we'd put the word about a few times in Belter's beforehand, like.'

Doogie could hardly believe that this was one of the same supposedly-educated young men who'd had their passports confiscated at the airport by the Guardia Civil just a fortnight before. 'And I take it you'd never even clapped eyes on this guy before, right?'

Jimmy pulled a do-me-a-favour smirk. 'Hey, like I told you before, man – we might be daft, but we're not fucking stupid, eh!'

'So, who is he, then?'

Jimmy rolled his shoulders. 'Well, I don't actually know his *name*, if that's what you mean.'

'OK, so what *do* you know about him?'

'Some sort of tour guide,' Jimmy said vaguely. 'As far as I could make out, anyway.'

'Oh, for crying out bloody loud!' Doogie erupted. 'Didn't you stop to think why this guy was unloading the stuff on you? The place was crawling with police and he offers you drugs for nothing, *if* you agree to do him a favour?' He shook his head in despair. 'What's happened to your brains, Jimmy? Leave them at the airport with your passport, did you?'

A feeble smile crossed Jimmy's face.

Doogie was on his high horse now. 'I mean, a girl dies, and you accept a *gift* of the same drug that killed her. Possibly even from the same batch. Can't you see you were stitched up by this guy? He was setting you up in case the police decided to frisk everybody in the place!' He grabbed Jimmy's shoulders and gave them a shake. 'Now come on, man – think! There must be something you can tell me about him. Nationality for starters!'

Jimmy raised his head, a look of panic in his eyes as the gravity of the situation began to dawn on him. 'English. Yeah, he might have been English,' he muttered. He paused to massage his forehead, then snapped his fingers. 'Yeah, English accent, and he was one of *your* lot ... the sky-blue blazer brigade!'

Doogie gave a mocking little laugh. 'You're trying to tell me one of our boys was wearing a Merryweather uniform in Belter's in the middle of the night? Do me a favour – it'd be more than his job's worth!'

'No, no, he wasn't wearing the uniform in Belter's last night. No, but I remember him from right here in the complex the other day. Yeah, he was picking up punters for a coach trip. Me and the lads were lazing about here having a few morning bevvies by the pool. Couldn't help noticing him, strutting about trying to impress the birds.' Jimmy wrinkled his nose. 'Fancied himself something bloody rotten.'

Doogie was becoming more intrigued by the second. He urged Jimmy to tell him more.

'Like what?'

'Like what day was he here?'

Jimmy had to think about that one, but he finally settled for the previous day but one. 'Yeah, the day before yesterday.' He grinned a self-satisfied grin. 'The morning after I finally got laid.'

'Congratulations, but just tell me where the coach trip was going, huh?'

Jimmy didn't have to think about that one. 'Easy! A trip to some distillery place up the island. Yeah, that's right – a few of the boys actually went along. Free samples of that blow-your-brains Mallorcan liqueur stuff. *Herbes* or something, they call it.' A smug look appeared on his face. 'I was too knackered to make the trip, of course. Geordie bird. Rough, but a fantastic hump. Went at it like a fuckin' rattlesnake all night.'

Doogie couldn't have cared less about the sordid details of Jimmy's love life. His mind was on more serious matters. 'Well, if what you say is right, I'll soon find out who lumbered you with the Ecstasy tabs. Just a matter of checking the Merryweather duty roster for Wednesday.'

But Jimmy wasn't listening. The faraway look in his eyes suggested that his thoughts were now firmly locked in Geordie rattlesnake mode.

Doogie gave him a nudge. 'Anyway, what's the favour you're supposed to do for this bloke?'

Jimmy blinked. 'Oh, right! The favour…' He dipped into his pocket again and produced a crumpled envelope. 'What I've got to do, OK, is give this address to the police before I get on the plane tomorrow.' He showed the envelope to Doogie. 'And I just tell the police that the guy who's supplying the Ecstasy to the pusher who supplied the Danish bird that died, if you follow what I'm trying to say, lives at that actual address, see?'

Doogie took the envelope. His heart skipped a beat as he read what was written on it. 'And the guy didn't tell you the name of the person who lives here?' he checked.

Jimmy indicated the negative.

Doogie stared long and hard at his still-bemused friend, then stated bluntly, 'Of course, you do realise that you can't go along with this, don't you?'

Jimmy gave him a puzzled look.

'OK, let me put it this way,' Doogie continued. 'What, precisely, had you intended doing with the pocketful of E's?'

Jimmy hunched his shoulders. 'Oh, just take them back home and flog them to –' He stopped short, suddenly realising the possible consequences of what he'd had in mind.

'Think about it,' Doogie said. 'You go to the Guardia Civil at the airport to ask, cap in hand, if you can please have your passport back to allow you to leave the country. Then you cheerfully confess that you know the whereabouts of the person responsible, directly or indirectly, for that young girl's death. Yeah, and all the while you've got a stash of the very drugs involved buried away in your suitcase.' He shook his head. 'You're pretty determined to spend the best years of your life in a Spanish nick, Jimmy, aren't you?'

'Shit!' Jimmy gulped. 'You're right!'

Doogie held out his hand. 'OK, for a start, you'd better give me every last one of those Ecstasy tablets.'

'And what are *you* gonna do with them?'

'I'm gonna flush them down the sewer with all the quick-release knickers, used condoms and other happy-holiday flotsam and jetsam I fish out of the pool's filters here.' He folded up Jimmy's crumpled envelope and put it in his own pocket. 'And as far as this address is concerned, you can forget it. Just don't get involved.'

Jimmy wasn't so sure, though. 'But the guy that gave me it... I mean to say, he's a tour rep, so what if I bump into him at the airport or something?'

'You claim you never met him before in your life, that's all. Just get yourself on that plane as inconspicuously as you can tomorrow, and then think yourself bloody lucky when you touch down safe and sound at Glasgow.'

It was as if the weight of the world had been lifted from Jimmy Brown's shoulders. He swayed forward to slap Doogie's shoulder again. This time, he found the target. 'Heh,' he said, managing to focus for the first time on Doogie's face, 'what's happened to your nose, man?'

Doogie had no intention of opening up *that* can of worms. 'Aw, nothing,' he smiled, 'just a mozzie bite.'

Jimmy tutted. 'You want to look after yourself, pal. Things like that can turn nasty!'

CHAPTER TEN

'ALFRESCO FRICTIONS'

IT TOOK ONLY A quick phone call to the Merryweather office to confirm what Doogie suspected – that Nick Martin had indeed been the rep assigned to the distillery trip that day. Of course, there was always the possibility that the stoned Jimmy Brown could have mis-identified him in the laser-flashing bedlam of Belter's. But Doogie didn't think so. Nick Martin had long been known for living beyond his means. He was forever lashing out far more than his Merryweather salary could justify to impress a succession of holiday bimbos in rip-off nightclubs, while simultaneously maintaining a reputation for having short arms and deep pockets when it came to paying his way with his workmates in reasonably-priced watering holes like Papi's Bar. It followed, therefore, that his flash, the-drinks-are-on-me routine in Papi's a couple of weeks ago had had Doogie wondering just where all the sudden cash had come from. Yet, until now, flogging drugs to kids in a disco was a sideline he'd thought too low for even Nick Martin to stoop to.

In the light of the furore being generated by the media following the Danish girl's death, it was clear that anyone who *had* been involved in supplying Ecstasy at Belter's would be keen to cover his own backside and, if the inclination and opportunity were there, to slip someone else the relevant jail pass. Seeing his own address on the envelope that Jimmy Brown had been asked by Nick Martin to hand to the police said it all for Doogie. The way he figured it now, Nick's intention could well be to plant incriminating evidence in his apartment before the police turned up with a search warrant.

Naturally, Doogie had other ideas of how the scenario should pan out, and old María's renowned watchfulness would be an essential element of his plan. However, to his astonishment, it wasn't María who met him on the landing when he returned home that evening...

'Angie! What the blazes are *you* –? I mean, it's great to see you. It's just that, well – we weren't expecting you for another couple of days!'

But Angie didn't return his smile. Her eyes filled with tears and she began to sniffle.

Doogie didn't need an explanation. 'It's old María, isn't it?' he said, grim-faced. 'What's happened?'

'A stroke,' Angie whimpered. 'The office phoned and told me. I got the first plane back.'

'So, how bad is it?'

'I don't know. I phoned the hospital from Palma airport when I got in half an hour ago. She's in a coma. That's all they would say.' Angie began to wring her hands. 'And it's all my fault. Bloody greed, accepting that promotion in Ibiza. I should've been here looking after Pedrito, instead of saddling poor María.' Unable to hold back the tears, she buried her face in her hands.

Doogie put an arm round her shoulder. 'Hey, come on now – you did it all for the best. And listen, old María wouldn't have had it any other way. She'd have torn a *right* strip off you if you hadn't taken that promotion.'

'I only hope she'll be all right, that's all,' Angie snivelled. She dabbed her eyes with a hankie. 'Honest, kid, I'd never forgive myself if anything –'

'Listen,' Doogie butted in, 'don't even *think* that way.' He gave her shoulder a squeeze. 'Now, come on into my – sorry, *your* place, and I'll fix you a nice, stiff G&T, huh?'

It had been Catalina who'd discovered María sprawled on the kitchen floor when she called by to see her at lunch time, Angie explained. Pedrito had answered the door, telling Catalina to be quiet, because María was having a siesta. Catalina had called a doctor, who had immediately arranged for an ambulance to rush María to hospital. That was about as much as Angie knew.

'And what about Pedrito?' Doogie asked. 'Where's he?'

'Julie at the office said Catalina was looking after him.' There was an abashed look on Angie's face. 'And that's the problem, kid – the office is closed now, and I didn't even ask where she lives.'

On the drive out to Capdellá in the little pool-maintenance van, Doogie told Angie all about Nick Martin's apparent involvement in drug-pushing, and about what could well be his plan to frame Doogie in the hope of diverting potential police interest away from himself.

Angie could hardly take it all in. 'My God, what a fucking low-life!' she growled. 'So, Tricky Nicky finally hits rock bottom, eh!'

'Well, it's about as low as you can get, even for a slug like him. I mean, he's got that young girl's blood on his hands, whether *he* actually sold her the Ecstasy or not.'

'Yeah, and stitching you up is his way of easing what little conscience he's got – as well as saving his own hide. What a lousy bastard!'

'Hmm, but he's got to plant dope in my pad to make his little scheme work.' Doogie stroked his chin. 'And how does he gain access? Breaking in's no good. That'd give the game away.'

Angie nodded, thinking about it. After a moment, she caught her breath and clapped a hand to her forehead. 'Dammit! The key!'

'The key? What key?'

'A couple of years ago. I let Nick borrow the flat for a fortnight while I was back in Nottingham seeing my folks.'

'Borrow?'

'Yeah. He'd just walked out on his wife. Carmen – Spanish – lovely kid – too good for that rotten bugger.'

'So you let him borrow your flat?'

'Yep – let the creep sweet-talk me into it. It was only for a couple of weeks, though. You know, just 'til he got himself organised with another pad and everything.'

Doogie knew what was coming next. 'And you never got the key back, right?'

Angie was inwardly kicking herself. 'I mean, I remember telling myself I'd have to ask for it back at the time, but then I just sort of forgot. Honest, it had gone right out of my mind, until now.' She batted Doogie's arm with the back of her hand. 'Listen, kiddo, you'd better get that lock changed, smartish.'

Doogie shook his head. 'Nah, no hurry.'

Angie glared at him. 'You're joking, of course!'

'No, I'm serious. What's the point in making things difficult for him?' Doogie allowed himself a self-satisfied smile. 'Yessiree, him having a key is the best thing that could've happened.'

Now Angie shook her head. 'You've lost me, mate.'

'It's easy! Look – don't forget that my pal Jimmy Brown is *not* gonna be grassing me up to the police at the airport, right?'

'Yeah, I've got that, but –'

'But Tricky Nicky doesn't know that, does he?'

'So what?'

'So, he's gonna be timing his dope-planting act for

sometime between when I leave for work in the morning and just before the time Jimmy arrives at the airport.'

Angie was beginning to see what Doogie was getting at. 'Well,' she nodded, 'you *could* be right.'

'Yeah, I reckon his idea will be to get into the flat and out again shortly before he thinks the drugs squad are likely to turn up with their sniffer dogs and everything.'

Angie still looked a bit confused.

'So, what we want,' Doogie continued, 'is for Nick to get into the flat trouble-free, OK?

Angie scratched her head. 'Yeah, I've got that, but –'

'But once he's in there…' Doogie waited for the penny to drop.

After a second or two of silent deliberation, Angie's face lit up. 'Ah, *now* I've got it! We turn the tables, right? The police have been waiting next door or wherever all along, and they come in and nail him with his trousers down – for want of a better expression.'

'That's it – in theory, anyway.' Doogie paused, a worried look on his face. 'But persuading the police to play ball could be a different story.'

Angie thought about that for a bit, then said glumly, 'I see what you mean. Your theory *is* a bit like something out of an episode of *Columbo*, I suppose. Slightly too pat to be believable.'

'Could well be,' Doogie conceded. 'And anyway, with all the publicity there's been, the police have probably got dozens of so-called *leads* like that to sift through.'

Suddenly, a smug little smile came to Angie's face. 'Aha, young O'Mara,' she said while tapping the side of her nose, 'but that's where your old Auntie Angie's murky past could come in handy.'

'Uh-huh? Well, tell me more!'

There was a dreamy look in Angie's eyes now. 'Mmm,' she drooled, 'Lorenzo Moll. He was only a highway cop in those days. Big motorbike, tight pants, long leather boots, mirror shades, all the gear.' She pouted reflectively, savouring the memory, before dragging her thoughts back to the present. 'But nowadays, he's a livewire in the Palma CID, or whatever they call it. So, leave it to me, lad, and you'll have troubles with nothing, OK?'

All this scandalous talk about drug-peddling and frame-ups had certainly taken Angie's mind off her own problems for a while. But Doogie noticed that, the nearer they got to Capdellá and the Ensenyat's farm, the more Angie became uncharacteristically quiet and withdrawn, fiddling with her fingers and staring blankly out of the window. There was no doubt that she didn't have her worries to seek. For, even if old María eventually made a complete recovery from her stroke, it was a foregone conclusion that her days of being a full-time babysitter for Pedrito were over. Of course, there was always an outside chance that Angie would be able to persuade the powers-that-be at Merryweather Holidays to post her back to Mallorca on compassionate grounds. However, even if they yielded to such a request, there was very little likelihood of their doing so before the end of the current summer season. And, as she still wasn't in a position to have Pedrito with her in Ibiza, there seemed no obvious way out of the mire for Angie. It was clearly playing on her mind…

'See, even if I came back here on my old wages,' she said after a while, 'I'd still have to hire a nanny, and by the time I pay one of them, I'm skint – or worse. OK, I'm making more money in Ibiza, but the same applies. I'd have to hire a minder for Pedrito there too, *plus* find the rent for a bigger flat.' She shook her head disconsolately. 'I just can't make it work either way.'

There was nothing Doogie could say to that, so he left Angie to return to her private thoughts.

It was only when they were entering the Finca Sa Grua farmyard that she came out of her shell again. 'Anyhow, my troubles are self-inflicted,' she piped up stoically. 'It's María I should be thinking about, the poor old thing.'

It was certainly old María that Pedrito was thinking about

131

as he turned round from where he was playing football with Rafael at the front of the house. Recognising Doogie's van, he rushed towards it shouting María's name, his face aglow with expectation.

'Hi, Pedrito!' Doogie smiled, getting out of the van and hoisting the little fellow up by the armpits to bounce him playfully in the air.

But Pedrito wasn't interested in any such fun and games. 'María!' he repeated, then squirmed free and rushed round to the passenger's side of the van. 'Where is María?'

Angie opened the door and knelt down to throw her arms round him. 'Pedrito, Pedrito, Pedrito!' she twittered, showering him with kisses. 'Have you missed me? Four whole weeks, eh! Hey, but just wait 'til you see what I've brought you from Ibiza!'

'*Hola*, Mamá,' Pedrito said, but with no more feeling than if he had last seen his mother only ten minutes ago. He wriggled out of Angie's arms and strained to see into the back of the van. 'María,' he called out again, his expression anxious now. 'I want to see María.'

Angie's face was a study in mixed emotions: pleasure, hurt, remorse, but most of all confusion. She just didn't know how to handle this situation.

Doogie stepped once more into the breach. 'It's OK, Pedrito,' he said as reassuringly as he could. 'María didn't come with us. She's having a wee rest – a sort of holiday.'

Pedrito turned and looked up at him with sad, appealing eyes. 'Has María gone to heaven to see Mario, Boogie?'

Angie had to gulp back the tears. She half turned away from Pedrito and whispered falteringly to Doogie, 'Mario Lanzarote – Pedrito's canary. He, uhm, he went to heaven. About a year ago.'

Doogie put on a cheery face and tousled Pedrito's hair. 'Don't worry about María, wee man. You'll see her soon enough, I promise you. Yeah, she's just kinda having a nice break while your Mum's home, that's all.'

But Pedrito was far from convinced. 'She was very sleepy,

Boogie,' he stressed. 'Still sleeping when the men took her away.'

Doogie realised that a quick digression was called for. He took Pedrito's hand. 'Come on,' he smiled. 'let's see how that new calf's getting on. Remember it?'

'Came out of the cow's bottom,' Pedrito recalled half-heartedly, his expression still doleful. 'I'd rather see María.'

Catalina appeared at the front door with her parents, their welcoming smiles barely concealing the concern in their eyes. Old María had been their neighbour for a long, long time, after all, and she was obviously someone very dear to them. Being sensitive to Pedrito's feelings, however, none of them even mentioned the old woman's name during the spell of polite small talk that followed Doogie's introduction of Angie.

As the conversation progressed, it transpired that Señor and Señora Ensenyat had taken a real shine to Pedrito, and they heaped Angie with praise for having brought him up so well. Even the normally laconic Rafael grinned and waxed lyrical about the little *guapo*, who had *un temperamento admirable*. *Sí*, he chuckled, and he had an even better right foot! *Claro*, he would play for Spain one day, this *chiquito*!

Angie could only smile appreciatively and assure them that she wasn't entitled to claim any credit for Pedrito's better qualities.

Señora Ensenyat gave a disbelieving little laugh, then linked arms with Angie and gestured towards the house. The three women would go to the kitchen to prepare the evening meal, she said, while the *four* men (she tapped Pedrito lightly on the head) would have their evening stroll, their *paseo*, to check on the fields and the animals ... the way men always did, she winked, when there was work to be done indoors.

Doogie realised that this was only Señora Ensenyat's diplomatic way of getting Pedrito out of earshot while she discussed old María's plight with Angie. Catalina would also have made her mother fully aware of Angie's personal predicament, and, from what he knew of Señora Ensenyat, Doogie guessed that she would try to provide Angie with at least a little verbal support. There wasn't much more she could do anyway.

Whether or not Pedrito sensed that Doogie had been telling him less than the whole truth about María, Doogie didn't know, but for whatever reason, the little fellow opted to tag on to Rafael during the prescribed male wander round the farm. Señor Ensenyat, for his part, could hardly have been more affable towards Doogie, swapping questions and answers with him about the similarities and differences between the islands of Mallorca and Arran. Yet Doogie felt there *was* a slight tenseness about him: an uneasiness brought about, perhaps, by Rafael's pointed ignoring of Doogie whenever a three-way conversation was attempted.

'Suit your bloody self,' was Doogie's inwardly expressed attitude towards Rafael's offhandedness. He had more to bother about than that at present.

It was dusk before they finally wandered back to the farmhouse. Twilight falls quickly in Mallorca, and the sun was already dipping behind the saw-tooth ridges of the Tramuntana Mountains, sending great flows of shadow spilling down their craggy flanks. An almost palpable tranquillity pervaded the warm, moist air: a serene silence broken only by the tinkling of sheep bells and by the occasional barking of a dog on a distant farm. Farther down the valley, the lights of the houses in Capdellá village were flickering now like fireflies hovering in the surrounding terraces of almond trees. Then, as though on cue, the liquid trill of a nightingale began to pour from a copse of evergreen oak on the mountainside above.

'Now *that*,' a captivated Doogie informed Señor Ensenyat, 'is something you *won't* hear on Arran!'

The table for the evening meal had been set outdoors in the *porche*, and although Señora Ensenyat's simple but wholesome fare complimented the lantern-lit setting of the old Mallorcan farmstead perfectly, there was an inevitable atmosphere of awkwardness about the occasion. Clearly, much had been discussed in the kitchen during Pedrito's absence, but nothing of what had been said could be relayed to Doogie while Pedrito was present. Also, the little chap's inclination to all but ignore his mother in favour of Señora Ensenyat, whose proximity and assistance he sought at the table, invoked hurt and embarrassment in the two women respectively. Maybe, Doogie pondered, this was Pedrito's way of expressing at last his hitherto unrevealed feelings about his mother having left him without adequate explanation – perhaps for ever, in his child's mind. Or maybe his apparent preference for Señora Ensenyat's company was simply Pedrito's natural gravitation towards an older woman, towards the familiar comfort of a granny figure. Towards old María, the one dependable cornerstone of his vulnerable young life.

Señora Ensenyat could do nothing but respond to Pedrito's overtures as warmly as she could, while offering a discomfited little smile to Angie when she thought she had caught her eye. Angie, all the while, was gamely attempting to present an air of insouciance by engaging herself in an over-animated conversation in Spanish with Rafael, who appeared enthralled by the attention being lavished on him by this Nordic-tinted 'sophisticate'. The speed at which Angie was drinking was a revelation of her underlying feeling of anxiety, however.

Like an automaton, Rafael kept refilling her glass from an earthenware jug of Señor Ensenyat's home-made wine.

Catalina nudged Doogie's knee under the table. 'I think Rafa he is *encantado*,' she whispered in his ear. 'He is bewitch-ed, no?'

Doogie glanced over the table towards Catalina's father. It was clear that Señor Ensenyat had noticed what he may well have taken to be this little flirtatious move by his daughter. Her mother had noticed it too. Señor and Señora Ensenyat exchanged glances, then looked apprehensively at Rafael.

Thinking fast, Doogie cleared his throat and said loudly, 'Yes please, Catalina. Some more salad ... ehm, *muchas gracias.*'

With a mischievous little smile, Catalina reached for the serving bowl and duly commenced to heap more salad onto Doogie's already full plate. '*Hombre!*' she murmured, locking his eyes in a melting stare for a second. 'You certainly know what is good for you, *si*?'

Pedrito soon fell asleep on Angie's knee during the drive back to Palma Nova, and this at last gave her the opportunity to tell Doogie what had transpired in the Finca Sa Grua kitchen during his pre-dinner *paseo* round the farm. Firstly, Catalina had phoned the Son Dureta Hospital in Palma for an update on old María's condition, but all they could tell her was that there was no change, although the old woman did seem to be holding her own. She was in intensive care and everything possible was being done for her, so all they could do now was pray.

'They said they'd let me in to see her tomorrow, though,' Angie said, her voice quivering, the strain of appearing to be at ease during the long evening now beginning to show. 'I've to phone them late morning – you know, after the specialist's done his rounds and all that.'

Angie's tearful eyes glinted in the glow of the dash lights as she looked down at Pedrito's head cradled in the crook of her arm. 'See his little face,' she said adoringly. 'His thumb in his mouth, his finger up his nose.' She gave a little choking laugh. 'He came out like that, the little bugger. Yeah, ten stitches it cost me.'

Doogie said nothing for a while. He realised that Angie was struggling to come to terms with the pain of what she saw as the affections of her own flesh and blood gradually drifting away from her.

'What's going to become of him, Ange?' he asked at length, his tone both understanding and candid. 'I mean, what the hell are you gonna do next?'

Angie started to sniffle.

'I'm sorry, Angie,' Doogie said, wishing he hadn't touched on the subject just yet. 'Look, I didn't mean to upset you – you know that. But, well, it's just that…'

'It's OK, kid,' Angie muttered, then wiped her nose on her forearm. 'It's all fixed.' She sniffled again. 'I mean, Pedrito doesn't know it yet, like. But … but … well, it's all fixed.'

Doogie waited for the details, but Angie just snuggled down and started to stroke Pedrito's hair, humming a nondescript little lullaby to herself. A lot of lost time was being made up for now, Doogie figured.

'Señora Ensenyat,' Angie eventually whimpered, the effects of having consumed such copious quantities of Señor Ensenyat's heady country wine adding to her already weepy state of mind. 'Pedrito's going to live with her – with Catalina's mother.'

CHAPTER ELEVEN

'IN THE HEART, OR IN THE HEAD?'

DOOGIE'S THEORY THAT DRUGS were going to be planted in
his flat turned out to be absolutely correct, but any notion he
may have been entertaining that Nick Martin would be
foolhardy enough to do the deed himself proved to be
completely off the mark. Not only that, but the miserable
junkie who was caught in the act by Angie's policeman friend
Lorenzo Moll and his team claimed he didn't even know the
identity of the person who had hired him. But whoever it was,
it certainly was *not* Nick Martin. The junkie had testified to
this after being shown a group snapshot, including Nick, that
Angie had taken at a Merryweather staff party a few years

earlier.

'*Por cierto*, this guy would have denounced Señor Martin if he had been the one,' Lorenzo Moll told Doogie and Angie on the landing outside her flat as the junkie was being led away. 'He has a lonely cell and cold turkey to face now, and he'd rat on his own mother if he thought it would make us go easy on him.' He nodded discerningly. '*Sí, sí*, I know these dope heads, believe me.'

As a consequence of Doogie's earlier outpouring of his story to Lorenzo Moll, Jimmy Brown had been apprehended by detectives at the airport before being reunited with his passport and allowed to board the plane home. They had made him sign a statement detailing his version of events, and had cautioned him that, if required, he would have to return to the island to give evidence in court. So, no matter how foxy Nick Martin was trying to be, the finger of suspicion still pointed directly at him. For how else, if Nick hadn't been orchestrating events, would an Ecstasy-toting intruder have turned up at Doogie's address right on cue, *and* in possession of a key to the apartment?

This was all still a bit too circumstantial for Lorenzo Moll, though. He and his colleagues would have more work to do before they could charge Nick Martin with a crime that would see him, if found guilty, spending up to ten years behind bars. An immediate search of his flat proved fruitless, however. Nick had been crafty enough not to make the mistake of 'shitting in his own nest', as Angie so colourfully put it. Still, Lorenzo Moll did have sufficient reason to haul him in for a grilling, after which Nick Martin was left in no doubt that his every move would be watched from then on. Though free, he was a marked man, the police's assumption being that, given enough rope, he would hang himself – and, Lorenzo Moll hoped, would take a few more of his rotten ilk with him.

'I reckon Lorenzo's bound to report all this to Manolo at the Merryweather office,' Angie remarked to Doogie over a hair-of-the-dog glass of wine on the apartment balcony. 'Even if it's just off the record. Yeah, 'cause they're old mates, that pair, see.'

'Good,' Doogie said. 'That'll save me the trouble.'

Angie looked surprised. 'It doesn't bother you, then – you know, that Manolo might do his nut?'

'He can't do his nut with me,' Doogie shrugged. 'I'm clean as a whistle. But,' he added, savouring the thought, 'it'll be interesting to see what he does about Tricky Nicky if Lorenzo does fill him in about all this.'

'Well, I wouldn't want to be in Nick's shoes,' Angie said ominously, 'because you can take it from me that old Sam Merryweather will be dragged into it.'

'And so he should be! It's his company's good name that's at stake, after all.'

Angie sat and thought for a while. 'I still can't understand why Nick did something as careless as handing over all those tabs to your mate in the nightclub.'

'Killing two birds with one stone, that's all.'

'Come again?'

'Think about it. Nick walked into Belter's that night with an envelope full of E's to flog, maybe not even aware that the Danish girl had just died, until he got the whisper that the place was crawling with plain clothes cops.'

'Yeah, yeah, my surname may not be Holmes,' Angie bristled, 'but I have grasped *that* much.'

'OK, so then it would have been panic stations for Nick, right? Getting rid of those E's fast would have been all he was bothered about, OK? And chances are that he might already have got the buzz in Belter's that Jimmy was looking for a fix. Tie that in with what his sick mind must've seen as a great chance to kick yours truly in the goolies, and there you have it.' Doogie hunched his shoulders. 'It was just his bad luck that he picked somebody who knew me, and my good luck that I bumped into Jimmy when I did.'

Angie nodded and took a sip of her wine. 'What an arsehole!'

'Aye, "a horse's arse with teeth" was how I once described his face, if I remember right.' Doogie gave a rueful little chuckle. 'I did horses' arses everywhere a right bloody disservice, though, didn't I?'

Angie mulled things over in silence again. 'It's the money side of it,' she eventually said. 'That's what I don't get.'

Doogie looked at her. 'The money side?'

'Yeah. I mean, you said the dope he gave your mate Jimmy must've been worth about three hundred quid.'

'At least.'

'And what would the amount of stuff that the junkie was trying to stash in here be worth?'

'Twice as much, maybe more,' Doogie shrugged. 'Your guess is as good as mine.'

'And the junkie would've been paid for his efforts, right?'

'No doubt, and whoever Nick got to hire him would've expected a backhander as well.' Doogie considered that for a bit. 'OK, so maybe the junkie would've been paid in dope after the event, but I see what you're getting at. Nick Martin has to pay his supplier for the stuff that's now either down the drain at the *Under-30 Club* apartments or in the hands of the police. A grand's worth, maybe?'

Angie nodded and took another sip of wine.

Doogie stroked his chin. 'Hmm, and he can't do any more pushing, because the cops are watching.'

'Absolutely.'

A wry smile crossed Doogie's face. 'I'd be starting to worry about my kneecaps, if I were Mr Martin. Yeah, and to quote the man himself, it couldn't happen to a nicer guy.'

Sam Merryweather's instructions regarding what to do with Nick Martin were short and sweet…

'Fire the bum!' he told Manolo on the phone from head office in England. Any schmuck suspected of hawking dope was friggin' guilty until proven innocent in Sam's view, and he didn't want no dog turd like that fucking with his business already. So, it was a sudden, '*Adiós*, Merryweather Holidays,' for Nick Martin.

Doogie got the news on his mobile while he was doing the

141

pool at the Hotel Tiempo Alegre later in the day. He was also told to report for duty at the office first thing in the morning – wearing his rep's uniform! With Nick Martin now out of the team, Doogie's continued absence could no longer be afforded, scarred nose or no scarred nose.

While feeling a certain pang of regret at having to end his short-lived career in swimming pool maintenance, Doogie was pleased to be greeted by an atmosphere of conviviality on returning to the flat that evening. Angie and Pedrito were in chirpy fettle, having just come back from Son Dureta Hospital, where the news of old María was excellent. She had regained consciousness, and her doctor had been happy to report that, although she was far from being out of the woods, her stroke appeared not to have left her with any serious after-effects. As Doogie and Angie had anticipated, though, a long period of convalescence would be required, and even then she would have to accept that a stress-free, restful lifestyle would be mandatory.

But that was all in the future. For the present, all that mattered was that she was alive and on the mend. To Angie's further relief, the old woman had even been able to hold Pedrito's hand for a few moments, and to whisper him a few words of reassurance that she didn't intend to go visiting Mario the canary for a while yet.

Adding to these causes for celebration, Catalina had popped into the flat on her way home to break the good news that, as from tomorrow, she was to be promoted from office junior to 'fully-fledged trainee tour rep' – thanks, of course, to the sudden and unforeseen demise of one Nick Martin.

'Hey, congratulations and welcome to the madhouse!' Doogie beamed. He gave her a big hug – a hug which Catalina wasn't slow to respond to, and wasn't too quick to release herself from either.

She kissed Doogie on both cheeks, but with noticeably more zeal than goes into the customary Spanish peck employed on such occasions. 'Oh, Doogie,' she cooed, 'it makes me so happiness.'

'No sex, please!' Angie scolded, then popped a champagne cork and squealed in delight as the bubbly gushed onto the floor. 'Not unless I'm in on the act, anyway!'

'Uhm-ah, excuse me,' a female voice said from the doorway. 'I hope I'm not interrupting anything, but the door was open and I just thought…'

'Jesus Christ!' Doogie gasped, his eyes on sticks as he turned his head to face the voice. 'It's *you*!'

'Quite,' Margaret Hyslop replied frostily. 'And it's nice to see you too!'

Doogie was still standing with his arms round Catalina, glued to the spot, his jaw sagging.

Angie, more concerned about not spilling too much champers than anything else, was busy filling glasses.

Pedrito, fresh from a visit to the bathroom, was standing gazing up at Margaret, his pants round his ankles, an appraising finger stuffed up his nose.

Margaret took in the scene with a look on her face that could have curdled milk. She dumped her backpack on the floor. 'Well,' she snarled, 'when you've quite finished snogging that girl, Doogie, perhaps you'll have the courtesy to introduce me to your … *friends*!'

'Wow, a wee party!' Senga McDuff soprano'd, grooving in from the landing looking like a ten-a-penny imitation of Dolly Parton with a two-week Mallorcan suntan and accompanying love bites. 'Got room for one more raver, have ye, Doogie darlin'?'

'You can take my place, *darlin'*!' Margaret huffed. She picked up her backpack, turned on her heel and exited the flat shouting, '*I'm* not accustomed to frequenting knocking shops!'

'Jesus Christ Almighty!' Doogie muttered as he disentangled himself from Catalina. 'The shit's hit the fan now, all right!'

'Somethin' Ah said, was it?' Senga enquired with a look of contrived innocence, then introduced herself to Angie and Catalina.

Doogie rushed out onto the balcony. 'Wait a minute, Margaret!' he yelled down to the street. 'It's not what you think! I can explain! Honest!'

'Fuck off, O'Mara, you perverted bastard!' were the genteel words that rose up in reply.

'Stuck up bitch,' Angie mumbled, then handed Doogie a brimming flute of bubbly. 'None of my business, of course,' she smiled. 'Cheers!'

'Listen, Ah'm not here tae intrude,' Senga said to the downcast Doogie. She gave Catalina the once-over. 'Ah can see ye've got yer hands full. Nah, Ah'm just on ma way tae the airport, like. Glasgow beckons. Aye, and Ah just asked the taxi driver tae drop me off here for a wee minute. Just wonderin' how yer nose and, ehm, yer *other* bits is doin'.'

Doogie was staring at the floor. 'Yeah, fine thanks,' he muttered absently. 'Good of you to drop by at that very moment.' He smiled an ironic little smile. 'Like you said last time, I owed you one.'

'Think nothin' of it,' Senga breezed, before strutting out the door in an invisible cloud of cheap perfume. 'Any time, darlin',' she called back. '*Ciao*, big man!'

Of a sudden, the celebratory atmosphere had degenerated to one of deep gloom.

'I can see now why you decided to shoot the crow for a while,' Angie told Doogie between swigs of champers. 'I mean, in all fairness, your friend Margaret isn't too well endowed in the niceties department, is she?'

'She smells of pee,' Pedrito chipped in.

Angie bent down to haul up his pants. 'It's yourself you're smelling, love. Learn to aim better.'

'I think the Margaret friend has the unhappiness for me to kissing you, Doogie,' Catalina offered, sad-faced. 'It is not the custom in Scotland for the kissing with the congratulatings, no?'

'No, they congratulate each other by swapping haggises and bits of coal up there,' Angie piped up in an attempt to re-inject some levity into the scene. 'Yeah, they only kiss when they're having a poke, see.'

'A … *poke*?' Catalina asked, wide-eyed.

'She's only pulling your leg,' Doogie said, unable to resist smiling at Angie's spiky sense of humour.

Catalina glanced down at her legs, then, her face a picture of puzzlement, she looked across the room at Angie.

With a dirty cackle, Angie rattled off something to her in *mallorquín* – only a few words with accompanying hip movements. Catalina blushed violently. The 'poke' word, Doogie gathered, had been duly explained.

The pervading atmosphere of gloom persisted.

'Ah, well,' Angie sighed, after an interlude of silent floor-gazing by her two young companions, 'doesn't time fly when you're having fun?' She looked at her watch. 'I'd better get Pedrito off to bed. Oh, by the way, Doog,' she said as an afterthought, 'old María insists I use her flat, so you can have your bed back in here. No need for you to doss down on the couch again tonight, you'll be pleased to know.' She stopped by Doogie's chair on the way out and laid a hand on his shoulder. 'No contest, incidentally, kid,' she murmured with a jerk of her head in Catalina's direction. 'Your Miss Arran Charm School 2008 can't even hold a candle.' Then, winking at Catalina, she said, 'And don't you be hanging about in here too long on your own with this hairy Scotsman, love. They don't wear nothing under their kilts for nothing, you know.'

Catalina's limp smile bore witness to the fact that she hadn't a clue what Angie had meant. Just as well, thought Doogie. Having *one* girl thinking him a sex maniac was enough to be going on with for the present.

They sat in a kind of pensive hush for a while after Angie and Pedrito had gone, Doogie on a chair by the table, Catalina on the sofa against the opposite wall. It was the first time they'd *really* been alone together, Doogie realised, but the embarrassment he felt in the aftermath of Margaret's ill-timed appearance and melodramatic exit was acute. It was dominating his thoughts. His mind was racing, rifling through the possible consequences of the event. What must he have looked and sounded like to Catalina, rushing out and shouting after Margaret the way he had? God, what a wimp! And as for Angie – it was all very well for her to throw in her tuppence worth, but it wasn't that simple. After all, his whole future could be at stake here.

It was Catalina who eventually broke the silence. 'I am thinking the Margaret friend,' she said quietly, 'she is wanting you very *mucho*, no?'

'Margaret wants everything very *mucho*,' Doogie muttered dejectedly. 'That's the whole problem.'

Another few moments of pensive silence.

'I am thinking she has a strong head, *sí*?' Catalina ventured.

'Headstrong would be the right way to put it in her case, but I know what you mean.'

'*Sí*, and she will fight to keep her Doogie. This I can tell.'

'But I'm not *her* Doogie. That's the whole point. I mean, more than anything else, it's that attitude of Margaret's that was behind me coming here in the first place.'

Suddenly realising what a self-centred whiner he must seem, Doogie went over and sat down beside Catalina. He took her hand and gave it a little squeeze. 'Look, I'm sorry, Cati,' he said. 'You've got problems enough of your own with Rafael and everything, so why should I be going on about my –?'

Catalina put a finger to his lips. 'But I have no *problema* with Rafael. I have told him the truth of what is here, in my *corazón*.' She moved her hand to her heart, then lowered her eyes and murmured. 'Do you know what is in yours, Doogie?'

Doogie feared that he did, but he'd managed not to admit it to himself so far. Hell's bells, things were complicated enough as it was! He tried to let go of her hand, only for Catalina to tighten her grip.

'Do you truly know what is in your heart, Doogie?' she said, looking directly into his eyes now.

Doogie glanced away. Yet another set of thoughts was running a three-legged race round his head, and he was trying desperately hard to put his money on the sensible one. But there was a new, more subtle contender competing for his emotions this time.

Catalina sensed this. 'Do you truly know, Doogie?' she repeated.

Doogie heaved a slow sigh, then put his arm round her shoulder. 'Aye, I suppose I do at that, but I'm maybe just scared to own up to it, that's all.'

'Why scared?' Catalina laid her head on his chest. 'You told me the words of the Señor Shakespeare, remember? Always to being true to yourself?'

'Ah, but if only it was always that easy,' Doogie said. 'You know, vet college and everything. I mean, I'm not going to be here in Mallorca working for Merryweather for ever.'

Still holding onto Doogie's hand, Catalina stood up. 'Perhaps,' she smiled, 'but we also have a saying in *mallorquín*... "Listen to your heart when it be fighting with your head. For, in the end, a sore head is more easy to curing than a broken heart."'

Doogie sighed again. 'Yeah, I suppose there's something in what you say, right enough, although it doesn't make things any easier.'

Catalina pulled him to his feet and wagged a finger at him. 'But if you are listening to your heart when the day comes to leave Mallorca...' She led him onto the balcony and rested her head on his shoulder. 'Look,' she said, gesturing through the palms towards the sun setting over the Mediterranean Sea. 'Can you ever be having a moment like this with the Margaret friend?'

Catalina's unexpected bluntness made Doogie laugh. 'No, I don't suppose I can at that. Not with the Margaret friend. And certainly not on Arran.'

She raised her eyes to Doogie's. 'And I also will fight to keep my Doogie. *Sí*, and this the Margaret friend will learn.'

Swallowing hard, Doogie tapped the end of Catalina's nose. 'Put those Spanish eyes away.' He pointed to his heart. 'They do strange things to my Scottish *corazón*.'

147

'And these are not nice things?' Catalina teased.

Doogie could see where this was leading, and, as much as the prospect appealed, he knew he'd have to let pragmatism win this particular three-legged race. 'Come on,' he said, resolutely guiding her back inside, 'I'd better get you home before your mother wonders where you've got to.'

Catalina turned and barred Doogie's way to the door. 'No, no, my mother will not to worrying.'

'But she *will*,' Doogie insisted. 'I know she will. Just look at the time.'

Catalina dipped her head, her expression a curious blend of guilt, surprise and self-congratulation. 'You see, I am telling my mother today that I am staying tonight with Angie and Pedrito.' She took Doogie by the hand again and led him towards the bedroom, pausing at the door to place her hand on his chest. 'Now come, my Doogie,' she whispered, 'and let your Cati teach you how to listen to your heart.'

CHAPTER TWELVE

'A BLAST FROM THE PAST'

NEXT MORNING, DOOGIE AND Catalina walked into the
Merryweather office to a barrage of good-natured whistles and
gibes from the girls…

'Oo-oo-oh! Arriving for work *together* now, are we?'

'Well, well, well, what put *that* smile on your face,
Catalina?'

'Been pulled at last by the pool man, have you?'

Over it all boomed Ingrid's hearty guffaw. He drew Doogie
aside once the catcalls had subsided. 'Hey,' he grinned, 'you
certainly put a spoke in Nick Martin's wheel, didn't you,
sunshine?'

'Fact is he spoked his own wheel,' Doogie shrugged. 'All his own work, really.'

Ingrid's smile was replaced by a concerned frown. 'He's out on his ass with no work now, though.'

'He's lucky to be out at all, work or no work,' Doogie snapped. 'How do you think the parents of that dead Danish girl think about trash like him walking free?'

Ingrid raised his hands. 'Hey, hey, sunshine, cool it, huh! I'm one of the good guys, remember?'

'Yeah, I'm sorry, Ingrid. I didn't mean to sound off at you. No, it's just that – well, why should anyone care about bloody Nick Martin's welfare? He had it coming.'

'Ah, but you haven't been gettin' where *I'm* comin' from, man.' There was a gently chiding edge to Ingrid's voice. 'Nah, it's *your* welfare I been thinkin' about, not Tricky Nicky's, right?'

'You mean me being back on the rep grind?' Doogie joked. 'Aye, it's a bit of a bummer after the cushy swimming pool number, but I'll survive, never fear.'

Ingrid's expression was solemn now. 'Never mind all that work crap, sunshine. We're talkin' about your personal safety here, get me?'

Doogie returned his look, but blankly.

'OK,' Ingrid continued, 'we're talkin' about Nick Martin here, right? Right, and he's one bad son of a bitch, believe me. Yeah, and one way or another, he's gonna be blamin' *you* for him landin' flat on his asshole.'

Doogie frowned. 'Maybe he will, but that doesn't –'

'Just look out for yourself, sunshine. That's all I'm sayin', OK?' Ingrid gave Doogie one of his melon-slice grins then thumped his shoulder. 'Now, let's see what kinda *nice* little job we got lined up for you today, huh?'

Shuttle-service gannet-droppings duty was the nice little job lined up for Doogie, as if he couldn't have guessed. Over and over again, it was one coachload of red and peeling holiday-end punters being ferried from hotels to airport, followed by what seemed like all the same faces (though milk-bottle white this time) being carted in the opposite direction. Still, the endless bombardment of questions, complaints, problems, boozy compliments and similarly-inspired insults helped keep Doogie's mind occupied and off the burgeoning complications of his private life. But not entirely.

Catalina had been assigned to help out at the Merryweather Holidays information desk in the airport's main concourse, so he saw her from time to time during the day. She would wave cheerily to him as he trudged past in the distance, followed by sweating, luggage-lugging hordes, desperate either to get to their flight check-in ahead of everyone else, or to grab pole position in the queue for their hotel-bound coach. The scenario, like the faces, never changed – only the names on the manifests.

Yet, all the time, thoughts of Catalina were in the back of Doogie's mind. What *was* he going to do about her? Clearly, she was taking things between them *very* seriously, and, in a perfect world, he had to admit that he'd have been happy to let events take their natural course. But it wasn't a perfect world. Far from it. For, no matter how much Catalina railed against it now, something still told Doogie that her 'presupposed' marriage to the moody Rafael would ultimately happen. It was the way of her people. In any case, the time would surely come when she would tire of the novelty of having a foreign *novio* like Doogie, of having her fling in this atmosphere of 'worldly freedom' that her new-found career had opened up to her. Yes, she would return to her country roots, to Capdellá, to be a farmer's wife one day. Of that, Doogie was sure – or was trying to be.

Then, taking her due place in his imperfect little world, there was Margaret. Margaret Hyslop, the key to Doogie's future security and, therefore, happiness. Or so she would have him believe. God, if only her storming out of his life yesterday had been a conclusive act, instead of merely one of her regular tantrums, one of her well-practised fits of pique. If only. Hell, if only she could have kept her bloody distance for just this one whole year!

'*Have booked into the Hotel Tiempo Alegre in Magaluf,*' the note pinned to Doogie's front door read when he got home that evening. '*Meet me there at 8 tonight. Margaret.*'

As it was already nearly nine o'clock, Doogie had a fair idea of what Margaret's mood would be when he did eventually turn up at her hotel. And turn up he must, because past experience told him that Margaret would still be waiting, and would continue to do so. And, if he didn't turn up tonight, the same sequence of events would be repeated tomorrow. Or, worse still, she would find out his daily schedule from the office and ambush one of his shuttle buses.

'Without your little harem tonight, I see,' she said by way of greeting as Doogie strode into the hotel lounge. 'Or are they following on behind with the eunuch guards?'

'Very droll, Margaret,' Doogie mumbled, then slumped down at her corner table – a table she'd chosen, he assumed, because of its position farthest away from the happy-holidaymaking riffraff at the bar. 'Or it *might* be droll,' he corrected, 'if I knew what you were on about.'

'The little gypsy slut you were groping when I stumbled upon your den of iniquity yesterday,' Margaret snarled. 'That's what I'm on about! And that's not to mention the two Brit slags and that dirty, little, bare-arsed brat with his fist up his nose.'

With a wry smile, Doogie calmly replied, 'The milk of human kindness fairly gushes from your breast at times, doesn't it, Margaret?'

A waiter arrived to take their drinks order.

'A Coke or something soft for you?' Doogie asked Margaret. 'Or will you stick with the venom?'

Margaret gave a derisive snort and turned her head away.

Doogie ordered himself a beer.

'*Muy bien*, Mister Sunshine,' the waiter grinned. 'Your usual *San Miguel* coming right up, *amigo*.'

Margaret's expression was one of shocked disbelief. She gaped open-mouthed at the departing waiter, then at Doogie.

'Mister *Sun*shine!' she gagged, looking as if she'd just been force-fed a live rat. 'Did I hear that waiter call you Mister *Sun*shine?'

He could have done without this, Doogie thought. But bugger it! Why spare her the details?

'Did you see a kids' entertainer doing his thing by the pool out there today?' he asked.

'That – that *clown* person?'

'Yeah, that clown person.'

Margaret scowled. 'What about him?'

'Just that I was him, until very recently.' Doogie savoured Margaret's dumfounded reaction for a moment, then added, 'And you probably noticed his female assistant as well, did you?'

Margaret nodded. 'What about her?'

'Just that mine was played by Catalina, the little gypsy slut you saw in my den of iniquity yesterday.' He smiled sweetly. 'OK then, Margaret, how does that grab you?'

Margaret looked ceilingward and shook her head in dismay. 'Catalina, is it? On first name terms with the local trollops now, are you?' She glared at Doogie, her nostrils flaring. 'I presume the half-naked urchin in your flat was just one of her ever-expanding litter of multi-fathered piccaninnies! Correct?'

Doogie chose not to answer, but sat waiting, poker-faced, for Margaret's next verbal lunge. It came soon enough.

'And just look at your nose!' She squinted at the scar, then raised her own nose in disgust. 'My God, don't tell me you've been brawling now as well!' She turned her head to glare at groups of her fellow hotel residents pressing noisily from the dining room into the bar. 'Who in their right mind would even want to associate with the likes of that bunch of Mallorca-struck Neanderthals, never mind get involved in fisticuffs with them?' She glanced fleetingly at Doogie's Merryweather blazer. 'Mind you, if you fly with the crows in Mallorca…'

Now it was Doogie's turn to give a derisive snort. 'You get the same Neanderthals, if that's what you want to call them, going on holiday to Arran, don't forget.'

'More's the pity.'

'Your father doesn't mind taking their money for stitching up their scrapping Rottweilers or pit bulls or whatever, though, does he?'

'That's an entirely different matter,' Margaret haughtily retorted. 'Professional ethics are involved.'

'Precisely! And if a certain mob of your Mallorca-struck medical college chums from Edinburgh Uni had had a modicum of the same, I wouldn't be sporting this welt on the nose for trying to protect *their* skins!'

Margaret looked away, her nose in the air again. 'I haven't the *fog*giest idea what you mean.'

'Precisely again, Margaret. And, if you'll just get off your high horse and stop jumping to all the wrong conclusions for a minute, I'll give you the facts – about everything. *If* you're interested!'

Still looking sideways, Margaret raised her shoulders in a suit-yourself shrug. But as Doogie's story unfolded, the more her attitude changed. She gradually turned to face him, her elbows resting on the table, her eyes never shifting from his face.

'So that's it,' Doogie said in conclusion. 'Senga McDuff and Angie may be of the honky-tonk variety, but to me they're still angels – total strangers who were good to me without making any big deal about it. And as for Catalina – well, she's just a nice, unspoiled country lass from a background not unlike my own. Small farm, hard-working parents.' He paused, then lowered his brows to glower at Margaret. 'And she's no more a slut than my own wee sister Mo, as it happens.'

Margaret, distinctly crestfallen, began to weave her fingers on the table, her eyes downcast. 'You don't think of this Catalina as a sister, though, do you, Doogie?'

Although Doogie had a feeling that something like this would be Margaret's response, he was still slightly taken aback. 'What makes you think that?' he said, cagily.

154

Margaret looked him in the eye. 'Have you slept with her?'

As accustomed as Doogie was to Margaret's penchant for not beating about the bush, he was caught totally off guard by her bluntness now. 'I, ehm, I – I thought I just told you she wasn't a slut,' he bumbled.

Margaret smiled condescendingly and looked down at her fingers again. 'That doesn't exactly answer my question, does it?'

Doogie remained prudently tight-lipped.

'Borrow them seats offa ya, mate?' a holidaymaker enquired, gesturing towards the two empty chairs at the table.

Doogie was thankful for this timely interruption. 'Yeah, yeah, help yourself, friend. They're all yours.' He exchanged nods of recognition with a few Merryweather clients over at the bar while awaiting Margaret's next stroke. She hadn't come all this way just to listen to *his* story – that much he did know!

'Father and Mother are asking for you,' she eventually said, tracing invisible rings on the table with her finger as she spoke.

'That's nice,' Doogie said cordially. 'Thank them for me. I hope they're both well.'

'Father's worried about you, Doogie.' Margaret's tone was sensitive now, her finger slowly spiralling closer to Doogie's side of the table. 'You know, he just doesn't understand why you've interrupted your studies like this.'

Doogie took a deep, exasperated breath. 'Look, I've just gone to great lengths to explain why, Margaret, but I really don't think you understand yet either, do you?'

Margaret reacted as if she hadn't even heard that. 'Come on now, Doogs,' she said in a way which, to Doogie, was bordering on the patronising, 'we go back too far to let anything, any*one*, stand in our way.' She looked round the room at nothing in particular and wafted a hand about vaguely. 'All this – all this *silly* holiday rep thing – let's be honest, it's just not you. All right, I'll admit that some of the people you've met along the way maybe aren't quite as bad as I

155

thought on first impressions, but even so… I mean, be fair, Doogie, they're just not *your* kind of people.'

Warming to her theme, she reached out and placed her hand on Doogie's. The slightly desperate look in her eyes reminded him of a puppy's owner who was making one final, tolerant plea to her pet to stop shitting on the carpet before she'd be compelled to get the whip out. 'Look,' she went on with redoubled intensity, 'Father now says he wants to retire as soon as you qualify. Not an indefinite few years after, but as *soon* as you graduate. All he wants to do is get out on that golf course.' She leaned forward and whispered excitedly, 'Just think, the practice will be yours! All yours!'

Doogie drew his hand away. 'You know I'll always be grateful to your father for the chance,' he said, trying to ignore the twinges of self-reproach pricking his conscience. 'It's more than any young vet could hope for, I know that, but as I've explained –'

'And there's us,' Margaret butted in. Her face was aglow with enthusiasm. 'It's like we always planned, Doogie. Just think about it. With any luck…' She looked heavenward and clasped her hands together in mock prayer. 'With any luck, I'll qualify as a doctor at the same time.' She was nicely wound up now. 'And, would you believe, old Doc MacFarlane back home has offered me a partnership. Yes, and him set to retire in a few years too!' She opened her arms and beamed, 'You see, Doogie? It's all going to work out just the way we wanted!'

Doogie shook his head. 'But that's the whole problem, Margaret. It's not what *we* –'

Margaret steamrollered over what he was about to say, her eyes sparkling with a kind of manic fervour as she delivered her coup de grâce: 'All you've got to do is jack in this Merryweather nonsense right away – or stick it out until the end of next month, if you *really* must – and you'll be ready to start the new term back at vet college in Edinburgh in September!' Before Doogie had a chance to reply, she added a stinging little appendix: 'OK,' she smiled, 'maybe nothing gained from your little career detour, but hopefully nothing lost either, hmm?'

Doogie could only laugh inwardly. It was either that or take the girl by the throat. And yet, underneath all her outward blustering and bullying, he could still recognise traces of the less complex, more contented Margaret he had known in childhood. The Margaret he had truly loved like a little sister. Oh, she had always been a bossy breeks, even as a toddler, but she'd always had a kindly side to her nature as well. And she was never selfish. Spoiled, yes, because that was the way she'd been brought up, but never selfish … as a child. No, that trait had developed later, at secondary school, as Doogie recalled. The will to succeed, to be best at everything she tackled, had been instilled in Margaret from an early age by her fastidious father, just as he'd done with Doogie after he took him under his veterinary wing. And Doogie readily admitted it was a discipline that had stood him in good stead ever since.

But with Margaret, it was different. Being a naturally gifted scholar, she'd soon found that she didn't have to work particularly hard to keep herself academically head-and-shoulders above her contemporaries. Consequently, she'd started to devote her superfluous mental energies to other things. To kicking back at classroom prejudices against what was universally regarded as her 'swottiness' by developing an aura of I-know-best superiority, of I'm-in-control loftiness, of almost blind I'll-show-you ambition. It had been a short step from that to the egotistic, unfeeling and, as Angie put it, stuck-up image she presented now.

Yet Doogie knew there was more to it than that. He remembered the material things that Margaret, as an only child of relatively elderly parents, had had showered on her – to the envy of every other kid in the village at that time. But it was much later, when the perplexing magnets of adolescence had set their emotions spinning, that he had come to realise that there had been one vital element lacking all along in Margaret's outwardly-idyllic family life. Love. A missing ingredient which, in her increasingly confused way, she had come to believe would automatically be found in her longstanding friendship with Doogie, but which her urgency to claim had only served to confound.

Doogie looked at her across the table, her face radiant with a kind of single-minded expectancy. It was the same expression that had disarmed him so often when, as kids, she would suddenly produce a pound note from her pocket and tell him to go and buy them ice cream from the van that had stopped, bells jangling, outside her father's house. And she was right in what she'd said a few minutes earlier tonight. She and Doogie did go back a long way, and he would never do anything to intentionally hurt her, no matter how much her browbeating ways got under his skin at times. Besides, who could tell, maybe her plans for them *would* materialise one day. But, and it was a big but, Doogie still needed time and space to work things out for himself before he could either build or demolish her hopes. And for the present, he knew that the only way to handle Margaret was to be firm with her.

'I'm sorry, Margaret,' he said, 'but the position remains the same as when I left Scotland. I fulfil my one-year contract of employment here, and we'll see what the future holds when the time comes.'

Margaret's face dropped. 'But my father,' she objected, 'he's expecting you to –'

'Hold on a minute, Margaret! I did write to your father telling him how I felt before I quit college, you know. *And* I've explained everything again to you tonight.' Doogie hunched his shoulders. 'It's my life, when all's said and done, and you've got to respect that, surely?'

Margaret got to her feet and smoothed down her clothes, her head held imperiously high. 'Fair enough, Doogie, you've made your position perfectly clear, I think.' She prepared to go, but paused by Doogie, who was standing now too, and smiled a thin smile. 'I'm leaving first thing in the morning. Back to the mainland to meet up with my friends.'

Doogie suddenly felt sorry for Margaret, just as she knew

he would. 'Oh, I – I see,' he stammered. 'I, uh, I was just about to ask if you'd eaten. There's a nice little place just around the –'

'I ate earlier, thank you. I can't get used to this strange Spanish habit of eating at bedtime, I'm afraid.'

'When in Rome?' Doogie dryly suggested.

'It's been nice seeing you again,' Margaret said flatly. 'I'll be coming back to Mallorca with my friends, by the way. Sometime in the second half of next month. They want to do some hill-walking here – rock-climbing, that sort of thing. That's after we've done Andalucia and, I don't know, maybe a bit of Portugal.'

It was all right for some, Doogie thought. 'We live in two different worlds, don't we, Margaret?'

'But my world's yours for the taking, Doogie,' she came back, the merest hint of pleading in the way she looked at him.

Doogie gave her a knowing smile. 'All I have to do is run out to the ice cream van, hmm?'

Margaret lowered her head, trying to hide the tears that suddenly welled up in her eyes. She produced a handkerchief and blew her nose. 'Damned hay fever!'

Doogie watched her struggling to regain her composure. He hated to see her this way, and anywhere else but in the crowded lounge of the Hotel Tiempo Alegre, he would have given her the comforting, reassuring cuddle she needed. Deep down, he knew that trapped somewhere inside that outwardly hard shell was the loveable wee Margaret Hyslop of old. It would just take someone with patience, understanding and, above all else, a thick skin to bring her back. But then, who else but Doogie knew her well enough to be bothered?

He bent forward and kissed her lightly on the forehead. 'Bye, bye, Margaret. Safe journeys. See you next month, eh?'

She looked up, her chin quivering, despite a look of dour determination that had returned to her reddened eyes. 'Just make sure you've got that fucking brain of yours sorted out by then, O'Mara!' she warbled. 'And that's an order!' With that, she turned and strode off – head up, shoulders back, cutting a swathe through the sea of Neanderthals like a man o' war in full sail.

CHAPTER THIRTEEN

'MIXED BLESSINGS'

MARGARET'S WHIRLWIND VISIT HAD left Doogie feeling
decidedly punch-drunk and, if anything, even more mixed up
than before. In one respect, he was pleased that the peak-
season rush was now in full swing, because there really was no
time for anything but work, work, work and more work – and
a little sleep, when you could grab it.

Life as a Merryweather Holidays rep was now just as
Angie had described it when, feeling like a fish out of water,
and with his emotions at sixes and sevens, he had first arrived
on the island. Whatever else, the few intervening weeks had
certainly taught him things about life, about people and even
about himself that he'd never been aware of before. For that he
was grateful – for the most part. Whether or not his new, more
street-wise, have-a-go outlook would help him in making
those vital decisions about his future was another matter

entirely, of course, but Doogie was tempted to let the pressure of work relegate all that to the back of his mind for the present.

Because of conflicting shift arrangements, even contact with Catalina had become irregular and invariably fleeting: usually only a few quick words as Doogie rushed past the Merryweather desk at the airport like a latter-day pied piper for adults. Catalina, meanwhile, seemed happy enough in her new post, yet Doogie could tell that the prevailing lack of opportunity to see more of each other was not to her liking at all. Nor was it to his, he had to admit, although he did his best not to show it. He'd persuaded himself that, all recent happenings considered, slowing things down between them for a while would make sense anyway.

Though reluctantly, Angie had duly returned to Ibiza after her traumatic flying visit to see old María. Angie's ongoing heartaches notwithstanding, at least the old woman's sudden and life-threatening illness had prompted Angie to bite the bullet and explain at last to Pedrito the reason for her prolonged periods of absence from him. Since then, the little chap seemed to have taken to his temporary 'foster' home at the farm of Catalina's parents with a kind of contented resignation.

'He is spending much time now at the *finca* of Rafael,' Catalina told Doogie during one of their snatched conversations at the airport. Rafael kept rabbits, she explained – for the pot, of course, but he allowed Pedrito to play with a few of the baby ones in a little wire-mesh enclosure he had made specially. *Sí*, they were becoming good friends, Rafael and Pedrito.

Doogie was pleased to hear it, in a way, but slightly envious too, although he didn't really know why. Maybe the image of Rafael providing the little boy with some of the simple pleasures of life on a small farm evoked almost forgotten memories of his own childhood when his father was still a young man. Or maybe, almost subconsciously, he just yearned to return to that uncomplicated rural lifestyle himself, no matter how unrealistic the notion or how impossible the dream. The fact of the matter right now was that he was nothing more than a penniless holiday rep, and a temporary one at that, with three more years of frugal student life in Edinburgh beckoning. And beyond that? Well, the sky could be the limit ... *if* Margaret had anything to do with it. But was he prepared to pay the price? And did he really want to reach for those particular stars in any case? Those were the dilemmas constantly nagging away in Doogie's mind. Hell, Rafael didn't know how lucky he was. He had a farm that provided him with a living, even if a modest one, in one of the most beautiful locations imaginable, and with the very real prospect, Doogie still believed, of a wonderful girl like Catalina sharing the rest of his life. But then, all other considerations aside, Mallorca was *their* world, its way of country life *their* heritage, and in reality Doogie was no more than a stranger passing through.

The more these thoughts played on his mind, the more Doogie became convinced that it was going to be less painful in the long term if he took the advice old Hyslop had relayed via his daughter Margaret – to pack in the Merryweather job at the end of next month and get back to his studies in Scotland. Realistically, what else was there to do? His staying in Mallorca any longer was only going to put his graduation back a year, as well as creating for Catalina and himself complications they'd probably both live to regret. He had to accept that fate had charted them different courses. It was as simple as that, and the sooner he came to terms with it, the better for all concerned.

Then in stepped fate herself – in the unlikely guise of old María.

She had continued to make good progress following her stroke, and had now been transferred from Son Dureta Hospital in Palma to a convalescent home in the mountain village of Valldemossa, about eighteen kilometres north of the city. Doogie had promised Catalina that, the first time they could wangle a day off together, he would drive her up there in Humpty Dumpty, Angie's trusty old Renault 5. The day arrived sooner than he expected – thanks, he suspected, to some crafty massaging of the duty rosters by the cupid-playing girls in the office, acting in response, perhaps, to a subtle hint or two from Catalina herself.

It was just after nine o'clock when Doogie pulled into the yard at the Finca Sa Grua on what promised to be a real scorcher of a day. He and Catalina were heading in the right direction, Señora Ensenyat told him, fanning herself with a cardboard egg tray as she watered a fine display of potted geraniums in the shade of the *porche* at the front of the farmhouse. *Sí,* there was always a breath of cool, fresh air up at Valldemossa. Oh, Catalina wouldn't be long, she assured Doogie, sensing a slight edginess about him. She invited him to sit in one of the two old armchairs by the doorway.

Catalina had just taken Pedrito to nursery school in Capdellá, she informed him. He went there three mornings a week now. Good for him to be with other children. Good for her and her husband too, she readily admitted. They weren't as young as they used to be, and they'd forgotten how exhausting looking after a four-year-old can be. Anyhow, they thought it better for Pedrito not to know about Catalina and Doogie's visit to old María today. He would only want to go along, and seeing María again might upset him, just when he was getting used to his new 'grandparents'. With a little smile, she laid down her watering can and went into the house, to reappear presently with two glasses of freshly-squeezed orange juice. She handed one to Doogie and plumped herself down in the other chair.

'*Madre mía*!' she panted. '*Qué alivio*! What a relief!'

Doogie silently revelled in the ambience: the mustiness of old hessian sacks folded neatly by his chair, the feathery smell of two chattering hens pecking optimistically in the sun-baked dust at his feet, the sleepy chirping of sparrows hidden somewhere in the leafy shelter of the old palm tree by the gate. He listened to the distant growl of a tractor labouring on one of the high mountain terraces, then gazed down the valley towards the ochre houses of Capdellá village, most of their windows already shuttered against the white heat of the day.

Señora Ensenyat caught his mood. 'It is beautiful, the valley of Capdellá, no?'

'Wonderful,' Doogie agreed, still marvelling at the scene. Indeed, he confessed, he had never seen a more beautiful valley. 'Evening, night and now morning. Every time of day different, yet each equally beautiful in its own way.'

Señora Ensenyat smiled and nodded her head. She followed his gaze over the valley, sipped her orange juice, then said quietly, 'You miss the life of the country, Doogie. I know. I can tell. I have watched you – from a distance, walking in the fields – and close up, saving the life of an animal.'

Doogie didn't answer. He didn't have to. He knew that this kindly woman, who had met him only three times, could already read him as easily as if she were his own mother. A lump came to his throat as he suddenly realised how much he still missed his parents, missed their simply being there when he needed them, missed that magic warmth of family that he'd always felt the presence of, no matter how far from home. How he could do with his mum and dad's words of advice now.

'Cati will miss all this too,' Señora Ensenyat continued thoughtfully. She turned her head to glance at Doogie. 'When she goes away.'

Doogie managed a heartening little laugh. 'No, don't you worry about that. She'll never leave here. She's too much a part of all this.'

Señora Ensenyat hesitated, then asked, a note of confusion in her voice, 'So, her opportunity in the Merryweather *turismo*? You think it is no good?'

She had put Doogie in a spot. The last thing he wanted to do was belittle Catalina's job, which she and her parents probably believed, in all good faith, to be a worthwhile career opening, but which would, in all probability, turn out to be nothing more permanent than one of Sam Merryweather's cheapskate 'work experience' scams. Doogie searched for the right thing to say…

'No, no, the opportunity's fine,' he bluffed. 'I mean, you know, if that's what she wants to do.' He weighed his next words carefully. 'It's just that, well, I don't think Catalina really belongs in that sort of life. To be honest, I think she's too good for it.' He forced another little laugh, hoping to sound suitably detached. 'No, no, she'll be back here to work one day – as a farmer's wife. Just you wait and see.'

It was Señora Ensenyat who laughed now. But hers was a hearty laugh that had Doogie grinning back, although he hadn't a clue why.

'You are thinking of Rafael,' she beamed. 'You are thinking my Cati and Rafa will one day be…' She stopped short and shook her head vigorously, the smile fading from her face. 'No, no, that will never happen. Never! I know my Cati. She is a modern girl and she knows what she wants and who she wants. *Sí*, and it is *not* Rafael!'

'Really?' Doogie gulped, but resisted the temptation to enquire if it was anyone he knew.

Once again, Señora Ensenyat seemed able to read his thoughts. She resumed her gaze over the valley and began to fan her face with the egg tray again. All traces of humour were gone from her eyes as she asked, 'You will return to Scotland soon, Doogie – to study again to be a *veterinario*?'

Caught off guard, Doogie didn't know quite what to say. 'Well, yes – but maybe not *soon*,' he floundered. 'But, yes, I suppose you're right. Some time or other I'll have to, you know, make some sort of decision about –'

Señora Ensenyat reached over and placed a hand on his arm. 'She is very precious to us,' she stated softly, but with undisguised concern. 'I understand that you have your own world to return to. And so I ask you – do not hurt her. Please.'

Doogie was spared the ordeal of attempting to make an appropriate response by the clattering arrival of the Ensenyat's ancient Citroën 2CV van. An aged and rusting jalopy it may have been, but, in Doogie's eyes, the girl who emerged from it

166

wouldn't have appeared out of place stepping from a stretch limo at the Cannes Film Festival. He had never seen Catalina looking like this before. The somewhat frumpy Merryweather uniform, he now realised, had been doing her no favours whatsoever. With a smile as bright as the day, she came tripping over the yard, the golden tan of her arms and legs accentuated by the white of her little cotton shift, her hair drawn up to reveal the classic Mediterranean beauty of her face. If Doogie had never seen her before, this first glimpse would have knocked him sideways.

'*Hola, Mamá!*' she called to her mother, though never taking here eyes off Doogie. She ran to him as eagerly as if she were welcoming back a long-lost hero and gave him the customary peck on both cheeks. Then she wrapped her arms round his neck and whispered in his ear, her lips hidden from her mother's watchful eyes, '*Te quiero*, Doogie.'

Doogie was flabbergasted, and it showed. No girl had actually told him she loved him before – not as if she meant it anyway, and certainly not in front of her mother!

'Uhm, me too,' he mumbled stupidly, the words seeming to spout from his mouth of their own accord.

Catalina giggled, then put an arm round his waist. Snuggling her head to his shoulder, she looked at her mother and said as spontaneously as if asking the time, 'We make a fine picture, my handsome Scotsman and me, no?'

Señora Ensenyat smiled and replied that they certainly did.

But Doogie detected a trace of worry in her eyes, a hint of anxiety in her smile, and he knew exactly why. He also knew how deep his feelings for Catalina had become. No matter how much he tried to convince himself that breaking from her would be in her best interests, he could see now that actually doing so would show him to be nothing but self-centred and callous.

The more he got to know Catalina, the more he realised just how accurate old María's description of her had been. Catalina was special. She wasn't just beautiful physically, but also in character, with a purity of spirit, of inner happiness and generosity that he'd never known in anyone before. It was just the naivety of a country girl, some would say, but he knew better. Catalina *was* special. And his leaving was going to break her heart. There was no point in trying to kid himself otherwise, because it was going to break *his* heart too. And what about her mother and father? Good people of his own kind, of whom he'd already grown very fond. Hurting them would be almost like hurting his own folks.

Yet the reality of the situation had to be faced *and* tackled … somehow.

As if aware of Doogie's thoughts, Señora Ensenyat came up to him and brushed his cheek with the back of her fingers. 'Be happy, Doogie,' she smiled. 'The troubles of tomorrow may never come, so why let the thought of them spoil today?' With that, she kissed them both goodbye, asked them to pass on her good wishes to old María, then shooed them off towards the car. 'And remember,' she called to Doogie as he opened the door for Catalina, 'look after our little girl.'

Pertly, Catalina placed her bottom on the seat. 'And I will make sure that you do,' she murmured to Doogie, while raising her eyes to meet his before swinging her suntanned knees into the car.

'I will, I promise,' Doogie called back to Señora Ensenyat, an involuntary yodel in his voice.

'You are liking my new dress, I think?' Catalina asked him, coyly.

Doogie fired up the little Renault's engine. 'You look beautiful. Yes, absolutely stunning,' he replied, trying to appear calm, but making a hash of finding first gear. 'Now, ehm, which way do we go?'

Catalina laughed, then told him to turn right at the end of the farm track. 'We take the mountain road for Andratx.'

Round the first bend, they saw a man on an open tractor, baling straw in a field by the roadside. It was her father, Catalina beamed. She pressed the car horn and waved to him through the open sun roof. Her father turned his head and waved back, his shirt wet, his face gleaming with sweat.

'Jeez, that must be murder in this heat,' Doogie muttered. 'And he *still* has to pick up and stack all those bales later. Hey!' he said, suddenly inspired. 'Maybe we could get back early. It's been a while since I flung bales about. Yeah, and it would do me the world of good to –'

Catalina placed her hand firmly on Doogie's knee and declared, '*Absolutamente* no!' She stretched over to nibble his ear. 'Today you are for me, *not* for the straw!'

That could be taken as a contradiction in terms, Doogie thought, judging by the way Catalina was acting this morning. 'But better keep your mind on the driving, O'Mara,' he warned himself. 'Remember what you promised her mother!'

And well may he have kept his mind on the driving. Leaving the Ensenyat farm, the road snaked tortuously upwards through a rolling, oatmeal landscape on which groves of almond trees grew ever more sparse as the little car toiled higher. Soon the switchback bends were hugging the contours of Sa Grua mountain, where the sagging limbs of aged pine trees hung in disregard for gravity from sheer, crumbling cliffs. Doogie had his work cut out just changing between first and second gears, the task made all the more awkward by the continued presence of Catalina's hand on his knee.

'*Lo siento*,' she apologised, then, with a glint in her eye, slid her hand to what she suggested would be a less obstructive position on his thigh. She started to hum one of the little Mallorcan folk songs Doogie had heard her sing to the kids during their *Mister Sunshine Club* days at the Hotel Tiempo Alegre. He was captivated by the childlike purity of her voice, although there was little childlike or pure about the way her little finger was now slowly tracing figures of eight in an area of his anatomy perilously close to the starting point for the taking of inside leg measurements.

'I thought you told me you used to go to a convent school,' he quavered, while wrestling the car round a hairpin bend cut through solid rock.

She nodded the affirmative without interrupting her song.

Doogie caught her eye and gestured towards her hand.

'Well, I'm pretty sure the nuns didn't teach you that.'

Catalina gave his thigh a squeeze. 'No need for teaching,' she shrugged. 'Is natural, no?'

Doogie glanced sidelong at the giddy drop now falling away to their left as the road began its descent into the next valley. 'Maybe so,' he muttered, 'but it isn't doing my concentration much good!'

'You want me to putting my hand away?' Catalina pouted playfully.

'I didn't say *that* exactly,' Doogie quickly replied. 'Just, you know – don't get too – well, you know what I mean.'

Catalina nuzzled her head against his shoulder. 'No, I do *not* know,' she said with almost convincing sincerity. 'Perhaps it is another thing the nuns have not been teaching me, *si*?'

After a while, the road levelled out to wind lazily through a wide, sheltered valley high in the very heart of the mountains. Natural scrub of wild olive and myrtle now gave way to row upon row of carefully cultivated grape vines that stretched away in perfect perspective for as far as the eye could see. A sign over an ornate gateway read, '*Viña Santa Catalina*'.

'They named their wine after you, I suppose,' Doogie teased, glancing down into Catalina's hair billowing in the hot air rushing through the car's open windows.

She looked up drowsily from his shoulder and gave his leg another squeeze. '*Si*,' she yawned, 'but only the sweet.'

There was something irresistibly soporific about this mountain air, its leafy fragrances tinkling with birdsong, its tranquillity pricked occasionally by the faraway bleat of a goat. The temptation for Doogie to pull over and lie down in some shady glade was almost too strong to resist, especially now that Catalina had begun to emit dainty little snoring noises into his shoulder. But old María would be waiting, and they still had a long way to go.

The little car zigzagged effortlessly, with only its brakes complaining now, through descending canopies of oak and pine towards another valley, where trim stone farmhouses sat scattered among orchards of orange, apricot and lemon.

Doogie gave the slumbering Catalina's hair a ruffle as they reached a T-junction overlooking a sleepy little town sprawled over the lower slopes of the mountain. 'Andratx!' He called out. 'The sign says we're coming into Andratx. Which way now?'

Catalina opened her eyes and blinked at the signpost. 'Estellencs! To the right for Estellencs!' She stifled a yawn. 'Oh, please forgive, Doogie. I must to have falling sleeps.'

'Think nothing of it,' Doogie said with a throwaway flick of his hand. 'It's this irresistible effect I have on the opposite sex.'

The road started to climb again, twisting its way towards the far perimeter of the Tramuntana Mountains, whose towering bulk dominates the entire north coast of Mallorca. Though wide awake now, Catalina remained quiet for a while. Doogie thought nothing of it. He was happy just to have her there beside him, her fingers drumming a slow, meditative tattoo on his knee. They had always felt entirely comfortable in each other's company without the need for small talk, so this present interlude seemed perfectly normal.

She had been dreaming when she was asleep back there, Catalina confessed at length, her tone strangely sad. She had been dreaming that Doogie had gone away, had been taken prisoner, accused of a crime he hadn't committed. He'd been accused of something silly, she said, like stealing grapes.

'From the vineyard of Santa Catalina, I suppose?' Doogie quipped.

But it hadn't been funny, Catalina objected with a vigorous shake of her head. It had been horrible. He had been shackled and blindfolded, unable to see her as he was led away. And she, as if turned to stone, had been unable to follow and help. She would never see him again, the jailer had shouted out. Never!

Catalina shivered. 'It was terrible, Doogie. *Sí*, and very, very real.'

'Hey, come on now,' Doogie chided. 'It was only a dream.' He glanced over and gave her a reassuring smile. 'Come on, cheer up. I'm not going to steal any grapes, and that's a promise.'

Catalina reciprocated his smile, but a hint of anguish lingered in her eyes. She fell silent again, and Doogie now understood why. He knew only too well what insecurities had triggered her dream, and he feared that, sooner or later, he was fated to make that dream come true.

After a long, steady climb along the wooded flanks of the mountains, the little Renault finally emerged into a setting that took Doogie's breath away – literally.

He swallowed his shock with a gulp as he looked down into the vast chasm that had opened up without warning, just a few heart-stopping inches from his driver's window. They were so high above the sea that the sails of a passing yacht seemed like the clipped corners of a postage stamp stuck to a vast envelope of blue. Leaning forward over the steering wheel, Doogie peered upwards to his right, where the mountain had discarded her wooded cloak and now stood naked, her rocky head held proudly against the sky.

The dizzy contrasts of depth and height had him reeling. He stood on the brakes and hauled the steering wheel to the right, skidding the little car to an unseemly stop at the 'safe' side of the road, and only just avoiding being hit by a horn-blaring tour coach lumbering at full speed in the opposite direction.

Catalina, rudely jolted from her post-nightmare thoughts, grabbed Doogie's arm.

He wiped a bead of sweat from his forehead with the back of his hand. 'Sorry, Cati, but I – I'm just not used to such big scenery where I come from. Phew! That was scary!'

Catalina looked at him, perplexed at first, then amused, seeing the funny side of the situation, yet fascinated by this unexpected chink in Doogie's armour. She started to laugh. They both did.

'I thought I was never going to get you to cheer up. Too bad I nearly had to kill us both to do it, though,' Doogie joked.

Catalina frowned. 'No, no, is not for joking. This road, he is very beautiful, but has much danger for the driving also.'

172

She nudged his elbow. 'But come – I know a place for the safe lookings.'

Doogie drove on for another mile or so, ever aware of the stunning scenery unfolding on either side of this amazing corkscrew of a road that seemed miraculously suspended somewhere between sea and sky. He curbed, however, any urge to take more than a fleeting sideways glance. After a few minutes, Catalina instructed him to pull into the car park of a roadside restaurant that materialised round one of the bends. The restaurant was already busy, judging by the number of cars and coaches parked outside. But Catalina pointed a little further ahead to a flight of steps that led up to what appeared to be a platform built onto a rocky outcrop, through which a short tunnel had been cut for the road.

'It is the looking place they call the Mirador de Ricardo Roca,' she said, then took Doogie's hand and hurried him along. 'Come and see. The *vistas* will take your wind away!'

She told Doogie to shut his eyes as they neared the top of the steps, and not to open them again until she said to. Blindly, he allowed himself to be led by the hand, conscious of nothing but the soft whispering of the mountains, of Catalina's excited mutterings in *mallorquín*, and presently of a gentle waft of warm air upwardly caressing his face as Catalina put a halting hand to his chest.

'*Ahora*!' she called out. 'Open now!'

'Fuck me!' Doogie wheezed. He staggered back from the edge of the bottomless void, clutching his heart, his eyes wide and unblinking.

Catalina dissolved into fits of laughter. She sat down on the low perimeter wall, clapping her hands. 'See,' she giggled, 'I did tell you it is taking your wind away!'

'You little bugger!' Doogie gasped. His heart was thumping, his knees quaking. 'Listen! I could've had a bloody heart attack there, you daft wee –!'

'No, no!' Catalina interrupted. She was still giggling, but shaking a finger at him now as well. 'No more speaking the bad words. Already you say the F one – the one you tell me is

173

prohibido.'

'Well, I'm sorry about that,' Doogie said remorsefully, 'but I really got a fright there, you know.' He stepped over to where Catalina was sitting and looked gingerly over the wall. 'I mean, just look at that speedboat down there. It looks like a water flea! Jeez, if I'd toppled over when my eyes were closed...'

Catalina flung her arms round his hips and clung on. 'Do not worry. Your little Cati is to saving you.' She tightened her embrace. 'My arms are strong – like *un gorila*, no?'

Doogie rested his hand on her shoulder. 'Hmm, not strong enough to fly, though. Wow! We must be about half a mile high here!'

Neither moving then nor speaking, they gazed out for a while over the Mediterranean Sea, watching a pair of seagulls slowly circling on upcurrents of warm air far below, counting the craggy headlands tumbling down from the high peaks in ever-fading shades of blue, and cherishing more with every passing moment the feelings that were binding them now as tightly as Catalina's arms.

It was almost noon by the time they reached Valldemossa, a quaint old town of narrow, cobbled streets and steep, winding lanes. Its charming clutter of beige stone houses huddle together in higgledy-piggledy terraces like cardboard boxes emptied from a sack onto the mountainside around the old monastery of La Cartuja. Doogie could see at once why this was an ideal location for a convalescent home. There was indeed a cooler, fresher air up here, and a wonderful feeling of tranquillity, even if there was a definite festive atmosphere about the place today.

It was, Catalina explained, the Day of Santa Catalina Tomàs, Mallorca's very own saint, who was born in Valldemossa over four hundred years ago. Later on, there would be a grand procession through the streets in her honour, and people would come from all over the island to see it.

'Aha, so they didn't name the wine after you after all?'

Doogie ribbed.

Catalina lowered her eyes and murmured, 'No, for I am no saint, I think.'

Doogie chuckled softly, but said nothing.

They found old María sitting dozing beneath a small palm tree (and under a huge straw hat) in the garden of her rest home. It was a rambling old house in the classic Spanish style, perched on a hillside not far from La Cartuja, with an uninterrupted view all the way down the valley towards the flat hinterland of Palma. In bygone times, the house had been the elegant summer retreat of rich merchants from the city, but now only lonely old folk sat, or were wheeled about, where once the elite of Mallorcan society strolled and idly chatted.

It took María a moment or two to recognise them after being awakened by Catalina's gentle proddings. But then her face lit up. She squealed '*Madre mía!*' and a string of other exclamations of delight while blessing herself repeatedly, then struggled to her feet to grasp them both in unreserved, though noticeably wobbly, hugs of welcome. *Hombre*! it was so good to see them, she twittered, before plopping herself down into her seat again and fanning her cheeks. And didn't they look a picture standing there, the pretty little Mallorcan princess with her handsome Norwegian? '*Qué romántico!*' And what about Pedrito, the little rascal? Oh, how she missed him! And why wasn't he with them? And how was Angie? Had she returned to Barcelona – or was it Madrid? And when would she come to visit her again?

María spilled out those and a dozen other questions in her little mousey squeak before she took breath for long enough for Catalina to even begin to answer. Then the old woman got to her feet again and took an arm of both her young visitors for a totter round the garden, while she listened to all Catalina's news.

The hospital had forecast that María's stroke wouldn't leave her with any after-effects to speak of, and mercifully (for her at least!) it didn't appear to have diminished her capacity for non-stop chattering. But her illness *had* taken its toll for all that. There was a frailness about her that hadn't been evident before, and her mind, though still alert, was clearly beginning to play tricks with her memory.

She was just not her old self at all, she confided when they stopped to rest on an old bench in a quiet corner of the garden, Catalina on one side of her, Doogie on the other. Her energy was gone, and she felt this sort of numbness down one side of her body at times – usually when she was tired, which was all too often these days. Still, she mustn't complain. After all, she might never have come out of that coma! She touched the crucifix at her neck with trembling fingers and whispered a little incantation.

Catalina watched her intently all the while, her lips smiling, but her eyes sad.

Old María took their hands in hers and looked at their faces in turn, her age-weary eyes suddenly shining and happy, as if she was being lifted by the expectancy of life that this young couple radiated.

'Ah, Cati and Boogie,' she sighed, 'the sight of you both together makes this old woman very happy.' Then, turning to Catalina, she went on, 'And now, *pequeñita*, I have a surprise for you.' She removed her straw hat and from it produced an old, yellowed envelope. Smiling and muttering away to herself, she pulled out a dog-eared parchment, carefully unfolded it and handed it to Catalina.

Silently, Catalina began to read the faded, hand-written words.

'But I do not understand,' she said after a moment. Clearly confused, she shook her head and looked at old María's beaming face. 'This document is – is –'

'*El título*!' the old woman grinned. '*Sí*, it is the title deed to my *finca*, my little farm at Capdellá!' She winked at Catalina and nudged her arm. 'So, my little princess, what do you think of *that* for your saint's day gift?'

Catalina was lost for words. Her expression changed from disbelief to puzzlement and back again. She gave an uncertain little laugh, then made to hand the document back. 'Aha,

176

Señora María,' she said, 'you are making a little joke, I think.'

But María, grinning more widely than ever, pushed the document back.

Catalina looked in utter bewilderment at Doogie, but what she got in return was an even more bewildered look.

Chuckling gleefully, María again took their hands in hers and told them, 'Do not preoccupy yourselves with my sanity, *queridos*. I know what I am doing.' Then, inclining her head towards Doogie, she pointed out, apologetically, that the farm would be in Catalina's name – at first. But later, when the day finally came that they tied the knot, as she had always known they would, they could put it in both of their names – if that was the thing to do with a dowry these days. She herself was not familiar with the modern ways – legal hocus-pocus and tax avoidance and all that new-fangled rubbish. Anyway, she shrugged, the farm was for them both. *Sí*, and this she declared in the name of Santa Catalina herself!

Before Doogie and Catalina could begin to recover, María went on to tell them that her flat in Palma Nova would be theirs before long too – plus whatever savings she might still have left in *el banco* after the thieving *bandidos* who ran this granny farm had had their share! 'You see,' she said, her tone quite matter-of-fact, 'I know my days in this life are numbered.'

'No, no, Señora María,' Catalina implored, 'you must not think that way.'

There was a placid look in María's eyes. 'When you get to my age, *pequeñita*, you know when your time is near.' With a kindly smile, she reached out to wipe a tear from Catalina's cheek. 'And don't cry for me, my little Cati. No, be *happy* for me. I have made my peace with God, and soon it will be time for me to go and find my Bartolomé.' She chuckled wistfully. 'Perhaps he will have another little farm waiting for me in heaven, eh?' A look of doubt spread over her face. She fingered her crucifix, murmuring, '*If* San Pedro ever allowed him to pass through the Pearly Gates in the first place!'

Still finding it difficult to believe that such a gift was

actually being lavished on her, Catalina was unable to say anything but an awkward, '*Gracias*, Señora María, but I cannot...'

For his part, Doogie really didn't know what to say at all. What a predicament he was in now! This was going to make his decision-making even more complicated than it already was, and that was saying something. Besides, while old María's good intentions were beyond question and her motives generous to a fault, the harsh reality was that, all other considerations aside, her little *finca* was only a semi-neglected clutch of fields and a dilapidated old house, located in an idyllic setting, admittedly, but in no way a potentially viable farm in this day and age. After all, even María and her husband had had to make their real living from running a hardware store in Andratx.

Suddenly, Doogie felt very much a stranger, an intruder in other people's lives. He was no more than a transient foreigner who had become the subject of an old woman's well-meaning but overly-romantic notions. He knew that he was being cornered into an unrealistic situation from which there could be no escape. No escape, that is, without great offence and hurt being caused to honest people to whom he was becoming more attached by the day.

He shook María's hand, hoping that his look of gratitude would disguise his embarrassment. 'María,' he said, 'what can I say?'

'Nothing! We have already waited too long!' The old woman hauled herself to her feet. 'We have an appointment at the office of the *notario*,' she declared. 'There are deeds to transfer!'

CHAPTER FOURTEEN

'THE STUFF OF … DREAMS?'

IT WAS ALREADY DARK by the time they reached Palma that evening, Catalina having suggested that it would be better to return home via the city after they saw old María safely back to her room. It was one thing to drive the spectacular coastal road in daylight, but at night…? No, the main road from Valldemossa to Palma, after a twisty but relatively short descent to the plain, was virtually straight all the way, so that would be the route to take.

Doogie had been little more than a fly on the wall during the sombre and protracted procedures at the notary's office. As everything was conducted in *mallorquín*, he hadn't understood much of what was going on anyway – except that, when they'd finally emerged back into the mellow sunlight of late afternoon, Catalina *was* the new owner of María's little farm at Capdellá.

Afterwards, a radiant María had insisted on treating them to a celebratory Mallorcan feast of *ensaimada* pastries and hot chocolate beneath what she informed them, in pious tones, was a 'rosary tree'. The café's elevated terrace overlooked the junction of Valldemossa's two main streets, from where, she had declared, they'd also be afforded an uninterrupted view of

179

the imminent procession honouring Santa Catalina.

And sure enough, as dusk fell, a raucous bugle-and-drum band had led a colourful parade of decorated floats and teams of swirling folk dancers through the crowd-lined street below them. The wooden effigy of the Saint, sitting atop her *carro triunfal*, her 'palanquin of glory', was escorted by an entourage of young men dressed, incongruously, as demons, who, Catalina and María assured Doogie, represented an important aspect of Mallorcan folklore. However, these ostensibly Saint-guarding devils had seemed mainly intent on making women in the crowd scream by leaping at them and lifting their skirts with their three-pronged spears. María had had a good giggle at all those goings-on, and, while also mindful of paying due respect to the Saint, said it was a pity she wasn't fit enough to be down there on the front line herself any more!

It had been an unforgettable day for Doogie and Catalina: a day when things, both simple and momentous, had taken place. Things that would leave their emotions and, perhaps, their lives affected for ever. So, little had been said during their drive back from Valldemossa, each electing to leave the other to quietly ponder the possible consequences of it all.

Catalina, though naturally overjoyed by María's totally unexpected generosity, had been acutely aware of Doogie's deep sense of uneasiness when the old woman had announced that her legacy was to be for them *both*. Catalina realised that this may have induced a feeling of entrapment in him, a feeling that she feared might now start to gnaw at the ties which had already developed between them both.

Doogie was alive to that possibility, too, and he sensed that it was playing on Catalina's mind, so changed was her demeanour from that of the carefree girl who had rushed over the farmyard to greet him that morning. Old María's little farm on its own, as he had learned before, would really only be worth anything financially if it were to be sold on to a rich foreigner for upgrading into one of the rustic holiday or retirement homes that were becoming ever more sought-after on the island. But Doogie already recognised enough of Catalina's staunch country character to know that she would never contemplate doing that – not if she could help it anyway. And so, despite her own and her mother's protestations to the contrary, the spectre of Catalina and Rafael together materialised again in Doogie's mind. It made even more sense than before, after all. It wouldn't just be the potential amalgamation of Rafael's and Catalina's parents' farms, but also the automatic annexation now of old María's. Although on a relatively small scale, it had the makings of the start of one of those landed dynasties that Doogie had already talked about to Catalina that lunch-time at Churchill's Restaurant in Palma Nova. And so what if old María had insisted her farm was for them both? It was now in Catalina's name and in her name only. Fair enough too. María was a lovely old soul, and Doogie was sure she was every bit as fond of him as he was of her, but at the end of the day, Mallorcans would look after Mallorcans. This was only natural – no different from how it would be anywhere else under similar circumstances.

Without a word being exchanged on the subject, then, Doogie and Catalina had managed to get themselves into a really despondent state. Why, they wondered, could things not have remained as simple as they had been during those few magic moments of greeting in the Finca Sa Grua farmyard that morning?

'*Por favor*, Doogie,' Catalina said as they approached the waterfront at Palma, an unmistakable note of anxiety in her voice, 'is good to stop here. We must to speak, I think.'

She motioned him to turn into a car park by a little lake that lies beneath the floodlit grandeur of Palma Cathedral. Doogie hadn't been here since he'd passed by in Ingrid's tiny SEAT 600 car in the early hours of his first morning on the island. He was captivated by the atmosphere of the place all over again. It was almost ten o'clock, the time when people in Spain start to think about eating dinner, and the city was just coming alive.

The succession of restaurants and bars lining the far side of the Avinguda d'Antoni Maura, a wide avenue which runs at

181

right angles to the seafront, were already filling with a lively mix of locals, tourists and, occupying most of the pavement tables, groups of white-uniformed American sailors from an aircraft carrier anchored out in the bay. There'd be a hot time in the old town tonight!

But such thoughts of revelry could hardly have been farther from Doogie's and Catalina's minds. Opting, without need for discussion, to stay well away from the buzz, they began to stroll through the near-deserted Almudaina Palace gardens on their own side of the avenue. Hand-in-hand, they wandered along pathways flanked by orange and lemon trees, the scent of blossom hanging heavy in the warm night air. Soon, they reached a stone archway, where a pair of black swans were gliding on a softly-lit pond at the very base of the palace walls.

Doogie didn't know if Catalina had planned to bring him here, or, for that matter, if she'd even known of the existence of this spot before. But, whatever the case, he now found himself standing by her side in a location that would have touched the most unromantic of hearts. Instinctively, he put an arm round her shoulder, and she rested her head on his chest in her now-familiar way.

Despite Catalina's urgent plea to talk, not a word had been spoken since they'd left the car. Both were content just to be with one another in that magical setting, and were reluctant, it seemed, to say anything that might break the spell.

'That dream I was having today,' Catalina finally murmured, with a tremble in her voice that revealed her sense of misgiving, 'it will be true, Doogie, no? You have decided to leave me soon, I think.'

Doogie felt a lump rise in his throat. Those few, searching words from Catalina had stung him into facing up to the realities of life that had been closing in on him like a gathering storm for so long now. Yet how could he tell Catalina the dilemmas, the doubts that had been haunting his mind? How could he explain what he thought about María's gift of the farm, without making it sound as if he didn't believe the old woman or trust Catalina? He took Catalina by the shoulders and turned her to face him. Her head remained bowed, but he folded his arms around her, gently stroking her hair.

'You know I don't want to leave, Cati,' he said. 'It's just that – well, my parents, you know – they worked so hard to give me a better chance in life than they had, and...' He swallowed, trying to steady his voice. 'And, I mean, it wouldn't really be fair to them if I didn't...' His words trailed away.

Long moments of silence passed, Catalina patting Doogie's chest, he still stroking her hair.

Then Catalina hesitantly asked, 'They were happy... your mamá and papá, *si*?'

Doogie did his best to disguise an emotional little sniff by clearing his throat. 'Aye, they were that,' he said hoarsely. 'Very.'

Catalina raised her eyes to his. 'You are still missing them very much, I think.'

Doogie could only nod his head.

'As I will miss you, when you go back to university in Scotland.' Catalina returned her head to his chest.

'It'll be three years I'll be away,' Doogie said with a sigh. 'And that's what I mean, I suppose. You know, you having María's wee farm now and everything. Three years. Well, a lot can happen in –'

Catalina placed a fingertip on his lips. 'Why do you believe that everything good and happy will be taken away from you? I cannot replace your mamá and papá, I know, but I will wait for you, Doogie. Not for Rafael or anyone else. Only for you … if you want me to.'

'I – I do want you to,' he quickly replied, though unable to suppress a hint of uncertainty. 'Of course I do, but...'

'But?'

Doogie was struggling to find the right words. 'Oh, I don't know,' he said with more than a trace of self-reproach in his voice. 'I suppose, knowing I'd be going back to university sooner or later, I should never have risked hurting you by letting things get this serious.'

Catalina gave a rueful little laugh. 'For me, then, you should never have walked into the *oficina* of Merryweather on that first day.'

Doogie had to admit to himself that the feeling had been mutual. The inescapable influence of fate, perhaps. He thought for a moment, then said, 'But three years. I mean, it isn't fair to expect you to –'

'Would your mamá have waited three years for your papá when they were young?'

Catalina had touched the very heart of the matter. 'Yes,' Doogie replied wistfully, 'I dare say she would at that.'

Placing her head on his shoulder, Catalina drummed her fingers lightly on his back. She started humming quietly to herself.

Doogie smiled. 'You're thinking again,' he said. 'I'm beginning to recognise the signs.'

'Mmm, I am thinking about the little *finca* of Señora María.'

'Uh-huh?'

'*Sí*, and I am thinking that perhaps you are feeling trapped, because the Señora María has been giving the *finca* to us both.' She glanced up at Doogie with a look of honesty in her eyes. 'And if you are feeling this way, like the Margaret friend is making you feel trapped because of the job her father is giving you, I will ask Señora María to take the *finca* back.'

Doogie gave her a reassuring hug. 'Don't you dare,' he cautioned with a laugh.

Catalina arched herself back against Doogie's arms to get a better look at his face. 'What do you mean?' she asked, her expression expectant, though also confused.

'Ah, well, I'm saying no more for now, but there's more ways of skinning a cat than one, as we say in the veterinary profession.'

'Skinning a cat? I do not understand what you say,' Catalina giggled, 'but I think I like it.'

Doogie wrapped an arm round her shoulder. 'Come on,' he smiled, 'I think it's about time I took you home to Capdellá.'

'Perhaps, perhaps,' Catalina replied, then slipped a hand into the hip pocket of Doogie's jeans. 'But I also think perhaps it is good to stop at your *apartamento* on the way.' There was a mischievous glint in her eyes that had Doogie going all weak at the knees again. 'For a … coffee, *sí*?'

'Well, well, if it isn't Magic Roundabout himself. Yeah, and complete with his sexy little peasant wench an' all!'

Nick Martin was standing in a shadow at the entrance to the car park.

Doogie couldn't see him, but the sound of Nick's voice made his flesh creep. 'Crawl back under your stone, Tricky Nicky,' he muttered as he brushed past him. 'You'll dry up and blow away if you hang about out in the open too long – with any luck!'

Nick Martin grabbed his arm. 'Not so fast, squire!'

'Get your slimy mitt off me, Nick! I'm warning you!'

'Come, Doogie,' Catalina whispered nervously, 'is better to ignore.'

'Don't push it, Dougal matey,' Nick Martin growled. 'And don't *you* try to warn *me* about anything – ever!'

He half emerged from the shadows, just far enough for Doogie to see that he was carrying a handgun with a silencer, and it was pointing straight at Catalina.

'Yeah, you were too busy gazing into your little spic bint's eyes to see me sitting outside that bar along there when you wandered off into the gardens for your quick screw, weren't ya?' He let out a menacing laugh. 'Just the chance I've been waiting for, squire. Oh, yes, have *I* been looking forward to this!'

Doogie glanced quickly about them. The little lake and the promenades around it were bathed in a bright glow from the floodlights of the cathedral opposite, but there wasn't a solitary soul to be seen this side of the busy Avinguda, several hundred metres away.

'No point in looking for help, Magic Roundabout, for there ain't gonna be any. Not for you *or* little Señorita Ensenyat

185

here.'

Doogie could make out enough of Nick Martin in the gloom to see that he was looking Catalina slowly up and down.

'Well, well,' he drooled, 'not a bad piece a' crumpet when you're all tarted up, are ya, Catalina babe? Yeah, is this my lucky night or what?'

Catalina cringed and hugged Doogie's arm.

'OK, Nick,' Doogie said, his heart pounding, 'just leave her out of this. If you reckon you've got a beef with me, that's one thing, but just –'

'A *beef* with you?' Nick Martin butted in, his voice oozing contempt. 'You only get me dumped from the easiest little earner I ever had in my puff, you drop me in it with the police, and you think I've only got a *beef* with you!' He pushed Doogie in the face with the flat of his hand. 'You total twat! Yeah, and have *you* got a lesson coming, farmer's boy!'

'All I'm saying is leave Catalina out of it, OK?' Doogie was doing his best to sound calm, though realised he wasn't making a very convincing job of it.

'Your tiny Hee-brides brain can't grasp it, can it, Mister so-called bleedin' Educated? Yeah, well let me spell it out to ya. I'm gonna make you fuckin' suffer, and your little bit of native totty here's gonna help me do it, ain't ya, darlin'?' At that, Nick reached out and made to touch Catalina's face.

As she shied back, Doogie instinctively lunged over and shoved Nick Martin's hand away. He was rewarded with a thump to his head with the side of the gun.

'Now then,' Nick snarled, 'here's what we're gonna do, Romeo and Juliet.' He grabbed Catalina round the shoulder and pulled her to him. 'No, don't try to squirm away, darlin'! Just you cuddle in nice and cosy to me. Yeah, and don't forget I've got a shooter pointed right at your pretty little guts.' He glared at Doogie. 'And don't you forget that either, Magic Roundabout. The slightest bleedin' hero act from you, and she gets dropped first, then you.'

'Just let her go, will you! Hell, I'd have thought you were

in enough trouble already without trying something as –'

Nick lashed out at Doogie with his foot and caught him squarely on the shin. 'Shut it, James Herriot! I could put your lights out right here and now, only it would be too fuckin' good for ya!'

'Is OK, Doogie,' Catalina whimpered, terrified. 'I'm OK. Please do what he is saying.'

'That's more like it, darlin'.' Nick tightened his hold on her shoulder. 'Now, just you walk along beside me here. That's it, smooch in nice and cosy.' He turned to Doogie. 'And you, Magic, you get on my other side. Not too close! Nice and natural. That's it – three chums out for a nice, quiet stroll.'

Doogie's mind was in turmoil. There was always the possibility that Nick Martin was bluffing, that the gun wasn't loaded, or was even a fake. But he couldn't take that chance.

They were shepherded through the most shadowy parts of the promenade, then over the street by traffic lights at the bottom of the Avinguda, and onto a wide grass verge running alongside the busy seafront roadway of the Paseo Marítimo. All the while, Nick was making sure they kept as far away as possible from the crowded pavement tables of the nearby hostelries.

'OK,' he ultimately grunted, 'we take a right.' He tugged Catalina closer to him. 'That's it, babes – nice and natural. Getting busy here, so keep it nice and relaxed.'

They were crossing a little square now; huddles of laughing people leaving bars, entering restaurants; clutches of American seamen ambling about in various stages of drunkenness, some already fixed up with clinging hookers. The area was bustling, but dimly lit. Nick Martin knew what he was about. But, Doogie wondered, would he dare use that gun in front of so many potential witnesses? He was tempted to shout out to a group of sailors coming towards them, to bump into them, create some sort of fracas, try to snatch Catalina away in the confusion. No, too risky. If Nick did carry out his threat, he could be into the crowd and away before Catalina hit the ground.

Beyond the square, they walked on through a warren of narrow back streets, each one with less people about than the last. They entered a dingy alley, where the only sign of life was a clutch of cats hissing and spitting in the gutter over the abandoned remains of a pizza. In the eerie stillness, Doogie could hear that Catalina was crying, and the sound cut into him like a knife. Unable to hold back any longer, he stopped suddenly and gripped Nick Martin's arm.

'For Christ's sake let her go now, you lousy bastard! What kind of sick kick are you getting out of this anyway? Is terrifying helpless girls what turns you on, eh? Well, *is* it?

Nick swung his arm round and struck Doogie hard in the stomach with the full weight of his gun. The ferocity of the blow made Doogie double over, gasping for breath. Catalina squealed in pain as Nick then took hold of her hair. He jerked her head back and thrust the pistol under her chin.

'You'll find out soon enough what turns me on, arsehole!' he shouted at Doogie, his voice shaking with rage. 'And if you try another move like that, your little tart here's gonna have her brains decorating the wall, savvy?' He aimed a kick at Doogie's leg then gestured towards a doorway a few paces ahead. 'Get in there!' he yelled. 'You first, O'Mara, then you, darlin'!' He shoved them forwards. 'And just remember, I'm right at your backs!'

Just then, there was the sound of footsteps and laughter entering the alley behind them. Doogie turned his head to see the silhouette of a tall man stumbling along while being propped up by a mini-skirted woman in stiletto heels.

'Forget it, Magic Roundabout,' Nick Martin scoffed. 'You're in the red light district, and that pissed sailor's interested in only one thing. Yeah, and that ain't your bleedin' welfare.' He kicked Doogie again. 'Now, get in there!'

Doogie opened the door to a scruffy hallway. It reeked of rancid cooking oil and was lit by a naked electric bulb dangling above a staircase straight ahead.

'Up them steps!' Nick Martin ordered. He prodded Doogie in the back with his gun, then motioned Catalina to follow.

'Hmm, nice, *very* nice,' he muttered, climbing the stairs a couple of paces behind her. 'That's a *really* cute little ass ya got there, darlin' – now that I get a proper gander at it. Oo-oo, yeah, nice pair a' pins an' all, from this angle!' He gave a low growl. 'Boy, what have I been missing all this time!'

Doogie was seething. He knew that Nick's randy remarks about Catalina were intended to get at him. Intended in part, anyway, but not entirely. That was being made blatantly obvious.

'Stand aside on the landing, the both of ya! Over there – faces to the wall!'

They heard Nick fumbling with a door key.

'OK, in here! Stand in the middle of the floor and don't move a muscle 'til I say so!'

They found themselves in a squalid room with a bare floor and flaking, whitewashed walls stained with dampness. A strip light glared from the ceiling onto a grubby double bed, two wooden chairs and a threadbare couch. The air was blue with smoke. Two men, Colombian sailors, according to Nick Martin, were sitting on the couch, bleary-eyed and sweating, a near-empty bottle of brandy on the floor in front of them, a half-smoked joint being passed from one to the other.

Nick closed and locked the door. He pushed Doogie down onto one of the chairs, then pulled Catalina over and stood her in front of the two men. He spoke to them in Spanish:

'*Bueno, muchachos,* I told you I would bring you a nice, tasty *chica*. So, how about this one?' He shoved Catalina even closer to the couch. 'All dressed in white like a little virgin, eh!' He rubbed forefinger and thumb together. 'Worth *mucho dinero* this one, no?'

The men, half out of their minds with booze and dope, eyed Catalina with undisguised lust. She recoiled as one of the men stretched out and tried to grope her leg.

'Hey, patience, *hombre*!' Nick Martin called out. He tugged Catalina back out of reach. 'We still have terms to discuss, *si*?' Then, turning to Doogie, he said with feigned courtesy, 'I hope you'll excuse my South American associates, squire. You see, they've been at sea for a couple of months, and they're a bit impatient to, well, get stuck in – for want of a better expression.'

Doogie was shaking with rage. 'You're not fit to breathe the same air as decent people, Nick. In heaven's name, let her go while you still can. Just remember, the police have been watching your every move since all those Ecstasy shenanigans after the Danish girl died.'

'*Police*?' Nick Martin threw his head back. 'That's your trouble, Magic Roundabout,' he guffawed, '– you live in wonderland. Get real, huh? No shit, I've got more mates in the Palma police than you've had hot haggises! Police watching *me*?' A smirk crawled over his face. 'Don't make me bleedin' laugh!'

Doogie returned his smirk. 'You're pathetic, Nick!' He took a glance round the room. 'I mean, look at this place. Yeah, and look at you. Pathetic! You couldn't cut it pushing drugs to kids, so now you're acting the pimp for the arse-end of animal life, like that pair of maggots over there.'

Nick Martin laughed again. 'Very good, squire. Trying to make me lose concentration by chucking insults about, huh? Oh, yeah, *very* bleedin' ingenious. Now shut it! Save your breath – what little you've got left!'

He turned to the two men and pushed Catalina closer to them again. 'OK, *muchachos*, here's the deal. The little virgin here – you get her for twenty minutes. Free, *comprende*?'

The two men swapped looks of approval, then hauled themselves clumsily to their feet, leering at Catalina.

'Whoa! *Un momento, un momento*!' Nick Martin cautioned with a shake of his head. 'Do you think I'm *loco*? No way are you being handed a cute little doll like this for a whole twenty minutes without there being *some*thing in it for me.'

The men glanced at each other again, raised their shoulders and grunted their agreement.

Dragging Catalina with him, Nick went over to a cupboard and took out a length of rope. He threw it to one of the men and ordered him to tie Doogie to the chair. 'Good and tight!'

190

He shoved Catalina back to where the other man was standing by the couch and told him to make sure she didn't budge from the spot. He then returned to rummage in the cupboard.

Desperate now, Doogie pushed the fumbling South American aside and attempted to lunge at Nick while his back was turned. But Nick was too quick for him. He wheeled round, aimed his gun and fired off a round which thudded into the floor just an inch from Doogie's feet. Catalina screamed.

'That's just to let you know,' Nick Martin rasped, 'that this ain't a fuckin' toy! Next time, you get it where it hurts!' With that, he pistol-whipped Doogie about the head until he fell to the floor.

The sound of Catalina's pleading faded from Doogie's ears as he slipped into unconsciousness. He had no idea how long he was out, but when he did eventually come round, he was back in the chair, trussed up with his hands behind his back, the blurred figure of Nick Martin slapping his face and shaking him by the shirt front.

'Wakey, wakey, Dougal! Get with it! The show's just about to start here!'

The pain in Doogie's head was excruciating. A foul-tasting wad of cloth had been stuffed into his mouth. Somewhere behind him, he could hear Catalina begging one of the mumbling South Americans to get away from her.

Grinning into Doogie's face, Nick Martin shouted at the man to cool it. He promised him he'd soon get his fun. All he had to do is keep the *chica* out of the way until the squire here was properly seen to.

As Doogie's vision cleared, he could see that Nick was holding a hypodermic syringe. It was filled with a cloudy liquid. The second South American was slouched by his side, a piece of string in his hand, a vacant, stoned expression on his face. The thought of this ugly slug and his crony getting their hands on Catalina made Doogie's stomach turn. He tried to shout through the choking gag, shaking his head in a frantic effort to dislodge it, struggling to free himself from the ropes binding his arms and legs.

'Wriggle away, Florence,' Nick Martin laughed. 'It'll make no difference. You're fucked, good and proper.' He gave Doogie one final slap on the face. A hard one. 'Now, if you're properly back from dreamland, this is the plan. In this here hypo we have smack – super-pure heroin – enough of the stuff to snuff anybody out. Yeah, but being a careful kinda bloke, I've added a little something else that'll make sure you don't come back from your *next* trip to dreamland.' Nick taunted Doogie with a smile. 'It's atropine, OK? A poisonous substance I'm sure you've come across in your anaesthetic lessons at vet school, yes? Putting dogs to sleep and suchlike, no?' He savoured the reaction in Doogie's eyes for a moment, then went on, 'And before you fade into oblivion, me and you are gonna sit right here and watch my two *amigos* performing whatever tricks they fancy on that there bed with your little lady friend. Now *that*,' he winked, 'is what I call a turn-on, O'Mara. How about you, hmm?'

Doogie tried to speak again, throwing his head from side to side in a desperate attempt to get the gag out of his mouth. He heard Catalina start to whimper somewhere behind him. He craned his neck round.

'Patience, my son,' Nick said casually, then seized Doogie's hair and yanked his head to the front. 'You'll get a good look at her in a minute or two, once the *muchachos* have got her unwrapped.'

Doogie was frantic to help Catalina somehow, yet totally powerless. It was the stuff of nightmares. Then he caught sight of Nick's gun, lying now on a chair by the door. If only Catalina could get to it, he thought, perhaps she could escape before…

Nick Martin could see what was going through Doogie's mind. He was wallowing in the warped pleasure it gave him, and he was about to make Doogie suffer even more.

'Yeah, Mister smart-mouth O'Mara, I've been thinking up some nice plans for the lovely Catalina since she fluttered into my little web tonight. Not that you'll be bothered, mind, 'cause come tomorrow morning you'll be just a statistic, only another piece of foreign shit lying in the gutter, dead from an overdose of dodgy heroin.' He smiled smugly. 'But I'll tell you anyway. I'm that kinda guy. Oh yes, and you're gonna like *this* idea, squire. It's got style.' He leaned towards Doogie, paused to nod in Catalina's direction, then confided, 'She ain't gonna leave here tonight, see. No, and tomorrow, her old man's gonna get a nice little ransom note.' He raised his hands and added cockily, 'OK, OK, OK, I know he's only a poor fuckin' peasant. But he owns a *finca*, and these days that means dosh. Yeah, some fat-cat Brit'll lob him the best part of a million for the gaff alone, and all those beautiful smackers, matey, will be mine, all mine.'

He told the Colombian to loop the length of string round Doogie's neck, then continued:

'And what do I do with the lovely Catalina while her old man's raising the gelt, I hear you ask? Well, I keep her working for me here, don't I? Oh yeah, there's always plenty horny seafarers sniffin' about this bit of Palma, and they'll pay ol' Nicky boy nicely for a short time with a classy little poke like her. Yeah, and the fact that she's not exactly willing makes 'em enjoy it even more.' He laughed in Doogie's face. 'Perverted bastards, huh?'

Nick instructed the sailor to tighten the string round Doogie's neck until a vein stood out, then nonchalantly said, 'Oh, and another thing, O'Mara, if you're thinking there's no way I'd ever turn your little bint over to her old man after she's seen and heard all this, you're absolutely correct.' He narrowed his eyes. 'When I'm good and ready, she'll end up with a neckful a' this stuff just like you. Yeah, and don't go breakin' your heart, eh? Gettin' screwed useless for a while and then dumped – it's bred into them half-Moorish slags.' He grabbed Doogie's hair and forced his head sideways onto his shoulder. 'Now, get ready for the trip of a lifetime, Magic Roundabout. Yes,' he grinned, 'time for bed, said Zebedee!'

Out of the corner of his eye, Doogie watched the syringe closing in 0n his neck. He felt the tip of the needle touching his skin.

Then, suddenly, the sound of Catalina's whimpering stopped. Doogie heard her let out a shriek, heard her minder howl in agony, heard her running across the room. She appeared in his line of vision, clawing at Nick Martin's face, beating him with her fists, screaming at him to leave Doogie alone, shouting at him that he could have her *finca* too, if he'd only stop all this and let them go.

Cursing, Nick Martin let fly with his free arm. He struck her in the face with the back of his hand, sending her reeling backwards onto the bed, blood trickling from her mouth. Catalina lay there, moaning to herself, stunned and helpless, as her erstwhile Colombian 'guard' came towards her, crouched in pain, clutching his crotch with one hand, his other raised in a clenched fist.

Doogie closed his eyes, unable to watch. Then came a timid knock at the door. It stopped the dope-befuddled Colombian in his tracks and caused his startled mate to let go of the ligature round Doogie's neck. Nick Martin glared at his two clients and raised a finger to his lips. He then calmly tiptoed over to the chair by the door and swapped the still-full hypodermic syringe for his handgun.

Doogie grabbed the chance to make as much noise as he could through his gag, while thumping his feet and the legs of his chair on the floor. His face twisted with rage, Nick spun round and aimed the gun two-handed at Doogie's head.

Doogie closed his eyes again.

When the bang came, however, it wasn't caused by a bullet, but by the door being kicked inwards off its hinges. It hit Nick square on the back, knocking him face-down, flat out and winded, his gun skittering over the floor.

Doogie opened his eyes just in time to trap the pistol under his feet.

A tall, ebony-skinned man in a contrasting white suit strode forward from the splintered doorway and plucked the gag from Doogie's mouth.

'Ingrid!' Doogie spluttered. 'What the hell are you doing here?'

'Just clearin' a path for me assault troop, sunshine,' Ingrid beamed. He gestured towards the doorway, where a diminutive blonde, wearing an ocelot mini dress and outrageously high heels, had taken up station, shapely legs apart, delicate arms akimbo. 'We been followin' you since back at the Paseo Marítimo, man. Sittin' there, we was, havin' us a coupla cocktails and checkin' out them American sailors for the *signs*, you know, when I sees Catalina and you, all walkin' along kinda palsy-walsy with Tricky Nicky.' Ingrid released his trademark Othello chuckle and started to undo Doogie's ropes. 'Seein' you three all chummy like that back there, I says to meself, "Somethin' ain't right, Björn baby. Better check it out!"'

In a confused flap, first one Colombian seaman then the other made a lurching break for freedom, only to be decked in the doorway by a flurry of flying kicks and karate chops from Ingrid's solo 'troop', who saved the best for last by booting Nick Martin's face in a perfectly-timed drop kick when he attempted to lift his head off the floor.

Doogie peered in near-disbelief at this deceptively dainty fighting machine as she exited the room, coolly dusting off her hands, tugging down the hem of her mini, swinging her hips seductively. 'Wait a minute,' he whispered to Ingrid, 'that's – that's –'

'Me live-in lover Fidel? Yeah, that's right,' Ingrid grinned. 'Face it, sunshine, you gotta be able to handle yourself when you go out at night dressed like *that* with all them sex-starved Yankee sailors about!' His laughter reverberated round the room's bare walls.

Doogie was dumbfounded. 'But I didn't think Fidel even liked me...'

'He don't,' Ingrid confided, while undoing the last knot at Doogie's ankles. 'But he was listenin' at the door there with me for the last fifteen minutes, you know, and he likes violence even less!'

Taking one look at the three felled bodies sprawled unconscious about the floor, Doogie arched an eyebrow and muttered, 'Aye, well, you could've fooled me!'

Ingrid nodded towards the bed, where Catalina was sitting in a daze, nursing her bruised mouth. 'Better see to your little lady there, Doog.' He nudged the comatose Nick Martin with his foot. 'I'm gonna phone the Guardia Civil – tell 'em come sweep this loada stinkin' garbage away once and for all.'

CHAPTER FIFTEEN

'ALL DOWNHILL FROM NOW ON'

FOR QUITE SOME TIME, it had been the industry's worst-kept secret that Sam Merryweather had been stalking his main competitor, *3-S Vacations*, with a view to a takeover. It was finally made public at the beginning of August that an offer from Merryweather Holidays had been accepted by the *3-S* board, and, further, that the amalgamation of the two firms had been given the nod of approval by the UK Government's Monopolies and Mergers Commission. However, the big question on the minds of everyone in Merryweather's Palma office on the day the news broke was not how this piece of big-business game-playing was going to benefit the customers, the shareholders or even the already-bulging coffers of their venerated employer himself, but simply whether or not any of their own jobs would be at risk. They didn't have long to wait for an answer.

Within an hour of the arrival of the fax heralding the successful takeover, another arrived from Merryweather HQ instructing Manolo to advise his team that, due to the unavoidable need to rationalise staffing requirements following the unification of the two organisations, it was regretted that the services of certain employees would have to be dispensed with at the end of the present calendar month – which, some cynics noted, just happened to be the end of the summer boom period as well. In fairness to all concerned, the fax went on, it had been decided, after much deliberation, that the shedding of staff would be on a last-in, first-out basis, and that the following personnel would have their contracts of employment terminated on August 31, or by mutual agreement as soon as was practicable thereafter.

Neither Doogie nor Catalina were surprised, therefore, to read their names fairly near the top of the list of those destined for old Sam's 'much-deliberated' bum's rush.

For Doogie, this bolt from the Merryweather blue served to put paid to any niggling doubts he still may have been harbouring about going back to Scotland to resume his studies at the start of the September term. Now there really was no choice. Even if he had wanted to, the chances of picking up another tourist-related job in Mallorca at the beginning of the autumn would be virtually nil.

As if decreed by fate (although more likely due to some forceful, long-distance lobbying by his daughter Margaret), a letter from old Hyslop, the Arran vet, had arrived for Doogie on the very morning of the 3-S takeover announcement. In it, just as Margaret had communicated in person, her father implored Doogie to have second thoughts about interrupting his studies. Such a hiatus in what was generally regarded as an onerous university course could prove difficult for him in the short term, and disastrous in the broader scheme of things. Old Hyslop had then stressed that Doogie should not forget the wonderful opportunities that waited on Arran for him – and

Margaret – once their student days were over. He closed by saying that he had already made a special point of meeting his old friend, the principal of the Royal Veterinary College in Edinburgh, to explain the 'emotional background' to Doogie's somewhat hasty decision to take a year out, and had come away with an absolute guarantee that Doogie's third-year place would be available for him to take up next month, 'as if nothing had happened'.

'As if nothing had happened,' Doogie repeated to himself. 'As if nothing had bloody *happened*? Jeez, if only they knew!' Doogie reckoned he'd probably seen more of life as it really is and had more things *happen* to him while working those past few weeks for Merryweather in Mallorca than he – or old Hyslop for that matter – could expect to experience in a whole lifetime of vetting on Arran!

And what was all this 'emotional background' stuff about? As much as Doogie liked old Hyslop, and as much as he would always feel indebted to him for providing the opportunity to learn from him over the years, and for guiding him towards a career as a vet, there was just no way the old boy could even begin to understand what had prompted Doogie to make the decision to divert from his seemingly pre-ordained route for a while. Coming from a relatively well-off family background, how could Hyslop ever know what it was like to see your own parents struggling incessantly to make ends meet, only to die without achieving anything for themselves, worn out and old before their time? Without achieving anything, except providing their children with the gateway to a life that they themselves had been denied, that is. Yes, all the Hyslops' easily-affordable extravagances lavished on Margaret would never compare in *real* value with the simple family pleasures and selflessly-won opportunities that Doogie's own parents had provided for his sister and him. And when it came right down to it, he knew in his heart of hearts which of the two fate-dealt hands scored higher for him.

If only the realities of life were different, though – less black and white, more compromising. If only. But they weren't. Everyone, no matter how idealistic, had to face up to that sooner or later. And so, Doogie conceded, it would be back to Scotland for him in a month from now. Back to the cheerless basement bedsit and the skint, rainy Sundays revising endless notes. And to a life without Catalina for three long years...

Catalina, Catalina. What would become of her now? Doogie had always suspected that her Merryweather job would prove to be no more than it had turned out to be. And, in many ways, he was glad it was coming to an end. He'd meant it when he'd told her mother that Catalina was too good for that way of life. Fine sentiments, no doubt, but sentiments come cheap. Where *would* she go from here? The same harsh realities of employment in tourism applied as much to Mallorcans as they did to foreigners, after all. Come the end of summer, the openings of last spring would be closing fast. Such was the way of things.

But the ill wind that cast such shades of impending sadness to Doogie and Catalina did blow away those same dark clouds from Angie's life. Because of the new company's rapidly adopted policy of staff 'streamlining', her position in Ibiza would now be assumed by her opposite number in *3-S Vacations*, while she would resume her old duties in Mallorca. It was a demotion in terms of wages, certainly, but one which Angie was delighted to accept – though not admitting as much to her employers.

'You know what the wags in the trade say the *3-S* in *3-S Vacations* means, do you?' she asked Doogie while walking to the car park after he'd met her off the Ibiza flight at Palma airport.

Doogie raised his shoulders. 'Sun, Sand and Sex, maybe?'

'Close. But no, it's "Stupid Suckers, Screw-'em-all" – referring to the unfortunate sods who work for them, of course. Telling you, kid, no wonder old Sam's been after that outfit for so long. He'll be able to cop that line for his company motto now!'

Doogie gave her a wry smile. 'Yeah, he's a hard

taskmaster, right enough, and damned ruthless when he fancies – as some of us have recently discovered to our cost.'

Angie slapped her wrist. 'Oh, trust bloody me! I was forgetting – you're gonna get your jotters at the end of the month, and here's me bellyaching about the new conditions of employment.' She laid a hand on his arm. 'Sorry, Doog. I mean, what a pain in arse. Yeah, and just when you were getting into the swing of things too.'

'Nah, no probs. It's probably all for the best. To be honest, I, ehm – I was having serious thoughts about going back to uni next month anyway.'

Angie threw him a sceptical look. 'The Margaret bird give you a hard time when she was here, did she? Put the old pressure on, did she, huh?'

Doogie opened the boot of Angie's little Renault and heaved her suitcase in. 'They don't get much past you, do they, Ange? Yeah,' he sighed, 'Margaret turning up didn't help any, I'll admit. Anyway, what the hell? It's all water under the bridge now, thanks to Mr Merryweather and his corporate capers.' He held up the car keys. 'You driving or me?'

Angie was already halfway in through the passenger's door. 'Daft bloody question. I've already downed three large, celebratory Vera Lynns since I said bye-bye to Ibiza this morning. Yeah, and that's on top of a right gutful at my farewell do last night.' She fanned her face with her hand. 'Phew! What a party!'

'Your mates were glad to see the back of you, then?' Doogie teased.

Angie gave him a playful punch on the arm. 'Less of the smart-arsed wisecracks, kiddo. Just drive.'

'Straight to Capdellá to see Pedrito, I take it?'

'Quick as you like. Poor little git that he is.' Angie's brows knotted. 'Boy, have I got some making up to do in the mothering stakes from now on!'

Doogie hesitated a moment, then said, 'I don't want to put a wet blanket on things. I mean, I know you're over the moon

201

about being back here and all that. But the thing is – what I'm trying to say is, who's gonna look after Pedrito when you're working now? You know, old María's health being the way it is. And Catalina's mother – well, maybe the strain's beginning to…' Doogie pulled himself up, thinking he'd probably gone too far. 'OK, sorry,' he shrugged. 'None of my business, but I just kinda wondered…'

Angie was quick to reply. 'No, no, you're absolutely right, love. I can't expect Señora Ensenyat to be lumbered any longer. Credit where it's due, she's been a diamond already. No, and anyway, like I say, I've got to shape up mother-wise, and pronto at that.' She forced a laugh. 'Bugger me, I *am* the little tyke's old lady after all!'

Doogie hesitated again, then repeated the awkward question: 'So, back to where we came in … who's gonna look after Pedrito when you're working?'

Angie tapped the side of her nose and gave Doogie a sly wink. 'Your old Auntie Angie's got plans, never you fear, kid.' She had a quiet chuckle to herself, before swiftly changing the subject: 'Anyhow, never mind me and my domestic problems – what the hell are *you* gonna do? That's what *I* want to know, mate!'

'How do you mean?' Doogie replied, deadpan.

Laughing, Angie gave his arm a thump with the back of her hand. 'Don't give me all that innocent, how-do-you-mean stuff! Come on, you know what I'm on about. Catalina and you, that's what!' She punched his arm again. 'Come on then, come clean! What's happening? Yeah, and don't tell me you're just gonna take off back to Scotland and say "Cheers, nice knowing you," as if it was just some little holiday fling the pair of you have been having.' Angie shook her head. 'I mean, don't give me all that crap, kid. It's your Auntie Angie you're talking to here!'

'I've got three years to do at uni, and that's it,' Doogie said with as much resignation as he could affect.

Angie gave him an old-fashioned look.

'OK, I'm not kidding myself it's going to be easy,' Doogie

conceded, 'but what can I do? It's not as if she can come with me. The student loan's not even enough to keep *one* person going, never mind two.'

'She could get a job,' Angie ventured.

'Nah, that would never do. I mean, what kind of life would that be?'

'You'd be together.'

'Aye, me at classes all day, studying at night, Cati stuck in some crap job in a bar or something, and both of us huddled into one tiny basement room in un-sunny old Edinburgh. No, no,' Doogie insisted, 'she belongs here in Mallorca, and I'd never ask her to sacrifice what she has here for what I've got to put up with before I qualify. It wouldn't be fair – on either of us.'

Angie still wasn't buying any of this. 'So, you're telling me you'll just see her once a year, like. Back here on your summer holidays. Is that what you're trying to tell me?'

'Who's to say I'll be able to afford to come back even once a year? Think about it – student loan – worse than broke – the system's got you in debt as well. Bloody purgatory, Ange.' Doogie was talking himself into a fine old state of doom.

'Mills & Boon,' said Angie.

Doogie noticed she was struggling to suppress a smirk. 'What are you on about – Mills & Boon?'

Angie started to snigger. 'Well, that or Barbara Cartland. Take your pick. You know, the usual corny sort of stuff – handsome young student falls madly in love with dusky native girl, but cruel fate and his conniving ex's rich old man force them apart, di-da-di-da-di-da. Still, at least you haven't got the evil villain to worry about. Not with Tricky Nicky in the slammer now.'

'As long as you can see something funny in it, go ahead and laugh it up,' Doogie muttered.

Still smirking, Angie smacked herself on the wrist again. 'Sorry, love. Must be the gin.'

'And she's *not* my ex,' Doogie pointed out.

'Oo-oo-oo-oo!' Angie goaded. 'Margaret still in the frame,

is she?'

Doogie wasn't in the mood for being ribbed, though. 'Give it a rest, Ange,' he frowned. 'You know the score.'

A look of remorse came over Angie's face. 'OK, I didn't mean to be hardhearted, honest. No, it's just that I don't see Catalina and you surviving for three years – you in Scotland, her here. That's all I'm saying. I mean, in this business, I've seen enough long-distance relationships and been through enough of them myself to know what I'm talking about, believe me, kid.'

Doogie was slightly taken aback and feeling more than a little embarrassed. 'Fair enough, Mills & Boon it may be, and you probably think I'm a bit daft saying this, but Catalina says she'll wait and everything, so…'

Angie patted his knee. 'No, no, you've got me all wrong, love. I'm not saying she isn't serious about that. It's a cert she is. Hey, I'm not *that* blind. No, what I'm saying is, her and you being away from each other for three years…' She shook her head. 'Well, I'll believe it when it happens.'

Doogie's expression became even more doom-laden. 'I don't see an alternative, Ange.' He thought for a moment. 'Not unless I flunk my exams, that is.'

'Oh, har-de-har-bloody-har,' Angie scoffed. 'A fat chance of that happening, I'm sure! Hell, with all the years you've been working weekends at the vet job, plus the time you've already put in at college, you probably know enough to pass your bleedin' finals right now!'

'Not quite as simple as that, I'm afraid.' Doogie stroked his chin, thinking again 'Although…'

'Yeah?' Angie pressed, all ears.

Doogie rolled his shoulders. 'Aw, nothing really. Just a daft notion I've got about that little *finca* of old María's.'

'Go on, then! Spill the beans!'

Doogie felt awkward, half wishing he hadn't brought the subject up. 'Nah, it's just pie in the sky. Just sort of – well, with me knowing about animals, and now that I've seen a wee bit about what the tourist caper's all about…'

Angie breathed an exasperated sigh. 'I don't follow you, kid, but as they say in the song, "If you don't have a dream, how you gonna make a dream come true?" So, go for it, whatever the blazes you're thinking about.'

'Well, we'll see,' Doogie replied. 'As that old movie guy Goldwyn said, there's a lot of water to be passed before that – or something along these lines.' Now it was Doogie who decided to make a swift change of subject. 'Anyway, Angie, first things first. For the few weeks I've got left here, what am I going to do about a place to lay my weary head at nights?'

'Don't be a daft Scotch lummox all your life! Did you think your Auntie Ange would kick you out on your cute little bum?' She tickled his chin. 'Cease your worries, child. You're OK in my pad 'til you collect your jotters and shoot the crow at the end of the month. So relax!'

Doogie cocked his head inquisitively. 'So, ehm, you and Pedrito – you'll be kipping in old María's flat again, is that the form?'

Angie stared straight ahead and smiled an inscrutable smile.

Doogie was confused. 'OK, but in any case, we still come back to the old problem – who's going to look after Pedrito when you're at work? It could be months before old María... And even then... And, as I say, Catalina's mother...'

'Why *do* you get your tartan knickers into such a twist at times?' Angie laughed. 'Blood pressure, boy! Being into the mysteries of medicine, you should know better than to worry about things that are never gonna happen.'

'You've lost me. What do you mean, things that are never gonna happen?'

Angie turned on the full, fake-coy act, wringing her hands, bashfully batting her eyelashes. 'Why, Doogie,' she simpered, 'haven't you noticed the overpowering fascination men have for me?'

'Well ... no!' said Doogie, deciding to play along.

'You bastard, O'Mara!' Angie hissed, then reverted to type, fluttering her eyelashes again. 'Certain men, that is,' she lisped. 'The, er, rustic type.'

'Well, I'm the rustic type, and you do bugger all for me.'

'Why do the words *fuck* and *off* loom before my eyes, Douglas?' she articulated with overstated politeness.

'Hey, that doesn't sound like Mills & Boon or Barbara Cartland lingo to me!'

'Yeah, but that's because we're talking about *my* love life now, kid, and I'm more into the Jackie Collins stuff. Now, back to business... The overpowering fascination *some* rustic men have for me, remember?'

Doogie looked at her blankly.

Angie tutted. 'OK, the overpowering fascination *one* rustic man has for me. Am I getting through to your heather-clogged brain *now*?'

Doogie did a double take at her face to check she wasn't kidding, but he still wasn't sure. 'Are you pulling my plonker?'

'As if I would!' Angie countered with a holier-than-thou toss of her head.

Doogie started to laugh. 'Not – not – Rafael?' He glanced at Angie for a clue one way or the other, but all she offered him was an aloof pout. '*You* and Rafael?' he checked. 'You're saying *you* and Rafael?'

'And what's so bloody funny about that, may I ask?'

'No, no, not funny at all,' Doogie promptly recanted, suddenly sensing that Angie might actually be serious. 'It's just that – what a surprise – I mean, who'd have guessed?'

'And you thought he only had eyes for Catalina, didn't you?' Angie smirked.

'I did,' Doogie readily admitted, then smiled approvingly as the jigsaw pieces began to fall into place. 'But Catalina didn't, did she?'

'Say again.'

'That night at her folks' place, when we were having the meal under the *porche*, remember? Yeah,' he nodded, 'Cati reckoned Rafa had the hots for you even then.' He shook his head. 'But, honestly, I wouldn't have believed in a month of

Sundays that –' He closed his mouth, realising he was about to put a foot right in it.

'Yes, I think you've made your point, young O'Mara,' Angie said dryly, then indulged herself in a self-congratulatory smile. 'But what you fail to appreciate, being an icicle man yourself, is the devastating effect the cool, classic, blonde, Nordic beauty has on the hot-blooded Latin male.' She pulled down her windscreen visor and checked the top of her head in the vanity mirror. 'Which reminds me, my bleedin' roots need doing again!'

Doogie was still having trouble getting to grips with this Angie-Rafael tie-up. 'So, how? You know, when–?' he fumbled. 'You being in Ibiza and him here and all that…'

Catalina had got it spot on, Angie then revealed. The magic between herself and Rafael had been there that night on the Finca Sa Grua terrace, sure enough – except she'd got herself too pissed on old Ensenyat's wine to realise it. But she'd met Rafael on a couple of other occasions on that same leave from Ibiza, when she'd been back at the Ensenyats' place fixing things up for Pedrito to stay with them and so on. One thing had led to another, the way it does. After that, Rafael had started phoning her in Ibiza – every day – and somehow, the way they do, things had got to the stage now when – well, if Doogie would pardon the pun, the scent of orange blossom was in the Mallorcan air, so to speak.

Doogie was stunned, but absolutely thrilled for her as well. 'You – you mean…' he stammered, grinning stupidly, 'you and Rafael – you're gonna get *spliced*?'

The sparkle of sheer joy in Angie's eyes spoke volumes, but she added a few words of her own. 'You bet your hairy sporran, Braveheart! And if that Rafa hasn't got down on one knee within two minutes of the big reunion today, I'll pop the question to the backward bugger myself!'

So, Angie was going to be a farmer's wife. Angie of all people! Doogie chuckled at the very thought. He could hardly believe it. Taking one hand from the wheel, he grabbed her round the neck and planted a kiss on her cheek.

'Let me be the first to congratulate you, Ange,' he beamed. 'Honest, I'm chuffed to bits for you, I really am.'

Yeah, and it would be really great for Pedrito too, Angie sniffled, tears rising in her eyes – seeing as how he'd taken so readily to Rafael, and vice versa, like. And being brought up in the country, on a farm, with all the animals and stuff – it would be the making of him, the little townie sod that he was. And as for herself? Well, she'd soon get into the way of things, she supposed. Not that she knew a bloody iota about farming, like. But, hell, like she'd told Doogie before, she'd learned plenty about wildlife and animals in all the years she'd spent working for Merryweather Holidays – especially during the annual Glasgow Fair holiday fortnight. 'Be fair, kid,' she concluded, 'dealing with domesticated livestock is gonna be a breeze in comparison!'

'So that's it,' Doogie smiled, 'your days as a holiday rep are over, eh?'

'I'll see the month out, stick with it 'til the end of the busy season – if Catalina's mother can cope with Pedrito for a bit longer, that is. That said, I don't owe Sam Merryweather any favours. But Manolo and all the troops – well, I wouldn't want to do the dirty on them.'

Doogie winked at her. 'You're an angel, Ange. I've said it before.'

'Hmm, maybe,' Angie mumbled, her smile fading. 'But a fallen one, all too often. Yeah, and have I got the bruises to prove it!'

'Hey,' Doogie chided, 'don't go knocking yourself. Rafael doesn't know how lucky he is.' He glanced at Angie's face, and noticed little creases of doubt etched on her brow.

'Thanks, love,' she said, 'but every time something good happened for me in the past, the arse always fell out of it – especially with the men in my life.' She lowered her voice, as if talking to herself. 'I can't believe I've got this lucky, that's all. Too bloody good to be true.'

Doogie reached over and squeezed her hand. 'Do you remember what you told me that night I arrived off the

Manchester gannet and I was feeling a bit lost and wondering if I was doing the right thing?'

Angie smiled wistfully. 'Yeah, all downhill from now on, wasn't it?'

'That's right. And that's how it'll be for you and Rafa and Pedrito. Just think about it – the three of you – and maybe half a dozen bambinos – freewheeling your donkey cart into the sunset.'

Angie was staring forlornly out of the window. 'Hmm, minus the half-dozen sprogs, it's a nice dream. I'll give you that.'

'Well then, do what the song says and make the dream come true. That's what you told me to do. So, come on, cheer up, Auntie Angie. There's a whole new life waiting for you!'

Doogie could see that Angie was struggling to overcome her nagging lack of self-confidence, to shut out her mistrust of the future.

'Yeah, you're right, Doog,' she finally chirped, putting on an air of optimism. 'Take it by the scruff of the neck and give it a good bash. It'll all work out hunky-dory – 'course it will. And listen, another thing!' She thumped Doogie's arm again. 'I'll be your next-door neighbour, give or take half a mile or so.' She paused, then added searchingly, 'When you come back to old María's *finca* in three years time, that is.'

'Aye,' Doogie said after a moment, his eyes fixed on the road ahead, his thoughts much farther away. 'When...'

CHAPTER SIXTEEN

'THE LITTLE FARM OF THE OLD WELL'

KNOWING THAT PEDRITO WOULD be at nursery school in the village, Doogie dropped Angie off at Rafael's farm and, not wishing to intrude on their 'big reunion', immediately drove the few hundred metres back down the road to the Finca Sa Grua. Angie's instructions to 'keep his gob shut' about her imminent betrothal were still ringing in his ears. In the Ensenyat's yard, Catalina and her mother, both looking drawn and worried, were saying goodbye to an elderly man, as sombre in appearance as his ancient black Mercedes. No sooner had the car left the yard than Señora Ensenyat hurried back into the house, her only acknowledgement of Doogie's arrival a cursory little wave of the hand and a distracted smile.

It was the doctor, Catalina told Doogie, her expression tense. Her father had had some sort of attack. He'd had them before a couple of times recently, but not as bad as this one. Just a slight pain in the chest usually, a kind of tight feeling. Nothing to bother about, he would say – just a touch of indigestion. But this time it had been much worse. He'd hardly been able to breathe – a huge weight on his chest, sweating hot and cold, pains piercing his arm. He'd slumped onto the floor, gasping, the colour drained from his face. He was dying, Catalina and her mother had thought. They'd sent for the doctor, who had come right away, had given him an injection of something or other, and some aspirin of all things.

Despite the tears in her eyes, Catalina attempted to sound upbeat as she added that her father did seem a bit better now, though – in bed, resting, but still not looking at all well.

'His heart?' Doogie asked rhetorically.

Catalina nodded. Mercifully, it hadn't been a full-blown heart attack, she revealed, but a severe warning, nonetheless, according to the doctor. Her father would have to take great care of himself from now on – wrap himself in cotton wool, the doctor had said.

'Which means he'll need help on the farm,' Doogie concluded. 'It's a good job you've got Rafael nearby.'

Catalina shook her head. 'Rafa, he has enough work on his own *finca*. Too much work, he is often saying. Oh, sure, he is sometimes helping Papá in the *emergencia*, like when the baby cow was coming. But, no, *normalmente* he cannot.' Although clearly worried to the point of distraction, Catalina took a deep breath, smiled at Doogie and added philosophically, 'So, it is good that the job of Merryweather is ending for me, no? Now I will be free to help my mamá to help my papá.' She raised her shoulders in a resigned shrug. 'It is natural. The way of the country people.'

Doogie knew that, despite this stoical front, Catalina was deeply disappointed that what she regarded as her escape into the modern world was coming to an abrupt end. But he also recognised that her family, and the present state of her father's health in particular, came before everything. Catalina, he was certain, would gladly do whatever had to be done to help her parents, with no thought of herself. It made him ponder how different his own family life might have been now, if only his outlook had been as selfless.

It was fortunate, Catalina went on, that this had happened to them when it had. August was a quiet month on the farm, with the grain crops already cut and the straw baled and stacked. But in a few weeks – *hombre*, that would be a different story! The almond harvest. The whole valley would be echoing to the sound of long canes rattling the branches of the trees, shaking off the nuts in their dry, yawning husks. Everyone, young and old, would be helping to gather the almonds from the big nets laid beneath the trees. Hard work in the September sun, but good fun at times too, with the families all working together. Catalina smiled at the thought. It was very much part of the old Mallorcan way of life, she reflected. *Sí*, it was natural.

She then fell silent, looking down at the dusty ground. Doogie stroked her hair, but said nothing. He knew what she was thinking.

'Will there be almonds to harvest in Scotland in September?' she asked at length, her head still bowed.

Doogie found it difficult to speak. 'No almonds, Cati,' he finally murmured. 'No almonds to harvest in Scotland.'

Catalina took Doogie's hand and looked up at him, a smile on her lips, but melancholy in her eyes. 'Come,' she said with as much cheer as she could muster. 'Come, and I will show you the *finca* of Señora María.'

Doogie hadn't really had an opportunity to talk to Catalina about María's farm since the day the old woman transferred the ownership: a day that ended in such horrendous circumstances at the hands of Nick Martin. In truth, he had been reluctant even to mention the farm again, ultimately thinking it easier on them both to pretend the matter didn't exist, until they saw what the future held in other ways. A lot could happen in three years, after all. But now that Catalina had broached the subject and they were actually overlooking the place from just a few fields away, he couldn't help being gripped by a compelling curiosity, a feeling which began to develop into a sense of real fascination the closer they got to the old farmstead.

The *finca* consisted of six little fields in all, Catalina pointed out as they walked through the first. Each one was enclosed by drystone walls and criss-crossed by rows of almond trees, with the occasional fig and carob as well, but also with plenty open land for growing crops or grazing animals. It didn't look much now, she admitted. And the reason it looked a bit forlorn and neglected was because her father had only been doing the bare essentials in recent years, the informal and impermanent lease arrangement he'd had with old María being what it was. But Catalina could remember the place when she was a child, when María and her husband were younger and fitter. Ah, *sí*, it had been very different then. Alive, lived in, lovingly worked and cared for, a wonderful little place. And, she remarked, there was a good well too – still as reliable as ever today, her father assured her – with abundant, sweet water. Water, a treasure worth more than gold to farmers in these parts.

Doogie was about to say to Catalina that there would be no restraints on her father restoring the farm to its full production potential now that she owned it, but thought better of it. In the light of the doctor's advice to Señor Ensenyat to 'wrap himself in cotton wool', increasing his workload would most certainly not be on his list of priorities.

Like many Mallorcan *fincas*, this one had a house that at one time had provided shelter for both humans and farm animals, little lean-to structures at either end of the main building being the original accommodation for a donkey or mule, a cow perhaps, or a goat or two. Nearby, but separate from the house, were some small enclosures – higgledy-piggledy constructions made from anything that had been to hand. One, which Doogie guessed would have been for poultry, had blocks of Mallorcan sandstone providing a crude foundation for gnarled, almond-wood posts onto which wire netting had been tied. Every expense had been spared, doubtless of necessity. Another enclosure took the form of a shallow pit, walled in with the same stone slabs, which had also been used to build a little, tile-roofed shelter in one corner.

That was the house of the family pig, Catalina informed Doogie, speaking in Spanish to get her message over more fluently. The pig, she emphasised, had been an essential and much-valued member of every country household in Mallorca until recently. November or December, she fondly reminisced, was the time of the *matances*, the pig-killing, when all the men and women from neighbouring farms would help each other with the cutting up and the salting and curing and sausage-making. This often went on for a couple of days at each place. 'And the singing and dancing every night!' she laughed. '*Madre mía*, such fun!'

'For everyone except the poor pigs,' Doogie suggested with a lopsided smile.

But so wrapped up was Catalina in thoughts of the festivities that she seemed not to have heard him. 'They are still doing it, the *matances*, in some farms in the high mountains,' she said with an eager nodding of her head. 'Such fun! *Sí*, and I will take you to see it this November or Decem–' She stopped abruptly, then murmured, 'I will take you to see it … one day.'

There was nothing Doogie could say. The nearer the time drew to the date of his departure, the harder it was going to be even to mention it. They both realised that. He put his arm around Catalina and they stood for a while looking at old María's gift, which, in other circumstance, would have been like an impossible dream come true for a young couple such as themselves. The realisation of that didn't make the reality of the situation any easier to cope with, however. To Doogie, it all still seemed unreal – like an impossible dream, indeed. Yet the dream was there, beside him and all around him now. And it *was* real.

He gazed at the neglected old house, absorbing its age-mellowed look, feeling the character of its honey-stone walls. With its vine-cloaked pergola over the front door bent and broken, its slatted shutters sun-parched and peeling, the house exuded a strangely wistful yet welcoming warmth. It was a house waiting to become a home again, and Doogie couldn't help but be captivated by it. He cast his eyes round the surrounding patchwork of little fields, descending gently towards Capdellá village on one side, stepping up in terraces towards Catalina's parents' farm on the other. And all around, the protective arms of those majestic Mallorcan mountains.

This was a good place.

'It is called the *Fincalet Pou Vell*,' Catalina said, as if reading Doogie's thoughts. 'The Little Farm Of The Old Well.'

'*Fincalet Pou Vell*,' Doogie repeated. A broad grin appeared on his face, although he didn't quite know why. 'The Little Farm of The Old Well, eh?' He nodded approvingly. 'Sounds good. Has a nice ring to it.'

Catalina was smiling now too, clearly relieved by Doogie's favourable reaction. 'But the house,' she said speculatively, 'it needs much work to make it how it was, I think.'

'Nah,' Doogie countered, 'nothing that a lick of paint and some honest sweat wouldn't put right. OK, a challenge certainly, but a nice one.'

'And the roof, it is good,' Catalina stressed. 'Papá is always keeping it good for Señora María. *Sí*, much *importante*, the good roof, he always is saying.'

Doogie looked up at the old ochre tiles and their matching 'bonnet' sitting soot-smudged atop the chimney stack. Here and there, leafy tendrils from the overgrown grape vine at the front door had ventured past the eaves and were weaving their way upwards over the roof, lending, like an artist's final brush strokes, a certain dramatic flourish to the unkempt beauty of the place.

Sensing Doogie's feeling of enchantment, Catalina nudged his arm. With a mischievous twinkle in her eye, she held up an old door key, which she'd had hidden in her hand. 'You want to look inside, sir?' she asked, while coyly canting her head to one side.

Doogie tapped the tip of her nose. 'Sneaky tactic. You should've been an estate agent.'

Giggling with anticipation now, Catalina turned the key in the lock and the weathered oak door creaked open. The sharp tang of wood smoke and a faint hint of cheese and old leather greeted them as they entered the house. It was dark as a cave after the dazzling light of the midday sun. However, clearly fully familiar with its geography, Catalina scurried this way and that, opening windows and shutters and chattering away with unbridled zeal about the house needing fresh air and the floors a thorough wash and the walls and everything a good dusting. But there were no mouses, Doogie would note from the scattering of empty traps, which her father always kept freshly baited with good, smelly Menorcan cheese. *Sí*, it was much *importante* to keep the mouses out of empty houses, her father always said.

Doogie stood in the doorway and blinked as Catalina's bustling efforts gradually flooded the place with light. The door led directly into a large kitchen, which appeared to double as a living room and dining room as well. This was typical of the old, un-modernised Mallorcan farmhouses, Catalina informed him, then pointed out traditional features like the huge inglenook fireplace in the corner, its mantle a roughly-hewn limb of olive wood scorched by centuries of lapping flames; the age-old terracotta floor tiles; the exposed wooden beams dangling with hooks for hanging hams; the chunky shelves made from slabs of local sandstone, whitewashed like the thick walls, whose bulk kept the house warm in winter and cool in summer.

An open-stepped, wooden stairway divided the kitchen from the only other room in this main part of the house. It was a huge barn of a room, and in the middle stood a long trestle table, surrounded by rickety chairs and an assortment of baskets, trays and boxes, some still full of almond husks. An old-fashioned washing machine with a mangle attached stood by a stone sink in one corner. On the walls hung rows of hand tools, some for tilling the land, others for pruning the trees. By a back door, wooden brackets protruded, on which hung what looked to Doogie like a miniature set of horse harness, its leather grey and cracked with age.

It was for a *burro*, a donkey, Catalina informed him, highly amused by his puzzled expression. And this room was the *almacén* – a storeroom, workroom and centre of everyday activities on Mallorcan farms in days gone by. And today, too, in some places.

'It's like stepping into a time warp,' Doogie gasped, wide-eyed. 'Magic, though. Yeah, really magic.'

Upstairs, a soothing and comforting atmosphere greeted them as they entered the simple, bedtime retreats of a Mallorcan peasant farmer and his family. Here was a haven of bygone tranquillity, a million miles from the package-holiday stir that throbbed, pounded, glittered and roared only twenty minutes away on the once equally-placid coast. Yes, Doogie decided, the *Fincalet Pou Vell* was indeed a good place.

Catalina led him through the four bedrooms in turn, hastily opening windows, apologising for the stuffy air, wafting her hand at the smell of mothballs in the cupboards. With increasing eagerness, she pointed out the views to each of the farm's fields, to its eponymous well with ancient, donkey-powered water-raising machinery still intact, to its orange grove nearby, to the neighbouring farms across the valley, and to the towering grandeur of Mount Galatzo dominating the skyline away to the north.

In the last and smallest of the bedrooms was a tiny alcove set into the wall, and in it a candle and wooden crucifix hanging over an old sepia photograph in an ornate gilt frame. Curious as to why it had been left behind in the otherwise empty room, Doogie lifted the photograph and took it over to the light of the window. It was a picture of two little children, a boy and a girl – about two or three years old, he thought. And they were dressed as cherubs, complete with tinsel halos

217

and wired muslin wings, as if for a fancy dress party, or, more probably, a saint's day procession, like the one he and Catalina had watched with old María at Valldemossa.

'The children of Señora María,' Catalina said, lightly touching the faded image with her fingertips, her expression sad.

Doogie was confused. 'But – but I thought old María had no family. I mean, I seem to remember you telling me that anyway.'

The two children had died shortly after the photograph was taken, Catalina explained. Although it had happened a long, long time ago, she had heard the story many times from her own parents, and also from old María, who would take her to this very room as a child to let her see the shrine of the little angels, as she called the alcove. It had been diphtheria or tuberculosis or a fever of some kind. Catalina couldn't remember exactly – only that María's babies had died of one of those illnesses which were common killers of infants in those days. María and her husband had never had any more children, but they'd kept this room, little Margarita and José's room, exactly as it had always been, until María left the *finca* for the apartment in Palma Nova after her husband's death ten years ago. And, although everything else in the room had been cleared out then, the faded photograph in the gilt frame remained – so that the souls of her little angels would always feel at home, according to a tearful María on the day she said goodbye to her house for the last time.

Doogie carefully replaced the picture. 'So, the Little Farm of The Old Well would have been María's legacy to them,' he said pensively. 'If they'd survived.'

Catalina didn't speak for a few moments, but stood looking at the photograph with Doogie, hesitating, as if gathering the courage to say what was on her mind. 'I think, Doogie,' she ultimately ventured, though still hanging back, 'that perhaps – perhaps this is why the Señora María … when she first saw us together…'

Doogie took her hand, which now felt strangely cold. 'I

know, Cati,' he said quietly. 'I know.'

They left the old house and its little angels to their slumbers and began to wander back up the valley, Doogie now with more thoughts than ever having those familiar three-legged races round his mind, Catalina content in the knowledge that the little farm, *their* little farm, had cast its spell on Doogie. Yet she still had niggling doubts. Doogie had to leave her. She knew that and, no matter how difficult for her, she accepted his reasons. There was nothing else for it. But would he really come back after three years spent in a life she didn't understand, in a world and with friends she didn't know? Friends. Some of them girls. One of them Margaret.

'Doogie,' she said, pausing to look back down over the fields to the old farmhouse, serene in its solitude once again, 'do you remember the night in the gardens of the palace in Palma, looking through the arch at the big black birds swimming?'

'The black swans? Yes,' Doogie replied with a little laugh. 'I reckon that's one night we'll both remember for ever, for *all* sorts of reasons!'

'*Sí*, but one thing you said…'

'Uh-huh?'

There was a confused look on Catalina's face. 'You said a strange thing – a thing about the *finca* of Señora María and undressing a cat two times, I think.'

Doogie laughed out loud. 'More ways of skinning a cat than one, you mean?'

'*Sí, exacto*!'

Doogie hunched his shoulders and smiled, awkwardly. 'Aw, it was just an airy-fairy idea that popped into my head, that's all.'

Catalina was even more confused now. 'Airy?' she queried. 'Fairy?'

'Oh, sorry. Airy-fairy. Well, it means – it means – let's see – yeah, it means "woolly", that sort of thing.'

'Woolly?'

219

Doogie scratched his head, thinking hard. 'Yeah, *impreciso*, you'd say in Spanish, I suppose.'

'Ah, *impreciso*!' Catalina waited with raised eyebrows for Doogie to continue, but when he said nothing, she asked, 'So, what is this idea of the airy fairy that you have for the *finca*?' She poked him playfully in the stomach. 'Come on, Scotsman, tell me! Tell me, or I will tickle your fancy!'

Doogie squirmed away from her probing fingers. 'OK, OK, I give up,' he pleaded. 'I'm a real scaredy-cat when it comes to tickle fights!'

'*Another* cat!' Catalina called out in exasperation, still stalking Doogie with her hands poised like claws. 'Now, tell me this idea of woolly!' Her eyes lit up. 'Oh, I can guess now,' she laughed, 'It is about sheep, no?'

Doogie now scratched his nose. He was feeling embarrassed, and it showed. 'No, well, yes – in a sort of way, partly,' he floundered. 'I mean, it's a daft idea really, and maybe I shouldn't have…'

While Catalina, her fingers at the ready for a tickle attack, crept towards him and stared threateningly into his eyes, Doogie shuffled away in reverse until his back collided with the trunk of a shady old fig tree.

'Tell me, or I will tickle your fancy!' Catalina threatened once more.

Doogie knew he was beaten. 'OK, OK, here goes!' he said, taking a deep breath. It was a notion, he revealed, that had occurred to him fleetingly on the best-forgotten first day he'd worked for Merryweather, when he'd been saddled with the job of guiding a hotchpotch busload of holidaymakers round La Granja, the old tourist-trap mansion with a host of associated 'traditional attractions' up in the mountains. They'd had a few farm animals there – only a handful actually, and nothing special, but a magnet, nevertheless, for mums and dads with small kids, he'd noticed. So, on that night in the Almudaina Palace Gardens in Palma, he'd got to thinking that, as old María's *finca* was too small to make a living from in the conventional way these days, maybe something involving tourism and his knowledge of animals could be developed. He'd wanted to sound out Angie on the subject earlier today, but hadn't got very far, as he'd still thought the whole concept a bit, well, airy-fairy.

A smile of admiration came to Catalina's face as she caught Doogie's drift. 'No, it is not a *concepto* of the airy fairy,' she said. 'It is a *concepto* much brilliant, *mucho estupendo*!' She grabbed Doogie by the ears and, as if to prove that she wasn't kidding, gave him what was, in her opinion anyway, a long-overdue kiss.

But Doogie was still feeling a tad reticent and more than a little unconvinced about the whole idea. 'You really think so?' he asked. 'You *really* think it could work?'

What he lacked in confidence, Catalina more than made up for in enthusiasm. '*Sí, sí,* but you must to tell me more!' she urged. 'Now, or I am exploding!'

Doogie took another deep breath. 'Well,' he began, 'it's actually what they call a farm park back in Britain.'

Catalina inclined her head to one side. 'Farm? Park?'

'Yes, a farm that's open to the public, set up specially *for* the public, where they can see all sorts of farm animals close up. And, of course, you always make sure you've got plenty of young ones – calves, lambs, chicks, piglets – for the kids to pet, or feed even. I mean, look how much Pedrito enjoys playing with Rafael's baby rabbits, for instance. And there are some places that even have rare breeds on show – types of cattle and so on from days gone by. Oh yeah, you'd be surprised how much interest there is in that. People are *always* fascinated by anything to do with the past, you know.' Doogie was warming to his theme, even beginning to convince himself of the viability of the idea. 'What I'm saying is that the farm park thing can be a good way to earn money on a place that's too small to be profitable in the normal way, simply because the visitors pay to get in. And there are millions of tourists coming to Mallorca every year…'

Catalina was sold on the idea already. '*Sí, sí,*' she chipped in, bubbling with enthusiasm, 'and there are ancient races of

Mallorcan animals too – cows, sheep, pigs, hens, goats, horses. *Si*, and all very little common!' She pursed her lips, adopted a serious look, then added, 'Some of them are looking to distinction, I think.'

Doogie chuckled. 'Facing extinction, eh? Well, there you go, then. Round up a pair of each and start breeding.' He could see from Catalina's expression that she thought he might be making fun of her now. 'No, honestly,' he assured her, 'you'd be surprised how many punters are interested in good causes like that. Good for publicity too. Yeah, and you never know, there might even be some sort of government grant available.'

'*Si*,' Catalina agreed, her confidence duly restored, 'and a shop on the farm for selling the *productos* to the punters, no?'

'Yeah, why not? And even a bar, with snacks and everything,' said Doogie, smitten by Catalina's infectious optimism. 'Mallorcan sausages and pies, *ensaimada* pastries, all that stuff. Mmm,' he nodded, 'and tractor rides through the almond groves. Town punters love sitting on straw bales on a trailer.'

Catalina was really fired up now. '*Correcto*! My *madre* can make the food and I will drive the tractor. *Si*, and we have the friends at the *oficina* of Merryweather and the *recepcionistas* at the *hoteles* for sending the coach tour punters to our farm park.' She gave Doogie another serious look. 'Much *importante* this, I think!'

There was no arguing with that, Doogie told her. 'Oh,' he said, as another important consideration came to mind, 'and don't forget, one of the biggest expenses in any business to do with animals is vet's bills.'

Catalina could see what he was getting at, and she liked what she saw. 'But, when you are a qualified *veterinario*...' she said leadingly.

'All free!' Doogie grinned.

Catalina whooped with delight. 'We can do it, Doogie! We can skin the cat, *si*?'

Doogie heaved a great, shuddering sigh. 'Well, we *could*, but...' He rubbed his forefinger and thumb together. '*Dinero*.

222

Being realistic, a project like that would take a lot of money to start up, and money's a commodity neither of us has much of, I'm afraid.'

Catalina shook her head vigorously. She wasn't about to let a little thing like the lack of money stand in the way of such a good idea. This was Mallorca, she reasoned, and the banks were always pleased to lend to people with good ideas related to tourism. And anyway, she would have three years to work and save while Doogie was away at college, *and* she would start preparing the *Fincalet Pou Vell* in the meantime too!

Doogie gave her a kindly but justifiably sceptical smile. 'All that and help your folks on their farm as well?'

'*Sí, absolutamente*!' Catalina was adamant. If you wanted something badly enough, you had to go for it, she insisted. You had to *make* it happen. She was young and healthy, so what was hard work to her? And she would not rely on ever getting any money from old María, either. After all, for all they knew, the old lady might well have to sell her flat to pay for her rest home bills now … if she lived long enough, which Catalina dearly hoped she would.

Doogie shook his head and chuckled softly at the look of obstinate determination burning in Catalina's eyes. 'Old María was right. The Mallorcan country women *are* pretty incomparable. Well, if you're anything to go by, that is…'

They could see four people in the *porche* of the Finca Sa Grua farmhouse as they approached over the fields. When they got nearer still, they heard the hearty sound of congratulations being offered and received, then the pop of a champagne cork and an outburst of cheering.

'Look – my father, he is there with my mother,' Catalina said, clearly concerned. 'Why is he not in bed?' Then, with a puzzled frown, she muttered, 'And Rafael with Angie… And the champagne…' She looked at Doogie to see if he knew what was going on.

Laughing, he held up his hands. 'Don't ask me. I mean, I've a fair idea what's happened, but Angie made me promise.'

Catalina's mouth fell open as the possible reason for the celebration began to dawn on her. 'Rafa and Angie?' she gasped. She looked at Doogie again, her eyes wide, a smile of incredulity on her lips. 'You mean, Rafael and Angie, they have…?'

'Better ask *them*,' Doogie grinned, then took her arm and hurried her on towards the house. 'I'm saying nothing!'

'Check *that* for a sparkler, kids!' Angie shouted without resorting to preamble as soon as she saw them coming over the yard. She flashed the diamond solitaire ring encircling the third finger of her left hand. 'Now, is that what you call a rock, or is that what you call a *rock*?'

Squeals and tears of joy were revelled in by the women, handshakes and macho shoulder slaps were exchanged by the men, with much hugging, kissing, congratulating and unrestrained displays of bonhomie all round. A bit like Hogmanay on Arran, Doogie reflected.

For once, the normally reticent Rafael was unreservedly outgoing and cheerful – even towards Doogie. Angie's classic Nordic beauty, dark roots notwithstanding, had evidently done the business. Another champagne cork popped. Rafael was pushing the boat out.

At the sound of all this jollity, young Pedrito came running out of the kitchen. '*Hola*, Boogie!' he shouted. 'Hey, did you know Rafael is going to be my new daddy?'

'Yeah, I just heard, Pedrito.' Doogie tousled the little boy's hair and gave him a wink. 'Good news, eh?'

Pedrito looked up at him, then said in a precociously reproachful way, 'You missed your chance, *amigo*!'

Catalina was now fussing over her father, urging him to sit down, warning him not to drink too much. And why, she wanted to know, had he got out of bed? He'd have to do what he was told from now on, or he'd have the doctor to answer to.

Her father patted her hand and tried to assure her that he was perfectly all right. And the doctor could go to blazes. Why, that miserable old goat would have him confined to his bed for the rest of his days, if he had his way! No, no, he knew best himself what was good for him, and joining in an impromptu fiesta like this was just the thing. *Dios mío*, he declared, there weren't enough of them in the countryside these days!

Catalina and her mother were clearly not persuaded, but being the head of the family, Señor Ensenyat had the last word. And that was that – in public, at least.

Doogie watched him closely all the while: the weary eyes behind the reassuring smile, the laboured breathing, that gaunt, exhausted look. He had seen the signs before, though he hadn't appreciated their ominous significance at the time. In Catalina's father now, he saw his own father of two years ago. Another relatively young man suddenly old and worn-out, overworked, before his time.

Catalina's mother caught Doogie's eye. She had been watching him observing her husband, and she knew what was going through his mind. She gave him an understanding smile: a sad, resigned smile, but with a look that said this was Angie and Rafael's moment. Pedrito's too. It was a moment of happiness that they deserved, and not to be diminished by thoughts and fears of things over which none of them, ultimately, would have any control. It was the same simple, fatalistic philosophy that Doogie's own mother had had – an attitude born of the country, where spring and autumn, birth and death are accepted features of nature's calendar, where the summer of life should be a time of celebration, without any pointless dread of the winter that will surely come round in nature's own good time. He returned Señora Ensenyat's smile with an acknowledging dip of his head.

'A penny for 'em,' Angie said, suddenly appearing by Doogie's side, her customary world-weary look washed away in a flush of romantic euphoria and several glasses of Rafa's bubbly. 'Still wondering how to make that dream of yours come true, huh?'

'Something like that, Ange. Something like that,' Doogie sighed. 'Anyway,' he continued brightly, 'it's your dream we

225

should be talking about.' He lifted her hand and took a close look at her engagement ring. 'Wow, Rafael really did come good!'

'Don't be personal,' Angie muttered with a smutty laugh.

'No, seriously – with the ring and the champers and everything, he's obviously been well prepared for the genuflect act.'

'*Gen*uflect?' Angie piped, half tiddly and enjoying it. 'I don't know *what* your language is coming to, young O'Mara, I really don't! Dirty-minded Scotch poultice!'

Doogie nudged her, signalling her to lower her voice. 'I mean the down-on-one-knee stuff,' he hissed.

'Oh *that*? Yeah, hardly in the door, I was. Wallop!'

'Wallop?'

'Yeah, you know…' Angie went all demure and useless for a second, then confided out of the corner of her mouth, 'Hidden depths of Latin passion, our Rafa's got. Not as slow off the mark as he appears, like!'

Doogie flashed her a smug smile. 'That's us country yokels for you.'

Angie leaned back and looked him up and down, her eyebrows sardonically raised. 'In your case, love, that remains to be seen!'

Letting that one pass, Doogie cleared his throat and asked, 'And, ehm, the big day … when's it going to be, then?'

'Oh, sometime next month,' Angie replied matter-of-factly. 'Soon as poss after I cut the Merryweather cord, we'll be tying the knot. Yeah, like I say, he doesn't believe in letting the grass grow under his feet, our Rafa.' Then, the fiesta spirit rapidly rising in her, she swung her glass-holding hand in a wide, theatrical arc, scattering its contents all over the place, while calling out, '*Música-a-a*! Let's have some party music for the new fiancés! *Ay-y-y, arriba-a-a*!'

Doogie took refuge in one of the old easy chairs by the door. Catalina settled on its arm beside him after she had produced a portable CD player, which was now honking out flamenco music for the clumsily fandangoing Angie and

Rafael. Before long, Pedrito had joined them, adding a final touch of disorder to the existing dance-floor mayhem. But the scene was a happy one – this spontaneous new family of three, laughing and dancing, delighting in each other's company, while their little audience clapped in time and laughed along with them.

Catalina slipped her arm round Doogie's shoulder, her smile reflecting the genuine joy she felt for the happiness that fate had bestowed so unexpectedly on her friends. Yet, deep inside, her heart was heavy, her concerns for her father's health impossible to set aside, the ever-increasing pain of Doogie's impending departure too real to ignore.

As were the little pangs of envy she felt for Angie and Rafael today.

CHAPTER SEVENTEEN

'ILL-MET BY TWILIGHT'

AS THE SWELTERING MONTH of August rolled relentlessly on, the long-suffering holiday reps' normal flusters and flaps increased apace. They were accustomed to such hassles springing from eternal flight delays, accommodation over-bookings and French air-traffic controllers' strikes. Then there were their clients' usual outbreaks of diarrhoea, constipation and sunstroke, panics about stolen travellers' cheques, lost air tickets and passports, and the occasional arrest of Brit 'gannet droppings' for offences ranging from urinating on the airport tarmac in broad daylight to attempted murder. But, for Doogie and his colleagues, such headaches were exacerbated now by the merging and pruning of the Merryweather Holidays and *3-S Vacations* work forces.

Knowing clearly where her priorities lay, Catalina had resigned her Merryweather post immediately following the news of her father's illness. Being at home to lend support to her parents was absolutely foremost in her thoughts. That aside, she'd also been mindful of the fact that the chaotic Merryweather duty schedules would have meant her seeing little or nothing of Doogie if she had remained working for them for the short period he still had left in Mallorca. This way, at least they would be able to share the few hours off that Doogie did manage to snatch every week.

He himself would much rather have followed suit by instantly severing his ties with the callous Merryweather regime. It would have allowed him to maximise the time available to be with Catalina, and also to muck in and help her father with whatever heavier chores needed to be done about the farm during those few final weeks on the island. But the economic realities of the situation had ruled out such notions, no matter how attractive. If Doogie didn't work out his full notice with the company, the company wouldn't provide him with a free air ticket back to the UK. A disaster in his current financial state.

Meanwhile, Angie, being Angie and a long-serving Merryweather trouper, had somehow managed to sweet-talk Manolo into keeping her on a part-time basis for the concluding month or so of her career, thus relieving Señora Ensenyat of much of the strain of looking after Pedrito, and allowing Angie ample opportunity to 'get her feet under the table and her slippers by the bed', as she put it, in what was to be her new marital home. She had also announced that, as soon as old María was able, she was to come and live with them, just a short way up the hill from her old home in her beloved Capdellá valley. God knows, the house was big enough, Angie had said, and if she couldn't provide some real family comfort for the old dear after all she'd done for her and Pedrito over the years, it would be a bloody blue do!

So, Doogie's short, eventful and unpredictably fateful spell as a sky-blue-blazered rep in Mallorca was drawing to a close.

And the closer the inescapable day for boarding that Glasgow-bound plane loomed, the more he dreaded the prospect.

He wasn't looking forward much to his second visit from Margaret Hyslop either. For a while, it had seemed that her declared intention to revisit the island had been abandoned, but on the penultimate day of the month (the timing characteristic of Margaret, Doogie reflected), he found a note pinned to his door when he returned home in the evening. The message was as brief and to the point as usual:

'*Staying at the Hostal Tramuntana*
in Andratx village. See you there
eightish tonight. Margaret.'

This, Doogie cursed, was all he needed after ten hours of non-stop airport duty. A fifteen-mile drive, in the opposite bloody direction, to Andratx! Typical – bloody typical! Still, there were things to be said to Margaret: things which she wouldn't particularly want to hear, he knew, but things that had to be said, nonetheless. So, no time like the present...

He found the Hostal Tramuntana in the high part of Andratx old town, tucked away in a steep alley just below the church. It was only a short hike – as he'd guessed it would be – from the foothills of the Tramuntana Mountains, which rear away northward for the best part of forty miles from this point. There would be plenty of hill-walking and rock-climbing potential there for Margaret and her mates, Doogie mused as he entered the Hostal's inauspicious little reception area. The room was dim, as cool as a crypt, with black-and-white marble floor tiles and antique Spanish furniture the colour of rosary beads. A solitary, white-haired old woman in black sat on a rocking chair in the corner, making lace and watching a Spanish-dubbed episode of *Neighbours* on an ancient TV. Its flickering picture, Doogie noticed, was a perfect match for the floor tiles. Margaret, he concluded, had certainly found herself a fun place to stay this time!

'Señorita Margaret Hyslop?' he said to the back of the old woman's head, hoping she wouldn't swing round to reveal herself as Anthony Perkins in a Spanish-dubbed version of

Psycho.

Without interrupting the slow, lace-hook rhythm of her spidery hands, or diverting her eyes from the telly, the old woman jerked her head sideways in the direction of an archway at the opposite side of the room. '*La terraza*!' she croaked with the voice of a laryngitic jackdaw.

'*Gracias*,' said Doogie, marvelling at this other extreme of Mallorcan tourism and resisting an impulse to enquire what time the bingo started.

Margaret was alone on the tiny terrace, a book lying open on the plastic table where she sat watching the gathering dusk paint grey shadows over the slab-sided wall of the church opposite. Doogie wondered for a moment if he should do the accepted Spanish thing and give her a peck of greeting on both cheeks, but something made him opt for the Arran alternative instead.

'Hi, Margaret,' he said, then gave her a cursory pat on the back and sat down opposite her. 'How's things?'

But Margaret had other ideas. 'Doogie!' she chirped, all welcoming smiles and flirtatious looks. She rose like a jack-in-the-box, stretched over the table and planted a singularly non-platonic kiss on his lips. 'How marvellous to see you again!'

'It's unlike Margaret, this,' Doogie said to himself. He was instantly suspicious, and it must have been apparent.

'My, my, I thought you'd be a bit more demonstrative in your salutations than that, after your little sojourn here amongst the natives,' she simpered, her attempt at disguising sarcasm with good-natured banter failing to come off.

'Well, don't forget I haven't been around as much as you, Margaret,' Doogie said dryly. 'Around Spain, that is.'

Margaret chose not to respond to that, but revealed her displeasure by sitting back down and adopting her familiarly haughty pose of looking away sideways at nothing in particular.

'While we're on the subject, how were Andalucia and the Costa Whatsit and wherever?' Doogie asked, the question emerging as another dig at Margaret, though not truly intended as such.

'Fine, Doogie, absolutely fine,' Margaret said huffily, still obliquely surveying fresh air.

How this type of pettish performance hadn't prompted somebody to slap Margaret's face and tell her to grow up long before now was beyond Doogie. However, he had resolved that 'Keep the head, O'Mara' would be his motto here. Persevere.

'Actually, I was expecting you and your chums to hit the island about a couple of weeks ago, according to what you told me before,' he said, persevering.

Margaret turned to face him again, a honey-sweet smile spreading over her face as quickly as it had disappeared half a minute earlier. 'Yes, that's right. We got here about ten days ago. Been exploring the mountains. Absolutely marvellous. Scenery to rival anything any of us have seen *any*where, actually.' She was slipping into her habitual patronising mode, lightly veiled behind a contrived smile. 'Honestly, Doogie,' she continued, 'it really is *such* a pity you've spent your time here in those horrible, concrete, holiday ghettos. There's just *so* much else to see on this island, if you take the trouble to get away from the dreadful places that attract all those – all those...' Margaret was searching for the most appropriate pejorative.

'Neanderthal low-grades?' Doogie prompted.

'Well, I wouldn't necessarily put it *that* way...'

'You were the one who put it that way before, Margaret.'

If she heard that, she pretended not to. 'I mean, the views over the sea from the mountain roads,' she went on, 'they're every bit as spectacular as *any*thing the Côte d'Azur has to offer.'

'Really?' Doogie swallowed a yawn.

Margaret was on a roll. 'Oh, and the quaint mountain villages – Banyalbufar, with all its a*maz*ing terraced fields – Deià, where Robert Graves the writer lived...'

'Robert Graves, eh? Just fancy!'

'Yes, the historical novel *I, Claudius*, you know.' Margaret

232

threw that away in a manner loaded with a presumption that Doogie *did*n't know, then proceeded with her condescending travelogue. 'And there's a little town called Sóller, famous for its oranges – particularly beautiful place hidden in an absolutely spec*tac*ular valley. Oh, and Valldemossa, of course – fascinating village, with its old Carthusian monastery – Chopin and George Sand spent a winter there once.' She shot Doogie a schoolmarmish glance. 'George Sand, the French writer, you know. A woman, actually – using a nom de plume, of course.'

'Gerraway?'

Paying no heed to Doogie's glazed look, and blissfully unaware that he had his own reasons foralready knowing the subjects of her lecture, Margaret drove on in top gear...

'And some of the viewing points high over the Med – *miradores*, they call them in Spanish, by the way – built at the most *breath*taking spots right along that coast! Honestly, there's one in particular near Valldemossa –'

'Called Miramar,' Doogie butted in, hijacking Margaret's spiel and leaving her gawping like a fairground goldfish. 'Built over a hundred years ago by the Archduke Louis Salvador of Austria, overlooking the place on his vast estate where he met and fell in love with a beautiful Mallorcan peasant girl, who used to go and pick olives there. Yes, I have managed to glean a morsel or two of local historical information during my little sojourn here among the natives, Margaret.' He kneaded his forehead in mock contemplation. 'Now then, let me see if I can remember the quotation... Ah, yes, it goes something like this – "The greatest wonder with which Mallorca regales the eyes of the soul and the soul of the eyes is here in Valldemossa – it is the superb headland of Miramar." The words are by one Miguel de Unamuno, I believe. And, uh, I won't bother to tell you whether or not he was a writer as well, Margaret, because I'm sure you already know.'

Margaret was even more slack-jawed now.

'Oh, the beautiful Mallorcan peasant girl died, by the way,'

233

Doogie added. 'Yeah, leaving the poor Archduke with a broken heart, from which he never recovered, they say.'

Margaret's dumbstruck expression morphed into a now-I-get-it smirk. 'Aha, and how is your *own* little peasant girl?' she goaded. 'Not planning any sneaky little ploys like that to break *your* heart, I hope.'

Doogie shook his head in disbelief. 'You're one in a million when the mood takes you, Margaret, you really are.'

'Oh dear,' she said, her eyes half-closed in mock pity, 'have I offended you? Tut, tut! Naughty me!'

Doogie stared at her for a few seconds, pensively tapping his pursed lips with his forefinger, inwardly debating whether or not he should simply leave right now. But he quickly came to the conclusion that it would be best to get everything out in the open once and for all. That's why he'd come, and that's what he would do, no matter how petulant Margaret had decided to be.

'I'm going back the day after tomorrow, you'll be pleased to know,' he said. 'Back to Scotland, ready for the start of the new term at uni.'

Margaret smiled smugly. 'There, I knew you'd come to your senses in the end. I just *knew* Daddy's letter would do the trick, and –'

'I got fired, Margaret. That's why I'm going back. Merryweather Holidays decided they could do without me, and I won't trouble you with the details of why. But that, together with personal reasons, which I needn't go into either, is why I'm going back.'

'Yes, but –'

'And for the record, as much as I appreciate your father's interest in me, I would prefer it if he left me to make my own arrangements with the principal of the vet college in future, OK?'

'Yes, but I only asked him to do that because –'

'Precisely, *you* ask and your father jumps. Well, that may be fine for you, Margaret, but those days are over for me. I've learned a lot about life and even more about myself since I came out here, and one of the main things I've learned is that, if you can't be true to yourself, you can't be true to anybody!'

Margaret now slipped back into supercilious mode. '*Really*, Doogie,' she sneered, 'paraphrasing Shakespeare may impress your little peasant wench, but it cuts absolutely no ice with me.'

'I'm making my own decisions from now on, Margaret. Do you get that? It's *my* life and I'm going to do what *I* want with it, all right?'

'Oh yes? And what great decision have you made about *your* life, may I ask?'

Doogie bit the bullet. 'Well, for a start, going back to Arran to take over your father's practice is off. No disrespect to your father, no lack of gratitude to him, but off. O-F-F, off, right?'

Margaret looked heavenward and gave a quiet, disdainful laugh. 'My God, you really have fallen under some gypsy spell or other, haven't you?'

'And what's *that* supposed to mean?'

'It's obvious! Where are you going to get another offer like my father's? I mean, come down to earth, Doogie! When you qualify – sorry, *if* you qualify, and there's no guarantee of that any more, the way your mind's gone since you came here – you'll have to find a *lot* of money to buy yourself a practice like the one Daddy's offered you for nothing.'

'And?'

'And you haven't got a pot to piss in!' Margaret was loosing her cool. 'The O'Maras never did,' she snapped, 'and that's *always* been common knowledge on Arran!'

Doogie shook his head and chuckled softly to himself. He was stung by Margaret's abusive outburst, yet somehow felt more pity for her than anger. He watched her weaving her fingers nervously on the table, her head turned to the side again, her emotions clearly torn now between remorse and an urge to hurt even more. As Doogie knew of old, Margaret wasn't accustomed to not having things her own way, and she was obviously having great difficulty handling this new experience.

235

'For you,' Doogie said calmly, 'money's what it all comes down to in the end, isn't it? Money and social status … whatever that is.'

'That's a typically simplistic view,' Margaret muttered. 'You fail to grasp the realities, and that almost goes without saying.'

'Oh, I think I grasp the realities perfectly now.' Doogie was composure personified, surprising even himself, under the circumstances. 'Why don't you admit it, Margaret? You'd have had zero interest in me if I'd stayed behind on Arran to help my father on the croft instead of going to vet college.'

'Oh, get real, for heaven's sake!' Margaret scoffed. 'That little patch of rented land couldn't even put enough food in your father's own mouth, never mind provide a living for you as well!'

'But maybe that shouldn't have been *my* priority, and that's something that *you* obviously fail to grasp.'

Margaret gave her hair a disparaging flick and looked away again. 'Educate me, do!'

'Maybe my first concern should've been to help my father, irrespective of what would or wouldn't be in it for me materially. If it had added a few years to his life, that would've been reward enough. I know that now.'

'And you would have followed in his footsteps, I take it – a penniless sod-buster, doing all sorts of unskilled jobs on the side just to scrape a living.' Margaret glared at Doogie. 'Is *this* the realism you're grasping?'

Margaret didn't realise how close she had just come to getting that much-deserved slap on the face. But Doogie kept the urge in check – somehow.

'I'd have managed,' he said. 'After all, I'm young and fit, I've got my wits about me, *and* there are more ways of skinning a cat than one.'

'Grow up! Only an idiot and a dreamer would think like that!' Margaret had stoked herself up to a full head of steam now. 'As my father always told me, none of us can survive in the modern world on dreams and romantic notions alone. You

236

have a duty to yourself to be everything you can be – to go for the first prize!'

'Fair enough, I suppose,' Doggie shrugged. 'But sometimes, Margaret, if you aim for *every*thing, you can end up with nothing. That's something *you've* still to grasp, and I just hope you don't end up learning it the hard way.'

Margaret gave one of her dismissive snorts. 'Don't you worry about me! *I* know exactly where I'm heading in life, and I aim to grab all I can on the way.'

'OK, but do try to be nice to people on the way up,' Doogie came back. 'You know what they say about meeting them again on the way down!'

Margaret allowed that remark to drift off into the evening air without response. Then, after a moment, she stared down at her folded hands and adopted the air of a little girl lost. This was a ploy Doogie had seen her use to great success many times in her life, usually when trying to wheedle something out of her father that he had already refused to give – a new dolly, a bike, or a car these days, maybe.

She looked over the table with pathos in her eyes. 'And us, Doogie,' she crooned. 'What about us, hmm?'

But Doogie wasn't about to take the bait. Instead, he bounced the question back. 'What *about* us, Margaret? What do you mean, what about us?'

'Well, you know,' she simpered, 'all the plans we had and everything...'

'All the plans *you* had. It never actually became a topic of discussion, remember? Just an assumption of yours. Yes, and because of that, an assumption of your parents as well.'

Doogie paused, waiting for a reaction, but Margaret merely resumed her hand-gazing act.

'We've been friends a long time, Margaret,' he continued firmly. 'Friends, chums, but nothing more than that. And for what it's worth, I really hope we can continue to be friends in the future ... *if* you can accept that I intend to settle for what you'd judge to be a much lower rung on the ladder than the one you aspire to.'

She looked up quizzically. 'I don't follow.'

Doogie braced himself. 'I'm coming back here when I'm through at vet college, Margaret. My mind's made up.'

Margaret half smiled, a disbelieving, almost derisory look on her face. 'To do what? You mean graduate in Scotland, then come *here* to practice as a vet?'

'No, not necessarily. I'm sure they've got enough well-qualified vets here already.' Doogie was being absolutely frank. 'No, in fact, when I think about it, I could probably do what we've got planned with the knowledge and experience I've got right now – if shove came to push and I flunked my exams or something.'

The penny-just-dropped expression returned to Margaret's face. 'Oh, I see,' she smirked. 'It's what *we*'ve got planned now, is it? Come on, don't tell me you're actually taking this silly holiday romance thing with your little gypsy tart *that* seriously. Infatuation,' she sniffed, 'that's all it is. The same sort of stupid crush every hair-brained Brit bimbo gets for the first dago waiter who gropes her arse and winks a big, brown, come-to-bed eye at her.' Margaret shook her head, disbelief writ large on her face. 'Honestly, Doogie, I thought you had a little more self-respect than *that*!'

Again Doogie successfully fought the temptation to smack Margaret one, but it was getting harder. 'I won't bore you with the details,' he bridled, 'but for your information, Catalina, the little *gypsy* you seem bent on slagging off at every opportunity, just happened to save my life since I last saw you. Hurled herself at a bloody psychopath who was about to ram a hypo full of poisoned dope into my jugular!'

Margaret threw her head back and let out a peal of forced laughter. 'I've heard it all now!' she jeered. 'Pocahontas and Captain Smith are alive and well and living in a Mallorcan dreamland! My God, if only you realised what a damned fool you're making of yourself, Doogie!'

He looked at her coldly. 'That's only your opinion, Margaret, and you don't even know what you're taking the piss out of. Yeah, right now I'd say it's you who's making a fool of yourself, wouldn't you?'

Effortlessly, Margaret swapped her mocking approach for a compassionate one. 'But you don't even *belong* here, Doogie,' she said with a consoling smile. 'I've told you that before, haven't I, hmm? And look, OK, I know your emotions were in turmoil when you came here, what with your parents dying and so on. And yes, of *course* I can understand that seeing this Catalina and her seemingly-happy family at their little Mallorcan croft or whatever must have made you think of home and how it used to be.' Margaret laid her hand on her chest and leaned forward to have a go at what Doogie guessed would be her trainee bedside manner. 'Yes, of *course* I appreciate all that. But, believe me, once you're back at vet college, you'll soon put all this Mallorcan nonsense behind you. You'll see the reality clearly enough then, I know.' She reached out to touch his hand. 'Come on now, you must know yourself that this girl's thing for you won't survive three weeks when you're gone – never mind three years. They never do, these holiday crushes,' she concluded, her voice oozing a kind of cod maternal sincerity. 'They never, ever do.'

Doogie drew his hand away and stood up. 'Thanks for the advice, Margaret.' He checked his watch. 'Now, I don't want to keep you from your friends any longer.'

'*Au contraire*!' Margaret breezed, as if the foregoing exchange had never taken place. 'They're waiting for us, dying to meet you! And listen,' she gushed, 'we've found this *amaz*ing little pub-type place – a *tasca* they call it in Spanish – right in the village here. Very unpretentious – a bit Bohemian, really. Run by a terrific Cambridge couple – he's a writer, she paints – they've been all over the world. You'll love them. Oh, and what's more, the food's good, old-fashioned, home-made British!' She got to her feet and made to thread her arm through Doogie's. 'So, come on, Doogs,' she grinned. 'Bygones is bygones, eh?' Margaret was treating Doogie like an uncooperative infant now. 'Yes, of course they is. So, hey, let's meet up with the gang and have some fun!'

'Sorry, Margaret,' Doogie said. He removed her arm from

239

his. 'My apologies to the *gang*, but I've got a prior engagement.'

Margaret gave the spirit of goodwill and reconciliation an instant red card. 'I hope you're not going off to see that little gypsy bitch!' she spat.

'No, Margaret, I'm going to the Hotel Tiempo Alegre, in fact – to pick up a coach load of Neanderthals for the airport. *Some* of us have to work, you know.' He walked away, paused in the doorway, turned and smiled. 'But, hey, enjoy the rest of your holiday with the gang … hmm?'

CHAPTER EIGHTEEN

'THE LAST SUPPER'

DOOGIE'S LAST DAY AS a Merryweather man was no different from any of the rest he'd experienced: the same helter-skelter dash-following-dash between airport and hotels, always trying to be cheery, mannerly and helpful beyond the call of duty for hour upon hour, with not even a monotony-breaking tour-guide trip to La Granja squeezed in for old time's sake. He'd have enjoyed that, too, being a bit better equipped with knowledge of the subject and certainly stoked with more plausible bullshit than he'd been on that first heart-stopping day on the job.

There *was* one good thing about this final day, though.

241

When he called into the office for the very last time at six o'clock, he knew there would be no last-minute order to be at the airport again at midnight to do an extra half-shift because of some unforeseen cock-up or other. And yet he couldn't help feeling disappointed when he saw off the last of his charges on a flight to Gatwick that evening. There was a real sense of anti-climax as he came to the end of what had turned out to be a short visit into someone else's world. A world where people lived on their nerves and worked on an emergency fuel supply day after day, week after week, yet emerged ready and willing (in the main) to accept anything the job threw at them. A bit like being a vet, in that respect, Doogie mused.

And, of course, there would be no farewell bash for *him*. After all, he was just one of several minions parting company with Merryweather Holidays, all clocking off their respective jobs at different hours, while the rest of the reps got on with things as if it were just another day. Which it was – for them. However, a going-away party *was* being planned for long-serving Angie, and Doogie had certainly been invited to that. But, with the new university year starting in a few days and Angie's shindig not due for another week or so…

Anyway, Doogie had said his individual goodbyes to as many people in the company as he could, he'd made a point of making a final visit to old María in the rest home up at Valldemossa with Catalina, and he knew he'd be seeing Angie and Pedrito 'for the last time for God knows how long,' as Angie would put it, at Catalina's parents' *finca*, where he'd been invited for a quiet farewell dinner tonight. Then, tomorrow morning at eleven o'clock, the moment he was trying not to think about – the departure of his flight back to Scotland.

'Sorry to see you go,' said Manolo, after Doogie had handed in his uniform at the office. 'You developed into a good rep. Good with the clients, patient, a quick learner, and a hard worker. Just the sort of persons we look for, but are not so easy to find.'

'Thanks, Manolo. I'm flattered. But, well, it wasn't my

decision to leave *just* yet, as you know.'

'Ah, but that, as we always say, is the package holiday business. No safety net for anyone.' He raised a shoulder. 'Next year, I could be the one with no job.'

'Maybe, but I doubt that,' Doogie laughed, 'and I certainly hope not.'

Manolo responded with a courteous nod. 'That's kind of you. *Muchas gracias.*'

'No, I really mean it. I won't say too much at the moment, but in a few years, I'd like to think I could come and ask for your support for a little idea that's –'

Manolo held up a hand, a patient smile just discernible under the overhang of his moustache. 'I know, I know, I know. Young Catalina has already spoken on the phone with me about it – and for more time than I can afford, I have to say.'

Doogie was caught on the wrong foot. 'Oh … I see. Sorry, I – I didn't know…'

Manolo's smile reached his eyes. 'A very persuasive and determined young lady, Catalina. Enterprising too. But yes, I think your idea is a good one, and I'll help all I can.' He stroked his moustache thoughtfully. 'And, who knows, perhaps even Mister Merryweather himself might be interested in investing in such a venture.'

Doogie was rendered almost speechless. 'Jeez, that's – that's magic!' His expression conveyed a curious blend of shock and guarded optimism.

Manolo stood up and extended his hand. '*Adiós*, Doogie. *Hasta la vista*, eh?'

'Yes, *adiós*, Manolo,' Doogie grinned. 'We'll, ehm, we'll look forward to maybe doing a wee bit of business in the future, then?'

'I do hope so, my friend.' Manolo gave him a cautionary look. 'If, of course, some enterprising young Mallorcan man hasn't stolen your idea *and* your young lady in the meantime, no?'

Doogie hadn't dared even contemplate such a possibility. 'Yeah,' he said with a pained smile, 'I suppose there's always that, right enough.'

Manolo laughed heartily and slapped Doogie's back as he accompanied him to the door. '*Buena suerte, amigo*!' he called after him. 'Good luck in your studies … *and* in whatever you decide to do with your life!'

A million dancing lights greeted Doogie when he drove through the gates of the Finca Sa Grua – a flying ballet of insects, hovering and gliding between the rows of almond trees, their tiny wings radiating the amber glow of the evening sun in the still, warm air. He stopped the car and got out to savour the scene for the last time. This was the same twilight that had been falling on the little terrace of the Hostal Tramuntana when he'd arrived in Andratx the previous evening. But now, instead of its shadows darkening the oppressively close walls of a church, its shafts of golden light picked out so many things of beauty in this Capdellá valley that were hidden in the dazzling glare of day. Things that he had never noticed before. Little details of the landscape, like the sail-less tower of an old windmill nestling among pine trees on a hillock by the village; the gable of a whitewashed farmhouse standing out from the shadow-brindled soil on the far side of the valley; rosy cliffs and dark clefts sculpting the green flanks of the mountains; the sun-bleached wooden wheel of the ancient well on old María's farm, down there just a few fields away.

Old María's farm. Catalina's farm now. *Their* farm. Their future … time and destiny willing.

For some reason, Margaret's words of the previous evening came back to him now, raking his thoughts and sowing seeds of doubt. Hell, she had a way of trampling all over your mind, that Margaret – of playing on your feelings and kicking your spirits into touch. Doogie had sworn that he'd never let her get to him in that way again. But she had, dammit, and there seemed nothing he could do about it.

'You don't *belong* here,' she'd said. 'That girl's family and their little farm are only making you think of your own home and how it used to be … Your head's in a Mallorcan dreamland … These holiday crushes never last … My God, if you only realised what a damned fool you're making of yourself!'

To see ourselves as others see us, Doogie pondered. Then he thought of what Manolo had said about some on-the-ball Mallorcan bloke maybe moving in on his idea *and* on Catalina. Had he been joking, just pulling his leg? Or was he saying the same as Margaret – that he didn't belong here, was only dreaming, heading for a rude awakening? Or was he saying the opposite, but marking his card in a way as well? Warning him not to be too complacent? Yeah, of course that was it. Hell's teeth, it was only Margaret's bloody-minded attempts at brain-washing that had got him reading something sinister into what had been an innocent and well-meaning remark on Manolo's part.

Or was it? For, when all was said and done, there was still no escaping the recurring thought that an awful lot could and probably would change in three years, no matter how sincere Doogie and Catalina's present commitment to each other. The world wouldn't stand still for either of them.

'Whatever you decide to do with your life,' were the last words Manolo had said. Doogie knew well enough *now* what he wanted to do with it, but maybe the passage of time and being away from the beguiling charm of this place *would* change all that. He had to admit it – the possibility was there, no matter how much he tried to persuade himself otherwise.

And then he saw Catalina, waving to him from the yard in front of the house and starting up the farm road towards him. She was dressed all in white again, smiling, her face aglow and her dark hair burnished by the late evening sunlight. This was old María's beautiful Mallorcan princess, stepping as if from a painting, and adding that final ingredient of magic to this entrancing scene. Doogie's heart skipped a beat. It seemed that all the doubts that had been invading his mind were already beginning to fade with the setting sun.

The kindness and generosity of Catalina's parents that

evening also served to confirm in Doogie's mind what he already instinctively felt – that here were honest people, who would gladly accept him as one of their own. And it was a genuine feeling, one of mutual understanding and growing affection. A feeling valued all the more by Doogie, perhaps, because he recognised this as the only family he would ever have now. But that realisation was warm and good. It wasn't something to be dismissed, as Margaret had cynically maintained. It wasn't simply a pitiful attempt by a still-grieving Doogie to replace his own parents and that lost feeling of home with people and things only superficially similar – right down to Catalina's father's illness.

'Listen to your heart,' had been Catalina's advice, and in his heart Doogie knew that he belonged here with these good folk. What was more, they trusted him, a total stranger until a few weeks ago. They trusted him not to hurt their cherished daughter, trusted him to believe in her, trusted him to keep his word and return to her … when the time came that he could.

'So, that was the last supper, huh, kid?' said Angie. She was sitting opposite Doogie at the big table under the Finca Sa Grua *porche*, where she, Rafael and Pedrito had joined Catalina and her parents for Doogie's farewell meal.

'For a while, I'm afraid, Ange,' Doogie replied, making no attempt to disguise his sadness. 'Back to Scotland for me in the morning.'

Angie said no more on the subject. She realised that, in that one clumsy question, she had already said too much.

In fact, there had been a noticeably subdued atmosphere throughout the evening, and not even Angie had tried to make light of it by coming out with her usual shafts of bawdy wit. She knew, as did everyone else present, what Doogie and Catalina were struggling to prepare themselves for. Doogie hadn't even felt hungry. Not that Señora Ensenyat's tirelessly-prepared Mallorcan dishes weren't as colourful and wholesome as ever, but his appetite just seemed to diminish as the evening wore on and the precious minutes in Catalina's

246

company ticked relentlessly by. Catalina herself had only picked at her food too: sitting beside Doogie, gazing at his face as he spoke with her father and Rafael about crops and animals and the coming almond harvest, her hand resting lightly on his knee, treasuring the touch that in the morning would be gone. She had often heard old María and women of her generation talk of the torture of the last few hours they'd waited for their husbands and boyfriends to go off to fight in the Civil War all those years ago. But she had never truly appreciated the pain they had tried to describe … until now. And the fact that Doogie wasn't going to war mattered little to Catalina. The parting and the sorrow would be the same.

Even little Pedrito had been unusually quiet during the meal, and Doogie had noticed that the little fellow had been watching him with a serious expression throughout, as though trying to fathom some complicated riddle.

'Boogie,' Pedrito said at last, 'why are you going away to Ibiza tomorrow?'

A stunned silence descended on the *porche*. Angie put her fingers to her lips, tears welling in her eyes as the poignancy of her little boy's question struck her. He had never once mentioned the word Ibiza in all the time since she first left him behind with old María when taking up her new job there.

Doogie, also touched by the significance of Pedrito's innocent though carefully considered question, could only murmur, 'It's Scotland I'm going to, Pedrito. Scotland.'

But Pedrito was still confused and, for once, his usual I-can-handle-it expression was beginning to waver. 'So … is Scotland in Ibiza too, Boogie?' he asked.

Angie took out her hankie and blew her nose. The others sat silently, apprehensively, knowing that to say anything would be an intrusion. This was between little Pedrito and Doogie: a delicate exchange that had its beginnings deep within the four-year-old's innermost thoughts. Hidden feelings, normal childish fears and insecurities, which he'd only once revealed before – on the day old María had collapsed and was taken to hospital.

Doogie smiled across the table at him, hoping the wee chap would stop staring with those truth-seeking eyes for a moment. 'It's not that far from Ibiza, Pedrito,' he said in as convincing a way as he could. 'Only a hop in the aeroplane as well. Not too far.'

But to Pedrito, this meant only that someone else he cared for was going to leave him. First his mother (and how could he know that she wouldn't go off to Ibiza again without telling him?), then old María, and now Doogie. And one of those times, one of them *would* go to see Mario, his canary, in heaven and would never come back.

Pedrito started to cry – struggling very, very hard not to, but unable to stop himself. He tried to seek refuge from his embarrassment by clambering down from his chair and running to his mother. But Angie was too cut up herself to do anything but pat his head with one hand and blow her nose again with the other.

Catalina's mother held her arms out to him, but he rushed past, still struggling to quell his tears, still determined to hide his emotions. He ran to Doogie and clung to him.

'Please don't go to Ibiza too, Boogie,' he pleaded. 'Stay here and play with Rafa and me and the rabbits. *Please*, don't go away too.'

Doogie couldn't speak. And anyway, what could he truthfully say, without causing more hurt, to a little boy not usually inclined to such shows of sentiment? What could he say to a confused and vulnerable kid, who had come to look up to and believe in him, if not entirely as a father figure, then certainly as a big brother? Doogie cradled Pedrito's head in his hand and brushed the tears from his cheeks. Then, hesitantly, he glanced round the table at the others. They were sitting with heads bowed, not knowing what to say either, not a dry eye among them.

Pedrito didn't utter another word for the rest of the evening. After the adults had falteringly resumed a semblance of conversation, he merely detached himself from Doogie and wandered quietly into the kitchen on his own. When Angie called him to go home soon after, he slouched out of the house, his head down, his hands in his pockets, and ambled off to the other side of the yard, where he waited in the shadows for his mother to say her goodbyes.

Doogie felt awful. 'I've hurt his feelings really badly,' he said to Angie.

She made a brave attempt at a smile. 'Don't let it get to you, Doog. No, it's my fault the little sod's like this.' She choked back a sob. 'We all know that.'

Doogie gestured towards where Pedrito was waiting. 'Do you think I should go over and, you know, try to…?'

Angie shook her head. 'Just let him work it out in his own little way, love. He'll get over it. Just give him a couple of days with them rabbits – you'll see.'

Doogie wanted to say that he *wouldn't* see. He wouldn't be here to, and the realisation of that was precisely what was hurting like a knife being turned in his stomach. But maybe Angie was right. Why make an already difficult situation even worse for the wee fella? Unwittingly, he had betrayed Pedrito's trust by deciding to go away, just as everyone else dear to the boy now seemed to, sooner or later. But Angie *was* right. The only thing that would heal Pedrito's wounds now was time … and the love and security of his new little family.

'I'll try to make it up to him some day, Ange, and that's a promise.'

Angie, who had been on the verge of breaking down since Pedrito first mentioned Ibiza earlier in the evening, finally began to bubble. She grabbed Doogie and put her arms around him.

'Come here and give your Auntie Angie a cuddle, you great big Scotch lummox,' she half-whimpered, half-laughed. After a few moments of mutual back-patting, she warbled into his chest, 'Bye bye, young O'Mara. We'll all miss you, kiddo.' Then, her face smudged with mascara, strands of her dyed blonde hair hanging limp and straggly with tears, she looked up at Doogie and told him through a chin-quivering smile, 'Sam Merryweather should've fucking sent you to Africa in the first place, the thoughtless old bastard!'

With that, Angie silently and hurriedly rounded up Rafael and Pedrito and was gone.

It was Catalina who suggested that she and Doogie should take a stroll to the Fincalet Pou Vell after her parents had retired for the night. It seemed right to him, too, that they should pay one final visit, during these last few hours together, to the little farm that old María had handed down to them, and to which all their hopes and dreams for the future were tied, no matter how uncertainly.

A new moon was already rising above the mountains. Stars shone large and bright in a cloudless sky, lighting their way through the little fields, where the dry husks of almonds, fallen early from the trees, crunched and cracked beneath their feet.

'When that moon up there is full,' Doogie said, 'we call it the harvest moon where I come from. The full moon of September. The end of summer and the start of autumn. The time to gather in the crops and make ready for the long, cold winter ahead.'

Catalina nodded thoughtfully. 'And yet here, autumn is really a second spring – a time, in the growing moon, to sow and plant all the things that would not survive the heat of summer. It is a season I think you would like.' She guided him towards the old house. 'And, *sí*, you would also like the winter in Mallorca, Doogie. A gentle time, warm and pleasant, but with great storms from the north too. The Tramuntana storms, with thunder and lightning, wind and much rain. But only for a short time, and then everything returns to *tranquilidad* – to the quietness – and the land smells fresh and new, and the leaves in the orange groves are shining and clean. *Sí*, for the winter is the time to pick the oranges, hanging heavy and ripe on the trees from November on. And in the new year, we have *las calmas de enero*, the calms of January – a little summer in winter that lasts for a week, sometimes two. This brings out the almond blossom, and the whole valley here is white, as if covered in snow. And then the seasons change, with more storms bringing rain to fill the wells, until the sun shines warm again to welcome the spring.' She sat down with Doogie on an old wooden bench under the overgrown grapevine by the front door. '*Sí*, I think you will like the winters here in Mallorca, Doogie.'

Doogie put his arm around her and gently stroked her hair. They sat looking down over the village, the distant glow from its windows flickering through the balmy night like the light of the stars reflected in the still waters of the *finca*'s old well itself. Nothing more was said, both wishing every passing second would last a minute, every minute an hour. An unseen choir of crickets chirruped sleepily all around, and the same nightingale, perhaps, that Doogie had heard on that earlier visit to this enchanted valley poured its heart out from a secret place somewhere high above the Fincalet Pou Vell.

CHAPTER NINETEEN

'IS PARTING SUCH *SWEET* SORROW?'

WHEN DOOGIE AND CATALINA arrived at Palma airport, it was in its normal state of chaos for this time of year. Organised chaos, as befitted one of the busiest holiday airports on the planet, perhaps, but chaos, nevertheless. Doogie was familiar enough with it all now, though, and being in the know, he was able to jump the already long queue at the check-in for Merryweather Holidays' Glasgow flight.

'No suitcase, Doogs?' the girl at the check-in asked.

'Nope, just this trusty old holdall I came with, and I'll carry that as hand luggage. Saves a lot of hassle at the other end.'

'Wow! If only they all travelled that light!'

'If they all travelled this light, you'd be out of a job,' Doogie cracked. 'Just like me!'

'Yeah, sorry to hear about that,' the girl said, in a way that suggested she really couldn't care less. Such things happened all the time, after all. It was par for the course in this game. 'Still, ne'er mind, eh,' she added, handing him his boarding card with a practiced imitation smile. 'Something'll turn up. See ya, love … NEXT!'

'YOO-HOO, DOOGIE!' came the call from the end of the queue.

Doogie recognised those stentorian tones. 'Christ, it's Margaret!' he muttered.

'The Margaret friend is on the same plane?' Catalina asked, a note of concern in her voice.

Doogie rolled his eyes. 'Seems like it. First I knew of it, though.'

Margaret was with two other girls and three lads, all similarly attired in multi-pocketed combat shorts, rolled-down woollen socks and chunky hiking boots. They were struggling with two trolleys heaped high with what appeared to be near-identical backpacks.

'What luck, being on the same flight!' Margaret grinned at Doogie, leaving her chums to do the struggling. 'Hey, if it's not full, we may be able to juggle things about a bit and sit together.' She threw a glance in Catalina's direction, then said offhandedly, 'Oh, hello. Let me see – Catherine or something, wasn't it? How nice to see you again. Now then, Doogie –'

'The flight *is* full, Margaret,' Doogie stated bluntly. 'Have a good one!'

He took Catalina's elbow and ushered her away through the milling crowds, leaving Margaret to stand gaping after them – fuming.

From experience, Doogie knew that the only place to find a measure of peace and quiet in Palma Airport at a time like this was the bar area in Domestic Departures. Instead of being chock-a-block with fed-up families preparing to head home to all points north in Europe after their annual holiday in the sun, this lounge was usually only occupied by a scattering of Spanish business people, sitting having a quiet drink while awaiting their flight back to the mainland. It was a haven of sanity in a sea of bedlam, and that's where Doogie and

Catalina took refuge, choosing a quiet corner table well away from the bar.

By now, there was less than an hour to go until boarding time. They sat, hardly even touching the coffees they had ordered, talking about everything and nothing, smiling at each other with nervous eyes, distractedly stroking one another's fingers on the table, willing the minutes to pass more slowly. And so they remained, oblivious to everything and everyone except themselves, until, with a final glance at his watch, Doogie stood up and said softly:

'It's time, Cati. I've got to go.'

Catalina bit her lip and nodded. 'I will come with you to the barrier,' she said, struggling to hold back the tears.

They walked hand-in-hand through the teeming masses in the main concourse, not saying anything, their minds numbed now with the inescapable realisation that the moment they had both been dreading was almost upon them. The final boarding call for Doogie's flight had already been announced when they reached Passport Control, beyond which Catalina couldn't pass. They could see Ingrid in the International Departures area beyond, ushering the last of the passengers through the gate marked 'Glasgow – Merryweather Airways MWA 104'.

Doogie laid down his holdall and took Catalina's hands in his. They stood silently for a moment, looking at each other, their eyes saying more than words ever could.

Then they heard Ingrid's voice booming out across the now empty hall:

'Get a move on, sunshine! This gannet's waiting for *you*! So shift it, *rápido*!'

'I will watch from the roof terrace,' Catalina whispered into Doogie's ear as they embraced for the last time. 'I will watch until your plane flies high over Sa Grua Mountain. And if you look down then, perhaps you will see the Little Farm of The Old Well, and you will think of your Cati, waiting for you to come back to her … one day, *si*?'

Doogie tried to speak, but the words stuck in his throat.

Catalina reached up and kissed him with tears on her lips,

then turned and hurried away.

Doogie watched her go, aching to follow.

'One minute, sunshine!' Ingrid's voice rang in his ears. 'That's what you've got before this gannet leaves without you. So *move* it!'

Doogie picked up his holdall, took one final look at Catalina weaving her way through the crowds, then headed off, trance-like, through Passport Control and over the departure hall towards the urgently-beckoning Ingrid. Suddenly, he felt totally alone, with an awful emptiness inside. He was consumed by a helpless sense of loss that he had known only twice before – on hearing of the deaths of his parents.

'Oh yeah, parting *is* such sweet sorrow, innit, kid?' Ingrid said as he tore off his half of Doogie's boarding pass. He grinned and slapped Doogie's back, hurrying him past. 'Now get yourself into that gannet's belly pronto!' His trademark guffaw resonated down the narrow passageway leading to the Glasgow plane's pier. 'And don't forget to send us a postcard frae Bonnie Scotland, huh? *Hasta luego*, sunshine, and haste ye back!'

Catalina stood alone, watching the sky-blue 737 taxi out onto the runway, waving her hand, trying to smile, teardrops trickling down her cheeks as the jet engines roared and the plane finally began its take-off dash along the runway. She watched it rise and climb out over the Bay of Palma, banking right and setting course northward towards the Tramuntana Mountains ... and to Scotland.

'*Adiós*, Doogie,' she whispered through her tears, sharing the agony she instinctively knew Doogie was experiencing as well – looking down, as he would be now, on Capdellá village and the Fincalet Pou Vell. '*Adios* Doogie, *y vaya con Dios...*'

She lowered her head as the plane disappeared from view, and began to sob into her hands.

'The gannet has flown, Mrs Sunshine,' a familiar voice said behind her.

She spun round, clutching her heart.

'The gannet has flown,' Doogie repeated, 'but this little gannet dropping stayed at home.'

Catalina didn't know yet whether to laugh or continue crying. 'But – I – you – what happened?' she stammered. 'You are being too late for the plane, no?'

'No,' Doogie said. 'I got there just in time. But when it came to it, I just couldn't leave you, that's all.'

'And you are not tugging at my legs?'

'No,' Doogie laughed, 'I'm not pulling your leg. So, how about a big welcome home, eh?'

Catalina ran to him and threw her arms round his neck, though still finding it difficult to believe that this was really happening. 'But the *veterinario* college,' she said, searching his eyes. 'The things your parents wanted for you. I – I cannot understand.'

Doogie nodded his head. 'Oh, I know – and I've thought about that an *awful* lot lately as well, but I reckon they'd have told me to do exactly what I'm doing now.'

'You mean, to be true to yourself, as the Señor Shakespeare said?'

Doogie tapped the end of Catalina's nose. 'That, and to recognise happiness when she's staring into my face with eyes as big and bonnie as yours.'

Catalina gave a bashful little giggle.

Doogie kissed her brow. 'Come on, Pocahontas. Time to take Captain Smith home to see your parents.'

'Pocahontas? Captain Smith?'

'Aye,' said Doogie. He picked up his holdall and put an arm round Catalina's waist. 'I'll tell you all about it sometime. But right now, there's something I want to ask your father.'

'*Sí?*'

'Yeah. Then there's an almond harvest waiting. And *then* you and I have to figure out the best way to skin that cat.'

THE END

Also by Peter Kerr

Bob Burns investigates
THE MALLORCA CONNECTION

ISBN 9781905170333

Price £6.99

"Whodunit fans will love this first in a new series ... a
murderhunt with funny and frightening results!"
Sunday Post Plus

Bob Burns is an old-fashioned kind of Scottish sleuth,
more interested in catching villains than brown-nosing
to get promotion. So, when his enquiries into a brutal
and bizarre murder are blocked by his bosses, should
he risk losing his career by carrying on his
investigations?

Encouraged by an attractive-though-maverick forensic
scientist and assisted by a keener-than-bright young
constable, Bob does it his way. The trail leads the trio
from Scotland to Mallorca, where intrigue and
mayhem mingle with the crowds at a fishermen's
fiesta. A rare combination of suspense and comedy,
with a real twist in the tail.

Bob Burns investigates
THE SPORRAN CONNECTION

ISBN 9781905170838

Price £6.99

In this new humour-laced Bob Burns mystery,
the droll Scottish detective is once again aided by
his game-for-anything forensic scientist lady
friend, Julie Bryson, and abetted by keener-than-
smart rookie detective, Andy Green.

When Andy becomes the unwitting recipient of a
drop of £100,000 in used notes, the trio become
enmeshed in a web of murder, intrigue and
Caledonian skulduggery, as the action shifts to
Sicily, New York and a remote Hebridean island.
The arrival of a Sicilian blacksmith as the
island's new laird leads to some hilarious
misunderstandings as the line between the good
and bad guys becomes increasingly blurred.

After many a Highland shenanigan, including a
vital kilt-raising stunt by Andy Green, the
mystery is finally solved … or is it?

Fiddler on the Make

ISBN 9781905170692

Price £6.99

When the sleepy Scottish village of Cuddyford is colonised by well-heeled retirees and big-city commuters, Jigger McCloud, a Jack-the-lad local farmer with a talent for playing the fiddle and an eye for the ladies, isn't slow to make a quick buck at their expense.

Life seems rosy for Jigger and his oddball-but-loveable family, until he tries his scams on a mysterious foreign millionaire, who arrives on the scene with plans to develop the area in ways that appeal neither to Jigger *nor* his milch-cow incomers. The folk of Cuddyford, native and otherwise, promptly close ranks.

Comic shenanigans, quirky characters and sinister ploys abound, and it's Bert, Jigger's scruffy little hamburger-craving dog, who turns out to be the hero of the piece as the McClouds and their beloved Cuddyford teeter on the brink of disaster.

Bob Burns Investigates
THE CRUISE CONNECTION

ISBN 9781906125158

£ 6.99

A strong cast of sharply-drawn and colourful characters gives Bob Burns and his two unlikely sidekicks plenty to cope with in an intriguing story of greed, guile, deceit and double-dealing that's sparked off by the discovery of a severed finger in a cruise ship passenger's quiche lorraine.

Does the finger belong to an alleged man-overboard victim? Was the man overboard pushed or did he commit suicide? Is it all just a cleverly engineered insurance scam? Does a shady Eastern European billionaire's interest in gaining control of a famous British football club have anything to do with this?

These are just a few of the many questions that Bob & Co. must find answers to as they travel to Mallorca to join the cruise liner *Ostentania* en route to the Canary Islands. Will they encounter trouble in Tenerife, lawlessness in Lanzarote or, perhaps, even grand larceny in Gran Canaria? Confusing coincidences pop up like mushrooms as Bob strives to solve what he initially considers to be an unsolvable crime – if indeed any crime has been committed at all.

Snowball Oranges: One Mallorcan Winter

Peter Kerr

ISBN 184024 1128
£7.99 320pp

'Look! The weather has come from Scotland to welcome you to Mallorca,' beamed Senor Ferrer. To our new neighbour's delight and my dismay, a cold mantle of white was rapidly transforming our newly acquired paradise in the sun into a bizarre winterscape of citrus Christmas trees, cotton wool palms and snowball oranges.

It's the stuff of dreams. A Scottish family giving up relative sanity and security to go and grow oranges for a living in a secluded valley in the mountains of the Mediterranean island of Mallorca.

But dreams, as everyone knows, have a nasty habit of not turning out quite as intended. Being greeted by a freak snowstorm is only the first of many surprises and 'experiences', and it isn't long before they realise that they have been sold a bit of a lemon of an orange farm by the wily previous owners.

However, laughter is the best medicine when confronted with consuming a local dish of rats, the live-chicken-down-a-chimney technique of household maintenance and attending a shotgun wedding. The colourful set of Mallorcan neighbours (including an eccentric old goatherd who eats worm-ridden oranges to improve his sex life) restores the family's faith in human nature and helps them adapt to a new and unexpectedly testing life in this deceptively simple idyll of rural Spain.

Full of life and colour, hilarious and revealing, and set against a backdrop of the breathtaking beauty of Mallorca.

www.summersdale.co.uk

Viva Mallorca: One Mallorcan Autumn
Peter Kerr

ISBN 184024 3805
Price £7.99 320pp

Autumn has arrived for the Kerrs on their fruit farm on the island of Mallorca...

The year's third season, 'winter spring', finds Peter, under the sharp eye of his long-suffering wife Ellie, struggling to shake off the relaxed Spanish tranquiloness that he has now mastered all too well. Old friendships have been established, and new ones are found as the Kerrs are introduced to Mallorca's champagne-swilling Filthy-Rich-Set and their eyes are opened by just how the other half lives...

Mosquito-repellent vinegar baths, delicious Mallorcan food, and with background support from dogs, donkeys, geckos, parrots and canaries, this is an autumn such as they've never known – Y Viva Mallorca!

Viva Mallorca is the third book in the award-winning series by Peter Kerr, following Snowball Oranges and Mañana, Mañana.

'An endearing insight into life in rural Mallorca and a characteristically humorous portrait of its colourful inhabitants' A PLACE IN THE SUN magazine

'Peter has hit the jackpot with tales from the sunshine isle' THE WEEKLY NEWS

'Although the shelves are overloaded with emigration stories, this is one relocation tale that makes for riveting reading, even on its third helping, thanks to Kerr`s lively writing style' SPANISH magazine

From Paella to Porridge: Farewell to Mallorca and a Scottish Adventure
Peter Kerr

ISBN 184024 5069
£7.99 320pp

The Kerr family say goodbye to their orange farm in Mallorca, and put it up for sale after three years of hard work. The Mallorcan experience comes to an end with a farewell fiesta for neighbours and friends, full of comic shenanigans but tinged with sadness. But now begins the return-to-Scotland adventure, and what a cultural shock is in store. Welcomed back by family, the Kerrs make plans to start a deer farm on a remote hillside, the beginning of a period of challenges and change, of buying and restoring houses in the lovely Scottish countryside. Meanwhile, Peter explores Scotland with fresh eyes, visiting such places as the 'Biarritz of the North' where Robert Louis Stevenson used to holiday, and giving us an insider's view of the world-famous Edinburgh Military Tattoo. There's never a dull moment in the Kerr household

'I was seduced by Peter Kerr. Not the man himself, of course, but his delightful books recounting life as a fruit farmer in rural Mallorca, having moved his family from Scotland' THE TELEGRAPH

'Kerr still has his light touch' THE SCOTSMAN

'...full of comic shenanigans but tinged with sadness' SPAIN magazine

For more information about our books
please visit

www.accentpress.co.uk